TART NOIR

TART NOIR

EDITED BY

Stella Duffy and Lauren Henderson

PAN BOOKS

First published 2002 by Pan Books
an imprint of Pan Macmillan Ltd
Pan Macmillan, 20 New Wharf Road, London N1 9RR
Basingstoke and Oxford
Associated companies throughout the world
www.panmacmillan.com

ISBN 0 330 48744 2

A CIP catalogue record for this book is available from
the British Library.

Typeset by SetSystems Ltd, Saffron Walden, Essex
Printed and bound in Great Britain by
Mackays of Chatham plc, Chatham, Kent

Stella and Lauren are dedicating
this anthology to each other in honour
of the total pleasure it has been to
do it together. As it were.

Contents

Introduction

Tart. It's such a potent four-letter word. Sweet, sour, sharp, sexy, with more than a hint of cheesecake.

This anthology embodies all of these qualities. It's a manifesto, a statement of intent. Just like all our first novels were, once upon a time. The crime writers who make up the majority of this collection wanted to invent a new kind of women's writing, to challenge and add to what had gone before. We set out to create crime novels in whose heroines we, and many other women, could see ourselves and our friends. Strong, funny, independent women who could hold their drink, go head to head with men and be the centre of their own universe. Women capable of saving themselves, who didn't spend the last chapters tied to a cellar wall by the serial killer as bait for the hero. Women who could dress up in stiletto heels and a pretty frock, save the world *and* get the cute guy. (Or girl.) Women having fun on their own terms, with not a token chick in sight. Girls, in other words, behaving badly.

We wanted to knock down the old stereotypes: the novels where the only female characters are markers to political correctness; drippy chicks who need saving; or dead, well – tarts. We'd had enough of thick-headed heroines slipping on their fluffy mules to go out, unarmed, in the middle of the night, with a serial killer on the loose, to investigate weird chainsaw noises coming from the deserted cemetery. (Without, of course, telling anyone where they're going.) Give us Geena Davis in *The Long Kiss Goodnight*, or Modesty Blaise, or Emma Peel.

All characters, incidentally, created by men. And hell, we need the boys to write great girls because books written by men are still in the vast majority when it comes to being nominated for, and winning, the big crime awards. Judged both by sales and quality of the books – from historical mysteries to psychological thrillers to hard-edged police procedurals – women crime writers are just as heavy hitters as the men. And yet that isn't translating to the equal respect of the establishment. Out of all the CWA awards since the 1960s, women were winners only 25–30 per cent of the time – and nominated, proportionally, much, much less frequently. Post-feminism is still a long way off.

We know that fans of *Tart Noir* are going to be men and women in equal quantity. We know this because that's the composition of the fans of our own novels. But we are strongly opposed to the idea that a certain kind of testosterone-charged novel, much as we love and admire many of those books, is the acme of crime writing.

This is one of the reasons why Tart Noir, as a group of like-minded women, was born. Lauren raised the idea with Sparkle Hayter, who went away and designed our fabulous website, www.tartcity.com, which has flourished like the green bay tree ever since. Tart City, run by Lauren and Katy Munger, is the place for like-minded tarts of both sexes to gather, gossip and plot world domination. *Tart Noir*, the anthology, was born in similar circumstances – Lauren and Stella spent far too long setting the world to rights in the ladies' loos at a book launch, and ended up deciding to edit an anthology of our own. (Partly out of frustration that we kept finding our work in anthologies where the ratio was fifteen male writers to five women, for no good reason that we could see.) Bringing together the writers for *Tart Noir* was blissfully easy. This is a fast-growing genre, and the writers in our anthology all have an individualism, a streak of wilful, in-your-face perversity, which perfectly defines the essence of *Tart Noir*.

With Stella based in London and Lauren in New York, we're ideally placed to present a transatlantic anthology to the world. And we are thrilled with what we have to offer. These stories cover all the bases from classic crime to magical anti-realism, hot sex to cold calculation. Many of the writers are pushing their own boundaries, using *Tart Noir* to help them touch on subjects they haven't tackled before – sex or violence or comedy, often all three. Some of the writers are not officially crime writers – and we're delighted to be their first taste of criminal activity. Others are simply doing what they do best, in fast, tight stories which offer fresh turns on old twists. There are series characters and brand-new ones just panting for half a dozen books of their own. Stories long and short, knowing laughs and nasty glances; some bittersweet, some as frothy and indulgent as a good cheesecake, some downright sad.

But what they all have in common is the Tart Noir criteria. We asked the writers to come with us, making a leap into what is the future of female crime writing. Written by women, and read by both sexes. The Tart universe welcomes, with open arms, readers of all genders and all persuasions. Just as long as they have a little bit of Tart in their hearts . . .

Stella Duffy and Lauren Henderson
May 2002

Acknowledgements

Thanks, first and foremost, to Sparkle Hayter and Katy Munger, without whose passion the Tart City website would still be just a lovely concept. And Beth Tindall, JJ Buch and Jennifer Blue, whose generosity, talent and originality have enriched the site so much. Our editors Beverley Cousins and Anya Serota, and our agents Eugenie Furniss, Stephanie Cabot and Anthony Goff, all of whom became as excited by Tart Noir as we did ourselves – which really helped. Marshall Mintz and Shelley Silas, delicious tarts themselves, bring out the tart in both of us. And much gratitude to Peter O'Donnell (Modesty Blaise) and Jamie Hewlett (Tank Girl), for proving that men can write tarts too . . . Finally, many thanks to L'Oreal for the nail polish which originally brought us together. Even if we disagree on what colour it was.

CHRIS NILES

Revenge Is the Best Revenge

'Randall, thank you for coming.' Serena Warner smiled briefly and opened a hand to indicate where she should sit.

Randall Burns's chest constricted. She thought she might well burst into tears. They were laying her off. That's what this visit meant. How awful. How banal.

Serena eased herself behind her rosewood desk. 'As you probably know, we're reviewing the skill sets of everybody in the company in the context of the merger with Trans-Mega with a view to maximizing our global potential, strengthening our core competencies . . .'

Serena Warner, vice-president of news-gathering. Screamer as everybody in the newsroom called her. Plain, talentless Screamer. How had she risen so far so fast? How had she ever reached a position where she could dictate Randall Burns's future?

Somehow she had. The interview was over in minutes.

'You have to leave the building immediately,' Serena said smoothly, almost as an afterthought while gathering up her papers. Standing up, moving on to the next kill.

'You are kidding?'

'It's procedure.'

'Whose procedure?' She felt like punching Serena. If she hadn't just had her nails done she would have.

'This is difficult for me as well.'

Sure, Randall thought. *My ass.*

Fifteen years and it came down to this.

The goon they'd hired to make sure she didn't go postal hunched gargoyle-like outside her office while she packed. When she picked up the phone to call a car, she found that her line had been disconnected.

Fifteen years of crap. Of clawing her way up from the grave-yard producing shift. Early mornings, overnights. All in the name of getting her face on network television.

She walked the length of the newsroom with her head up. She felt like a refugee, if refugees wore Lacroix.

She walked blindly along Madison. Her preposterous shoes bit at her heels and toes like tiny demons. She had never walked home in her life. By the time she got to 72nd Street, her feet were bleeding.

She had an appointment with her personal trainer at six – he came three times a week for power yoga and Tantric meditation. She cancelled it. In this state she could not even begin to think about merging with the Ultimate Divine. She called her lawyer. He told her he would make the network pay and she believed him.

Nobody treated Randall Burns this way. Nobody.

The next day in the papers the president of the newly merged company promised a lean organization ready to rule the twenty-first century airwaves and every other means of communication besides. Several hundred people had been sacrificed to appease the gods of the old and new media.

Randall tried to be positive. There would be other jobs, for sure. She had a following. She had been in the nation's living rooms for five years. That practically qualified her as royalty, didn't it? Trouble was, in all that time she had never been described as 'America's Sweetheart'. 'Sweetheart' meant people would stick with you through the good and the bad, laugh when you laughed, cry when you cried. They had seen her, but had they loved her? She couldn't be sure.

She tossed around her options while she attended a kick-boxing class at Equinox. The exercise studio was full of spindly, anxious twenty-somethings loathing imaginary rolls of fat – fighting it with all they had. Randall was forty-four. Most days she was happy with what she saw in the mirror. Today she winced. Botox time.

But where was her future, if not in television? The lecture circuit was a possibility. Lecture circuit. Yeah, sure. People paid three hundred bucks a ticket for a polystyrene meat product and a chance to feel secretly sorry for the schmuck on the podium who'd once been at the top of their game. Well, no thanks. She wasn't ready for the sidelines.

And there was that publisher talking about a book. An offer which would now, no doubt, go away. New Yorkers thought failure was more contagious than a disease. Nobody wanted to know; there were no fund-raising ribbon campaigns for losers.

After the class she swam fifty lengths of the bijou pool. Pushing herself until she could barely breathe, she climbed out shaking. She sat in the steam room and reviewed her options. Twenty minutes later she had decided. Serena Warner, the bitch, had to die.

The immediate question was how. As she mulled over the logistics, Randall realized this was going to be more difficult than anything she'd attempted. She had mastered character assassination during her years navigating the treacherous straits of newsroom politics, but, despite extreme provocation, she had never gone any further. Usually, when faced with a difficult task, she did what most New Yorkers in her social bracket did and hired a menial. But Randall didn't know where to find a hitman – or hit-person as she supposed they were now called – and she didn't suppose that any of her Upper East Side friends did either.

There was another thing: she wanted to see the expression in Screamer's eyes when she knew she was going to die. She wanted her truly to regret that she had ever thought she could take on Randall Burns and win.

She called her producer, Trace Currer, and invited him over for drinks.

'Sorry you were axed, babe.' Trace Currer was tall and thin with thick black hair and a pale complexion. As current fashion dictated, he wore a goatee, which made him look like an Eastern European pimp. 'I'm sure I'm not far behind you,' he said flatly. He had a phlegmatic disposition. He was the only man alive who could call her babe and live to tell the tale. Their professional relationship had outlasted both of her marriages.

'What's it like at work?' Randall asked as she mixed drinks on the terrace.

'Carnage.' Trace bent his body in half, propped it on the railing and looked over at the crawling rush-hour traffic on Madison. The evening was mild and a soft sky sparkled above them. 'Half of them are sobbing, the other half want to get laid off so they can stay home and work on their screenplays. What's your plan?'

'To pack a truck full of explosive and park it outside the office.' Randall handed him a glass.

Trace showed his teeth, the expression that for him passed as a smile. 'Very funny,' he said and glugged the martini.

Later, after Randall had explained that she wanted to find some information on the Internet, Trace showed her a website.

'Who do you want to dig the dirt on?' he asked, his long, delicate hands poised above the keyboard.

'Oh, nobody special. I'll do it afterwards, when the martini's worn off,' Randall said. 'Come and have another drink.' She didn't want Trace around while she was delving into Serena Warner's life. He was way too sharp.

'Sure,' Trace said, although he stayed where he was. 'I'll be along in a minute. Just want to check my email. You never know, they might have fired me online.'

The information Randall bought showed Serena was from a wealthy Dallas family and had graduated with honours from two good universities. She had spent a number of years abroad as a producer for a rival network. She spoke Russian and French and had lived in Moscow.

Easy for her, Randall thought. Serena didn't know what it meant to lift yourself up by your bootstraps. She hadn't had to marry money, so she wouldn't have to worry about where the next pair of snakeskin slingbacks was coming from. Serena lived alone in a loft in TriBeCa. Like Randall, she had trashed two marriages. She had no kids, no pets, no criminal convictions, no blotches on her credit rating. She was a model citizen. A model citizen with days left to live.

Death by drowning? Serena never went near water deeper than her bathtub. Suffocation? Randall had read that it left the fewest clues, but it would mean sneaking into Serena's apartment while she was asleep and Randall could barely open her own door with the correct keys. Learning to pick a lock was out of the question.

A gun was the obvious answer, but Randall, who had been overwhelmed by tears when she covered the Million Mom march, was opposed to guns. She didn't believe they had any place in a civilized society.

Randall mulled over the options as she followed Serena around for a week. It was amazing how *unaware* Manhattanites were. All those years of aggressive beggars and squeegee men in their faces meant upstanding citizens saw nothing and in turn hoped that nothing saw them.

One night Randall realized that someone was following *her*. Serena was at a Russian bar in the East Village listening to dreary folk songs. It was cold outside – a sudden snap – and Randall had been about to give up her vantage point in a doorway across the street. When she turned suddenly she saw a dark-clad figure staring at her from under a defunct lamp post. A wave of sick dismay almost made her throw up. How long had he been there? What did he want? She started walking. Made a sudden right turn on 2nd Street. A sneak glance. So did the person following her. Past hipster bars and clubs. She turned left on to First Avenue. Saw a taxi and took it. When she looked back, the figure had gone.

The next night Serena was enjoying a post-movie Cosmopolitan at the Screening Room bar. Randall had slipped in while Serena visited the bathroom and was occupying a rickety chair on the mezzanine. She had an excellent view, so she was able to see a figure in a dark raincoat stop at the doorway and peer in. He was wearing a hat so she couldn't see his face. Randall held her breath. The figure turned and walked away.

Randall gulped down her drink for courage. *Get over it*, she told herself. Manhattan was full of people and some of them were going to be on the same streets as her sometimes. She was losing her nerve, that was all. She couldn't stop now because imaginary monsters were dogging her.

Serena had returned from the bathroom and was chatting with a handsome young bartender. Randall watched her scrawl something on a business card and push it across the bar along with a ten-dollar tip.

'You haven't got a prayer, Screamer,' Randall said under her breath. The bartender, a red-head with lazy eyes, smiled politely.

Randall followed Serena to her loft, which was nearby on Lispenard Street. She watched the lights go on in her second-floor apartment. Something, the hunter's instinct, made her hang around.

Later, as she slunk into the back doorway of the Chinese furniture store which faced Serena's, she heard brisk foot-steps. She pressed herself against the rough brick wall. The footsteps slowed as they came closer. Randall peered around the corner. The man had stopped to consult a piece of paper. Newly confident of his direction, he slipped the paper into his pocket and crossed the street to Serena's apartment.

It was the waiter from the bar.

'Damn,' Randall whispered as she watched his butt, every bit as delicious as his face, disappear into the softly lit lobby. It wasn't enough that Serena had fired her, the twisted old crow was even getting laid more often.

Serena wasn't at the bar the following evening when Randall dropped in and discovered that the barman's name was Teddy and he was a poet. *Shame*, Randall thought. A body like that buried in books was just plain wasted. He had a sexy voice too. Deep timbre with a twang of the South. She practised imitating it later as she walked along Canal looking for a cab. She was good at accents. Most of Manhattan's fashionable restaurants were more difficult to get into than the space programme, so it was sometimes useful to pretend to be Tom Brokaw or Ivana Trump when making a reservation.

When she went out that night to let her long-haired dachsund irrigate the sidewalk, she thought she saw a tall figure in a dark overcoat vanish around the corner of Madison. But it could have been any one of dozens of Euro-trash who littered her neighbourhood. *Get over it*, she told herself. Cold-blooded murderers do not cringe at shadows.

Later that week Randall lunched with Marcee Beckwith Mermelstein, a senior editor at a Fifth Avenue publishing house. To her surprise the publishing offer had not gone away. Marcee wanted Randall to contribute to an anthology about the art of simple living. Randall did not believe for a moment that life was supposed to be simple – you didn't look taut at forty-four from granola bars and gratitude – and she didn't suppose that couture-clad Marcee did either. But here they were. Thinking of ever more subtle ways to fleece the public out of their hard-earned cash.

'We're exploring the issue with a number of prominent women,' Marcee said as she picked delicately at chilled Sevruga. 'There's a sea change going on. The public is tired of consumerism. Going to the mall does not fill the emptiness in their souls.'

'Then they shouldn't shop at the mall. They should shop at Saks.' Randall said. 'Only kidding,' she added when she saw the look of alarm on Marcee's face. Marcee paused a milli-second and then laughed politely.

'Humour is so important – in a simple life.' Randall's agent, Karin Schrecter Doonan, frowned at her and lifted her index finger slightly. *Don't blow it*, that finger said.

'And you work in television. You've had all those marvellous years of experience. The Dalai Lama must have taught you something . . . Nelson Mandela.' Marcee gave a little sigh and looked reverent. 'These people have such insights.'

'I guess you pick up the knack of living simply when you're in jail.' The words popped out before Randall could censor them. Jail was on her mind lately.

'If you're not interested . . .' Marcee's surgically smoothed face was beginning to display a hint of pique.

'Oh, but she *is* interested.' Karin put her hand lightly and briefly on Marcee's arm. 'And she'll write a beautiful essay. Randall is a very spiritual person, Marcee. She instinctively cultivates her inner life. Even through all the horror of network news politics Randall has never lost sight of what keeps her grounded. She knows that money and status don't mean a thing.' Karin shot a glare at Randall that Marcee couldn't see. 'And now that she's lost her job . . . well. She's gained a whole new . . . depth . . . a new *level* of spirituality, haven't you, dear?' Karin's face showed the sort of strain you can only feel when big bucks are backing out the door.

'I have realized that money isn't everything,' Randall said after thinking about Serena Warner for a moment or two.

'I know now what will give me lasting satisfaction and what won't.'

'Lovely, darling,' Marcee murmured. 'Lovely.' She raised her glass of sparkling water.

Normally before a big assignment there were hair and make-up and pastel-coloured power suits. Researchers' notes to read up, voice exercises to perform. This time she simply dotted some tinted moisturizer on her cheeks and put on her lucky La Perla underwear. She was in deep disguise tonight – chain-store clothing. But the Italian silk briefs provided some measure of comfort. She pulled on the new black jeans and turtle-neck sweater bought from Old Navy and slipped on an old pair of Adidas sneakers. She packed an equally nondescript change of clothes into a supermarket bag, tucked her hair up into a Mets baseball cap and grabbed the Emmy award she had won for mussing her hair during Hurricane Andrew. She had carefully unscrewed the base and dismantled the statue to remove the plaque, which identified her as the winner of the Outstanding Coverage of a Breaking News Story.

On her way downtown on the subway Randall reread a memo that had been emailed to her by a former colleague, who had used many hours of company time to figure out how to hack the newsroom computer's dead file. It was from Serena Warner to the network president and was short and to the point. The layoffs, Screamer insisted, were also a chance to 'get rid of some dead wood'.

Randall ripped the memo into tiny pieces and dumped it in the trash.

If she had had any intention of backing out, she didn't now.

Randall's surveillance had established that Serena was an early riser and so was usually home at around eleven. This evening was no exception. The lights were on and nobody had gone in or out of the building for some time.

As she approached Serena's apartment, Randall could have sworn she heard the network news sting. Ba-ba-BA-ba-ba. High orchestral notes followed by a trill of percussion. Ba-ba-ba-ba.

She pressed the buzzer. Serena's voice came out crackly, 'Hello?'

'It's Teddy.'

A small silence. The news theme was pounding louder. 'Ba-ba-ba-BA-BA-ba. Ba-b . . .'

'Teddy?'

'If you're busy . . .'

'No . . . no. Come on up.' Serena sounded as flustered as a schoolgirl. 'Just give me a moment to prepare.'

Ba-BA-BA-ba-ba . . . The news theme dimmed. Randall waited nervously. Prayed that nobody would come by. This part of Lispenard Street was usually quiet at night.

Eventually the door opened and she was inside.

Breathless with fear, she climbed the stairs to the second floor. Serena's door was ajar. She pushed it. It opened straight on to a large living room scattered with modern sticks of furniture. Doric columns kept the fourteen-foot tin ceilings in place. Open-plan kitchen. Nobody.

'Hello?' Randall gripped the Emmy. The temptation to turn and run almost overwhelmed her. An open door? What if this was a set-up? Another glance around the room.

A sound came from a room to the left. The tip-tap of high heels on hardwood. Then the door opened and Serena stepped out.

'You!' she said.

Randall realized then that the Internet report had not told her everything about her old boss. Had, in fact, omitted the most interesting information.

Serena was in full bondage gear. A black rubber bustier laced up the front with red leather, matching undies, a whip. Thigh-high patent-leather stiletto-heeled boots. Randall winced with embarrassment. It was cheap gear, in every sense of the word. It didn't even look like real leather. Not to mention the fact that flabby Serena simply didn't have the body for it.

She was quick on the uptake, though. She knew immediately that this wasn't a social call. 'Get out.' She raised the whip, her face flushed under the leather mask, a trace of white powder on her upper lip. Randall ignored her and advanced, gripping the Emmy. Serena aimed the whip at Randall's face and flicked her wrist sharply. Randall ducked, but the braided leather came down on her shoulder.

'Ow. That hurt!'

Serena raised the whip again and euphoria surged through Randall like electricity. This was the way disputes between real women should be settled. Honest and upfront. Free of subtext. She swung the Emmy back and brought it down with all her strength.

Leather mixed with blood and dyed blonde hair. The blow caught Serena behind the ear. Serena remained standing. The Emmy broke neatly off at the feet.

'Damn,' Randall muttered as the solid base rolled merrily away, leaving her with the statue. Useless. How typical of television: even the awards were all style and no substance. She dived after it, grazing her knees on the polished floor.

Serena was just as quick. She planted both patent-leather boots on either side of Randall's prostrate body and flicked the whip near her ear. Randall groaned. If this case ever came to court there wasn't a jury in the land who would convict her – this was a view of Serena Warner that nobody should have to see.

Serena slashed the whip and a stinging taunt caught Randall on the neck. Randall scrambled out from under, covered her face with one hand, reached for the base with the other. Serena was kicking her now with the pointed toe of her cheap boots. Definitely not real leather, Randall decided, as she lunged for Serena's standing leg and brought her crashing to the floor.

Serena was quick. She wriggled out of Randall's grip and with a neat backward swipe smacked Randall's ear with the handcuffs she had fastened to one wrist. Randall gripped the Emmy base and swung it again. Another glancing blow. It would have felled a normal person, but coke-fuelled Serena merely wiped blood from her eyes and lashed at Randall again with the handcuffs. The flat metal caught her on the side of the face.

Randall spied the delicate winged statuette lying a few feet away. The curved figure holding a globe aloft. The wings so sharp her maid had once drawn blood dusting them. She backed off from Serena, crawling backwards like a crab. Then both were on their feet. This time Randall had the statue. Wings first, she rushed at Serena.

Ba-ba-ba-ba-BA! A final, crushing lunge and Randall heard the flourish of timpani. The wings connected with Serena's windpipe. Another thrust and it was in all the way and then out again. Serena's eyes opened wide in comic dismay. Her mouth sagged open. The leather whip fell to the ground. Serena's legs gave way. She landed on her knees, swaying. For a moment Randall thought she was going to get up again. But Serena's life was over. She fell straight forward, crashing on to the parquet with a muffled thump, face first.

Crying with relief, Randall stripped down to her underwear, changed into the clean clothing and bundled the blood-stained gear along with the whip and the handcuffs and the broken Emmy into her bag.

A quick look out of the front door confirmed Lispenard Street was deserted. She tucked the bag under her arm. She walked fast towards Canal Street subway, then changed her mind. She was juiced, she'd walk down Broadway.

Several times she glanced around to see if she was being

followed, but the streets were clear. Like her head. She felt exhilarated. More joyful than the day she'd done her first network stand-up. A traffic pile-up on I-95 which had left twenty-five people and one golden retriever dead.

The Staten Island ferry was almost deserted. Randall took a seat in the bows and clutched her bag to her chest as the squat orange vessel churned out of the terminal. It was a clear summer night and the city sat as pert and bright as a socialite's breast job between the Hudson and the East Rivers. As they glided past the Statue of Liberty, Randall walked casually up to the rail and leaned over, dangling the bag in her hands. Then she felt a firm hand on her shoulder.

'How deeply disappointing,' Trace said. 'You're a Mets fan.'

Randall dropped the bag into the sea, but as she let it go Trace snatched it and held on. He'd shaved off his goatee. He looked younger, more vulnerable. She felt a prickle of excitement. God, she was horny.

'Lovely night.' Trace leaned against the rail, staring out towards the Verrazano Bridge. Holding up the bag. Weighing it in his hands. Looking around. There was nobody else at the bow.

'Don't lecture me,' Randall snapped.

'Checked the tides lately?' Trace said patiently. 'Know where all the backward running eddies are?'

Randall shook her head.

'See, you need to check the tides and the currents. You don't check the tides and you can bet your bottom dollar this will wash up and there'll be awkward questions. Very awkward questions.'

'Is that so? And I suppose you have a better idea,' Randall hissed.

'Well.' Trace shrugged modestly. 'I am your producer.'

It took a long time to make the ferry trip back to Manhattan and then get in Trace's ancient BMW and drive to a deserted lot in Red Hook. They made one stop – to post the handcuffs and whip through the grating of a storm drain off Atlantic Avenue. Then Trace incinerated the bundle of bloody clothing, using the can of gas he kept in the trunk.

'Red Hook's run by the Mafia,' he explained as he threw a match on the gas-doused clothing. 'So even if people see something, they're too well trained to do anything stupid like blab to the cops.'

'Terrific,' Randall snapped, tapping her foot, expecting a carload of wise guys to pull up any moment. But nobody showed. The lot remained deserted long after the last thread of clothing had been reduced to ashes.

'All gone,' Trace said, dusting his hands. 'You OK?' He put his face close to hers. She nodded wearily, put her hand on his neck, rubbed her finger over the tiny hairs at the nape.

Somehow they got back to his apartment.

Inside, they flew to each other. Hands, bodies, mouths. She wanted Trace. He wanted her. There was nothing between them but skin and sweat.

The awful, gut-hurling realization of what she had done dawned the next day. Randall woke at eight, groaned and rolled over and buried her face in the pillow as the memories of last night rolled in with fresh horror.

What madness had driven her to do such a thing? What on God's green earth had she been thinking? Was she insane?

'I fucked my producer,' she whimpered, sitting up in bed and putting her face in her hands. 'I fucked my producer. I can't believe it.'

During five years on the road together this had never happened. All the other travelling journalists went at it like the Sixties had never ended. But not Randall and Trace. It had crossed her mind, of course, on the late nights in dirty shit-holes when they'd had five too many from the mini-bar, but she had always assumed that Trace preferred women who were the very opposite of her – those dark-eyed Boho girls who wrote bad songs and lived in fifth-floor walk-ups in the East Village.

Randall stumbled out to the kitchen. No Trace. No trace of Trace. She turned on the television. Serena's death was busting out over the airwaves. 'Publicity hound,' Randall muttered as she flipped channels. 'Even dead, she won't fucking shut up.'

Baby-chick reporters with lipgloss for brains seemed less shocked by the murder than the discovery that a network executive liked kinky sex. All the stations promised 'special reports' that evening. 'High ratings, high risk – the chances successful people take that jeopardize their careers,' smirked Randall's former colleague, Bridge Winter. 'You should know,' Randall muttered as she buttoned the television in order to call for her messages. There was just the one, from her agent.

'It's Karin, darling. Good news. Marcee called last night. We've agreed on a figure for *Beautifully Simple*.' She named a sum that was far from simple. 'Anyway darling, we sign on the dotted line next week. They want to see a draft in two months.'

Randall shrugged. What did she know about the subject? What did it matter? She'd park herself in her draughty country house in Stockbridge, down a couple of martinis and cull a few platitudes from Oprah magazines. After last night she could do anything she damn well pleased.

Except for Trace. Where was Trace? Out giving the cops a nice long statement? Over at the newsroom filing his exclusive news report? Polishing his Emmy acceptance speech for his series, *Why Anchors Kill*?

What to do . . . what to do. Randall's panic mounted as she watched the pictures on the mute television. Serena's apartment, cops goldfishing to reporters, the owner of the sex shop where Serena bought her gear, preening himself for his fifteen minutes' worth. Her breath came in gasps. She was done for. They would find her. Trace had already told them. Trace had set her up. He had withheld some vital piece of evidence. Maybe he'd even had a hidden camera. What to do . . . what to . . . wait a minute! Why not kill Trace too?

Randall's fevered brain raced as she looked around for a weapon thinking, not for the first time, that dating in New York was a complete nightmare, etiquette-wise. No wonder she hardly ever went out. And the kitchen had very few useful weapons. A Dualit toaster looked substantial, but wasn't. A knife, a knife, where the hell were the knives? She yanked open drawers. There were no carving knives. Like many in New York, Trace's state-of-the-art kitchen was entirely for show. And she couldn't very well kill her producer with a coffee machine. Think of the headlines.

The freezer. Randall yanked the door open. Bingo! There was a frozen bottle of vodka, nearly full. She reached in and grabbed it. The ice clamped the glass to her fingers.

'Shit,' Randall dropped the bottle and it bounced on Trace's grey rubber floors and whacked her big toe. She cursed in pain. 'What the hell am I doing?' she moaned. She slid to the floor and, because no other options presented themselves, she opened the bottle and took a swig.

Minutes later Trace loped into the apartment with a bag of groceries. He set it on the granite counter and pulled up juice, coffee and bagels. Randall still had the vodka bottle in hand.

'Gee, not for me, but you go ahead.' He bent and kissed her as he took the bottle away. Randall's insides went to goo. Neither of her ex-husband's bank accounts had made her feel that way. She fastened her hands around Trace's neck and pulled him down beside her.

'Are you planning to blackmail me?' she asked as Trace unbuttoned her shirt and kissed her shoulders. Randall reached for the buttons of his Levis.

'Blackmail? How very un-post-modern.' Trace nuzzled her neck and breasts, soft as a baby fawn. He slipped the shirt off her back, running his fingers, maestro-like down her spine.

'It's a story,' Randall said, pulling his jeans over his slim muscled legs. 'It would make your career.'

'I have other priorities.' Trace's fingers tripped merrily down her stomach. Lower, lower.

'What, exactly, would those priorities be?' Randall gasped.

'Well, we have a good working relationship, right?' Trace's fingers feathered her so lightly she thought her head might explode.

'Uh . . . uh . . . uh . . . under the circumstances I couldn't deny it.' Randall's legs twitched with agonizing pleasure.

'I didn't think so,' Trace said complacently, still busy. 'I'm resourceful, intelligent.'

'E . . . eee . . . Eager,' Randall added, breathless.

'I speak several languages,' Trace added. Then there was silence while he showed her how gifted his tongue could be.

'So, what I'm saying is this,' he continued a few minutes later when Randall thought, nay knew, he was going to kill her with pleasure. 'I think we make a good team.' He nibbled at her ear with his teeth. 'I'm sure you agree.'

'Yeh . . . yes, yes!'

'We've built up some trust over the past five years . . .'

'Don't stop,' Randall whimpered. 'Please, not now . . .'

'I won't stop,' he whispered. 'What I start, I finish. And I'm not going to turn you in. I was following you to make sure you didn't botch it.'

What to do, what to do . . . Was he just spinning her along, having his evil way before he called the cops? Did he want to get his hands on her money? Oh, my God! Too much sensation! Randall couldn't process it all. Had sex ever been this good? Was it Trace or the danger? She sobbed for breath. 'Can we . . . talk about this later?'

But Trace took no notice. In the same soft tone, as though he was murmuring endearments, he whispered, punctuating his sentences with a nibble on her ear.

'This is just the first round of layoffs, remember. In my last job performance review Screamer called me workmanlike.'

'Oh . . . oh . . .'

'Exactly,' Trace whispered gently, sadly. He nibbled and dabbled some more.

Through the haze of delirium, Randall noticed the broken Emmy sitting on the table. Trace must have cleaned it because it shone as brightly as the day she had won it.

'So here's what we do.' Trace ran his spare hand through her hair and smiled. He looked about fourteen when he smiled. 'I give you an alibi. The list of people who hated Screamer is probably epic but the cops might come around.' His fingers increased their tempo.

'And?' Amazing she had any breath left in her body.

'And you take me with you to your next gig. Since we're such a good team.'

'Oh . . . oh, my God . . . But I might not get another gig.'

'You will.'

A decision had to be made. Could she trust Trace? He seemed to be smitten with her, but how long would that last? On the other hand, why the hell not take a chance? She could keep him in thrall to her, she knew a few tricks. And besides a certain amount of tension was essential for any relationship. And if *she* grew tired of *him*, well. There was always that Emmy . . .

'What do you say?' Trace leaned on one elbow, watching her face screw up, eyes tight. Whole body straining towards one, glorious moment.

'Oh, yes . . . Oh, yes . . . Oh, my God, yes!'

'As good as a handshake,' Trace said as he kissed the inside of her thighs. 'Y'know, I have the feeling this could be the beginning of something great.'

VAL McDERMID

Metamorphosis

Fingers rippling down my spine. Lips nuzzling my neck. Trimmed fingernails leaving their marks on my skin like vapour trails in a clear blue sky. Teeth nibbling my shoulder blades, sinking into the long muscles of my back. Hands fierce on my buttocks, clawing and spreading them. A tongue rimming me, unimagined waves of pleasure spreading deep inside me from the tight scrunch of my anus. A fist forcing its way into me, so deep I think I'm going to split open. Like when I gave birth. The smell of sex and sweat and something more earthy. The sound of a voice I barely recognize as mine, moaning, 'I'm your bitch, fuck me harder.' The moans that turn to cries as my body gives itself up to her.

How the hell did I get here?

I'm a stranger in my own skin. Nobody who knows me would recognize this wanton sprawled on a hotel-room bed, possessed by a desire I never even thought to conjure before. I never fantasized about having sex with a woman. I never fantasized about dirty, nasty sex. I've always been a soft focus sort of girl. Candles meant romantic flicker to me, not hot wax on nipples.

Yet now this strange addiction has me in its grip.

I tell myself the story of how it came to this and I am none the wiser. I list the chain of circumstances, as I am trained to do, and it still sounds entirely alien, something so far outside my life that it can have no connection to me.

Cause and effect, action and reaction, the steady building of a

19

case. That's what I do for a living, and that is where the story begins. I am Jane Sullivan, barrister at law, called to the Bar twelve years ago. I am a criminal barrister on the Northern Circuit. I am a happily married woman with two daughters aged nine and seven. My husband David is a lecturer in philosophy at Manchester University. We live in a three-storey Victorian house in a quiet cul-de-sac in the part of Didsbury that hasn't been colonized by students and young graduates taking the first steps in their careers. We have two Volvos and a labrador called Sam.

We are embarrassingly middle class. And I like my life.

So how the hell did I get here, groaning with animal delight at the hands of a woman with six body piercings and three tattoos?

Stevie walked into my life and my chambers six months ago. The client was accused of attempted murder, the solicitor not one of my usual providers of briefs. They'd come over from Leeds on the recommendation of a local client who thought I'd done a good job in a similar case earlier in the year. Stevie was there to give the client moral support. The story was broadly familiar, though not one I hear nearly often enough.

The client had been living in a women's refuge after her boyfriend had put her in hospital once too often. In spite of a restraining order, the boyfriend had tracked her down and burst into the refuge. He'd found her in the kitchen and in his haste to attack her he'd slipped and fallen. Simultaneously she'd had the presence of mind to smash the milk bottle she was holding against the edge of the sink. As he stumbled to his feet, she stabbed him in the neck with the jagged edge. And now she was the one facing the full weight of the law. Stevie, it turned out, was working part-time at the refuge while she completed her master's degree in psychology. The client trusted her, which wasn't something she could say about many people she'd met in her twenty-three years.

To be honest, I didn't pay much attention to Stevie that day. I registered the black hair, the dark brows, the blue eyes and the creamy pale skin that signals a particular set of Irish genes, but I felt not a flicker of attraction. My focus was on the client, my mind already racing through the possibilities of having the charge reduced to a Section 18 wounding.

I took instructions, gave as much reassurance as I could, then went home to read my children a bedtime story and eat supper with my husband. I didn't give Stevie another thought until the case was called at Leeds Crown Court.

The client was shivering with fear and Stevie was rubbing her hands when we met outside the robing room. The client was beyond sensible discussion, so I directed my points at Stevie. I explained that I'd already seen the prosecution counsel and he wasn't inclined to reduce the charges. Paradoxically I thought that might work in our favour: a jury would be more reluctant to convict on the greater charge once they had heard the evidence of what the victim had done to my client in the past. I was intent on running the self-defence line. Anyone who had suffered what my client had suffered at this man's hands would have reasonable grounds to be in fear of her life.

The trial didn't go well. My client was the worst kind of witness; defensive, contradictory, inarticulate. The victim cleaned up well and managed a good stab at the heartbroken remorseful lover role. But I was determined not to lose this one and, even if I say so myself, I delivered the kind of closing address to the jury that barristers have wet dreams about. The judge summed up late on the second day and I fully expected the jury to be out overnight. That's why I'd kept on my hotel room.

But to my delight they came back inside half an hour, and with a not guilty verdict. I congratulated the client, who was a soggy bundle of tears by then, shook hands with Stevie and headed back for my hotel to pack my bags and catch a train back to Manchester.

I'd barely thrown off my suit jacket when there was a knock on the door. I opened it, expecting housekeeping, or the man who recharges the mini-bar. Instead, Stevie was lounging casually against the door jamb, a bottle of champagne dangling from her hand. 'I thought you might fancy a little celebration,' she said.

'I was just about to check out.'

One corner of Stevie's mouth lifted in a half-smile, a dimple creasing her cheek. 'Go on, you know you want to,' she said. 'That was a hell of a performance in there. You deserve the chance to rerun it with somebody who knows you're not bull-shitting.'

'I really should . . .'

'Besides, nobody's expecting you back in Manchester, are they? We all thought this was going to run into tomorrow.' She raised the bottle and waggled it gently. It was, I couldn't help noticing, rather a good marque.

In spite of myself, I was smiling back at her. I opened the door. 'Why not?' I said. If I'd known the answer to that question, I'd have slammed the door in her face.

I took a couple of glasses out of the mini-bar and we sat in the armchairs on either side of the little round table in the window. The last of the light glinted on the tiny fragments of diamond that crusted the outer rim of Stevie's eyebrow ring. She opened the bottle with remarkably little fuss and poured the champagne into the tilted glasses. 'Here's to crime,' she said. We clinked and sipped. 'You were fantastic in there, you know. I thought we were goners, but you turned the whole thing round.'

I shrugged. 'It's what they pay me for.'

She shook her head. 'It was a lot more than that. I've seen enough barristers in action to know the difference. You were very special today.'

I felt mildly flustered; I could sense an edge of flirtation in her

voice and I wasn't sure whether I was imagining it. 'I'm supposed always to be special,' I blurted out.

She gave her crooked smile again. 'I don't doubt you manage
it.' She nudged the ashtray on the table with a long, slim finger.
'Do you mind if I smoke?'

'Feel free. It's not as if I'm going to be spending the night
here.'

She opened her shoulder bag and took out a tobacco tin. To
my astonishment, she started rolling a joint. 'You've been walking around in the court with a pocketful of dope?' I knew I
probably sounded like her mother, but I couldn't help myself.

Stevie grinned. 'Hardly a pocketful. About a caution's worth,
I'd say. Jane, nobody was interested in me today. I could have
been shooting up smack in the ladies' loo and they'd never have
noticed.' She must have caught my look of horror because she
added hastily, 'Not that I touch the hard stuff. Only joking.'

She lit the joint and took a deep drag on it, holding the smoke
for a good fifteen seconds, her eyes closed in pleasure. Then she
held it out to me, her eyebrows raised in an amused question.

I don't know why I took it. Perhaps I wanted to show her I
wasn't as straight as she assumed. Perhaps I wanted to revisit
the carefree student I'd once been, before ambition and its
satisfaction had given me too much to risk losing. Or perhaps I
had the first subconscious inkling that there might be something
lurking beneath the surface here that I'd require an excuse for
afterwards.

Whatever the reason, I shared that joint. And the next one.
The champagne slipped down and we began to unwind, our
public faces unravelling as we shared something of our stories.
It seemed to make sense to order another bottle of champagne
from room service. We were halfway through the second bottle
when Stevie said, 'I should be going. If you're heading back to
Manchester, you'll need to think about getting a train.'

My dismay startled me. I didn't want her to go and that shook me. But I couldn't remember the last time I'd felt so relaxed. She got to her feet and moved towards the door. I couldn't think of a way to stop her, so I followed. She opened the door and turned towards me. 'I'll say goodnight, then.' She stepped forward and kissed me.

My mouth was open under hers. I felt the flicker of her tongue inside my lower lip. Then my hand was in her hair, pulling her into me, the blood pounding in my ears. Suddenly we separated. I couldn't read her eyes. I had no idea if she could see the darkness of the desire in mine.

'I don't think it's a very good idea to stand snogging in a hotel doorway,' she said coolly. 'Don't you think you'd better close the door?'

A wave of mortification brought a red flush to my neck. 'I'm sorry,' I said, every inch the stiff lady barrister again. I stepped back to shut the door, but before I could she was inside the room.

'You do want me on this side of it, don't you?' It was, we both knew, an entirely rhetorical question.

A tangle of clothes and limbs, a stumble of legs and hands, a mumble of words and lips and we were naked on the bed. There was nothing seductive or sensual in it; we'd performed the foreplay with our earlier words. This was simply a total carnality I'd never known before. It was appetite fed, satisfied, then fresh hunger aroused purely to be appeased. Time slid past us in a chaos of glutted lust. She did things to me I had never known I desired. And, without giving it a second thought, I acquiesced.

More than that, I gave as good as I got. I discovered instincts I didn't know I possessed. My mouth, my hands performed with a sureness of touch I couldn't have believed possible. Language was reduced to a primal state.

'There . . . oh yes. Harder . . . Please . . . Oh God . . .'

Somewhere around dawn, I think, we slept. I woke to find her sprawled face down next to me, the tail end of a sheet across the hollow of her back. The room reeked of sex, with a sweet base note of marijuana. The clock read seven thirty-four and I remembered my life. David would be getting the girls up, ready for the school run. He'd wonder why I hadn't called the night before, but not in an anxious way. He knew that when I was absorbed in a case I didn't always want to be dragged into a different, distracting mental space.

I knew I should be consumed with guilt, but it was entirely absent. All I felt was a kind of grateful wonder, an astonishment that there was room in my life for something so remarkable.

Stevie stirred and lifted her head. Her eyes opened a crack and she laughed softly. 'I thought you'd be long gone, beating yourself up all the way to Manchester,' she drawled.

'I want to see you again.' The words tumbled out before I could consider their wisdom.

'I know you do. And you will.' She propped herself up and kissed me. 'Like the song says, we've only just begun.'

I travelled back on the train, understanding for the first time the notion of the body electric. I was tingling in every limb, invigorated and exhilarated. I'd thought I understood the power of sex, but I'd been seeing a coloured world in monochrome.

Of course, I had already convinced myself that this was an entirely physical thing. It belonged in the domain of the senses, not in the heart. As such, there would be no real and present danger in seeing Stevie again. We would be occasional lovers, it would gradually lose its glamour and we would drift apart. My only real concern was whether Stevie would fall in love with me. If that were to happen, it might pose a threat to my life. But somehow I didn't think that was probable. I couldn't see Stevie picturing a future with someone as conventional as me.

What never occurred to me was that I would be the one who would become besotted. I saw her again the week after the Leeds trial, down in London. This time, the sex was more extreme, more rooted in the exploration of outrageous fantasy. This time there was cocaine to sharpen the edge of desire and loosen my non-existent inhibitions. It enraptured me. I was hooked on her.

I found myself seeking out briefs that would take me away from home so I could spend the nights with Stevie. I couldn't get through the day without talking to her on the phone, conversations that always revolved around sex and usually ended in orgasm. I knew my advocacy was suffering because I was spending more time mooning after Stevie than I was absorbing my briefs. I was taking the kinds of risk that could destroy my life and the lives of the people I had, until Stevie, loved more than anything in the world.

That, then, is the chain of circumstance that has brought me here, brought me to my knees again before a woman who is clearly tiring of me. She makes excuses now, where before she made plans. Sometimes when I call someone else is there and she won't talk. And I cannot bear the thought of her lying in someone else's arms, this woman who has stolen my comfort and ripped a hole in the fabric of my life. A day without the sound of her voice leaves me hollow, picking at my food, snapping at my children.

I fear what I will do when she leaves me. I know now what it is to be driven by an obsession that is beyond control. I understand the mentality of stalkers because that is what I am becoming. Her leaving will bring my house down in ruins about me because I will not be able to let her walk away. The need in me is too fierce.

I fear what I am becoming. I look in the mirror in the morning and see an edge of madness in my own gaze. I have run too many defences not to know the damage that this could wreak if I let it spiral further out of control. The only thing I can do to save myself, to save my life, is to act now, while I am still capable of organized, rational thought. If I wait till she leaves me, as she undoubtedly will, I shall be beyond such niceties.

And so I have made my plans. This will be our last night

together. The room is booked in Stevie's name. What she doesn't know is that I have already ostentatiously checked into another room in a motel on the far side of town; the sort of place where nobody sees you come or go. I made sure she got here first tonight and I will sit it out until I can lose myself in the early morning departures and go straight to court. I've been very careful not to touch anything that would take a fingerprint; I know better than to wipe down the surfaces because that would be a sure sign that someone else had been here with her.

We're going to play bondage games tonight. I asked her to bring her toys with her and she has because she still cares enough to want to give me pleasure. I've been reading up on cases of auto-erotic asphyxiation. It's mostly a male thing, but there have been cases where women have died playing the sort of games that are supposed to enhance sexual pleasure. I've worked it all out. Her feet bound to the foot of the iron bedstead. Her hands tied in front of her. The orange spiked with poppers in her mouth. Then the noose round her neck, fastened to the bedhead.

The tragic accident.

The hardest part will be avoiding her eyes.

VICKI HENDRICKS

Stormy, *Mon Amour*

It's a breach birth and soon as I see the tail slip out between my legs I know I am caught. The doctors start to mumble about fixing 'her deformity': 'replace rubbery grey hide with skin grafts', 'sculpt feet from the finlike appendage', 'separate muscles and bones to create legs'. But I'm filled with pride and wonder at her beauty – and at how I widened the gene pool. 'Don't touch her,' I tell them. She's perfect.'

Roger figures it out on the way home from the hospital. 'Jesus Christ,' he screams, 'it's Stormy's isn't it? You fucked that dolphin! You fucked that dolphin!' He glares into my eyes and I can only worry about him keeping the car on the road.

'Only you, Cherie,' he says. 'Only a fuckin' French bimbo like you would think you could pass it off as my kid. I always said you'd fuck a snake – but fuck a fish? Christ.' He stares straight ahead. His hands are bloodless on the steering wheel.

'He's a warm-blooded mammal,' I tell him. 'He loves me.'

I sit back and look out of the window. Roger shakes his head and makes a hissing noise between his teeth, and in my mind I'm outta there. I'm sick of him telling me to use my brains instead of my heart, to 'Grow up, grow up, grow up.' He must have told me a million times that the world is a tough place and I'd better get used to it. He says I'd be found dead on the highway if he wasn't around to protect me. But it seems to me the only one I need protecting from is Roger. Before I got pregnant he smacked me hard enough to put a tooth through my lip and one time he dislocated my shoulder. He was so sorry I forgave him, but now I have a daughter to think about.

'Well, Cherie, I'm not stupid enough to support that fucking fish and let her father off the hook. Get your stringy little blonde French ass outta here. Take that thing and hit the road before somebody finds out.'

I don't bother to mention that she is a mammal also, a mermaid – or to explain how I fell in love with a dolphin. Roger is mumbling how he'd rather see the likes of her on a platter, but I ignore him, the swine. He's making it easy for me because I hate him more now than I have over the whole three years we've been married.

He wants me out by the weekend, tells me to charge a flight to my mother's in Quebec. But I figure the next day, when he's at the restaurant, I'll hop a Greyhound for Islamorada. Asshole owns the car. All the time I'm asking myself why I handed my life over to a pudgy forty-year-old redneck who cooks animal flesh for a living. When I hitch-hiked out of Canada, I never expected to become a redneck myself, a country girl in the sticks of central Florida, taught everything by Roger. Now I'm twenty-one, legal, and have all the courage of a new mother to make a life for myself and my baby. I don't care about the rest of the world and what they might think about me and Stormy. We understand each other and that's it. He trusts my judgement with every rubbery inch of his slick hard body and, with that to hang on to, I can make it work.

The next morning I wrap Mineaux's fin in a diaper and a wet blanket and slide her bottom into a plastic Winn-Dixie sack, so she's moist and comfortable for the long bus ride. The hundred bucks I've saved is in the diaper bag alongside canned tuna and sardines I scrounged from the pantry. It's a short walk to the station and we're on the bus in no time. I know exactly where to find the new father. He was taken out of the show for sexual behaviour towards the female swimmers – really just me – and put in the isolation lagoon, where he had to learn tricks for his supper. I've been suffering with love ever since and I can't wait to see him. Love, *mon dieu*. No stopping it. There's a legend that pink dolphins in Peru change themselves into human shape to seduce the village girls, make them fall in love. The dolphins wear hats made from dried fruit to cover their blowholes. Stormy never needed a hat.

I nurse Mineaux every time she wakes, napping in between, until Key Largo. Then I hold her up to see the shining water, my eyes searching for dolphins from every bridge, even though I know he's not there. It's a beautiful place to start a fresh life. I get a cab from the bus station to Theater of the Sea. I'm not sure how to sneak Minny and me into the pool with Stormy and I have to heal a few days before I can get in the water, but at least I can show him his new daughter.

It's four o'clock when I walk through the gate. Only an hour left. I step right up to the window and charge the admission on Visa. I hope Roger hasn't thought of cancelling. I tell them I don't want to swim, but they still make me pay to get inside. It's expensive. I wonder how long till I can get a job. Childcare might be a problem.

My spirits rise with the glimpse of Stormy's lagoon. I nearly skip across the concrete down the path and across the grass to the edge of the pool where I last saw him. There are no shows going on and no theatre employees in sight. I search the surface of the water for the roll of his shiny grey head or a snort from his blowhole. I'm just starting to worry he's been taken away when I catch a glimpse of him gliding along the glassy edge. He's fast and sleek. Sunlight glints off his head and makes him shine like mercury as he rolls and sinks. I'm not sure if he's seen me, but I'm in awe of his perfection and can't break the moment.

When his head emerges at the far side of the pool, I greet him with the series of squeaks I've learned. We don't understand each other's signals exactly, but the specifics aren't important.

Stormy dives under and makes a run. He surfaces in front of me and flings a set of drips off his nose that glint in the setting sun. I recognize his mannerisms. He's full of glee. I hold Minny to my side and squat on my heels as his grey vinyl face looms up. I tilt forward to touch him with my cheek. He catches the scent of the baby and sinks slowly back into the water, holding there without the flicker of a fin, his eyes bright and level with the bundle in my arms. I gently unwrap Minny, who is sleeping through all this, and set her down on the smooth rock edge in front of him. Her upper body skin is pink and soft, but her tail is thick tough hide, the best combination of us both. She opens her eyes and begins to squirm. The black in Stormy's eyes deepens. I can feel his love and wonder welling up around us.

We're the perfect family, even if a photograph wouldn't show it. He nudges Minny with his beak and I think he wants me to put her into the lagoon beside him. It worries me in case I'm misinterpreting his intentions. I look at his upturned face, his snout making an upward jerking motion, the same as when he wants fish, but there's love in his eyes, unmistakable. He knows he's the father and he wants to see her. He holds still a little way out, in the calm lapping of wavelets. I lower her slowly and put her tail into the water a few inches. She isn't used to the temperature. Her fin pulls up and she looks at me with her face scrunched and starts to cry. I gather her up, wet tail dripping against my body, and look around to make sure we are still safe.

Stormy hovers impatiently. 'Just wait a few days, *mon amour*,' I tell him. I'm afraid. I want to be able to get in with her. I know he's hurting for a touch, but I rewrap her. She's so tiny and he can be a little rough. She squirms and nuzzles to nurse, so I slip my shirt up and she goes at it while Stormy watches with a father's love. I can see how much he wants to flop up on the grass beside us and he has the strength to do it, but he holds back. When Minny dozes off I set her down behind me, with the blanket bunched up under her head to keep her comfortable, and crawl back to the edge. I lie down so my head is close to the water. Stormy has been watching from somewhere under the surface and he raises up and rubs his face against mine over and over like a cat, only more primitive, and stronger. I ache to get in the water with him. Ever since I met him that's where I want to be.

I put my arms around his round, smooth shoulder area and hold him, touch one finger to the rim of his blowhole and stroke it gently like he enjoys. The sun is low and the air still. Minny is peaceful. I would be happy to stay like this for ever.

'Park closing' blares on the loudspeaker and startles me. I sit up and glance around, but there's nobody in sight. I dry my arms on my shorts as Stormy watches from a few feet out. He waits there and I blow him a kiss, pick up Minny, and walk back along the path. I look over my shoulder every few steps so he knows I really don't want to leave.

I have to be careful, so I only bring Mineaux back once in the first week. I don't put her in the water, although she already takes an interest in it and reaches out toward Stormy. 'Dada,' I tell her. 'That's your Dada.' She might have the instinct to swim from birth, but I'm not healed and I want to wait till I can get in, just to be sure.

Luckily for me, right away I get a job at Lorelei's down the road. It's a nice dockside restaurant with a giant mermaid out front to attract attention – a colossal Mineaux. I get out of the motel I've been charging to Roger and move into a tiny apartment across the street from the restaurant, for rent by the week. Lorelei's agrees to let me work lunch and early afternoon. People are nice in the Keys, helping me work everything out. That way I can leave Minny during her nap and get a free meal a day, besides saving enough tips to pay the rent. My only costs are diapers, the expensive admission charge, and a little food. I don't like leaving her alone, but she sleeps sound and I can't think what else to do. Two times in the next week I get her up after work and walk her over to see her papa. It's almost all the life I need. I don't miss Roger.

After two weeks I feel safe to get into the water. I have no way to tell Stormy why I haven't joined him sooner, but it's one of those things he accepts on trust. Never a complaint out of him. On the first night I can swim I wear my bathing suit under my shorts, and when I stand and peel off the shorts he lets out a throat-full of wild, high-pitched whoops. I have a little extra stomach on me, but one of the best things about Stormy is that he always thinks I'm beautiful. I slide in next to him in the cool water and, for the first time since the day we met, I wrap my arms around his body, the supple hardness no man can compete with. He's able to change the texture of his hide according to his mood and he turns himself into velvet, sliding around and nudging across me with his catlike grace. He puts his erection under my arm – a touch like chamois over steel. He tows me around in his circles of glee until I get dizzy and let go.

I want to take my suit off, but I don't dare. If Minny starts to cry, someone might hear and the staff come running. I have to be quick. I hug that thick smooth hide and cling to Stormy's satin underbelly, my legs around the curve of his back, feet locked over his side fins. He nuzzles me and brings out his flat grey tongue, letting it rest outside his mouth. I twist around his head, swiping his tongue across my shoulders, sending tingles down my back. I yank my top down and lower myself till his tongue is on my nipples and his mouth covers my whole chest. I fasten myself tighter against it, feeling the hot rush I've longed for, his mouth and tongue like smooth rubber and fine suede nearly swallowing my chest.

I glance behind me. We're at the far end of the spit of land and so far nobody has wandered back after the last show, but it's still a risk. I find his erection again with my foot and rush his foreplay. It's a spike I can stand on with no problem, but I have no fear when I pull my bottoms aside and slip myself down over it as he rises under me, stretching me to my limit. He lies on his back to let me take control and holds level in the water while I work myself up and back, my own moisture making me more slippery than he is. The water warms up around us with the heat of our feelings. I hold him close, my face near his huge clear eye, like a crystal ball, as I feel the orgasm building inside my whole body. I let loose. Sky and water blend into a sparkling blur. Stormy holds still, tilted in the water, his fin waving slowly under us to keep my head above the surface, while I stay locked around him and float in a daze against his pure grey body.

Voices coming from down the path shock me back into the world. I scramble to get out, dress, and pick up Mineaux. A man and woman smile as they come to stand beside us and gaze at Stormy in his pool. They have no idea what they missed, but I'm shivering in my wet clothes and feeling the effects of a lucky escape.

A month passes fast. Stormy and me are the happiest couple I can imagine. Minny has grown to double the size expected for a normal baby and I feel safe to put her in the water. It's July, plenty warm, and one night I dip her in to the hips. Her face shows surprise, but I make happy noises until she coos. Then I lower her waist-deep, even with Stormy's face on the surface. He nudges her side like a kitten and she puts her pink baby fingers flat against his skin. He makes a soft squeak in his throat and she answers him with a sound I can't imitate. She smiles. It's an instant connection. 'Mineaux loves her daddy,' I tell him. He hovers there, not making a sound, but his eyes are fixed on her. We're just like a real family, except there's no yelling, no hitting and no money problems to worry about. I glance behind me. Nobody watching, but it's time to go.

On our next visit, a few days later, I hold my breath and dip her face. She screeches, blinks and opens her eyes wide as I bring her up. Instinct kicks in. Her arms flap and her tail pulsates so strong I can barely hold her. Stormy nudges my arm and I know he's telling me to let her go. I'm not ready so soon, but I can't let them miss this moment. I take a breath, ready to plunge in beside her, and let go of her waist. She takes off in a straight path just under the surface of the water. Her arms streamline to her sides and she pumps to her own rhythm across the lagoon. Stormy is stunned for a second, but then he's by her side, gliding and watching as she surfaces for air, her face glowing with a baby smile I know isn't caused by gas. They begin to play, circling each other, Stormy letting out his most joyous shrieks and Mineaux rising up like an angel from the water, able to stand on her tail beside her father. They race in the glow of sunset. It's beautiful. My heart is bursting with love. I'm straining over the edge, enjoying their special bonding, and there's only the slightest pinch in my heart because I can never share in their world completely.

After a few minutes I get in and try to swim with them. They help me to overcome some of my human weakness in the water, holding me between their sturdy skins at the right angle for a smooth ride. I learn to pulse my legs and keep up with the help of a tiny arm on one side and a fin on the other.

It would be a fantasy come true, if we didn't have to beware of the rest of the world. As I take her out that night I see the sadness in Stormy's face, the slight downturn of his mouth. The scary thought that he wants me to leave Minny with him runs through my head. I know that he's lonely and unhappy doing tricks all day for his food in that small lagoon, and we are the only thing in his life he cares about. He's beginning to look lean and pale, even though he always has that built-in dolphin smile. His eyes are dull and his head is breaking out in small bumps. I know that dolphins can commit suicide by closing their blowholes and refusing to breathe, and I'm worried. He's suffering. I read in his eye that he wants her there, but I can't leave her.

I'm walking past the office with Minny on my hip, heading for the exit, when a man steps out in front of me. He has a mean look on his face and I know he's seen me several times. I'm sure there's been talk from the staff about me hanging around. I make the choice to defy him even before he can get any words out.

'I'm reporting you to the police,' I say. 'You've got a dolphin in here against his will and it's cruelty to animals.'

He shakes his head and frowns. 'We've had nuts like you here before – cutting our gate, trying to free the dolphins. The police are on our side.'

I hold Minny tight against me. 'I belong to Feta,' I say. 'We're not well known like Peta, but we protect the fish in this universe. We're tough.'

'Dolphins aren't fish,' he says. He walks past me laughing.

'I know that,' I yell. 'We protect them too.'

He looks back at me and his eyebrows go up, like he thought he heard words come out of my mouth but decided it's only mosquito buzz. I turn towards the exit to get out of there with the baby. Right then a light comes on in my brain. It's as dim as a nightlight, but there's enough glow to see that all my life I've been a pushover, somebody to ignore or boss around, and it's my own damn fault. I never stand up for myself, just run away from trouble and get nowhere. I've spent the last two months living as if Stormy was going to raise up on his hind fin and swoop me over some threshold into my dream world. But it's up to me to make a life for myself, my lover and my daughter. Soon I'm going to get caught and jailed – and if they find out about Mineaux she might become a test subject – a million bad things could happen. Nobody will ever understand me and Stormy. It's time for me to do something.

I watch the guy as he goes into the office. If he reports me I could get banned from the grounds. I have a feeling there's going to be trouble and I need to get Stormy out of there fast before I get cut off or his condition gets worse. I think it's from nerves, the sadness that comes from seeing what life could be for us if we had our freedom. He's helpless and hopeless.

I leave the park before anything can happen, but I know the man can identify me. I've been getting weird looks from the staff for a long time. I have to remind myself that this relationship – so natural to me – is still extreme to the rest of the world.

Roger would say, 'Put your blonde brain into overdrive,' and the memory spurs me into a plan to beat them all. It's just one chain-link fence that separates Stormy from the open water and all I have to do is cut a dolphin-sized hole. Then I can follow him down the Keys and find a new place to stay, where he can visit whenever he wants and roam the ocean like he's supposed to naturally. It's the first time in my life I realize that sometimes it's right to break the law. Tonight is the night of the full moon, so it's my best chance, for reasons of light and luck, to get him out.

I quit at work and tell them I'm sorry. I have no choice. I'll call about my pay in a week. I'm ready to cry, so they don't ask questions. They were my first friends since I married Roger. I leave at four and cross the street to my apartment. I'm in a nervous hurry because I have to rent a kayak before the guy closes and then take a taxi to rent the bolt cutters. I put my key into the door to unlock it, but it locks instead. I forgot to lock up when I ran over during my last break. I turn the key back and step inside feeling panicky, realizing that Minny has been there for a couple of hours when anyone could walk in. Roger is sitting in the big chair by the window. He looks rougher than ever, with white stubble on his chin and his usually short grey hair now grown into a skinny, greasy ponytail. He's smoking a cigarette. A Bud is on the table next to him. '*Merde*,' I say. 'Fuck.'

'Cherie, baby. I'm here to take care of you, honey.'

My hands are shaking and I hold the door half open, dreaming that he could possibly slither back out. I'm unable to run because of Minny in the bedroom and I'm unable to shut myself in with him. He stands up, walks over and slams the door.

'How'd you get in, Roger?'

'Landlord gave me the key.' He goes back to the chair. 'What's a matter, sweetheart? I want to forgive and forget. I can't live without my little honey. I'm fallin' apart without you, babe.'

I dart down the hall, not taking my eyes off him until I'm out of sight. I check on Minny and she's sleeping soundly and her diaper and blanket are still wet inside the plastic bag. I close the door to the bedroom and take a big breath before dragging myself back to the living room. All I can think about is that I have less than an hour to get rid of him and rent the bolt cutters and the boat.

'How d'you find me?'

'Pooh. I knew you were here since you used that Visa card. Where else would you go, anyway?'

I shrug.

'I wasn't thinking right when I told you to leave, baby doll. It's not like you cheated on me with another man.' He laughs and shakes his head, but his eyes are flat. 'This is special. It's a beautiful thing. We'll never have to work again. We've got a genetic miracle here and they'll pay us big bucks and fly us all over the world. The kid'll be famous and so will we.'

I sit down on the rattan couch. All I can think is to fuck him fast and send him off to some bar. He isn't going to leave until he gets it and feels back in control. We did the split-up routine a couple of times during the marriage when I didn't have the sense to stay gone, so Roger figures I'm sucker enough to try us again. Then he'll be happy to head for the next bar down the road and I'll head further south with Stormy – maybe all the way to the Tortugas – and never have to see Roger again. I don't like cheating on Stormy, but it's my only choice, and since Stormy can't ask questions I'll never have to lie.

I smile and go over to sit on Roger's lap. His human stench closes around me and I throw my head to his shoulder and fake a gag into a sob. 'Hold me, big honey, I've been so lonely.'

It's a nauseating idea to touch Roger's foul mouth, but I

concentrate on closing off my senses and becoming a machine. He takes me into his hairy arms and pulls my head back to start sucking at my lips. I taste and remember the hot sick slime of human spit passed from him to me, and I dig my nails into his back to brace myself while he sucks and slurps. He smears his sloppy tongue and lips over my face until I feel clammy. He crams my mouth full of his tongue so the sharp bite of cigarettes stings the back of my throat. Beer burps thicken the air I breathe. I try to think of salty spray. I'll bathe myself inside and out before I touch Stormy and expose him to foul infected human mucus.

There isn't much time, so I swallow my disgust and pull my shirt over my head and step out of my shorts. Roger wedges off his shoes, toe to heel, and I squat to unbutton his shirt while he yanks off his socks. I slip the shirt off his shoulders, unhook his belt, and rip down his pants. He's ready to go, as big and hard as most humans can get. I put my legs around him, sit down on his purplish cock, and work myself up and down, applying all the pressure I'm able so he can't hold out for long.

'Oh, yeah, that's my little gal,' he drawls. 'Yeah, man.'

I make some squeaky noises of my own, like I used to, but I'm spoiled by Stormy's fresh fish smell and smooth, thick, steel-hard organ. This doesn't even feel like sex to me any more, much less can I confuse it with anything called love. Roger's skin is hot and squishy and when he starts to sweat I think I'll puke. He's fast, thank God. His ears go red, and he gives out that call like a bull elephant. I don't mean to insult the elephant, but Roger could do sound effects on Discovery. He's in and out of me in less than a minute. His head lolls and he leans back to doze in the chair. I take his hand. I can't leave him there with Minny and I need to lock up and get a move on.

'Hon, I have to go back to work. There's a nice place down the road where you can wait for me. Beer's much cheaper than at Lorelei's – almost free. Unless you want to stay here and watch Minny? She might wake up with a dirty diaper and then you could change her for me and give her some cereal.'

He opens his eyes and lets his jaw drop, then makes a smacking noise in his jowls. 'Yeah, toots. I'll take your first suggestion. I'm pretty thirsty after that workout. Mmm, mmm. You're still one sweet little thing.'

His ass rises off the couch in an instant, like I knew it would at the mention of childcare, and he pulls on his clothes as fast as I've seen him move when his burgers were burning on the grill. I watch him walk down the sidewalk and he makes a turn into the driveway, where a car is parked. It's a new one. He's been spending money, probably counting on Minny as a gold mine.

I put on my clothes and check her. She's sound asleep and I can only pray she stays like that. I take the two days' tips I've saved and my laundry quarters and my driver's licence, in case they require some kind of security. It's a hot walk the short distance to the kayak rental and I sweat my way down the street, moisture pouring off me from rushing and planning a lie. No other way. I can't move Stormy before dark, so I'll have to rent the kayak for an hour and steal it, at least temporarily. It's the only way I can get to the gate and cut it. I never did anything like this before.

It's a young guy, smoking some herb, and he lets me pay for one hour and takes my expired driver's licence as a deposit without even looking at it. It has my right name, but I intend to bring back the kayak the next day anyway. I'll just have to pay off the bill gradually. I take my life preserver, get in, and paddle out of sight of the rental guy, to a piece of land alongside the park, on the other side of the fence. I tie up to the overhanging mangroves, nice camouflage. I have to take the chance that nobody will wander over there and grab the boat. I have to leave a lot to fate, but I know it will work because I'm doing the right thing.

I walk back to the road and cross to the Tom Thumb grocery.

I call a taxi and wait. It's only five-thirty, so I'm OK so far. The time stretches to five-fifty when the cab pulls in, and I'm getting frantic thinking about how long this is going to take, Minny all alone, and Roger less than half a mile away.

I tell the driver to wait while I go into the rental place for the cutters. Behind the desk the man looks at me odd, like he knows I'm up to something, but it's the Keys, after all, so he doesn't say anything. I fill out a form and leave the Visa card as a deposit. I don't know if I'll be able to return the cutters, so Roger will have to take care of it when the bill comes. It's lucky for me he decided to make his fortune on Minny and never cancelled my credit. If it wasn't for my Catholic school upbringing, I could have used the card plenty to my advantage, but those nuns just never let loose. I feel them grabbing at my ankles now, even as I keep on moving in what I know is the right direction in the long run.

The taxi driver turns to look, but I drag the bolt cutters on to the seat and tell him to take me back to the Tom Thumb. I think he's on to me too, but I don't give a rat's ass as long as he doesn't try to stop me. I have him drop me near the path to the water. I hand him my last four dollars and change, and it barely makes the fare and a small tip. He hands me a dollar back. 'You might need this, girlie.'

I smile and thank him. I don't know what I'll do with a dollar, but it's good will, and that pumps up the hope in my heart and brightens my face into a smile as I swing the bolt cutters on to my shoulder and shut the door.

I walk the short distance to where I tied the kayak. I smear my arms and legs with jungle-strength Deet I brought for mosquitoes. I climb into the plastic boat and drag the cutters from shore and plunk them between my legs. At this moment it occurs to me that I might not be strong enough to cut the chain-link fence that jails Stormy. I have no idea how much muscle it'll take. But I have no choice. I tell myself I can do it. I will do it. It's right. It's good for everyone.

I dip my paddles and ease out on the silvery surface, following my long skinny shadow over dark water where grasses grow and unfriendly sea creatures are, no doubt, lurking. I have maybe a mile to paddle around the point to the area of the man-made lagoon where Stormy is captive. The last rays of the sun are warm on my back and I glide slowly, not wanting to reach the gate until dark. My mind is racing with thoughts of Roger so nearby and Minny probably awake by now, hungry and wet with urine that could turn her luminous scales to dull grey blisters, her version of diaper rash. She's delicate that way, despite her hardy appetite and advanced swimming ability.

I reach the edge of Stormy's lagoon while it's still light and tie up under the mangroves to wait. The mosquitoes thicken with the night, but finally the moon comes up like a mother-of-pearl saucer, lighting my heart with hope and courage. I make my way to the chain-link barrier where my love waits. I hear his blow three times before I see him. He senses my presence on the other side of the spit of land and waits, probably wondering why I didn't come to see him at my usual time and spot.

As I round the corner to the high-fenced area, he rears up and looks me in the eye through the links. I reach two fingers inside and caress his silky nose and purse my lips to kiss the smooth tip. Under his gaze I lift the bolt cutters, which are heavy just to hold, and put the pinch on a piece of chain link at surface level. I use all my strength, squeezing the handles hard and getting nowhere. I take a breath – one, two, three – a hard punch, all I've got. I feel the blades bite and the link snaps. I'm ecstatic, yet there are many more to go. I'll need to cut a big door to peel the fence back far enough to fit Stormy, but now that I've done one link, there's no stopping me.

I crouch low in the kayak to get the right angle, resting after each effort. I work myself into a sweat fast. It takes all my strength each time and my arm muscles are shaking when I'm only a third of the way. I can't let Stormy see, but I'm crying silently. I'm worn down and sick with fear, thinking of Minny at home, and it's nearly midnight. I can only hope Roger found some drinking buddies to keep him out late. It's the Keys, I remind myself, so that's a given.

I have to get into the water as I work lower, taking breaths and going under when my arms can't reach. I'm cold and shivering, even though the water is probably above eighty degrees. Finally, I make the last necessary cut and try to bend open the door I've created. It's tough. I climb back into the kayak and wedge the nose in the open space to widen it, and swing the boat against the cut flap to crush it against the immovable part of the fence. I smash the boat into it a few times, to make sure the crease will stay and Stormy will have plenty of room so as not to scratch himself swimming through. I pull the boat out and back off, giving him space to make his break for freedom. He lifts himself to his tail and takes a look through the fence before making a move.

'Let's go, honey,' I whisper. I'm panting from excitement and exhaustion, my teeth chattering with cold. I motion with my hand. 'Swim through the hole.' I know he doesn't understand my words – not like anything he's been taught – but he can see that his way is clear. I don't know why he's hesitating. He can't realize that somebody could find us at any second and close us off for ever. I wish I brought a fish or two to lure him out faster.

Stormy sinks under the water and I think he's ready to shoot on past – still he waits. His eyes are wide open, but dull with the ill health that's been creeping over him. I wonder if I'm too late and he's weak. Maybe he's scared to leave his daily portion of dead fish. He hasn't survived on live fish for years and can't know that I'll keep him supplied. He floats silent and still. His eyes look from me to the hole and back again, but there's no flicker of motion.

I plead. 'Sweetheart, go, go, go . . . Please. Stormy, *mon amour*, swim . . . Come with me. We'll live together – in freedom, *cheri* – with our baby.' *Plût à Dieu!* . . . I flop off the boat and swim through the opening and grab his top fin. I kick with all my strength and try to pull him forward, but the fluttering of my skinny legs, in comparison to the churning power of his mighty tail, is nothing but sound and splash. I kick and pull and kick until I wear myself out. My face slips underwater. As I lift myself for a breath, I choke and Stormy puts his fin under my arm and boosts me up. I quit coughing and start to sob. He's not going anywhere, ever. He's too well trained.

I hang there on Stormy, crying and shaking, while he rests solid as a mountain in the wavelets. For the first time I wonder if he has ever shared the hot sharp pain of unfulfilled love between us, the need to be together or die that made me put my soul to the test and rise above my ordinary self to commit this deed. The cold dawn of awareness is terrifying. I want to sink below the surface and stop breathing, like he can, never face the air and the world again. It's clear that he has never experienced the passionate longing I've read in his eyes. He has never loved me in human terms – and I am an idiot.

I gain back my senses and realize that I have to go home to Mineaux, but I can barely pull myself into reality. I look for the kayak, but it's drifted away. I can't spot it across the vacant moonlit water. The park will be locked if I go that way, and it's a long walk back around the point to the road, but it's the only choice. I've stolen the kayak and the bolt cutters and lost them both – I'm a criminal with no money and no reason to live – and a crippled child to care for.

I swim out through the hole and turn back for one last look at Stormy. He's waiting and watching, as he always does when

I leave. I don't know what is inside his brain. I never did. I'm freezing and weak, but I breast-stroke down the long line of fence toward a shallow place where I can climb out. I see moving lights in the distance, from the road, a road I had hoped to go down and never come back.

One set of lights moves in a different direction and, as I swim, it seems that this might be a car driving towards me on the point of land that I have to walk down. I pass the last piece of fence and climb out on to the rocky edge. It is a car, getting closer. I lower myself back into the water to hide. It must be the police. In a few minutes the car pulls up and stops. There are no beacons, only headlights. I realize the perimeter fence is blocking the way from here. The door opens and a man gets out. He walks to the fence and his face catches moonlight – it's Roger.

He looks into the nearest pool on the other side of the fence and then sits down on the hood. Somehow he knows I'm here. He's planning to wait. I don't know what to do. I can try to swim past him without making a sound and hide in the brush until he turns back. I'm ready to give it a try when I hear crying. Good God. Minny's in the car. I haul my dripping self up the rocks. Roger sees me and stands watching as I take a few steps and stop to cough.

'I knew it,' he says. 'Blonde French bimbo.'

'I need to get the baby, Roger.'

'I was in the Tom Thumb buying cigarettes. Saw you get into a taxi with bolt cutters.'

'Oh.' I twist my hair and wring it behind me, walk past him, and open the car door. Mineaux smiles at me from her baby-seat on the floor. I reach for her and hold her against my shivering wet body, taking her warmth, knowing she doesn't feel the cold.

Roger stands looking down at me. 'I thought maybe you were picking up tools for your boss, so I went on back to the bar, but I couldn't quit thinking about it. It was midnight by the time I got back to your place. I knew exactly what you were up to.'

He purses his lips and nods his head – like he's so clever and I'm such a loser. He's half right. 'What kind of a mother are you, anyway, leaving your kid all night without food – and nearly dry? I changed her, fed her and rewet her blankets. I don't know what you'd do without me.'

'You changed her?'

'Protecting our future, hon. Don't expect it to happen again.'

I look at his face of broken blood vessels and his stubbly grey chin, and I sob into Minny's blanket, with nothing left except the painful knowledge of my lunacy. Roger motions me into his arms, but I turn and scoot into the car and close the door. He gets in on the driver's side and flips on the heat to warm me up. I'm going with him and that's all he cares about. If I have to share Mineaux with the world, maybe I should. I don't know what Roger will expect from us, but I know all that Stormy never had to offer. The world is a tough, lonely place and I can only hope to survive.

Minny reaches a finger toward the light of the radio dial and bubbles a baby sound of wonder from her pink mouth. I smile. I made a big mistake, but I did a damn good job of it.

KAREN MOLINE

No Parachutes

The body's response to fear is simple: fight or flight. Either lose your cookies while scampering off to safety, or hope to find an incontinence pad before being embarrassed to death by an unsightly accident. There's no shortage of people who've confessed that being scared witless set off their bowels. But how many have confessed that being scared witless set off their libido?

I confess. I was once scared witless at 33,000 feet. And not from a fear of flying.

Picture this: I'm dozing on Sardine Air, heading back from Rio to New York many years ago. I'd gone down there with my girlfriend Teri, under the misguided impression that I might meet some eligible beach bum who'd put some pina in my colada for a holiday romp. It's now 2 January and I still have a raging headache from the New Year's Eve we spent on a yacht in Copacabana Bay, watching a million Cariocas singing and dancing in front of bonfires they'd lit on the beach. (Just so you know what a glam evening this was, our Brazilian idyll was punctuated by the charming sound of a dozen seasick Italians, puking over the side all night; they'd had too much champagne when we boarded and forgot that the ocean tends to have – oh, you know – *waves*.) But all that ribald revelry was a distant memory by the time we were awakened at four a.m., got to the airport, sat around for five hours, and were then herded aboard our plane. Sardine Air, the charter airline from hell, had reconfigured this 747 to one egalitarian Fish-in-a-Can Class, cramming in as many narrow seats as humanly possible. By some major miracle Teri and I scored seats at the very front, in what had been first class in another lifetime, so there was almost (*almost*) decent leg room. She was a Hollywood publicist and used to travelling around the world, sleeping at odd hours, and she promptly fell asleep. I, on the other hand, squirmed around, hoping to nap through what was going to be fourteen hours of pure boredom.

Several dreadfully skin-moisture-sucking hours later, somewhere over You-Don't-Want to Crash-Here near the equator, busy reading the calorie content on the back of a packet of stale peanuts, I heard a noise I never want to hear again. It was a noise bouncing through the thin partitions of Sardine Air, amplified by the confined quarters. It was a woman, screaming. Screaming for her life. Screaming bloody murder.

Oh great, I thought, *we're being hijacked. We're going to Cuba. We're going down. What a perfect way to start the new year.*

Everyone who'd been sleeping woke with a start. The flight attendants dropped their peanuts and ran back to where the woman was screaming, the sound of their trampling feet echoing loudly. For a second or so it seemed as if the plane actually tilted down towards the left, panicking in the air as we were in our seats, as if the force of the running flight attendants forced it over.

Don't be ridiculous, I chided myself, *the plane hasn't tilted because some crazy woman is screaming and we're going down, down, down, to Cuba. To wherever. To the rainforest and all those endangered species which would be wiped out when we crashed and then what would Sting sing about? Sardines in the Amazon?*

It's amazing what your mind does to you when it doesn't know how to process information. A human brain isn't wired immediately to understand screaming at 33,000 feet. All it wants is flight. But we were already *on* a flight. Panicked confusion had strapped us to our seats more securely than the buckled belts. There was nowhere to fly off to. Except down, down, down.

The screaming continued. Male voices started shouting.

'He's got it!' one man yelled. 'He did it.'

'No, he did it!' another shouted. 'That one!'

'Stop him!'

'Get your hands off me!'

'You sonofabitch!'

'I'll kill you!'

'I'll kill you first!'

'Where's a doctor? We need a doctor. Is anybody a doctor?'

The pilot, flanked by several flight attendants and several brave male passengers, rushed past us, hurrying back to the noise. We all turned around to watch him, though we could see nothing. And that's when I noticed the guy sitting a few seats over. He was a dirty blond and broad-shouldered, with bright blue eyes. He was a babe. A dead ringer for Robert Redford (in his earlier less-grizzled incarnation as the Sundance Kid). He looked at me. I looked at him. He smiled. I smiled back. I felt a sudden, sharp ping, deep inside.

It is deeply gratifying to know that, even when suddenly confronted with inexpressible terror, when jolted from dozing boredom by an involuntary rush of adrenalin, when faced with a potentially fatal disaster high in the sky, this girlie's brain was still wired to flirt.

Sundance leaned over the aisle to me. 'Are you a doctor?' he asked softly.

'No,' I said, the screaming suddenly far less frightening. 'Are you?'

He shook his head. 'Are you a cop?' he asked.

I shook my head. 'Are you?'

'Well, then,' he replied, 'I guess we'd better sit tight.'

I certainly wouldn't mind sitting tight with you, I was thinking as the screaming stopped. A few minutes later the pilot hurried back to the cockpit. Then he came on the intercom.

'This is Pilot Stevenson speaking,' he said, his voice calm and unruffled. 'We've had a slight situation, but everything is now under control. I've also been advised that there's an, uh, weather situation in the New York vicinity, so we may have to divert to Barbados. I'll inform you as soon as we've been apprised by air-traffic control. Thank you. The flight attendants will now be coming through the cabin with drinks.'

'Why Barbados?' I muttered.

'Large enough runway for a jumbo,' Sundance said, smiling at me as he ran his hands through his hair, leaving it seductively tousled. 'Jumbos can't land just anywhere.'

But your jumbo could . . . I shook my head. I was being ridiculous. Too anxious to keep still, I got up and tried to walk nonchalantly into the nearby galley. 'What happened back there?' I said to one of the flight attendants, who looked more than a bit frazzled as she filled a bucket with ice. 'Do you need any help?'

She shook her head. 'One guy pushed his seat back, and the guy behind him didn't like it and pushed the seat forward, and the first guy got mad, and they started punching each other. Then a bunch of other guys started fighting. One of them got stabbed. That's when the wife of the first guy started screaming.'

'Stabbed badly?' I asked, appalled.

'It doesn't seem to be more than a flesh wound.'

'That's a relief.'

'Yes, and there are several doctors back there. You'd think they'd be able to afford another airline,' she said savagely, putting the bucket on the cart with a loud thud.

'Is that why we're going to Barbados?' I asked.

'We'd try to land in Caracas if it were a medical emergency, but we were going to have to divert anyway. There's a huge blizzard in New York. Just what we need. A bunch of drunks and a blizzard and no one can find the knife.'

'The knife? You mean the weapon?'

'You got it,' she said as she filled her coffee pots. 'All the guys who were fighting have been handcuffed to their seats in the back, but we don't know who did the stabbing.'

'Won't the police take over once we land?'

'Yup. Those idiots back there. I hope they all get what they deserve.' She sighed. 'I'm going back to catering. It's got to be easier than coping with this.'

Fight or flight. Fight on a flight. Fists and a knife – had been flying. And now, so was I, armed with a reason to connect to Sundance.

Collective terror is a great ice-breaker. You're immediately linked with everyone else who's endured the same experience. You want to talk about it, reassure yourself that things'll be OK, calm your racing heart. Or, in my case, keep that heartbeat racing.

So I told everyone in our section what had happened. Sundance's smile deepened. Said his name was Jonathan (not Robert), that he was so, so successful as a real estate developer but (naturally) spent all his spare nights rehearsing his rock and roll band. Then he leaned over and asked me, with a dazzling Ultra-Brite flash of his perfectly even teeth, what was I doing when we got back to New York . . . and did I think I might want to be doing some of it with him.

I was about to tell him that his teeth were as gleaming as Robert Redford's when the pilot came back on. We were, indeed, going to Barbados until the runways in New York could be cleared. It might be a long wait. Sundance winked again, said he was going to have a nap till then and promptly conked out. I was too revved up to sleep. I'd thought I was going to die and instead got busy plotting an airplane tryst.

Now I'm a cautious person by nature. I don't normally jump into dalliances without at least the pretence of trying to get to know someone over the course of a date or two. But the horrid sound of that woman's screams was still bouncing around in my brain, and the worry that the knife someone had used to cut another man's flesh was still missing, and another passenger might have it and go berserk again . . . and base instinct took over. I had to do something to shut it off, and fast. Was it a subconscious Darwinian drive to procreate in the face of danger, no matter what? Was it the simple need to touch another living, breathing human being, to prove that all the nerve endings hadn't been short-circuited by fright?

I looked at Sundance, fast asleep. He had fat, kissable lips and long lashes, darker than his dirty blond hair. (I don't know about you, but Boris Becker-like pale lashes are a total turn-off to this girl.) I didn't have a clue about him and, frankly, at that moment I didn't care. He was there. A warm, buff body with fat, kissable lips. He liked me. He wanted to connect, too. We were still alive, but I wanted more. I wanted to know I could still feel, and hang the consequences because the adrenalin of fear had instantaneously transformed itself into the adrenalin of lust. And I was determined not to be helpless in the grip of lust as I'd been for those few seconds when, gripped by fear, I was sure we were going to die.

There's only one thing to do when helplessly gripped by death-defying (literally) lust. Get a grip on the nearest available body and don't let go until the lust fades away. Then, I hoped, the last lingering shreds of fear would fade away as well.

Once we'd landed, we all sat in our seats as the police boarded the plane and took off half a dozen men, each one shouting that he was innocent. No one said peep about the missing knife. We were told we could go into, but not leave, the terminal until our flight was called, and we stepped outside into blinding sunshine and down the metal staircase. There I saw the strangest sight:

on either side of us stood dozens of 747s, lined up in a perfect row like giant winged creatures, all massively still. All waiting. We went down on to the tarmac like the rest of the passengers. It was a totally appalling breach of all security concerns, but what did we care? We'd already cheated death. That knife wasn't going to harm me now.

'Come along,' Sundance said, taking me by the hand. We strolled into the small terminal, into a horde of aimlessly milling, sunburned tourists as bleary-eyed as we must have been. There wasn't a seat to be found, or a hidden niche or nook where Sundance and I could have a sweet moment's grope to ourselves.

'This calls for a drink,' he said, leading me into the duty-free shop. We waited patiently in a long line of weary customers, hoping to get to the cash register before the spiced rum and mixers ran out. After what seemed like ages, we had several bottles in hand and walked back out into the glare of the sun. My darling clever friend Teri had a picnic spot ready for us. She'd spread our airplane blankets on the hot tarmac and was reclining on several of our airline pillows. 'Wait right here,' she said as she hurried up the stairs to the plane. We plonked ourselves down, too tired to wonder what was worth waiting for, and opened the bottles. Teri came tripping down the steps a few minutes later, smiling broadly, a large bag slung over her shoulder.

'What have you been up to?' I asked, grinning.

'Making the best of a hideous situation,' she said, grinning back. 'I'm not a publicist to the stars for nothing.'

'What do you mean?' Sundance asked.

'I had a nice little chat with the poor overworked flight attendants, and I traded four tickets to the premiere of Mel Gibson's next flick for a bucket of ice, a few sandwiches and some absolutely indispensable plastic glasses.'

'Now that is what I call an absolutely fair trade,' I said.

'Bottoms up,' Sundance said as he mixed our drinks.

And so we had a blissful, drunken, spiced rum picnic in the shadow of dozens of jumbo jets.

By the time we stumbled back on board, Sundance and I could barely stand up and we couldn't keep our hands off each other. Teri laughed and obligingly switched seats, and we got several blankets. The lady across the aisle frowned at me. I thought about my mother. For about two seconds. Then I turned that thought right off and turned to Sundance. He pushed the hair out of my eyes, poured me another rum punch, and kissed my eyelids, my ears, my forehead, my lips. That was it. We made out like lovesick teenagers under the blanket for what was now a blissful flying time of three hours and forty-seven minutes. The lady across the aisle couldn't believe her eyes.

'You ought to behave,' she hissed at me when I came up for air. 'You ought to know better.'

I did know better. Better than she did. I was alive. I wasn't stabbed. I wasn't going down, down, down. If anyone was going down, it was going to be Sundance, just where I wanted him to. My body was on fire. I had Sundance's hands cupping my breasts, unzipping my pants, roving hungrily under the blanket. If we hadn't been so exhausted and so bombed and so squashed into Sardine Air's midget-sized seats, we undoubtedly would have been cupping something else.

'Mind your own business,' I told her.

An hour before landing, Sundance dozing in his seat, I got up to stretch my legs. I took my make-up bag and walked all the way back to one of the lavatories. I stared at my flushed cheeks and shining eyes in the mirror. My lips were tingling, swollen with kissing, and I ran my fingers over them, delighted.

Fight or flight, I thought. Why worry about that when Sundance was waiting?

Sighing happily, I tried to pull out a tissue from the box. The tissues were jammed in there, so I yanked them a little too hard. The whole box spilled out and there was an odd clank on the floor. I looked down and saw a small, folded penknife. My heart started racing. *This must be the weapon,* I thought. Stashed by the stabber. I put some tissues in my hands, then gingerly picked it up. I handed it to one of the flight attendants in the back and she smiled at me with genuine relief.

'You think this is the weapon?' I asked.

'Might be,' she said. 'Why else would it be in a tissue box?'

'I don't think I want to know,' I said and hurried back to the arms of my dirty-blond stud. We sat entwined, lost in a delirium of smooching, until the plane taxied to the gate. Applause broke out when the engines whined their last. We'd been in transit for nearly thirty hours and at that point all I cared about was crawling between the sheets.

Hopefully with Sundance for company.

Except I couldn't. Not right yet. The police were waiting as I got off the plane, to ask me a few questions about the knife. I mumbled in response, too tired to care. Teri and Sundance both sat with me, their heads drooping. What seemed like hours later, but was probably only a few minutes, I heard the magic words, 'Escort you home.'

Never had a knife made me more happy. It had brought me Sundance and a ride to my blessed bed. There was a foot of snow on the ground and not a taxi in sight for all those hundreds of weary, waiting passengers.

The cops drove us home carefully, first dropping off Teri, and then depositing me and my new beloved on the stoop of my brownstone. Wearily we hauled our bags up the stairs and into my apartment. Sundance kicked off his shoes, pulled off his pants and shirt, kissed me briefly, then fell into bed. I stripped off my travel-stained clothes, stood under the spray of a wonderfully hot, stinging shower, then fell into bed beside him. It seemed perfectly natural to have him in my home, I thought happily as I fell asleep.

And then . . . and then . . .

And then how does this delightful tale end, you may ask?
Did Sundance and I awaken into orgasmic consummation,
zooming off into ecstatic raptures of pleasure? Did we fly off
into the sunset, naming our gorgeous children Rio and Rumba,
reminiscing as we grew old about the flight that had brought us
together?

Hardly. As it turns out, it was just my luck that Sundance
was completely useless in bed. It was over before you could say,
Whaddaya mean, I wasn't upgraded? Not even *Wham, Bam*.
When we awoke there was a grunt and a shove and then he
rolled over and fell asleep again. *Well,* I thought, shocked, *he's
still exhausted. Give the Kid a break.* But several hours later,
when we were both awake and refreshed, his performance barely
improved. Later that night, when I was on top and he nodded off
mid-tumble, I realized I'd unwittingly discovered what necro-
philia felt like. For a man with such nimble, roving fingers at
33,000 feet, his ineptitude on the ground was astonishing. I'd say
it was all about foreplay with him, except, once the clothes came
off, there was no foreplay. There was no play, period. Grumpily
I confronted him when he arose (ha, not like that!) the next
morning.

'Sorry,' he said, shrugging. 'I know I'm a lousy fuck. I'd rather
play with my band.'

Yeah, and I'd rather play with myself.

Worse, he somehow neglected to mention that his so, so
successful real estate business consisted of a bunch of neglected
slum buildings in Harlem and his band was a bunch of session
musicians he paid through the teeth to put up with his guitar
noodling. I'd nearly gone down with a talentless slum lord.

The moral of this tipsy tale?

I'll never take a charter flight again.

MARTINA COLE

Enough Was Enough

Shona looked at the two little boys asleep on the back seat of the car and she smiled to herself. Such good-looking boys, everyone said so. Blond-haired and blue-eyed, both had sturdy bodies and friendly smiles. They were very confident little people who assumed they were welcome anywhere and who settled down within minutes in a strange environment.

But then, why wouldn't they? Both adored, both loved so very much by each of their parents.

She saw her older son Tom's leg quiver as he slept and guessed he was finally right out of it at last. He fought *everything*, especially sleep.

She yawned. She was tired herself. It had been a long day and an even longer night.

All that fighting and arguing had taken it out of her.

She glanced at herself in the mirror above the dashboard. Adjusted it so she could see herself properly. Long blonde hair that saw the benefit of the hairdresser more often than it was needed and a full-lipped wide mouth that made her look sexier than she actually was.

Wide-spaced blue eyes, so like her sons' and the creased forehead of a woman who had a lot on her mind.

She relaxed her face and stared at herself for long moments.

She glanced at her husband as he moaned and ignored him completely.

He was always moaning lately. She had a feeling it was

because he was much more interested in being with the woman from the swingers' party than being with her or the boys.

She closed her eyes and laid her head back against the car seat. It was comfortable and she could easily sleep now, but she forced herself to stay awake.

Joseph had stopped his noise and she was glad of that much at least. It took a lot to shut that man up.

She remembered when they had first met and the memory reminded her of how much she had loved her husband once. How much he had loved her.

When they drove along then, there had been no moaning about her and the kids. He would suddenly slip his hand from the gear stick and trail it up her skirt. Making her hot for him, the sheer pleasure from the feel of his fingers on her skin was overwhelming. She would feel her mouth go dry and she would close her eyes and let the feelings of embarrassment tinged with shame wash over her as his fingers parted her legs and she would open herself to him.

He had enjoyed her discomfort as much as he had enjoyed the pleasure he gave her.

She still felt hot at the thought of it. The same confused emotions washed over her and she wanted him to do it again, one last time.

But she knew it wouldn't happen.

His fingers were trailing up other skirts, making other women come while he drove.

She felt the sting of her tears and swallowed them down.

Why wasn't she enough for him?

Why did he need other people?

She studied him again, her handsome husband. All her friends had been so jealous when she had bagged him. She had asked him once what had attracted him to her and he had laughed at her. He had laughed at her a lot in those days. Still did, come to think of it. Only then it had been with pleasure and with love not with ridicule and contempt as it was now.

He had answered that it had been the way she seemed so remote; it had been her remoteness that had attracted him. He had honestly not understood why this answer had upset her so much.

He was cruel, really. He didn't like women as much as he thought he did.

When Tom had been born he had dropped her off at the hospital and taken the car to be valeted. Her waters had broken on the front passenger seat and he had been like a demented maniac at the thought of the cleaning bill.

She remembered feeling upset at the time, hurt that he could care more about the car than her or their child. But that was Joseph all over.

She giggled at the memory of his face when he had come back hours later to see his son emerge from inside her. He said he couldn't believe that his child was hanging out of his wife's body.

He had been so amazed that even the midwife had laughed.

When he talked about it afterwards at dinner parties he always made it sound as though *he* had done all the work, that *she* had just been peripheral to the whole procedure, and people had believed him. It was a way he had.

He was a fucking bully; at least that is how she described him in her mind. He was nothing more than an emotional bully who came across as all sweetness and light to everyone, except, of course, to his wife and children. The life and soul of the party, but a terror when you got him home.

Her head was aching now from all the thinking.

That had always been her problem, even as a child she had lived too much inside her head. School reports reported her as dreamy, inattentive. Living in her own world.

Well, so what? Who wanted to live in this one all the time? Not her, that was for sure.

She watched his hands move around. Once, she had loved those hands as much as she had loved him. Those hands had given her so much pleasure. She had tingled just thinking of him coming home to her. (That was in the days when he had still come home to her, of course!) Now someone else tingled at the thought of his fingers and his mouth. Someone else ran to replace lipstick on bruised lips and rearrange breasts in bras that were as uncomfortable as they were impractical.

Those bras she had worn for him were all too big for her now; perhaps she should give them to the new woman in his life. Her breasts had all but disappeared since the boys had arrived, but she still looked good. She was *determined* to look good even if he rarely saw her.

The first time he had taken her to one of *those* parties she had been amazed at some of the women there. Big women overweight and under-dressed. Tits and arses hanging out for all the world to see. Joseph had loved it. She saw his eyes popping out of his head at the antics of the people there.

But they were ugly people, ugly inside and out.

He didn't think so, though, he thought they were great. Funny, in touch with their sexual personalities was how he had described them.

Fucking exhibitionists was how she thought of them privately.

But she had gone along with it as she had gone along with everything he wanted. It was how you kept someone like Joseph beside you. By doing what *he* wanted instead of what *you* wanted.

Like the handcuff escapades and the pretend rapes.

She wondered what he thought about the handcuffs now.

He was obsessed with sex. Any kind of sex.

Now it was sex with perfect strangers.

She had quite liked having sex with the woman, though. She

had wondered at that, it had happened in a bedroom without everyone watching and looking on. She had been trying to escape the sight of her husband on the floor with all those people. Had sneaked into a bedroom and been followed in there by the pretty, dark-haired woman.

It had taken her by surprise, the way she had responded to the dark-haired woman with the smooth hands and the even smoother tongue. It was as if she had disappeared into her own body for the first time in years.

She shook the memory away, disgusted with herself for her feelings.

That was what he had reduced her to. A lonely, sad person who got off on someone being *nice* to her, because the woman *had* been nice to her. Had told her she knew how she was feeling and how only another woman could understand her predicament.

They had sought each other out after that.

It had annoyed Joseph because she had connected with someone and according to him that was not what the parties were all about.

They were about anonymity.

It was weird taking the kids to school and seeing neighbours who had fucked her husband acting normally and talking about the children and the washing machine and how hard it was to find a good au pair these days.

Fucking surreal.

She was swearing in her head a lot these days. Effing and blinding all the time.

It was creeping into her everyday language as well.

Even her mother had remarked on it. Her pinched mouth had expressed sorrow that her daughter, *who had everything*, could talk in such a disgusting manner.

Good job she couldn't listen to what went on inside her head, it would blow her away completely.

She would love to be a fly on the wall when this latest debacle became public knowledge. She would get the blame, of course, she got the blame for everything.

Her eyes wanted to cry and she was bravely stemming the flow of tears. Tears got you nowhere and gained you nothing. She should know, she had cried enough of them.

The first time Joseph had stayed out all night she had cried. Innocent to the ways of the world then, she had been frantic. Believed something had happened to him, a car crash or something.

Wrong!

He had looked at her crying as if she was something he had dragged in on the bottom of his shoes.

He had shaken his head as she had screamed and created. Laughed at her bloated face and blotchy skin. Informed her how stupid she looked, a grown woman expecting her husband of three years to remain faithful.

Was that when she had changed towards him?

She peered at him once more. His handsome profile as he sat in the driving seat of their Mercedes making her heart jolt because he still had that power over her. The power to make her want him.

He was talking away, but she was not listening to him.

He talked about the kids now! Oh yeah, *now* he wanted to talk about the kids. Now it was too fucking late! Usually he found them a boring topic of conversation.

Now suddenly it was important for him to see them grow up, see them become men.

She watched his lips move, but the words were not making sense to her any more, but she could hear the desperation in his voice. She was enjoying his fear, she could almost smell it.

But then desperate times meant desperate measures she supposed.

And this was one desperate and terrified man. At last she had his undivided attention, maybe she should have done something like this years ago.

She had finally had enough and he knew it.

He had taken her and degraded her, he had used her and abused her. He had given her two children and had then promptly dismissed them from his life along with her.

Now suddenly they were all *so* important.

She had gone along with anything he wanted to keep him by her side and nothing had worked.

He had thrown it all back in her face.

Enough was enough as her mother used to say.

Enough was enough.

The policeman looked into the car and shook his head in despair.

The two little boys looked asleep, as did the woman. In fact she was smiling as if she was having a wonderful dream.

But the man who was handcuffed to the steering wheel looked as if he had been through hell. His head was cut and bruised, there had been violence and it had obviously been directed at him. His wrists were torn and bloodied from his attempts to slip them from the handcuffs. He had fought for his life, all right.

He had managed to smash his head through the side window of the Mercedes; it must have taken some effort.

But it had made no difference. The garage had filled up with fumes and it had just taken him longer to die.

He stepped out of the large garage and looked down the sweeping drive to the electric gates that told intruders this was private property so keep out, and waited for the pathologist and the ambulance to arrive.

It was a lovely day, bright and sunny. He could hear the sounds of summer, buzzing flies and birds singing in the trees. It really was an idyllic setting.

The imposing house with its gables and its moneyed air looked lonely in the brightness of the morning.

Bereft of life, it seemed to be looking out at the world with a weary expression.

The policeman thought of his wife at home with the kids and his homely face broke into a small smile.

Suddenly, he wanted to see them this very second. Make sure they were all OK.

But instead he waited as he was expected to.

LIZA CODY

Queen of Mean

With half a glass of red swirling down my plug-hole throat I wrote, '*Psychotic? Yes. Minimalist? Never. Naked Lunchbox is the band to give indie miserabilism a good kicking. Don't miss it.*'

I hit send and bunged it down the line to Steve at the *Gigz'R'Us* office. Stolen words, junk phrases, meaningless concepts slither down their own electronic plug-hole. Do I care? I do not. I had a good night and I'm saying so.

Was the band psychotic? Hardly – it was young, totally unknown and mildly silly compared to bad-boy bands I knew and loved. Would it give indie miserabilism a good kicking? I very much doubt it, even if I knew what that particular junk phrase meant. Or if the band knew. Or Steve at the office. But Steve will print it. Oh yes, of course he will, because he's a poseur who admires junk phrases that juxtapose blue-collar attitude with intellectual name-calling.

I've worked out what Steve likes, which is why I lifted and reworked the phrase from a *Guardian* review in the first place.

'We gotta meet,' Steve said a few months ago. 'You sound like my kinda groover.'

'Think so?' said I with a husky hoot.

He invited me to the *Gigz'R'Us* New Year thrash. I accepted, but I didn't go. A week later, after he'd read my Ban She copy he rang and said, 'Why didn't you come? I was looking out for you.'

'You were not,' I said. 'You seemed to have all the action you could handle.' How did I know that? I didn't, but I do know how Steve likes to see himself.

'I did, didn't I?' he simpered.

'And *I* don't run with the crowd.'

'No?'

'No.' And I cut the connection. But after that he began to pay me more and he printed my byline in bold. Then he asked me for a photo.

'It's my opinions you're paying for,' I retorted, 'not my face.'

'All the same . . .'

So I sent a photo. It was a beautiful thing, but it wasn't me I wasn't at that stage ready to be visible.

Steve had never seen me, but I'd seen him. This is the age of the spy, after all, the age of surveillance. Young dudes expect to be looked at and listened to, and I'm nothing if not obliging. If Steve dresses for attention and walks loose-limbed, choreographed to catch the eye, if he spends a small fortune on his hair and face, it means he wants to be watched. He has a website, for God's sake – he's telling the world he wants attention.

But that's cool. I was not looking for a hippy. Had I for one moment believed that Steve was editing a street magazine, chock-full of alternative opinions, for nothing but idealistic reasons, I wouldn't have bothered. Right from the beginning I sussed that *Gigz'R'Us* was more Steve's personal CV that it was a magazine. It was a manifesto which said over and over again: I am young and hip. My opinions, the opinions of this paper, are what's happening. Everyone else better shuffle off and die. You don't count.

To enforce his reputation as a thrusting young carnivore, Steve naturally rubbished what was popular and promoted his own recherché tastes. A brave and cheeky iconoclast, oh yes, and the group of writers whose opinions he published were just like him – young, hip, iconoclastic, affected, always up for a little name-bashing. And then there was me.

If Steve had known who he was employing he would have been astonished, to say nothing of mortified, embarrassed or shamed. But he didn't know. He was a hi-tech narcissist who thought I must be another reflection of himself.

It was a situation I would find hard to explain to anyone who already knew me and it all happened because I wasn't ready to shuffle off and die with dignity. And because of a sad little conversation I had with my oldest, closest friend at the Tate Modern.

We'd wanted to look at some Louise Bourgeois drawings, but the morning was spoiled by two camera crews vying for the best locations. One was filming a media pundit talking about Rothko and the other was filming a legendary photographer on a fashion shoot with five legendary models.

Penny herself was a model in the Seventies – before models were superstars, before a shoot was a media event in itself.

'At least we had a small place in the sun for a short time,' Penny sighed.

'*You* did.'

'You did too,' she said – generously, 'but I never thought of posing in pretty frocks as a career for a grown woman. If I'd known then what I know now—'

We looked each other in the eye and laughed. Thinking, presumably, about the wealth of knowledge we'd hacked out between green tick and tragic tock. There are so many mistakes a woman can make between men and menopause.

The biggest mistake of all was the belief we both had that you must deserve the prize: if you work hard, sacrifice, put others first, do enough to merit it, the trophy will be yours. Bollocks, cobblers, in a pig's patootie: awards are made regardless of merit and you can steal any prize if you are young, hip and relentless in the art of self-promotion.

'Even so,' Penny put in, 'I wouldn't want to do it all again.' She still has the perfect bone structure, of course. It's just the skin that sometimes reminds you of badly fitting tights. 'I don't think I'd actually want to "self-promote",' adds the woman who was picked out of a cinema queue when she was fifteen by a bored photographer. 'It just isn't dignified,' added the friend whom I once hated because at the age of seventeen she could make strong men weep and rich men give her their homes.

This same woman can still summon enough elan and allure to snag a cab merely by lifting a hand. I walked.

On the Embankment I met . . . ah, who did I meet? I really do wonder about that. She said her name was Lucy Satin, but come *on*. Who the hell is called Lucy Satin?

'You're making that up,' I said.

'Only in the sense that all names are made up.' She smiled a crooked smile, revealing strong white teeth. Imperfect cheekbones, I thought, remembering Penny, but young. All you have to be is young. Youth is better than bones.

I'm not sure how we got talking. I was looking at a piece of sculpture outside the Ministry of Defence – a perfect portrait of metamorphosis, from a man to hero to corpse, all in one figure. I may have said something about all human aspiration ending in doom and death.

She said, 'It's the price you pay for dreams. It's what happens when you twat around with destiny. Destiny bites back.'

'Aren't some dreams worth the price?'

'You tell me,' she said, smiling her crooked smile. 'You're paying.'

'Then, yes, they're worth the price. If nothing else, I want to travel further than I can walk.'

'What else do you want?'

I suppose, in the back of my mind, I was still running with the thoughts stirred up by my conversation with Penny. I can't think why else I would have told a total stranger, a woman young enough to be my daughter, 'What I want is a younger, more perfect body.'

'Whose would you like?' she asked, and she sounded just as if she were behind a counter at Selfridges offering me a squirt of perfume.

I burst out laughing, but she said, quite soberly, 'You see, that's my business. I give people more perfect bodies. I am, in fact, a body double. If you go to the movies or watch much TV you'll have seen me. It's no good looking at my face – you won't recognize that. You wouldn't recognize my bits either – you'd think they belonged to . . . well, whoever. I am what you might call an enabler.'

At that moment the sun came out and reflected off the pure white walls of the Ministry of Defence, almost blinding me. I blinked and then saw that she was handing me a card. It read: Lucy Satin. Body Double. Dreams Come True. Strictest Confidence.

'Thanks,' I said, trying not to giggle. But Lucy was staring at the metamorphosing sculpture, which now looked black and threatening against the blinding white stone wall.

'Advice,' she said. 'I wouldn't automatically opt for a woman's body if I were you. Women's bodies are boringly over-exposed these days. Think about it. There's still a huge advantage to androgens.'

I laughed outright. I couldn't help it. 'If I could choose,' I said. 'If. It isn't only the matter of a young body. It's a question of, well, attitude. When I was young you didn't put yourself forward. You waited to be asked. You couldn't *use* what you had without feeling—'

'What? Cheap? As if you're cheating? Oh come on! How old *are* you? It isn't about "taking advantage" or "showing off" any more. It's about self-respect. Deserving it. Living up to your full potential.'

'Going for it?' I asked sarcastically.

'Which is exactly what you didn't do,' Lucy said dismissively. 'What *did* you do? Remind me. A couple of books, and a handful of high-profile lovers? And that's it?'

'How the hell do you know?' I was suddenly incensed and somewhat scared.

'I recognized you, stupid. You had your picture on the dust jackets.'

'That was ages ago. They've both been out of print for years.'

'Yes. And why? Because you didn't push or kick up a fuss.' Lucy's expression, what I could see of it with the white glare behind her, looked contemptuous. 'You never maximized your potential. Which is why we're having this conversation, or are you just gobbing off and wasting my time? You want a second crack at it, right?'

'Well—'

'Oh, fuck it,' Lucy said, turning away. 'Just forget it. If you don't know what you want, you can't blame anyone but yourself if you don't get anything.' She turned back suddenly. 'You're just going to let me walk away, aren't you? Why?'

'Because you're a lunatic,' I said.

'Actually,' she called over her shoulder, 'it's because *you* are a wuss. You *like* being as boring as you look.'

So I ran after her and whacked her with my handbag. For the first time in my life. I have never hit anyone before, I swear.

I burst into tears – not because I was upset. I wasn't. I was relieved, nothing more. And nothing less. It was as exhilarating as the beginning of a romance. Which, in a sense, it was. And Lucy? Lucy Satin just laughed.

After that day I began to notice several things. Not all at once – the consequences weren't immediate. For instance, in the next month, I won three small amounts on the lottery. My cat left home, never to return. My son got a job and stopped asking for handouts.

'What are you up to?' Penny asked. 'You never seem to be in when I call these days. Got a new man?'

'Who says I need a man?'

'No need to bite my head off. What's got into you?'

'Must be the hormone gel,' I said and hung up. I felt Penny was holding me back. Old friends resent change. New friends take you at face value.

'I think I've found the perfect man for you,' Lucy said. 'His name's Steve. He wants to be famous. He's vain, venal and promiscuous. Wildly ambitious.'

'Good-looking?'

'Pretty tasty,' she told me. 'Well, *he* certainly thinks so. Check it out – he eats at Gnosh. It's a fit little package we're looking at.'

I was having trouble with the way she talked about people as if they were commodities, but I found that, with practice, if I disciplined myself to think 'it' instead of 'he', I could free myself from considering his humanity.

'Humanity? Boring,' Lucy said. 'Whatever made you old dames think you were better than them? All it did was turn you into a bunch of overworked prigs. Once you accept you're as bad as the worst of them, you can start to have fun.'

So in the interests of equality I started to refer to my own body as 'it'. Steve was not the only commodity I was shopping for. I joined a health club and realized that, with a little work, soft flesh could be a renewable resource: I began to notice the transmutation of wibbly-wobbly dross into toughened gold. Well, it certainly looked more gilded after I hit the sunbed.

Then, following Lucy's direction, I sat close to Steve at trendy Gnosh and witnessed what, only laughingly, could be called an editorial meeting.

'He wants to be the smartest cookie in the jar,' I told Lucy, 'but he isn't very smart. What's his degree in – woodwork?'

'Ooh, saucer of milk for you,' Lucy said.

'Although,' I added, 'if trashing people were smart, he'd be a genius.'

'Way to go! Accentuate the negative. You're learning.'

In fact, sitting close enough to Steve to overhear his conversation gave me my first opportunity. Quite loudly, he said, 'I wish we had someone to send to the Ratrun gig. It's about time someone cut them down to size.'

So I went to watch Ratrun, and afterwards I wrote: *Constant adulation would make anyone sloppy and tonight was no exception. It's as if the audience has forgotten why they liked Ratrun in the first place, and Ratrun has forgotten how to be hungry. In the Kama Sutra of avant-garde rock, Ratrun has now assumed the missionary position.*

I signed my piece 'Kaa', after the snake in *The Jungle Book*, and I added a note which said, 'I suppose you will be publishing your usual sycophantic review, but I thought maybe you'd like to know what's being said at street level.'

Steve rang the next day. 'I liked your piece,' he said. Well, he would, wouldn't he? He more or less told me what to write so he didn't question my opinion. And I failed to mention that I didn't know Ratrun from a rat's bum.

He said, 'By coincidence we couldn't send a staff reviewer so I'll use your piece. I don't know how you're fixed, but we're always looking for a fresh young take on stuff. So how would you feel about freelancing for us?'

My opinion was nasty enough to pass as 'fresh' and 'young'. I was in.

About that time I began to feel silly in a skirt and I saw, to my surprise, that women's slacks ballooned on my hips like jodhpurs.

'I can't believe it,' I told Lucy, 'I've got *acne*. What're you doing to me?'

'Don't shout at me,' she said. 'Slow down. Adjust the dose. You're showing all the signs of 'roid rage.'

'Don't tell me what to do.' I slammed down the phone because I was sure I could hear her laughing. But later, after I'd chilled a bit, I realized that I *was* becoming itchy and antsy. There was something tick-tick-ticking at the back of my neck, saying, 'Get on with it, get moving, stop wasting time.' Oddest of all – shopping drove me crazy. I wanted to race in, tear something off the rails and race out again. Trying on was out of the question.

'What's the matter with you?' Penny wailed. 'You're no fun any more.'

'Got to work,' I said. 'I told you. I've got some freelance—'

'No need to snap,' she said.

I'll have to dump Penny, I thought. She's so . . . so what? So girlie? So old? So mummy-fied? Let's face it, honey, my best friend Penny was a drag – always on about clothes, kids, diets and relationships. Well, I was one relationship she could cross off her achingly long list.

I wrote, *O'Donnell's is the sort of after-hours joint where bouncers go to gut-barge each other between sets. The house band stinks . . . of pure testosterone.*

Gigz'R'Us printed the piece and Steve forwarded the free beer voucher O'Donnell's sent him by way of thanks. That was lucky – I hadn't known what to say about the band except that it was crude and drab. But that wouldn't do for Steve, and it wouldn't do for Kaa either. I was on safer ground when I could say something like *Imagine Sun Ra on a bad hair day.* Or *This is clearance sale Krautrock without any roll.*

Next time I saw Lucy she was sucking on a long black cigarette, leaning against a wall, in the middle of a thunderstorm. It was after midnight and rain tumbled like diamonds out of the shattered sky, but she was wearing a skinny, strapless number and her bare shoulders steamed. She seemed wreathed in smoke.

'Who are you sticking the knife into tonight?' she asked. 'You're getting quite a reputation, you know. I saw one of your reviews quoted on an ad last week.'

'I'm getting there.'

'Where exactly?' Rain boiled and vaporized on contact with her skin. Her cigarette end glowed scarlet in the dark. Mine was too wet to smoke. I dropped it into the gurgling gutter.

'Having fun,' I said defensively.

'Don't knock it,' she said. 'Don't settle for it either. Is that all you want? Is that what having another bite at it means to you?'

'I can't go much further than this. I'm just a voice trapped in wire, the words in the machine.' I felt let down. My limitations had become too apparent to me. 'I can spy on Steve from a distance,' I said, 'but I can't go to his poxy party. If he sees me, I'm blown. He'd die if he met me.'

'Hmm,' she said.

'You know, he's taking credit for my reviews?' This was something I'd found out only that morning. A guy with a grudge copied and sent me Steve's application for a job presenting a youth media show on Late Nite TV. In it he said that as well as being MD and commissioning editor for the 'new street-smart, opinion-forming magazine, *Gigz'R'Us*', he was out there himself, reviewing under such sobriquets as Tony Vole and Kaa.

My guess was that the guy with the grudge was Tony Vole, although in his email to me he called himself 'Mole'. And why not? Steve was pretending to be me. While I was pretending to be . . .

'This is what's happened all my life,' I told Lucy. 'I do the work, he gets the credit and I can't confront him. It's so unfair.'

'Hand me a tissue,' she said, 'and wait while I have an ickle blub.'

'Well, what do you suggest I do? I can't exactly stomp in and nut him.'

'*I* would,' said hot young Lucy, 'if he was ripping *me* off.'

Of course, I was ripping off other reviewers, left, right and centre, but, in my defence, I was *not* stealing their identities and I *was* adding my own venomous spin. I was beginning to wonder if maybe I was getting my come-uppance when I saw Lucy staring at me, eyes narrow, critical. 'Thinking's bad,' she hissed.

'Why?'

'Dunno. Just is. People who think just sit on their bums in front of computers making excuses. Like you have all your life. I thought you wanted to change.'

'How?'

'Get your hair done,' Lucy said. 'There's nothing like a good stylist to change your life.'

The stylist worked in a salon called Shape Shifters. He sat me down in a front of a machine which took my picture from several angles. On a computer screen he morphed a variety of styles and colours of hair on to my image. Lucy watched over his shoulder. They didn't consult me.

'Queen of mean or king of sting,' Lucy mused. 'What d'you think, dahling?'

'We could go either way,' said the stylist, twitching his mouse.

'Stop when you get to one *you* like.'

'Hey,' I said weakly, 'it's *my* hair.'

'I told you, dreams are expensive,' Lucy snapped. 'Today they're costing you your hair.'

'Masterful,' sighed the stylist. 'Ooh, look, Lucy-Lu, I could almost fancy that myself.'

'Me too, almost,' Lucy agreed. 'It's very . . . um, Peter-with-painted-toenails.'

'Harry-with-handbag,' added the stylist.

'Make your mind up,' Lucy said to me. 'Boring middle-aged

woman? Or younger Harry-with-handbag who can stomp into
Steve's office and nut him?'

'What sort of choice is that?' I asked.

'The one you wanted,' says Lucy.

Actually, I was amazed at the transformation. A whole layer of
myself fell with my hair to the salon floor and was swept away
to be burned, leaving me bereft and bewildered.

'What you see is what you get,' said Lucy, grinning her
crooked grin at my unfamiliar reflection. 'What you get is up to
you. Try to get what you really want this time.'

It's always easier to know what you *don't* want, and I told
you at the beginning that I didn't want to shuffle off and die.
The game is always won by the young and hip. But if you can't
beat 'em and you can't join 'em, your only option is to steal
from 'em – if you can get away with it.

I was getting away with it. I was Kaa, my own creation.

But that night I sat alone in my flat without even a cat for
company. I tried not to think about my hair. I refused to think
about the cost. Instead I counted the cigarette burns on the arm
of the sofa and wondered how long I'd been so careless of the
soft furnishings. I remembered my son, always wanting to eat in
front of the TV and me saying a sofa was not a dining table.
I remembered running around behind him putting down the
lavatory seat, wiping the basin after he cleaned his teeth. I
remembered his giggling girlfriends with their feet up on the
coffee table, their bags stuffed with lipgloss and condoms.

Now the coffee table was covered with trade papers and
notebooks and I asked myself when it was my cleaner stopped
coming, and when I had stopped noticing the smell. My car was
spotless, but the flat was a tip. Still, as Lucy says, everyone can
see your car so it'd better gleam, but no one's going to look at
your interiors unless you invite them in.

She's right. When did anyone ever get famous for wiping the

green stuff off the fridge door? I realized I simply didn't care any more, I'd lost patience for invisible, repetitive tasks.

What I wanted, at that dark moment, was a bloody red steak to cheer myself up, but when I looked in the freezer, all I found was broccoli quiche and neat little tubs of pasta sauce. I caught myself asking what idiot had put them there. I went out.

Night is the best time these days. Daylight seems to sear my eyes and give me headaches. I used to complain of sleepless nights until I realized how easy to solve the problem was. Now I sleep longer and deeper, but not at night.

Night is for prowling, searching for live acts, something to get my teeth into. Opinions form, words flow, Kaa speaks, another boy-band bites the dust.

Tonight I go looking for Steve in his favourite canal-side haunt, Odd Bags. The hag on the door looks like a Nazi, but his blusher gives him away.

'Not seen you before, have I?' he says, and the high denomination note concealed in my fraudulent handshake vanishes. He eyeballs my hat, my hair, my threads and my Church's shoes. 'Got anything to make the evening go with a bang?' he asks.

'No.'

'Want some?'

'Oh why not,' I say, and another note changes hands. I pass. Oh yes I do. I am wearing a fedora, the light is dim, but I pass unquestioned. This time last year he would have tittered in my face. Tonight neither age nor gender have let me down and I pass.

It was karaoke night at Odd Bags. There was a man on stage dressed up as Diana Ross who was belting out 'Come See About Me' to a bunch of other Diana Rosses, Dolly Partons, Marthas and the Vandellas, Chers, Edith Piafs and Bette Midlers.

I was shocked – I'd been led to believe that Odd Bags was one of those cool, hip, dark places where cool, hip guys like Steve cruised. Glitter balls came as an unwelcome surprise. I was mortified to be surrounded by a bunch of guys who seemed to know more about the art of being glamorous women than I ever had, even in my heyday.

My first instinct was to run. If Steve was cross-dressed, I wouldn't recognize him anyway. All the work I'd put into becoming what I thought he wanted was in any case wasted when surrounded by so many wigs, ball gowns and suspender belts. As a man I was redundant; as a woman I would never have cut it even in my wildest dreams.

'Looking for someone?' breathed a six-foot-tall Blondie.

I must have been dithering. Cardinal sin. 'Whatever you do, don't faff around,' Lucy told me many, many times. 'Go for it. You deserve it.'

'I'm looking for a man,' I said idiotically.

'Join the queue,' he sniggered. 'Will I do?'

'No. I mean yes,' I stuttered. 'I mean you look superb.'

'Thank you, darlin', but you just missed me. I did *the* definitive "Heart of Glass", to *rapturous* acclaim I might add.'

'Well you've certainly got the legs for it,' I babbled.

Blondie hooted. 'This isn't your scene is it, darling? Poor little lost boy. Pity, you'd have made a luscious mid-period Patti Smith.'

'No shit!' I said, horrified. 'Actually I was looking for someone in particular.'

'Tell Debbie, darling, she knows *everyone*.'

So I told him and found out that Steve was the bustier-clad Madonna sitting between Kate Bush and Tina Turner at a table covered with streamers and champagne bottles.

So many famous, talented women. So much in-your-face female sexuality. And all without the foul whiff of genuine degrading oestrogens. I thought about Lucy Satin, body-double to the stars. Would she, too, be redundant here? Or would she stomp in and nut Madonna?

'Steve's partying,' Blondie said. 'She just landed the job she wanted at Late Nite TV, the bitch. Some people take it all. *And* she's too stringy for Madonna.'

The coquetry and spandex turned my guts. I went to the bar and downed a sour with the tab of zing I'd scored off the doorman. Refreshed, enabled, emboldened, I ordered a bottle of Bollinger for Steve's table. I hung around till the waiter pointed me out to him. Then I flicked the brim of my fedora, meeting his eyes across the seething sequinned crowd between us as I turned away and made for the door.

I didn't think he'd come. I wouldn't have. If some strange guy sent me an invitation, an expensive drink, a follow-me gesture, I wouldn't have followed him. But, then, I am a woman. And Steve, for all his silly top and fishnet tights, is a man. For whom there is no danger he can't handle. No man he can't beat.

Did I nut him? Well, I have to confess that, however far I've travelled down my chosen route, I still cannot get interested enough in men fighting to learn the appropriate techniques. I'm ashamed to report that first I pulled his wig off, then I went for his face – forgetting that I no longer have effective fingernails – and finally, in the clinch, I bit him. His tin tits were boring into my back, his forearm was locked around my throat. I just sank my teeth into his strangling arm and hung on, grinding, until he let go. My blood was boiling. His was dripping off my chin.

I don't care what you say, women's party gear renders the wearer vulnerable. Had Steve been wearing a decent jacket like mine I would never have even bruised his skin. He has only himself to blame. As I told Lucy, after the story appeared on *London News* a couple of days later.

'I didn't attack him,' I protested. 'He attacked me.'

'Don't be so wet,' Lucy said. 'He was probably only trying to cop off. Can't you tell the difference?'

'Not always, no,' I said truthfully. 'And he didn't give me the chance to tell him who I was or what my beef was.'

'Sex and conversation don't mix. But it's just as well, seeing

that his condition is critical and the police are waiting at his
bedside to question him.'

'I still can't believe it,' I said. And I couldn't. When I ran off
that night, Steve was on his feet using the foulest language
imaginable.

'Blood poisoning,' Lucy said, with relish. 'Septicaemia. Toxic
shock.'

'Men don't get toxic shock.'

'Steve did. That's some set of fangs you've got.'

'It wasn't me,' I wailed. 'It couldn't have been.'

'If there's one thing I can't stand, it's guilt. You did it – suck
it up. You wanted a new life and you took it.'

'Not like that. Anyway, he might recover.'

'Mmm,' said Lucy.

Two days later, the headlines were calling it 'A Bizarre Death',
and Lucy was saying, 'OK, so he's dead. Boo-hoo, move on.'
And Lucy was saying, 'There's a job going at Late Nite TV.
You're qualified – Steve nicked your work and your name to get
it. It's yours by right. Go for it.'

'I can't! Lucy think about it. A TV presenter – if anyone sees
me I'm blown.'

'Steve saw you and you weren't blown. You've changed.
When are you going to start believing me? You can be who you
wannabe. Come to think of it, you'd been stalking Steve for
months and you didn't recognize him.'

'He only saw me in the dark. And I didn't recognize him
because he was in drag.'

'That's your answer then. Present a show in drag.'

'Lucy,' I say, 'you're going too far. This even turns post-
feminist irony upside down.'

'So?' she says.

'So . . .'

'Wimp out now and we're through,' says Lucy Satin, body-
double.

What the hell, I think – what've I got to lose? Lucy begins to leaf through a wig catalogue and I pick up the phone. Outside, the night rain falls, and faintly through the double glazing I hear a rumble of thunder. What is life anyway, if it isn't a performance? None of it's true. And I look at my fading reflection in the window and I think, *Yes, this is me, this is what I'm doing, and I do deserve it.*

LAURA LIPPMAN

What He Needed

My husband's first wife almost spent him into bankruptcy. Twice. I am a little hazy about the details, as was he. I don't think it was a real bankruptcy, with court filings and ominous codes on his credit history. Credit was almost too easy for us to get. The experience may have depleted his savings, for he didn't have much in the bank when we married. But, whatever happened, it scared him badly and he was determined it would never happen again.

To that end, he was strict about the way we spent money in our household, second-guessing my purchases, making up rules about what we could buy. Books, for example. The rule was that I must read ten of the unread books in the house – and there were, I confess, many unread books in the house – before I could bring a new one home. We had similar rules about compact discs ('Sing a song from the last one you bought,' he bellowed at me once) and shoes ('How many pairs of black shoes does one woman need?') It was not, however, a two-way street. The things he wanted proved to be necessities – defensible, sensible purchases. A treadmill, a digital camera, a DVD player and, of course, the DVDs to go with it. Lots of Westerns and wars.

But now I sound like him, sour and grudging. The irony was we both made good money. More correctly, he made decent money as a freelance technical writer, and I made great money editing a loathsome city magazine, the kind that tells you where to get the best food/doctors/lawyers/private schools/flowers/ chocolates/real estate. It wasn't journalism, it was marketing. That's why they had to pay so well.

Because I spent my days instructing others how to dispose of their income, I seldom shopped recreationally. I didn't even live in the city whose wares I touted, but in a strange little suburb just outside the limits. Marion was an unexpectedly pretty place, hidden in the triangle created by three major highways. It should have been loud. It wasn't. It was quiet, almost eerily so, except when the train came through. Our house was Victorian, pale green, restored by the previous owners. It needed nothing, which seemed like a blessing at first, but gradually became unsettling. Houses were supposed to swallow up time and money and effort, but ours never required anything. We were childless, although we had a dog. When my husband found the house and insisted we move from the city, I had consoled myself by thinking the new place would absorb the energy I never got to put into raising a family. But its only demand came on the first of the month, when I wrote the mortgage cheque.

One day last January I came home and tossed a bag on the kitchen table. White, with a black-blue logo, it was from the local bookstore. Christmas was past, no one's birthday was on the calendar. I had no excuse for buying a book. I hadn't read anything in weeks, much less the required ten. Which is not to say I always obeyed the rules. I broke them all the time, but was careful to conceal this fact, smuggling in purchases in the folds of my leather tote, letting them blend with what we already owned until they took on a protective colouring. 'This sweater? I've had it *for ever*.' 'That book? Oh, it was a freebie, came to the office by mistake.'

But on this particular January day I came through the kitchen door after dark, let the dog leave footprints over my winter white-wool coat and threw the bag down so it landed with a noticeable smacking sound. My husband, who was preparing dinner, walked over to the table and opened the bag. It contained a first novel, plump and mushy with feeling. I steeled myself for his response, which could range anywhere from snide to volcanic. I was prepared to tell him it was collectable, that this first edition would be worth quite a bit if the writer lived up to the ridiculous amounts of praise heaped on him.

But all my husband said was, 'That looks good,' and went back to his sauce.

Over the next few weeks, I brought more things home. CDs, which I didn't even bother to remove from their silky plastic wrapping. More books. A new winter coat, a red one with a black velvet collar and suede gloves to match. Moss-green high heels, a silk scarf. He approved of everything, challenged nothing. He began to think of other things we could buy, things we could share. *Season tickets to the opera?* Sure. *A new rug for the dining room?* Why not? *Built-in bookshelves?* Of course.

One night, in bed, he asked, 'Are you happy?'

'I'm not unhappy.'

'That's what you always say.'

True.

'Why can't you talk to me?'

'Because when I tell you what I feel, or what I'm thinking, you tell me I'm wrong. You tell me I don't know my own mind. I'd rather not talk at all than hear that.'

'You don't know what you want.'

This was true.

'You were a mess when I met you.'

This was not.

'Everything you've accomplished is because of me.'

'But,' I pointed out, 'I haven't actually accomplished anything.'

'Are you going to leave me?'

I gave the most honest answer I dared. 'I don't know yet.'

He threw himself out of bed and ran downstairs. I went after him, found him in the kitchen, pouring bourbon into a stout glass of smoky amber. He had not approved of those glasses when I bought them, but he used them all the time. He finished his drink in two gulps, poured another. I got a bottle of white wine from the refrigerator and sat with him.

'Do whatever you have to do,' he said at last, 'but understand there will be consequences.'

'Consequences?' I assumed he meant financial ones, perhaps even a blow to my reputation. In my circle of friends and business associates I was famous for being happily married, if only because that was the version I insisted on. His absence made it an easy illusion to sustain. Although I had to socialize a lot because of my job, my husband never came along. He liked to say I was the only person whose company he craved. He thought this was romantic.

'You will come home one day and there will be blood all over the walls,' he continued, not unpleasantly. 'I'll kill myself if you leave. I can't live without you.'

'Don't say that.'

'Why not? It's just the truth. If you don't want to live with me, then I don't want to live.'

'You're threatening me.'

'I'm threatening myself.'

'A person who would kill himself has no respect for life. It's not a big leap from killing yourself to killing someone else.'

'I'd never hurt you. You know that.'

We stayed up all night, talking and drinking, debating. We had done this in happier times, taking the opposing sides on less loaded topics. He demanded to know how he had disappointed me. I couldn't find any real answers. A few minutes ago, I had been not unhappy, but I had assumed my condition was my fault. Now, all I could think was that I was a prisoner. A thug was threatening the life of someone I loved, had taken him hostage. That thug was my husband, my husband was his hostage. I was trapped.

But, then, I had always been trapped. By my job, which I hated, and this house, whose only requirement was that we make as much next year as we did last year. I could give up books and CDs and coats with velvet collars, but those economies of scale would make no difference. Like everyone else we knew, we were addicts. We were hooked on our income. He was hooked on my income. My servitude made his freedom possible. I wanted to be a freelancer, too, to leave the world of bosses and benefits. One day, he promised, one day. And then we bought the house.

I couldn't talk about this, for some reason. Pressed about the concrete reasons for my discontent, I couldn't say anything, except to complain about the train, the drag of commuting. We had only one car, so I took the local train to work, which jounced and jolted, making five stops in eleven miles. It was wonderful in the morning, the paper in my lap, a travel mug of my own coffee in hand. But the last train on this line left the city at seven-thirty. At day's end, I always felt as if I was on the run, a white-collar criminal returning to my halfway house. I talked about the train until three or four in the morning, until my eyes dropped with sleep, his with boredom and bourbon.

When I came home the next day, there was a new Volvo waiting for me in the driveway. Green, with a beige leather interior, and a CD player.

'Now you won't have to take the train any more,' he said.

The car was just the beginning, of course. We responded to our marital crisis in the acceptable modern way: we threw fistfuls of money at various people in what is known as the mental health profession. I found them in my magazine's 'Best Doctors' issue. His psychiatrist. My psychiatrist. A licensed clinical social worker who specialized in couples therapy and who believed in astrology and suggested bowling as a way to release aggression. A specialist in social anxiety disorders, who prescribed various tranquillizers for my husband. Another licensed social worker, whose beliefs seemed more sound, but whose work yielded no better results. He gave us homework, we did it dutifully, but neither one of us could see how it was helping. I wanted to talk about the suicide threat, which I considered vile. My husband disavowed it, downplayed it. He wanted to talk about my secret plan to 'stabilize' him so I could leave with a clear conscience. The social worker said we both had to give up our insistence on these topics and move on.

'Are you scared?' my shrink asked me in February.

'Very,' I said. He told me to search the house for a gun the next time I was left alone, but I was almost never left alone. Finally, he went to the grocery store, but I didn't find a gun. I was almost disappointed. I wanted hard evidence of the fear I felt, I wanted to be rational. I did discover that my husband was stockpiling the tranquillizers from his doctor. He had claimed to have trouble sleeping since I admitted I had thought about leaving. *Why?* I wanted to ask. *Are you watching me all night? Do you think I'd slip out then?* How little he knew me if he thought I'd leave that way. I imagined him killing me as I slept, then killing himself. I began to have trouble sleeping, too, and it was my turn to get a prescription, my turn to stockpile.

But how would he do it, my sceptical sister asked. 'He can barely summon up the energy to change a light bulb, he's not organized enough to buy a gun. I hate to say it, but he would be lost without you.'

Her words hung there, making us both glum.

'I'm not saying you should stay,' she added. 'Only that you shouldn't be scared of him.'

'But you're saying what he said, more or less. If I leave, I have to be prepared to face the consequences.'

'Are you?'

'Almost.'

I had no reasons to stay, but I had no reason to leave. Until, it seemed to me, he said what he said, revealed how far he would go to keep me. I believed in my marriage vows, if not in the God to which I had made them. My husband didn't hit me, he didn't cheat on me. I knew no other reason to leave a spouse. Oh, yes, he was lazy, and he liked to tie one on now and then, upending the bourbon bottle in his mouth to celebrate this or that. Or, more frequently now, to brood. But I couldn't fault him for that. I couldn't really fault him for anything, except for the fact that he was willing to ignore my misery as long as I stayed. He was prepared to make that deal, to do whatever he could to keep me there.

I thought there were rules for leaving, a protocol. I thought there would be a good time or a right time. I realized there would never be a good time.

'What can you get out of the house without him being suspicious?' my shrink asked me in early March.

'Myself,' I said. 'Maybe a laptop.'

'You can't take a few things out, over several days?'

'No,' I said. 'He'd notice.' And it was only when I said it that I realized it was true: he was keeping an inventory. He was going through my closet while I was at work, checking my underwear drawer, looking under my side of the bed. He was spying on me as surely as I had spied on him when I went looking for the gun he hadn't bought. All those things – the CDs, the books, the shoes, the clothes, the Volvo – were meant to weigh me down, to keep me in place. That's why he had allowed me to have them. He was piling bricks, one by one, in front of the exit, burying me alive.

'Then it will have to be just you and your toothbrush,' my shrink said. 'Call from your sister's house after work and tell him you're not coming back.'

I came home from that session planning to do just that. But

my husband knew me too well. He could see it in my face, in
my eyes. He backed me into a corner in our bedroom that night,
demanding to know why I was unhappy, how I could turn on
him. For ever and ever, I had said, I who valued words and
vows above all else. How could I think of leaving? He did not
touch me. He didn't have to touch me to scare me. He demanded
every secret, every fear, every moment of doubt I had ever
experienced – about us, about myself. I sat in the corner, knees
to my chest, shaking with sobs. I began to think I would have to
make up confessions to satisfy him, that I would have to pretend
to sins and lapses I had never experienced. He stood above me,
yelling. Somewhere in the house our dog whimpered. I would
have to leave him, too. Leave our dog, leave the car, leave the
clothes, leave the CDs and books, lose the opera, and *La Bohème*
was next. Of course, it would have to be *La Bohème*. It was
always *La Bohème*. The fact was, I'd even have to lose my
toothbrush. He was watching me that closely now. I'd be lucky
to get out of the house with my own skin.

I did the only thing I knew to do: I capitulated. I asked for his
forgiveness. I brought him the bourbon bottle and he poured me
a glass of my favourite wine, a Chardonnay he usually mocked
for its lack of subtlety. We drank silently, pretending a truce. We
crawled into bed and watched one of his favourite DVDs, a
Sergio Leone Western. I would start to doze off, then pretend to
be wide awake when he asked if I was sleeping. He didn't like
me to fall asleep with the television on. I think he resented how
easily I slipped away from him every night and was secretly
pleased when I joined him in insomnia.

On our television a boy stood beneath his brother, who had
been suspended on a noose. If the boy moved, his brother would
die. Henry Fonda stuck a harmonica in his mouth. 'Play,' he
said, 'play for your ever-lovin' brother.' Of course he couldn't
stand there for ever, harmonica in mouth, hands tied behind his
back. He staggered forward and his brother died.

By the time the sun came up, I realized an unpredicted snow had been falling all night and the streets were near impassable, even for a brand-new Volvo.

But I had to go to work or be docked a day's pay, snow or no snow, binge or no binge, Sergio Leone or no Sergio Leone. I said goodbye to my husband's slumbering form and headed out of the door. I wore jeans, snow boots, a black turtleneck, the new winter coat, suede gloves and a felt hat. I turned the key in the lock. I wanted to take it from my ring and throw it in the nearest drift, but I knew I couldn't. I'd have to come back. I walked to the train. I did my work. And that night, when the train stopped at our station, I wasn't on it. I was at my sister's house. She wasn't approving, but she was sympathetic. She listened as I called and told him, in a choked voice, that I was never coming back. He didn't say anything. The line went dead in my hand.

He didn't have a gun, after all, so there was no blood on the walls. But there was all that booze, and all those pills, his and mine, squirrelled away for the sleeplessness we had never tried to cure. Because I didn't go back for forty-eight hours, things were pretty bad. The dog, luckily, had survived, and without resorting to anything desperate or disgusting. I had filled his kibble dish the morning I left. Still, it was bad, and everyone felt sorry for me, wanted to ease my guilt. So sorry that the suburban police said it must be an accident, and the coroner agreed, and the insurance company gave up fighting after a while, so the mortgage was paid off in one fell swoop with the life insurance. There was no suicide note, after all. And while there were all those threats, dutifully reported to all those mental health professionals, they proved nothing. He had mixed booze with pills, despite warnings. True, it was suspicious he had taken so many pills, but I was able to report in all honesty that he had often ignored dosage advice, taking two, three times what was recommended. He also had an amazing capacity for liquor.

It never occurred to anyone that he was probably dead the

morning I left, that my phone call home that night, overheard
by my sister, had been completely for show. Or that the pills
had been chopped up and dissolved in his bourbon bottle days
ago, in hopes such an all-nighter would come again, and soon.
It had been hard, waiting, but it was worth it. I had not noticed
the snow falling because I was lying in bed, listening to his heart
stop.

He had always said he would kill himself if I left. All I did
was hold him to his word.

DENISE MINA

Alice Opens the Box

If Alice had anything left to give, she'd give it. She'd given her life for Moira already and she'd given it happily. They'd never let her out after what she'd done for her, but she wanted to give more. She looked up. The grey woman was watching her through the glass, a silver badge flashing on her chest. When Alice looked up, the guard looked down at her papers. Alice saw that look all the time, but today, day of days, it cut deep, kicking the breath out of her. She crossed her legs and covered her face, folding in on herself.

The guard watched Alice through the glass, wrapping her hands around her skinny, withered face, coughing or something, bucking from the chest. The guard was glad that she wasn't going in the car. Most of them in here were just unfortunate, but it would sicken her even to touch a woman like that. No one wanted to go with her, no one wanted to talk to her. Alice didn't want to talk to anyone else anyway, she had said about three words in the seven months she'd been here. She had never cried, that's what they said about her, not one tear, even in the hospital. Women prisoners will cry because their tea is cold. The guard looked at her again. Alice had stopped coughing and was sitting calmly, a blank look in her eyes, a hand smoothing her greying hair.

Alice had cigarettes. They were the only thing she had left that was worth anything. She had six from a ration of ten for the day, had them in her pocket and she'd give them to Moira when they got there, as a sign between themselves that she loved her. And she did love her. She wanted to throw her hands out and wrap them around her, hold her in tight and not let go.

The guard looked up and saw Alice lift a knee and throw her arms around it, as if she was going to pull her own leg off. She had a skirt on and the guard could see the crotch of her pants, the red and blue skin on her inner thighs. She was sickening. It was as if she wanted to be sickening. The buzzer shrieked and Hannan spoke through the intercom.

'Hannan and Arrowsmith. Here for Alice Paterson.'

The guard let them into the office.

'There, she's there,' she said pointing through the glass.

Hannan and Arrowsmith looked in at her, crossing their arms, contemptuous.

'Did you two run over the governor's dog or something?'

Hannan snorted. 'We're getting brownie points.'

'Yeah,' said Arrowsmith, 'and we're the only two on today who haven't got kids.'

'That poor baby,' the guard shook her head.

'Aye,' said Arrowsmith, 'died after just six hours. As if she knew who her mother was.'

Alice saw them watching her and talking. Whatever they were saying, she knew it wasn't good. They all hated her; even before Moira they wouldn't look at her. The two guards disappeared from the office and the grey metal door in front of her buzzed alive. Hannan pushed it open and stepped back.

'Let's go, Alice.'

Arrowsmith was standing in the corridor, nodding and pursing her lips.

They were rougher than they need have been. She'd nearly dropped the box on to a table and they were pissed off with her for that. Hannan held her upper arm tightly and shoved her towards the car, digging her nails into the skin. Alice felt disgust in the stiffness of Hannan's fingers, in the way she kept her body distant. No one wanted to be here. Neither of them would look at her in the eye. They spoke in single words. 'In,' said Hannan, capping her head as she pushed her into the back seat of the car.

It was hard to hold the box in both hands and get herself into the seat. The side of the box was too deep for her to hold it with one hand. Alice wanted to put it down on the seat, but knew it would make them hate her more. She held it underneath and bumped her arse along the seat, her hand feeling the contents slide to the side, a gentle shift in weight.

Arrowsmith followed her into the back seat, soft thigh pressing hard against Alice, shutting the door behind her. Hannan got into the car through the other door. Like mirror images they slid their belts on, clipping them next to Alice's hips. The driver locked the doors. Arrowsmith passed a belt over Alice's lap, making her lift the box as she handed it across. Hannan took it, clipped it shut. 'Go,' said Hannan to the driver.

They watched the gate open. A wall of grey slatted metal rolled upwards, splinters of sun glinting off the surface. Beyond the gate lay another barrier, a solid metal wall. An electrical impulse shook it awake and it slid back. Alice hadn't seen outside the gates since the last day of the trial. It was green outside, big hills in the distance. Cars passed them as they waited to join the road, clean and dirty cars.

'How long will it take to get there?' asked Alice.

Hannan looked at her. Alice was not known for being chatty. It was the longest sentence she had said since she came in.

'Half-hour,' said Hannan and turned away to look out of the window.

The heater was on full in the car, a hot whingeing breath. Alice looked out of the window, resting her hands on the box, feeling under the lip of the lid with the tips of her fingers. Screw nuts, small, but she could still get hold of them. She looked at

the box and smiled. She'd been planning this. She was going to
see Moira once more, whatever the consequences, and she was
going to give her the fags. They were all she had left.

She looked at the guards. Hannan was watching the road,
Arrowsmith was doing the same on the other side. They couldn't
bear to look at her and it was a good thing. The driver was
watching the road, not checking the mirror as often as he should.
His eyes were ringed with brown skin, tired and sickly. Keeping
her elbow down and her hands still, Alice turned the metal
screw below the lid with her fingertips. It was stuck, wouldn't
move. She pressed it hard, keeping her arms slack, pressing on
it, stopping when they turned their heads towards her, when
their eyes might fall on her hands. She breathed in, keeping
her breathing steady. Finally, just as her fingers were about to
spasm, she felt the screw give.

The driver slowed for a roundabout and a woman crossed in
front of them. She wore a dirty anorak and carried a shopping
bag. She looked annoyed and her bare legs were slapped red by
the cold wind. Alice watched the woman pass, turning her head
to let her eyes linger. Lucky cow, lucky cow. Going shopping for
messages, mince and tatties and a mag with puzzles or some fag
papers. Lucky, lucky and not even knowing. Alice had a coat
like that, with a hood and deep pockets. She wore it for the four
winters before the police came to their door. That coat got rained
on and snowed on, she wore it against the wind and too long
into the summers. It was pink with purple squares and white fur
around the hood. She never cleaned it, that she remembered.
Never got round to it. It was clean when she bought it in Oxfam
and then, suddenly, four years later she looked at it and it was
too dirty to clean.

Her fingers turned slowly, undoing the screw. She pulled at
the edge of the lid. Sensing movement on the lip, she slid her
hand along the wood to the far edge and began to press another
screw. The four winters were hard and unkind, the four winters

when she did what she shouldn't have. She knew she'd done wrong, knew what she was doing was wrong but it all happened slowly and she couldn't see how it might have been different. She did love him. Charlie. Even the name made her feel hot, sent a flush up her neck. She lived to see his face and would lie in bed at night, staring at the ceiling, amazed that he was with her.

When she first saw him, sitting in the corner of the pub, he was surrounded by laughing men, laughing himself. He lifted a hand, brushing hair from his eyes and she saw gold glinting on his pinkie. A long time afterwards, sitting on the stained sofa watching him eat a curry off his knee, she realized that laughing along with a crowd was as unusual for him as it was for her. He wasn't comfortable in company, wanted to be alone, to have peace and quiet. It was important to him. She was lucky he moved in, that he forgave her the kids. It was hard to keep them quiet. She thought it was their ages, three to seven, but all she wanted was for them to keep quiet. It didn't seem too much to ask.

The car juddered to a stop at a set of lights, throwing them all forwards on their seats. The box slipped along her thighs, banking against the front seats, dropping at the corner. They all heard the contents hit the side. Hannan and Arrowsmith looked at her, appalled. Arrowsmith lifted the box carefully into her hands again.

'Do you want me to take it?' Hannan said it like a threat, as if Alice couldn't even be trusted to hold something. It wasn't her fault, the car had stopped sharp, but they hated her already and couldn't hide it. She liked the men better. They didn't judge so much. The women were cows. Fat cows who couldn't get a man. Charlie.

Alice shut her eyes. Charlie in the bath in Lomond Street, wet hair, rubbing his face with a flannel. She could see the muscles on his back when he moved his arms. He was thin, Charlie, always slim. He said he was going bald. *No, you're not. It's thick at the back.* She opened her fingers on the back of his head, pushing them up through the thick yellow hair, feeling the sharp ends run through her fingers. *Shut those fucking kids up.* He was a wonder to her. She would look at him when he was watching telly, wondering at him being here with her, despite the kids, despite herself and everything she lacked. She couldn't even cook nice.

She finished the corner screw and moved her hand slowly over to the next one. Charlie was in Perth now. They weren't allowed to phone or write to each other and she could see that it was a good thing. While he was there she couldn't see straight, honestly couldn't see what they had done was wrong. She just wanted them to be quiet. When Charlie was near he filled her eyes, she couldn't see past him. Even when the police came to the door and lifted the floorboards and found the kids. They were crying. They climbed out themselves, she watched them. She'd looked at Charlie and knew it wasn't so bad. She just wanted them to keep quiet. She kept explaining to them, if they kept quiet she wouldn't need to punish them, wouldn't need to take the belt to them or wet them in the cold bath or put them in the dark place. She didn't enjoy doing it, but they needed to learn to keep quiet or she'd be alone again, in that flat again, for years with no one to talk to, for years with no one. *Shut those fucking kids up.*

She didn't mind sitting in the box in the court, being looked at as long as Charlie was there beside her. She was big with Moira then, her stomach swollen in a big round ball. They were taking Moira away, whatever happened in the court, the social worker said. Because of the cuts on the other kids, because they'd gone bad. But Moira would always be her child, the social worker said. They were made of the same stuff. And Moira might find her when she was eighteen, she'd have the right to look for her. She'd know who her mother was.

In the court a man said she sacrificed her kids for her man.

Those unhappy children, he said, unhappy children who suffered her for a mother. What a thing to say. She was doing her best. He'd leave if they didn't keep quiet. She dressed them and let them watch telly, it wasn't much to ask them to keep quiet. James, her oldest, agreed with her. He kept them quiet when he could, made the smaller ones stop running when Charlie was home. James was small for seven. Deep down she knew the man in the wig was right. The jury looked at her and she knew they thought it too. Charlie and James and her, three against all of them. The man in the wig was right. The screw on the box was done and she moved her hand over to the final one.

'We'll be there in a couple of minutes,' said the driver.

Hannan and Arrowsmith looked at her, reading her face and seeing nothing. They looked away.

'Now, we're going to have to cuff you in a minute, Alice,' said Hannan, trying to be kind, 'I'm sorry but that's how it has to be. Governor's orders.'

Alice's fingers worked and worked, turning the last, the very last chance she had to see Moira. The car slowed as it turned into the drive, passed through the high metal gates and crunched through deep red gravel. Alice slid her hands into her pocket, wrapped her fingers around the fags, breaking them because she was so overwhelmed. With the other hand she wrenched the lid off the box, breaking the wood, the loud crack filling the car. The car stopped suddenly. The driver turned to look, shocked and disgusted. She couldn't see because her eyes were hot and brimming over. Hannan and Arrowsmith's faces blended together. *Stop it, you fucking mental bitch.* Alice pressed the fags into the box shouting, *Moira, sorry, sorry, Moira, sorry.*

Christ, stop her. They pulled the box out of her hands, dragged her out of the car and cuffed her hands behind her back. Alice looked up and, among a field of gravestones, saw an angel in white stone, wings outstretched as if she was just taking off, heading home. She kept her eyes on it while they fussed around her, sat the box on the back seat, tried to fit the broken lid back on.

She hadn't shed a tear in hospital. She knew she was doing right. She pressed and pressed the face until the chest stopped moving. Pressed the face into her own tender breast, hurting herself while the breathing stopped. Moira. As she laid her face down in the cot, her body was still raw from her, her stomach still swollen.

Hannan was crying, looking into the car at the box and crying like kids do, with her chin all tight and her hands limp by her sides. Behind Alice, Arrowsmith was panting hard, yanking the hands up her back, hurting her shoulders.

'How can ye?' she said over and over, 'How can ye?'

'Who is Moira?' shouted Hannan, 'Who's Moira?'

The man in court said she sacrificed her kids for her man. Now, it was different, now it was better, now it was her for the kids. She looked into the car. The small white box had the broken lid sitting on it, snapped fags around it on the seat and on the floor. Inside the box, precious white box, lay Moira, black hair, skin of milk, blue lips. Moira, the happy child who would never suffer Alice for a mother.

SUJATA MASSEY

The Convenience Boy

'Miho! You'll miss the train if you don't get up right now!'

Miho Haneda was too tired to groan as her mother pulled off the quilt she was huddled under. She'd been awake for a while, going over the memory of the night. The hands stroking her body, then the mouth. She had wanted to stay in bed for a thousand years. Now there was chilly air on her skin – the atmosphere of a typical Japanese house in late autumn. Getting out of bed was hard enough on any workday, but these last few mornings the process had been utterly miserable.

'Ara!' Mrs Haneda shouted. 'Naked again and in December! You will catch pneumonia if you do not wear pyjamas. Go to the bathroom now, get dressed, and I'll have some hot soup for you.'

Miho stood up, not bothering to hide herself. For much of her twenty-three years, she'd been embarrassed about her body, but lately she had been feeling so alive that she'd stopped minding that her knees were so bony and her bottom too flat. She'd stopped minding that nobody seemed really to notice her as she went about her tea-making duties at Sendai Electronics, where a year after university she'd become an office lady just like all the others: navy blue uniform, sheer hose, artificial smile, voice pitched at the high, breathy point that the male bosses expected.

As she went into the bathroom, turned on the little water heater and splashed warm water on her face, Miho counted. Twelve times – or was it thirteen? There had only been two nights missed in the last two weeks since he'd started visiting her bed. Thirteen times, yes, that was it. She was having more sex now than she'd ever had in her life – and to think it was under her parents' roof! It was convenient, all right. Convenience Boy, she called him in her mind, because he did exactly what she wanted – all without her having to tell him, and all without knowing his name.

As Miho sleepily brushed her teeth, she thought again about how all she wanted was a chance to know who he was. See his face. Just once she would find a way to turn on the light and see who her stealthy lover was.

But last night, when she'd stretched out a hand towards the lamp, he had whisked it out of reach, then flipped her over on her stomach and begun loving her in a new way that had her biting the quilt for the next fifteen minutes. It didn't matter who he was, Miho had thought, as her core splintered into a hundred shining fragments. It didn't matter at all.

The woman who opened the door to the first-floor apartment in an old stucco house regarded Miho blankly. 'Yes?'

Miho blinked because this woman was younger than she'd thought – a girl, really, in her late twenties, with brownish-black hair cut in a short, cool-looking spiked cap. She wore a tight-fitting T-shirt that outlined high, typically small Japanese breasts, and black nylon running shorts. Her legs were long and slender and would have been perfect by modern Japanese standards, if the thighs hadn't been so muscular. When Miho saw the Asics trainers on the girl's feet, she understood the thighs. She was a runner.

'Excuse me, hello, it's the first time we are meeting,' Miho began in the high-pitched, polite way she'd spoken ever since she was old enough to realize that was what girls had to do. 'I'm Miho Haneda. Are you Miss Shimura?'

'I am. And I know about you because my cousin called me to

say she'd made the referral. Actually, I was just going out to jog. I expected you at noon, not eleven.' The woman's voice was lower pitched than usual and had odd stresses on certain words. *Half Japanese*, Chika had said. Not a regular Japanese. Chika had said that the fact Rei Shimura was a foreigner would make her less judgemental of Miho's situation.

'My office manager changed my schedule, so that's why I'm early. I'm sorry, but when I called to tell you the line was always busy—'

'You're right, it's been engaged. I apologize, but I was receiving a fax from Scotland that took most of the hour.' Rei made a face as she motioned Miho inside.

While Rei sat down to untie her running shoes, Miho stepped gracefully out of her pumps and up on to the tatami mat flooring of the apartment. This was the strangest apartment she'd ever seen. Rei had decorated the walls with kimonos – old ones, the kind that Miho's grandmother wore – and had tied old kimono sashes into soft sculptured shapes that were grouped on the top of antique wooden chests. An old kitchen cabinet held more pieces of blue and white china than Miho had ever seen, outside of a shop. The apartment looked like a museum of Japanese folk art, not the home of a jogging detective.

Rei picked up a tea pot from an antique tea table and went into the kitchen. 'Is green tea good? Or do you want *kocha*?'

Miho's stomach leaped excitedly at the thought of foreign, black tea. '*Kocha*, please. I'm very grateful you could see me.'

'It's no problem. But let's get to the point of the consultation. I don't know if Chika told you, but I generally bill six thousand yen an hour.'

Miho gulped. Rei certainly was plain spoken. 'That sounds reasonable. I can gladly pay you for today and for the advance hours.'

'Excellent.' Rei came back to the coffee table, beaming. 'Here, is this chair comfortable enough for you, Miss Haneda? It's an old Korean piece. If you like it, I can easily find you another from my source in Kyushu.'

'I don't want to buy a chair. And please call me Miho. I'm younger than you.' Then Miho blushed, realizing what she'd said sounded insulting. 'Not that you're old at all – you don't look thirty! And I know you have a famous business selling Japanese antiques—' Miho cut herself short, she was making small-talk.

'It's true that my work generally involves Japanese antiques. I must tell you I'm a bit confused about why you're here, Miho-san. Why don't you just tell me what you want?' Rei asked, sounding kind. 'Don't worry, nothing's too strange. I've had plenty of unusual requests since I started my consulting service.'

So Miho told her, keeping her gaze steadily on the cup of black tea Rei had set before her, since it was too embarrassing to look at this stranger, no matter what she said.

She started with the first night, the time she'd awoken to find a warm, hard body against her. She talked on, at times in a whisper, about how she'd been afraid at first, but then headlights from a passing car outside cut briefly through the room, and revealed a bit of the boy's face – showing incredibly beautiful, gentle eyes. Then, she'd reached out a hand to stroke his cheek and it had all begun.

The person she'd thought of as an intruder turned into a boyfriend she thought she could love – even though he'd never said a word to her over the hours they'd spent together. She didn't mind the silence; after all, the sincerity of loving touch meant far more than words. Or so she thought.

On the fourteenth night he did not come to her room. After that, she'd waited in vain. Now, two weeks later, he had still not returned.

By the end of the confession Miho's tea was cold and she and Rei were staring at each other. There was an expression on Rei's face which Miho couldn't read. Could it be arousal? Miho had noticed Rei recrossing her legs a few times during her more explicit descriptions. That gave Miho a little rush of pleasure, followed by a sensation of shame.

At the end of Miho's confession Rei asked a few questions: the name of the current prime minister; what day of the week it was and to count backwards from a hundred in multiples of four.

Miho answered the questions patiently, then said, 'You think I'm crazy.'

'I'd think that most people telling a story like yours would be fantasizing,' Rei said slowly. 'I asked those things to see how connected to reality you are. Chika told me you were very rational, but this story – I've never heard anything like it.'

'I thought you might not believe me. That's why I brought photographs.' From her Celine handbag, Miho whipped out a white folder containing her evidence; the telephoto shot showing the outside of her window with the damage to the latch, the scuff marks that looked as if someone had climbed up the six feet to the window and the trampled mulch around the camellia bushes just under the window.

Rei was silent for a moment. Then she said, 'Miho-san, these photos don't prove anything. You could have made all these marks yourself on the house wall. The footprints don't look that mannish to me, anyway. They're no bigger than mine.'

Miho looked at Rei's feet, which actually were larger than the footprints left in the garden, and guessed they were a legacy of her half-American heritage. Then she shook herself, feeling irritated at how Rei had taken her off course. 'Why would I fake something like this? It would only bring trouble with my mother. I'll die if she finds out about Benri-kun.'

'What did you call him? *Kun* means "boy" or "guy", but Benjie is not a Japanese name I've ever heard—'

'*Ben-ri.*' Miho exaggerated the R sound so that Rei, who was used to English Rs, would catch on. 'You know, convenience. I think of him as a convenience boy.'

'But . . . why?' Rei's eyes widened.

'Well, don't you know that some girls call their boyfriends "Mr Rice" if they're using them to get meals, or "Mr Transportation" if they can always drive them. There's even a kind of man called "Mr Donor", who gives plenty of money when you need it.'

'Convenience Boy. It sounds so – mercenary,' Rei said, laughing a little as if she wanted to sound cool. Why was she nervous? Miho wondered, watching Rei shoot a glance over to a tansu chest draped with an obi, upon which sat two framed photos. The first one was framed in traditional black lacquer and showed a sober-looking, but handsome, young Japanese man standing in muddy boots and jeans in a garden. The other portrait was framed in silver. It showed another young man, happier looking, with red-gold hair, green eyes.

'Who is the foreigner?' Miho asked, following Rei's gaze.

'A guy from Scotland.'

'And the Japanese one?'

'Never mind.' Rei straightened her shoulders and leaned forward. 'Listen, Miho-chan, I must tell you that the kind of searches I do generally are for antiques – not convenience boys.'

'But in the past you've found *killers* – which is very serious business! All I'm asking you to do is find someone I care about. And if he doesn't want to meet me, I want you to ask: did he run away because he lost interest – or because somebody saw him go through the window? And then I want you to tell him I want him back.'

Rei shook her head. 'He might be upset to find out that I know what's going on. I mean, there are American Marines who've gone to prison for breaking into Japanese teenage girls' bedrooms. And that was for fondling, not for rape.'

'It never felt like rape to me,' Miho said, voice trembling. This was the reaction she expected from the police, not a sophisticated foreigner like Rei-san – a woman so cool she kept framed pictures of two lovers. 'Please, Rei-san. I've got a few ideas of Benri-kun's identity – that is, if he's someone who knows me, who maybe sees me every day, but is afraid to act. I'll give you this list; it shows their names, the places they work and their telephone numbers. I was hoping you could check out these men for me, without, of course, revealing what's going on. If what I've been doing became known – well, it would ruin my reputation.'

'Indeed,' Rei said. 'You're only twenty-three. It's natural for you to want to explore fantasies, but in a couple of years you'll probably get married.'

'You haven't married,' Miho pointed out.

'OK, I'm not married,' Rei answered crossly. 'I don't know if I ever will be. But I can tell you it's not all fun and games being a twenty-eight-year-old single woman in this country. Those of us who don't live with our parents have to deal with outrageous rent and gas bills and flying cockroaches in the summer—'

Miho cut her off. 'I'll pay you, no matter what you find. And if you can actually get Benri-kun to come back to me, I'll pay you double the hourly rate! I can afford it. I live with my parents, so I can save my entire salary.'

'Well, I don't.' Rei sighed. 'And since this is a lean month I suppose I could make a few enquiries. But, first, we'll need to draw up a contract. And, if you don't mind, I'll need a small deposit and a couple of photographs of you.'

'Thank you!' Miho opened her handbag and retrieved the fat envelope she'd already stuffed with seventy thousand yen: a week's pay for pouring tea and muttering sweet inanities to the male employees at Sendai. It was a lot of money, but nothing, really, in comparison to the sensation of Benri-kun's tongue flickering between her legs. To get that back, well, she'd pay anything.

For Miho, the next few days passed very slowly. Benri-kun still hadn't come through her window and Rei seemed to be moving through Miho's list of suspects at the languorous rate at which it took soybeans to ferment into miso paste. In fact, Miho was so bored with waiting around that she actually helped her mother make the salty paste, which was the perfect flavouring for soup.

'You will be a good wife now that you know this procedure,' Mrs Haneda said approvingly after five days, when Miho's bowl of beans had begun to turn into a nice brown slurry.

'Wife? But I'm just out of school – hardly started my job at all—' Miho slammed down the lid on the underground compartment in the kitchen floor, which was used for chilling the miso so it fermented at a natural temperature.

'But you're *ready*. I've been searching for matchmakers since last week. It's up to me now, since you have never found a serious boyfriend of your own.'

'But I don't want to!' Miho was filled with horror at the thought. Many Japanese marriages were arranged by go-betweens, but it wasn't what she wanted. The kind of geek who went for an arranged marriage could never have the skill of Benri-kun. If she allowed her mother to proceed, her life would be like a prison sentence.

'Miho-chan, you're just twenty-three now, but you'll be twenty-five before we know it: a Christmas Cake. The price of Christmas Cake is high before December the twenty-fifth, but nobody will touch it after the holiday has passed. You're a lovely girl. I wouldn't want that to happen to you.'

Miho was so upset that she walked straight out of the kitchen and into the wide-screen TV her younger brother had set on the floor. As she cried out at the pain of her bumped shin, Nao cursed her for blocking his view of the screen.

'You wretch,' she snarled at him as she went upstairs to her room. There, once her door was safely closed, she whipped out her cell phone to call Rei Shimura.

'What's the latest?' she hissed. 'You've got to find him before my mother forces me to get married.'

Rei laughed at first, but sobered up when she heard how serious Mrs Haneda was becoming. She told Miho that she'd whittled down the list to three strong possibilities.

'Who?' Miho asked, feeling her heart start to pound.

'I'll fill you in next Saturday afternoon! Can you meet me around noon at Never Never Land? It's a casual restaurant in Sakuragi-Cho, just across from Mister Donut. I'll explain what I'm doing first and then I'll run a test on the three suspects.'

'Yes, I can meet you there. But why are you testing them with me there?'

'Unless you're there, it's impossible to measure their sexual attraction.'

'But what is the test?' Miho persisted.

'I can't talk about it over the phone. It's too sexy.' There was a hint of laughter in Rei's low voice. 'But don't worry about anything. Your privacy will remain complete.'

'How can I be sexy in front of someone yet private?' Miho wondered aloud, but felt a frisson of excitement race through her. She hadn't felt this way since Benri-kun had last touched her.

'I'll explain at Never Never Land. One o'clock and dress as you would for a lunch date with a girlfriend, OK?'

This was not something her mother would approve of. Still, if Rei Shimura, the woman with two lovers, had a plan that was remotely naughty, Miho knew it had to be good.

Rei was the opposite of the athletic woman Miho had met when she walked into Never Never Land that Saturday afternoon. She was dressed in a snug red suit that ended at mid-thigh and black fishnet stockings, and her lean but large feet were strapped into spike heels that looked like Jimmy Choo, a designer line that was only in a few top Japanese department stores. Rei couldn't afford Jimmy Choo shoes if she was complaining about paying her bills – or could she?

Suddenly Miho – who was wearing a pair of neat khakis and a simple blue sweater – felt a rush of anger at Rei for telling her to dress casually. Rei looked better than she did. The plan that had seemed so enticing over the phone had to be a trap, one that wouldn't work in anyone's favour but Rei Shimura's.

'You look perfect,' Rei said, sliding down across from Miho in the snack shop's booth, setting down two chocolate doughnuts and a coffee for each of them. She hadn't asked Miho what she wanted and at this point Miho was too stressed to eat.

'No, you're the one who looks good. Are those Jimmy Choo shoes?' Miho asked sourly.

'Yes. But they're hand-me-downs from my mother, actually,' Rei added, deflecting the compliment in the proper Japanese manner. 'I dressed up because I'm posing as a dating service director.'

'Oh!' Miho gulped.

'I sent each of the men on your list a phony letter offering a chance to meet five girls willing to date them for no obligation. The letter said I could promise them any kind of woman imaginable; high school girls, young housewives, office ladies, nurses, whatever. I even included photos that I clipped from magazines and had scanned into a headsheet. See?'

Rei handed Miho a sheet of paper headlined 'Fantasy Dating Club'. Beneath it were colour pictures of various women in sexy poses, similar to the seedy ads you saw fluttering around on subway platforms.

'I figured that any guy who crept through your window would be the type to get excited about a dating service. Out of your list of ten, three responded by sending in a card wanting to try a first date. And, interestingly enough, all three men specifically requested Cherry Blossom Girl, who – if you haven't already noticed – is *you*.'

'What?' Miho gasped, then looked again at the picture of a woman in a sequinned red evening dress, with a shoulder-length pageboy and cheerful smile. 'But that's not really me. I don't own a dress like that . . .'

'I know. I had a friend who's good with computers slightly alter the facial features and he added a similarly proportioned, but different body in a glamorous frock.' Rei explained that she'd engaged in the subterfuge to avoid letting Miho's colleagues and acquaintances know that she was actively looking for a partner. Of course, the three men who showed up to meet Miho would be hit with truth. But, Rei reasoned, these men would be likely to avoid gossip since Miho would have the power to reveal to their colleagues that they'd registered with a dating service – and requested her.

'So who asked for me?' Miho felt herself begin to flush with pleasure at the idea of being sought after.

'From the office, that young salaryman who works on the floor below you. Mr Sakamoto? I found out he lives in a very nice area of west Tokyo, by the way.'

'That's right. Kenji Sakamoto.'

'You sound disappointed,' Rei said, a smile playing about her lips – lips that were too full to be Japanese. Miho envied her that, as well as the cool, brownish-red colour she wore on them.

'Well, he's all right, I suppose . . . but not my favourite. Who else?'

'Mr Nagai, the manager at Keikyu Supermarket in your neighbourhood.'

'Oh, Ryo-kun.'

'Kun? You mean you're good friends with him?'

'I've known him and his sister, Kyoko, since we were all in elementary school. They both still live in their mother's house a few blocks away. I suspected him because he had a big crush on me in high school . . . and his sister, who works in the supermarket too, seems really shy every time she sees me, as if she knows something's up.'

'Women usually know the truth,' Rei said, nodding. 'Well, it's nice to have a shared history with someone, if this Ryo turns out to be Benri-kun. I think that since he lives so close to you, he's the most likely candidate to be making it through your bedroom window. After midnight the trains and buses don't run, so Mr Sakamoto would have a hard time getting back and forth from Tokyo to see you. Not to mention, he'd be pretty tired if he had to work those long hours demanded of salarymen.'

'I suppose so,' Miho said glumly. 'Ryo Nagai is definitely sexier looking than Mr Sakamoto . . . but my mother would never approve. Who's the third candidate?'

'Hold on, why wouldn't she approve of Ryo Nagai?' Rei persisted, a frown marring her perfect lipline.

'Managing a supermarket is hardly as prestigious as running financial analysis for Sendai. And Ryo's family is a little strange – his mother is sickly and his sister is painfully shy. Believe me, my mother and the marriage broker would make a big deal out of that kind of family history.'

Rei rolled her eyes and said, 'The final contestant is the car salesman who sold your parents their last Honda.'

'Mr Tanaka!' Miho said, smiling slightly.

'If you didn't already know, his first name is Akira and he is forty-five years old and *married*.'

'You don't approve,' Miho said.

'Listen, it's your business.' Rei sighed. 'I just wanted to be sure you knew, since you seemed interested in having an on-going relationship.'

'So, what are you going to say to them?' Miho asked, changing the subject because Rei was making her nervous.

'I've asked all three men to come at different times during the afternoon to that restaurant you mentioned. I'll be there to meet them and, as I launch into my talk, I'll have you walk across the room. I think the man who really wants you won't be able to miss seeing you. His glance will linger, or he'll blush, or something like that. And if the man gives himself away, I'll ask him politely if he wants to meet you. You can go from there.'

'But if it's really me walking by, I'll be recognized,' Miho said, sounding panicked.

'And you'll know *they* registered with a dating service. Don't worry; neither of you can possibly be embarrassed.' Rei reached out and patted her hand. 'Even if you wind up dating a man who turns out not to be Benri-kun, it won't be a total loss. It might be *better* to hook up with someone who doesn't crawl through bedroom windows.'

Miho answered by drawing back her hand from Rei's intrusive touch. Miho knew it was silly, but like most Japanese she didn't like to be handled – not by acquaintances, anyway.

The restaurant Rei had suggested – Never Never Land – was a casual drinking spot that provided, alongside your beverage, a complimentary bowl of edo mame, the steamed soy beans which were both healthy and addictive. When Rei ate three soy beans in quick succession, it meant that Miho was supposed to walk slowly past Rei's booth.

From her vantage point in a booth at the back of the room, Miho watched as Rei chatted with Mr Sakamoto. His mouth didn't seem to be moving much. Miho guessed that Rei was expounding on the rules of the fictitious dating club – either that, or talking about what a wonderful person Miss Cherry Blossom was.

Watching them, Miho could hardly believe that Mr Sakamoto might be Benri-kun. He struck her as potentially a very straightforward kind of lover, while Benri-kun was quite devious. He was an expert with his hands and mouth and hadn't even got around to using his *chin-chin* yet. He'd used other things, too

– fruits and vegetables, things that Miho had never imagined possible.

As Miho felt herself relaxing into an erotic reverie, she kept her eyes on Rei. Finally Rei popped three soy beans in her mouth, and chewed them in an exaggerated fashion. It was time to move.

Miho left her booth, making sure that her coat and purse were still obviously there, so the staff wouldn't think she was trying to leave without paying. She walked slowly, remembering something she'd heard about sucking your stomach in and moving as if there was a hundred-yen coin tucked in your bottom.

She kept her gaze forward, as if she was headed in the direction of the tiny, unisex bathroom, then realized that was a pretty embarrassing place for a potential lover to see her headed. She cast about wildly for something to look at and in the process caught a glimpse of a woman wearing dark glasses, who was staring at her as if she knew exactly what was going on. How embarrassing. She whipped her head back and saw Mr Sakamoto. He, too, was looking right at her, and he stood up and made a quick bow.

'Miss Haneda, isn't it?' He greeted her cheerfully. 'Hey, do you live around here?'

Miho stopped and pressed her lips together. Was he trying to throw suspicion off himself by pretending surprise at her neighbourhood? 'I – I was out shopping,' she said, striving to be elusive.

'Oh. May I introduce Miss Shimura. She's a – new friend,' Mr Sakamoto said.

'Hello,' Rei said, and murmured the ordinary pleasantries.

'Well, I'll be going. See you at work,' Miho said and almost reached the door before realizing she couldn't leave. Not with all her things in the booth and not with two more men to inspect. She slunk back, forgetting the model's strut. She shouldn't have worried. Mr Sakamoto was bent close to Rei, talking to her about something new, talking as if Rei was the girl he was really after.

According to the plan, the two women were not to speak until after all three men had shown up for their appointments. Mr Tanaka, who arrived just five minutes after Mr Sakamoto left, turned up not in the usual grey suit he wore when selling cars, but a pair of Tommy Hilfiger jeans and a half-buttoned black shirt. He seemed to have a lot to say to Rei and looked anxious. The two hadn't spent more than ten minutes together when Rei made the soy-bean signal. Hoping against hope that Mr Tanaka wasn't the one, Miho started toward their table.

She needn't have worried. Mr Tanaka glanced at her without recognition and without stopping his chatter to Rei, which Miho now could clearly hear was about the virtue of her buying a new car. Miho went to the restroom – she'd drunk a couple of beers and was needing relief – and when she came back, she saw Rei pointing to her watch, as if to shoo Mr Tanaka out.

When he was gone, the two women exchanged glances. *No*, Rei mouthed at her.

Did she mean, *No, Benri-Kun's not Mr Tanaka*, or *No, he's not either of them*? Miho spent the next thirty minutes wondering about it because the last candidate, Ryo Nagai, never showed up. After forty minutes Rei took the bill up to the restaurant's main counter and paid.

Rei and Miho caught up with each other around the corner in the shelter of a bookstall. It had started raining, ruining Miho's carefully blow-dried hairstyle.

'I don't have good news,' Rei said. 'I don't think either of the two are Benri-kun. Mr Sakamoto seemed friendly enough, but he didn't show a serious spark. And as for Tanaka, the car salesman, he was completely oblivious. The only reason he contacted the service is that he thought he could sell cars to a bunch of women! I could have killed him.'

'Well, there's still Ryo Nagai. But if he didn't show up, he must not want me.'

'Maybe he had to work.' Rei paused. 'Or he was so consumed by feeling for the real Miho that he couldn't bring himself to meet the fraudulent one.'

Miho looked at Rei. 'Do you really think that could be true?'

'We won't know until we confront him.' Rei snapped her fingers. 'I've got it. Why don't we go to the supermarket?'

'But – but that would just embarrass him, wouldn't it?'

Rei frowned. 'I'm the only one who would seem out of place. I know, I'll lurk in the background, pretending to shop. Since you have a long-established friendship, you can talk to him while you're buying something. I know this is hard, but try to say something out of the ordinary, that lets him know you find him attractive. Then just walk away. I'll watch to see if he gazes after you or gives some other sign of adoration.'

'But what could I say?'

'Compliment him. I don't know. Look at the shirt he's wearing and say the colour suits him.'

'But that's so personal. It's not typically Japanese to be so personal—'

'Miho, that might be the direction we need to go in. I feel rotten about how little progress I've made. The dating service strategy didn't work, but I'm not ready to give up. Are you?'

Miho shook her head. This final effort was the least she could do.

It was only a twenty-minute walk to Keikyu Supermarket, but because of the rain Rei insisted they take a taxi. In the taxi she brushed Miho's wet hair and lent her the fabulous lipstick.

They entered the supermarket separately. Miho picked up a plastic basket and began her trek around the store. She decided to look for nice-looking fruit on sale that would please her mother. But all she saw were bruised nashi – a fruit that was a cross between an apple and a pear – and withered-looking oranges.

'Miho-chan, how are you? It's been a long time.'

Miho looked up from the shrink-wrapped tray of oranges she had been contemplating. It was Ryo's sister, Kyoko, wearing blue jeans and a striped T-shirt that showed the unfortunate broadness of her body. Kyoko must have had the day off because as a store clerk she usually wore a pale blue smock.

'I'm fine. Are you just leaving the store?' Miho said. She hoped this was the case because she would die of humiliation if she had a witness to her first awkward flirtation with Ryo.

'Um, not exactly,' Kyoko said. 'I stopped in to speak to my boss. Actually, I've missed a lot of work lately because we've had some trouble at home. My mother went into hospital for minor surgery and the medicine she had to take afterwards made her quite depressed. So at night she wakes up and can't be soothed.'

'Oh, I'm sorry,' Miho said, trying hard to mask her excitement at the possibility Kyoko had raised in her mind. Maybe Ryo really was her lover and if it turned out he'd stopped visiting her because his mother was ill – why, that was completely understandable. 'Is your mother better now?'

'She has at least two more weeks of the medicine, unfortunately. After that I hope things will be better. It's a terrible thing to lose so much sleep – but maybe you already know. I gather women tend to have these symptoms more than men . . .'

'I believe so,' Miho said, breaking into a smile. 'Thanks, I mean, it was good to see you, Kyoko-chan. I'd better move on – I promised my mother I would find her some nice fruit for dessert.'

'Did you see the canteloupe?'

'No.'

Miho followed her to look at the shrink-wrapped halves of melon laid out in rows under a sign proclaiming their outrageously high price. Despite this, and the prohibitive covering, the melons looked luscious. The flesh was a deep, succulent orange pink, with a reddish-pink line defining the inner edge, which surrounded a lush pit of seeds. Miho felt an internal quivering and blushed. As she picked up a melon half, holding it lightly in her hand, she was flooded with an aroma of fruit that reminded her, almost, of the way her bed had smelled the last time she'd enjoyed Benri-kun's ministrations.

'It's my favourite,' Kyoko said softly. 'How about you?'

'Is your brother here?' Miho asked abruptly.

'Today's his day off. Did you want to see him?' The expression on Kyoko's face was tight. *Oh no*, Miho thought. *She thinks I want him. I'm not really sure that I do. I just want to know—*

Miho stammered, then said, 'Oh, I just wanted to pass on my best wishes for your mother's recovery.'

'Very well, I'll tell him. And I know Ryo will be sorry you missed him.'

Miho took her fabulous melon half to the check-out counter. She saw Rei out of the corner of her eye, motioning that she was going outside. Five minutes later the two women were safe from the pounding rain in the shelter of the nearest fibreglass bus shelter. Miho explained to Rei that Ryo hadn't been working; his sister had confirmed he was off for the day.

'It's interesting, don't you think?' Miho said. 'He wasn't working today. It must have been that he went to the restaurant and he lost his nerve. And Kyoko said something very interesting – their mother is ill! She has problems at night. That's a very good reason why he might have stopped coming.'

'Hold on. That woman in jeans, the one you were talking to in the produce department, is Ryo's *sister*?'

Miho nodded.

'Does she – live with Ryo?'

'Of course. Like I told you, they're normal Japanese children. Kyoko and Ryo will live with their parents until marriage . . .'

Rei was shaking her head. 'Do you think, then, that mail for Ryo and Kyoko would be placed in the same mailbox?'

'Yes, I suppose so.'

'It makes sense. She must have opened and responded to my dating service flier. I know she wants you because I saw her looking after you with the most wistful expression—'

'Kyoko?'

'Yes! I saw her earlier today in the restaurant, sitting in a booth by herself wearing sunglasses. She must have hoped to get a glimpse of the girl who looked just like you. Then, I got suspicious when I saw her appear suddenly in the supermarket. I didn't know she worked there, but I assumed she had followed us.'

'She couldn't have been at Never Never Land. If she was, she *knows*—'

'She was definitely there and she must have followed us in the taxi to meet you here. I caught a glimpse of her watching us when we were talking outside. There was something in her face. I don't know if it was jealousy, or what.'

'Jealousy? But why?'

'Miho,' Rei said, her voice suddenly much lower, 'I want you to tell me exactly how far Benri-kun went with you. The things he did. And whether you truly felt, um, his *chin-chin*—'

'He was a very generous lover – he didn't expect me to touch him.' Miho chewed her lip, remembering. 'It was impossible, anyway. He was always dressed. I figured it was because he had to leave quickly.'

'Gosh,' said Rei in English. 'I don't know how you're going to feel about what I have to tell you—'

'Don't say it.' Miho finally understood. The sensuous tongue. The skilled touch, as if the lover knew exactly how every part of her body felt as she touched it. The fact was, no man would know how to do all that. No man could be that sensitive!

Could Benri-kun have been Ryo's sister Kyoko?

'I think I need a drink,' Miho said.

'I do too,' said Rei.

Rei bought the first two rounds of Cosmopolitans; Miho bought the rest. Two hours later they were still laughing and crying. Lesbianism was not something Miho had ever thought about. In Japanese there wasn't even a word for it. But, Rei assured her, it was an option for women all over the world. And there were places in Tokyo where women could go.

'No,' Miho said. 'I could never do it.'

'I'm not talking about sex – just have a drink with her.' Rei yawned boozily. She went on to explain that she'd heard about some bars in Tokyo for women only. They could have a few drinks, dance, talk

'I don't know how I feel about loving a girl,' Miho said.

'I wouldn't either,' Rei said with a wink. 'You're going to have to be the brave one and find out.'

The brave one. The one who did something before even Rei Shimura had tried it? A pleasurable shiver ran through Miho.

'No,' Miho said again, but her voice was softer.

'An arranged marriage wouldn't be so bad . . . if you had someone on the side, would it?'

Miho bit her lip, thinking. Japanese housewives had all day to themselves, from seven-thirty in the morning till about ten at night. Her mother didn't do much with the day except cook and clean. Would Miho dare to do more?

'Since Kyoko lives so near to you . . . do you want to walk by her house on your way home?'

'It's not my normal route,' Miho said.

But when the two women went out to make their separate ways home, the rain had stopped. It wouldn't be much of a hassle to take a short detour past Kyoko's house. So Miho did just that.

JENNY COLGAN

The Wrong Train

Pinkie and I had had fun. It had been one of those whirlwind evenings that are so short and sweet in London. North of the river, not an area I was really familiar with. I should have got a cab, I know, when Pinkie went, but instead I spent my last cash buying a round for two gorgeous Norwegian students I thought were part of our party. They turned out not to be and conversation was limited, to say the least, but nonetheless it was twelve-thirty when I emerged. I realized immediately I should have gone with Pink instead of staying far too late, talking to strangers into a work night. I groaned inwardly. It would have to be the tube.

The Norwegians had made polite indications that, if I wanted to, I was more than welcome to accompany them to their youth hostel, but I wasn't exactly in the mood to bunk down with sixteen people right at the moment. They were students – as usual, I told them that I worked in a public audit office, and watched their eyes glaze over.

It is slightly embarrassing and stupid what I really do for a living: I work for MI6. Yes, really. The Secret Service. And no, I don't do any spying. I'm a Civil Service administrative assistant, to all intents and purposes, and push a lot of paper around all day. Nothing exciting really ever happens and, as you're not allowed to know what everyone else does, it is kind of dull. My boss is hardly even there; he's always flying off to health conferences, of all things. That's why I like hanging out with

Pinkie. He works there too. We're good chatting mates, and I was thinking about fancying him but hadn't quite got my head around it. Still, he's someone I can talk to about work, as long as we're careful.

I circumnavigated the station laboriously until I found the entrance. There was a metal sliding door covering most of the entrance way, but it wasn't locked and I slipped past it. No one in the ticket hall, but I supposed they'd be downstairs sweeping up McDonald's boxes, chocolate wrappers and copies of *Metro*. The lifts weren't working; however, the lights were still on, and the barriers fixed open. The station clock was broken. I went to check my watch, then remembered Pinkie had borrowed it for a trick which involved smashing it, and it hadn't come out right (technically trained to the eyeballs and he couldn't pick up a non-specialist piece of equipment without dropping a pint glass on it. Bless him).

Stairs it was, then. There were 272 to the bottom. I don't like those old circular staircases at the best of times. I hopped down the outside, trying to make a reassuring amount of noise. As I clopped down, I looked, as always, at the handle-free doors set into the walls. Where the hell did those things go? How many levels were there?

As if in answer to my question, I suddenly heard a sound. I stiffened and tried to peer round the spiral staircase. About ten feet below me two voices were having a whispered argument.

'Not tonight!' one of them hissed.

'I'm telling you, she's coming through,' insisted the other. There was a muttered expostulation, then a clacking noise, then I was alone again in the stairwell and feeling frightened.

I shook my head briskly to clear it. Suddenly I felt sobered up. It had been two drivers having an argument about the conductor. Or two cleaners complaining about their supervisor. It was fine, I was fine, and it was twelve miles to south London, so I'd better get my butt down the stairs if I didn't want still to be walking to Balham at five a.m.

I rounded the next corner tentatively, but there was nobody there, just another sealed door set into the wall.

The platform was completely deserted. Two sheets of newsprint danced at the opposite end and out of the corner of my eye I caught sight of the omnipresent rats scuttling over the tracks. I paced up and down the middle, reading the chocolate machine, the advertisements for finance brokers and strange philosophy schools, anything to take my mind off the fact that I had made a mistake. The electronic display board wasn't displaying anything – not that this was unusual in itself, but I couldn't stop thinking that I had done something stupid, and had 272 steps up and a very long walk home ahead of me.

Finally, the papers on the track began to dance more briskly and that strange, familiar hot wind started to blow its way through. The lights of the train were careening crazily towards the station: this was one driver desperate to get home. I didn't blame him. For the life of me I can't understand how people used to shelter down here during the war. It must have been foul.

I stepped back instinctively as the train rattled through, abrasively loud. My eyes narrowed as I took it in. It was one of those old carriages that you almost never see any more, the red ones, which must date at least from the Fifties: probably before. This one, however, looked strange and as it began to slow I realized that, instead of just being the odd carriage, the entire train was made up of old rolling stock. The windows were too grimy to see through. The thing came to a shuddering stop in front of me and I glanced once more, uneasily, around the deserted station, and watched as the old doors gradually started to open.

I moved up to step into the carriage. It was nearly dark inside, lit only with a faint glow. The door shut, much more quickly than normal. Already the platform was slipping away and the train was off, belting into the night.

'Didn't think she was stopping here tonight,' said a growly voice and I peered around for the first time. To my left, a man with a large white moustache, wearing an old-fashioned uniform, was addressing a similarly dressed man opposite him. This man said nothing, but shook his head.

The carriage was about half full. But it wasn't your traditional late-night tube crowd. People were sitting quietly, staring straight ahead. There were families, with mothers shielding silent children. One man sat glowering into mid-air, with no one around him. One looked on the verge of tears. They were thin and pale. I didn't get this at all. A couple of the women shot glances at me, but otherwise I was completely ignored.

They must be workers, I thought. Night-shift workers. On their way from one end of the network to the other. I must have got on a special workers' train. Yes. I smiled apologetically – not even thinking about the children, not then – and leaned against the side of the seating – for about one second, until the train hurled itself through the next station without stopping. If anything, we started to speed up. Appalled, I watched the stations through the window as they flashed past: Chalk Farm, Camden Town, Mornington Crescent. No one else on the train was paying the least attention. I sidled up to the man who had spoken, the one with the moustache.

'Excuse me,' I said.

He was staring at the floor, nervously jangling a ring of keys. Slowly he lifted his big head to look at me. His face suddenly registered concern.

'Yes?' he said gruffly.

'I—'. Suddenly I was lost for words. 'I think I'm on the wrong train . . .'

'They all say that.' That was his lugubrious companion, sitting opposite. The man I was talking to, however, looked shocked.

'Where the hell did you spring from?' He picked up a sheaf of papers from his lap and started to shuffle through them.

'I got on at Hampstead, remember?' I said. 'Why? What's the matter? Why isn't the train stopping?'

The man rubbed his moustache and looked gruff.

'I knew this would happen eventually,' said the man slumped in the opposite seat.

'Be quiet, Wayland,' said the man, sharply. The train rocketed on past deserted platforms. Completely dark, lit only by the ghostly glow of the Exit signs. Exit signs where I was no longer sure there were any exits. By my reckoning, we must be under Euston somewhere.

'Is this – is this a workers' train?' I proffered timidly. He raised his head to mine. His eyes had big dark circles underneath them. He stared at me for a long time and I drew back.

Wayland sniffed heavily.

'Yes,' said the man with the moustache, as if grabbing at the idea. 'Yes, yes, it is.'

'Well, can I get off?'

The man looked at Wayland as if for confirmation.

'Waterloo,' he said, finally.

He spoke rapidly into a remote control as we flashed onwards. Whoever was at the other end was furious. He turned his head away so I couldn't see him speak. I looked around the carriage. The people were still dead silent, staring straight ahead. Finally the man turned to me.

'Waterloo,' he said again, then, as if remembering he ought to be charming, added, 'this is just our night workers' train, you know. I don't know how you slipped past the barrier, young lady.'

The train started to slow. It was so dark it took me a while to make out the rough shapes and pointers that revealed we were coming into Waterloo. A tall, shadowy shape of a man stood there. Was he waiting for me? Inexplicably, I felt cold. The great train screeched and gradually pulled up. Behind Wayland I noticed a woman start impulsively and the man beside her squeezed her arm.

'Get out!' said the moustachioed man. Then, as if he realized his brusqueness, 'Quickly, please. We've got a – ehm, a workers' schedule to keep to.'

I looked towards him. On the platform the tall dark man stood silently, waiting for me in the pale, modernist station.

'Go,' he said. 'The doors won't be open for very long.'

'And you don't want to come where we're going,' said Wayland. 'Joke,' he said, when the man gave him a strong look.

The doors rattled open and the man in the gloom walked forward. I stepped out and the doors immediately slammed shut behind me. As quickly as I had seen an underground train ever move, it *reversed* out of the station, rattling speedily on its way.

'Follow me,' said the man.

He was silent as we walked through miles of corridors. The walls were covered in posters for things I'd never heard of and things I wouldn't expect to see advertised in the tube – cigarettes, nylon stockings.

'I should fine you,' said the man eventually, as we wove up through the dimly lit passageways. 'Instead—'. He stopped. 'I'm going to ask you not to mention what you saw tonight.'

'Why?' I said. 'I just made a mistake.'

He coughed and looked around, feeling in his pocket through his heavy set of keys.

'We don't need any old person thinking they can catch a late train and get away with it.'

'Huh?'

'Trains stick to timetables,' he said grimly and took my name and number. 'We'll not go any further this time,' he said, staring at me intently. 'But keep it to yourself or we may have to prosecute.'

I was more than exasperated by now.

'For God's sake!' I said. 'Are you telling me—'

'Please,' he said desperately. He'd stopped in front of something you couldn't tell was a door until you looked closely at the outline. 'We shouldn't have let you on that train. Someone cocked up, OK? I'm asking you to leave it alone.'

'OK,' I said. Suddenly I was desperately tired and all I wanted to do was go home.

'Just walk straight through,' he said, 'and take the emergency exit. If you're in there for more than a minute the alarm will go off. Go quickly.'

And he opened the door and pushed me through.

I stumbled forward a few paces, then stopped and gasped. At first I couldn't work out where the hell I was. Then gradually I took it in. I was standing on the stage of the Old Vic Theatre. Hundreds of seats rose up ahead of me eerily. I turned round to see where I'd come in, but there was no sign – just lots of scenery pieces, ropes and the occasional gap of pale brickwork. The proscenium arch rose up in front of me. Mindful of the warning, I hopped down the steps to make it through the exit door before I really did get arrested.

I woke up at about ten the next day – after a long cold walk home – wondering if I'd dreamed it all. It felt so unreal. I supposed the people on the train looked as drawn and miserable as any tin can of commuters at seven-thirty in the morning – they were just doing night shift, that was all. And where were they going? Wherever the track needed fixing, I supposed. But the children bothered me. Why would you haul children out to work in the middle of the night? My instinctive middle-class liberalism chided me as I headed into the lifts at Balham tube. Not everyone could afford childcare, after all.

I wouldn't tell anyone. I might just ask Pinkie – randomly, a propos of nothing – if he knew how people worked late at night in the Underground. Pinkie knew everything.

Pondering this, I made my way up to the top of Vauxhall tube in a dream and wandered, head down, into the MI6 building. So much for a secret service – this was one of the most high-profile buildings in the capital. They'd even let them use it in the James Bond movies – as the secret service building. Like, d'uh. This tended to make people wonder if the real building was in fact elsewhere, but I knew that wasn't true – it just went down a lot deeper than people thought, that was all.

I fumbled for my pass as I approached the entrance and practically collided with someone I recognized from the sixth floor. Over his shoulder, for a split second, I noticed someone retreating, wearing a hat, a scarf half covering his face. For an instant, I could have sworn it was Wayland, the man sitting opposite the conductor in the train. I blinked and when I opened my eyes again he was gone.

Pinkie was sitting in the basement cafeteria, troughing what looked like his fifth cup of coffee of the morning. He had red hair, pale skin and small pink eyes from staring at a computer too long, hence his nickname.

'Hey!' I said, bouncing down next to him with a latte for me and a double espresso for him. 'How's it going? By the way, I think you're fantastically clever.'

He smiled good-naturedly, knowing immediately I was after something. Pinkie knew how everything worked – whether it was fixing printers or explaining the American election system. He was hotly in demand for quiz teams.

'Hey,' he said. 'Sorry about your watch. Did you get back all right?'

'Forget about the watch,' I said. 'Listen. The weirdest thing happened to me last night.' And I told him everything, apart from thinking I'd seen Wayland this morning – that seemed just a little too crazy.

He listened. By the end, his mouth was hanging half-open.

'Are you sure, Frankie, you weren't in some mad alcoholic haze and dreamed up the whole thing and woke up in the gutter?'

'No!'

'Not a gutter then. A pavement?'

I bounced on my hands in frustration.

'Well then,' he said, 'very odd. Where were they going to work? And surely shift workers talk or, at least, chat to each other. And they'd have the crèche at the start of where they worked, not the destination – that would change all the time.'

I hadn't thought of that.

'What was the route again?'

'Hampstead through Camden and straight down to the river.'

He shook his head. 'That's the path of the old Fleet river. That's the route they used for the old unmentionables.'

'The what?'

'Oh, like plague carriers. People with nasty diseases. This is way long ago – before Elizabethan times, even. Used to drift them down the Fleet and turn them out on the river. Sink or swim. Even if you swam, of course, you'd catch a proper nasty from the water bugs and die anyway in screaming agony after infecting another area. They finally cottoned on and stopped doing it.'

'Oh,' I said, in shock. 'That's absolutely disgusting.'

My office on the fourth floor was unusually quiet when I went in. I said my normal cheery hello to Grace, the receptionist, but she could scarcely look at me. I pirouetted around to my usual cubicle. Worse and worse. It was tidy, for starters. And my boss, Peter, was sitting on the edge of it, clearly waiting for me to come in.

'Hi there,' I said, as casually as I could, trying to gauge the situation. He looked at me and, almost, for a moment, seemed quite sad.

'Miss Johnson,' he said. He *never* said this, not ever. He always called me Frankie. 'Miss Johnson, can you come with me, please?'

The next half-hour was a complete blur. The head of human resources – a drippy woman whom I'd only met once at my vetting interview – sat in the corner like an enormous humming bird, making agreeing noises every time Peter pulled out something else.

'—anomalies in the accounting expenses passed by you – automatic termination of contract—'

I felt numb. Nothing he said was sinking in. I might not understand everything on every piece of paper that came across my desk, but I did my best . . . but all I could think of was the times I hadn't followed things up, or the small mistakes I'd covered up. Then I saw they were standing up.

'Can I have your pass please?' Peter was saying.

'I'm – I'm *fired*?' It was unreal.

'I'm afraid I'm going to have to escort you out.'

I followed him blindly. The human resources woman nodded and hummed one last time. Down the lift and through the atrium. Just before we reached the revolving doors, I looked up at my erstwhile boss.

'Peter,' I said, pleading with him. 'What the *fuck*?'

His eyes darted around nervously. There isn't a single private space in the MI6 building; we're all aware of that. You can be seen, and heard, from almost any point at all by people with the right clearance.

He tried looking at me and stuttered.

'Good luck, Frankie,' he managed finally. 'And, you know, how you've always been told to keep things quiet? You know people have said that *every day*?'

Well, I knew my Official Secrets Act, yes, thank you.

'You know you've been told *every day* – right up to yester-day?'

What on earth was he talking about?

'Well, pay attention. OK? And look after yourself.'

And I was through the revolving door for the last time.

In fact, no one talks about the Official Secrets Act at all in the service. It's a given; it's assumed that everyone knows about it. The last person to mention keeping things quiet to me was the man in the tunnel. Yesterday.

I didn't know where to go. Numbly, I wandered up and looked at the river. It was dark, deep and foreboding in the early November chill. The water looked gloomy and endless. What would it have been like, I wondered, to have taken the long trip down that lonely stream – sitting, terrified, in the boat? Then falling, being pushed or falling into the murky, filthy water, choking and crying out for air until you couldn't breathe any more and the great Thames swept you along and carried you out to sea.

I checked my watch before remembering that I no longer had one. It was nearly time to meet Pinkie for lunch, as we had arranged that morning. God, I didn't care what he had to say about stupid plague ships now. I just wanted to let out some of my anger and frustration – without, for fuck's sake, without breaking the Official fucking Secrets Act. This was impossible. The shock had worn off and pure anger had taken its place. What the hell did they think they were doing? Bastards! What had I done, really?

I wished I knew.

Pinkie wasn't in the restaurant. I waited for him for a good three-quarters of an hour. I couldn't believe he'd stood me up. Especially now, when I really needed someone to talk to. Maybe he'd heard the news already. But we were friends.

I decided to catch up with him as he left work, but I had to fill in the time beforehand. I walked along the Embankment until I reached Vauxhall library. Sitting in a booth in the corner, I went through as much London history as they had. God! It was true!

. . . people often known as the 'Unmentionables' were
rounded up, for suspected typhoid, cholera or tuberculosis,
and put on the 'sweep ship'. This was meant to carry them to
the harbour, where they could seek safe passage, but was
often found 'accidentally' to capsize with the loss of all
passengers who, in their weakened state, would often not
survive the water – this was before the understanding of the
passing on of disease through drinking water. It had largely
died out by the time of the Great Plague.

The tuberculosis mention rang a bell. It was on the rise,
wasn't it? Being brought into the country, but resistant to drugs.
I had read something about that at work. My boss Peter had
done some work on it. No, Peter was now my ex-boss. Christ.

Finally Pinkie emerged from work. I had been hanging about
outside for ages.

'Pinkie!' I shouted. His face turned quickly; then as he saw
me he half-grimaced.

'Hey, what happened to you at lunchtime?'

I touched his arm and he pulled away roughly.

'What's wrong? Did you hear about me being fired?'

'Look, I'm sorry,' he said grimly, keeping his head down and
keeping on moving. 'I'm not supposed to talk to you.'

He elbowed me away and disappeared into the Underground.
I paused a second, then followed him. My hand shook as I
pushed money into the machine, picked up the ticket, then
headed over to the gate. I could just see the top of his red hair
disappearing down towards the Victoria line.

I pushed my ticket into the gate, but the red cross came up.

'Excuse me, miss—'. The attendant came towards me.

'The ticket's being denied,' I said hurriedly. 'Can you let me
through? I'm in a bit of a rush.'

'This ticket isn't valid, miss,' he said.

'Don't be stupid, you just saw me buy it over there.'

I indicated towards the machine.

'This ticket isn't valid, miss,' he repeated.

'That's crap,' I said.

Out of the corner of my eye, I saw a woman with a pushchair being ushered through the beeping open gate. I feigned to go left, then dashed off to the right, just making it in behind the woman with the pushchair and nearly knocking her over in the process.

'Miss! Come back!' The attendant was gesticulating wildly at me. Another attendant was coming towards me and I ran towards the escalator.

'Miss!' The man behind me was galloping down too, taking two steps at a time. I speeded up. My heart started to pound in my chest. At the bottom of the escalator I could just see Pinkie rounding a corner. Thank God he was tall.

Pinkie half-turned and spotted me. He looked very, very frightened. As we reached the northbound platform for the Victoria line I sensed, even before I saw, the train at the platform. The doors were still open. Pinkie speeded up. So did I. So did the man running after me. I was conscious of hitting bystanders; of bags and rucksacks in my way.

'Sorry!' I yelled. 'Sorry!'

The back of Pinkie's neck was bright scarlet. He jumped into a carriage. The doors began to close. Breathlessly I threw myself towards the train. By the skin of my teeth, I was on; the doors slammed behind me and the train started to move. I turned around and saw the attendant on the platform. He had pulled out a walkie-talkie and was barking into it urgently.

Pinkie wasn't in the same carriage. He was at the end of the next. As soon as he saw me, he got up and started to move towards the far connecting door.

'Pinkie!' I yelled, but he slipped through and was gone. I pursued him down the narrow aisle – and through the next carriage and the next. The last one was completely empty. Pinkie stood at the end, looking hunted and forlorn, with nowhere else to go.

'What the *hell* is going on?' I asked him, panting and sweating, as the train rocketed under the Thames.

But before he had the chance to answer me there was a massive screeching noise, as the train pulled up, shuddering to a rapid, screaming halt in the tunnel and all the lights went out.

We stood motionless for a second, conscious only of our rasping breaths.

'Oh God,' said Pinkie, almost to himself. 'Oh God, oh God, oh God. Why the hell did you follow me? Wasn't it obvious? And now look what you've done.'

'What?' I said.

The train was still swaying gently in the darkness. Even though I knew the river was far above us, I fancied I could feel it move.

'Well, think about it.' He was furious. 'I had people in my office today threatening me – seriously threatening me if I spoke to you again. That's why you got fired, you idiot. You've clearly seen some – shh. Did you hear that? Somebody's coming,' he whispered. 'Up the next carriage.'

By screwing up my eyes to see through the glass at the other end, I thought I could make out the dim shape of somebody, going from seat to seat, checking people out, carrying a torch.

We looked at each other in agony. The handle to the carriage slowly opened, and a face appeared. The torch came in our direction and instinctively I blinked to avoid its glare. A heavy-set, but youngish man moved slowly towards us.

'Hello, there,' he said, pleasantly. 'I just happened to be on the train – I'm a policeman, Inspector Crawford's the name – and when we came to such an abrupt halt I thought I'd better check if everything was all right.'

I looked at him closely. He seemed well-meaning.

'I think somebody stopped this train because they're looking for us!' I blurted out. I told him, as quickly as I could, what had happened. He stared at me in disbelief.

'It's true. They're definitely after her,' muttered Pinkie. 'Me, too. Can you do something about it?'

Crawford looked bemused.

'Well, certainly. You can come down to the station—'

Suddenly there was a crackle over the intercom. I watched Pinkie's head snap up, the colour drain from his already pale face.

The train announcer cleared his throat.

'We'd like to apologize for the delay to this train. This is caused by a problem in one of the carriages. As soon as we have found this fault, the train will start moving again.'

'That's us! We're the problem in the carriage!' I hissed. And Pinkie was staring down the other end of the carriage, where the door was opening once again.

Crawford followed our gaze.

'I'm sure we'll be able to sort this out!' he said jovially, stepping towards the person who had moved inside. In a split second, I realized the man who had walked through the door was Wayland.

'Crawford!' I shouted. 'No! It's one of them!'

Crawford moved in front of me. There was a noise like 'ffnut', and suddenly Crawford was sinking down towards the floor. I grabbed him on the shoulder as I got there and he moaned. My hand came away sticky.

'What the fuck!' I screamed at Wayland as he came closer. I threw out my own arm at him. My fist connected with something metal, and with all the force I could muster, I thrust it upwards.

'*Christ!*' Suddenly Wayland was staggering about in the twilight. There was blood streaming from his nose and both his eyes were shut.

'Shit!' shouted Pinkie from the other end of the carriage. 'Quick! We have to get out of here.'

He was fumbling with the door and had managed to work the emergency lever and swing the door open. I crouched down beside Inspector Crawford. His hand was clasped to his shoulder. Wayland was still bent double, cursing. From the looks of things I'd broken Wayland's nose and possibly caught his eye with the pistol cock, too.

Wayland was staggering up, waving the silenced gun around. Together Pinkie and I started to pull Crawford towards the rear end of the carriage. Blood was coursing down his suit. Tube trains are about six feet off the ground. Beyond was pitch darkness. I hate the dark.

'Which rail is live?' I asked desperately.

Pinkie jumped down and landed on what sounded like gravel.

'The middle one. But don't stand on any rails. Come on. There'll be a digger's hole along here somewhere.'

Crawford landed heavily, only a caught breath betraying his pain. Now it was my turn. Pulling the door closed behind me, I took a deep breath of my own and jumped into the black.

It was hot and airless in the tunnel. I pressed my back against the old stone wall. I could hear my blood frantically pushing itself around my panicking body.

'Inch your way to the right,' Pinkie commanded. 'Away from the train.'

Our eyes were adjusting once again and there were dim bulbs set into the walls every twenty-five yards or so.

'OK,' said Pinkie, ahead. 'We're under the Thames, so there won't be any access to the surface.'

Up ahead we could just see that the tunnel met another coming the other way.

'We should switch tunnels,' Pinkie went on. 'That'll confuse them, and we can head north, to Embankment.'

Crawford was struggling with something.

'What is it?' I said.

He puffed. 'Getting my police walkie-talkie. Radio back to base. They'll come and help us.'

'Wait,' said Pinkie suddenly. 'Don't tell them which way we're going. I'm not sure we'd like the kind of help that might pick up the radio.'

Just then I thought I heard a foot crunching on gravel.

'Wayland,' I whispered.

We started a kind of sideways crab trot, Crawford with his hand firmly clamped to his shoulder, and we reached the interchange of two tunnels. We stood for another second, catching our breath – and we could hear another noise, a familiar low, roaring rumbling. A train was coming.

'We'll cross to here,' Pinkie hissed, indicating a space two tracks away beside a stone pillar.

'We've got to cross those?' I said, looking at the six heavy metal bars on the ground between us and the dark hole in the distance. There was another crunch on the gravel behind us.

'Yes.'

Pinkie set off, hopping carefully and slowly between each individual bar. He was holding Crawford's good shoulder and practically pulling him along behind him. The monster appeared from nowhere. Out of the dark, the noise was a deafening torrent, and two enormous headlights suddenly flashed on to us. The train looked inches away. And Crawford froze in shock, right in the middle of the tracks.

I screamed. The light bouncing through the girders made the scene take on a nightmarish strobe-like quality. Pinkie tugged desperately at Crawford's shoulder, but in shock he was completely immovable. It looked as if the great train was going to swallow both of them – it was so close I could see the driver, his eyes wide, standing up, taking his foot off the dead man's handle.

Then the place Pinkie had been disappeared, taken up with the flashing lights of the carriage as the train flashed through.

Crawford was blown aside in the side-slip. Trying to save his ruined arm, he fell on to a rail as the train set up a great shrieking. I closed my eyes, in horror that he might hit a live one, but as the sparks from the wheels on the rails flashed past, I could see him, lit up from the front, desperately trying to raise himself up. I jumped forward and took hold of him.

After what felt like an hour, the train was past, still screeching and sparking. Crawford fell back, sitting limply between the rails. But I was looking towards the other side; the rail where Pinkie had been only seconds before.

'Ohh, Jesus,' I gasped. 'Ohh, Jesus.'

Then, slowly, like a zombie rising from the ashes, Pinkie stood up from the other side of the track. One side of his body was entirely black from where he'd thrown himself against the wall.

'Pin—' I started to shout, but immediately he shushed me. Twenty-five yards down the tunnel to the left a second train was stopping.

The three of us limped up the second passageway. Crawford was gasping and we had to drag him along. At the third side hole, Pinkie indicated us in. We sat Crawford down. He was the first priority; he was losing a lot of blood. I ripped up his shirt to use as a tourniquet and wiped the sweat off his forehead. He held up his radio again, panting.

'I have to get through to them,' he said. 'I have to tell my boss. They know where we are now anyway.'

We both nodded, and I continued pulling the cloth tightly around his arm. The radio crackled into life. Crawford barked out the story between ragged breaths.

'Tell them we're going to Embankment,' said Pinkie. 'Northern Line. Tell them to meet us at the platform.'

Crawford nodded and continued to speak hoarsely into the receiver.

'There are some officers near the station,' he said to us. 'They're getting down there now.'

We stumbled on, always careful of the rails, through endless near dark, and to fight the panic threatening to overwhelm me I thought of the unmentionables, the other people, sitting in their own train, heading into the dark. Where were they going? Flushed down the sewers like rats – the rats I saw scuttling ahead of us.

The tunnel curved on way ahead of us. Nobody spoke for some time, although we were conscious of Crawford, labouring to keep up with us. The makeshift bandage I'd put on him was drenched in blood.

Then, finally, round a long curve, with several rails heading into an interchange, the tiny lights of a platform showed up in the distance.

'Thank God!' I said. 'There it is!'

'Ssh.' Pinkie hushed me again. 'We have to go faster. They're coming this way.'

Crawford could only grunt. I snatched his walkie-talkie.

'Hello! Hello? Sierra Foxtrot?' it crackled.

'We're nearly there,' I said into the receiver. 'Make sure there's an ambulance.'

'Roger. We've cleared the station.'

But still we could hear them coming behind us, out of the dark. Boots, and hoarse shouts, and a clattering noise that sounded like someone running a pipe along the wall.

We were terribly out of breath now, and I wiped the sweat off my forehead, kicking out at another rat, but thinking, 'It's nearly over. We're nearly there.'

Then the tunnel lit up like the Fourth of July.

The fluorescence shot through the tunnel like dominoes toppling. We fought to cover our eyes. Light after overhead light went on, creating an illusion of motion across the ceiling.

I looked back. There were four of them about fifty yards behind us, big and beefy. And in the middle of them stood Wayland. With his gun.

'Go!' I screamed, as the first shot rang out.

'Everyone stop! This is the police!'

We hit the floor and crawled along the ground, crawling towards the platform.

'Everyone stand up! Hands up!'

I lifted my head and saw a man on the very edge of the platform with a loudhailer. The shooting stopped. Gingerly we started to stand up. Then another voice shouted,

'Stop!'

I could make out the whole platform now. On the left-hand side were several policemen, including one with a loudhailer. On the right were another group of people, including, to my utmost shock, Peter, my boss. He was now wielding a loudhailer of his own.

'Frankie!' he yelled.

Everyone – the policemen on the platform, the men behind us – suddenly stood stock still.

'Frankie!' he yelled again. I found myself shaking all over. *'This is over your head. This is MI6 business. Anyone from the Met – you have no business here. You can go.'*

Nooo. This couldn't be true. I felt Crawford grasping my arm.

'I'm here with the CDC. That's the Centre for Disease Control. We're just preventing outbreaks, Frankie, that's all.'

I thought of the pale faces in the carriage.

'Frankie, do you really want to be known as the girl who brought TB back to London? Typhoid Frankie – is that what you want?'

There was silence in the tunnel.

'Nobody was hurt, I promise. We just take people somewhere they can be looked after.'

Another pause.

'*Look – just come over here, there's a good girl. Everything will be fine. Sorry about Wayland – he took matters into his own hands.*'

The lines of policemen were still standing there, looking confused and discussing the situation with each other.

'*It'll be OK. Just come up on this side. We can even get you your job back.*'

'*Bullshit!*' screamed Pinkie suddenly. Then he grabbed me full on the face and kissed me on the lips.

'*Come on!*' he screamed as he pulled away. And he made a leap across the rails, towards the policemen's side of the platform. I saw his long body, his skinny white stomach visible between his trousers and his T-shirt as he leaped. His curly hair was outlined against the fluorescent light like a halo and he looked like an angel falling as Wayland shot him down.

Chaos erupted. Without pause both sides of the platform hurled themselves at one another. One of the policeman charged up the passageway to Wayland and rugby-tackled him: I had a brief snapshot of them both tumbling over on to the live rail, which lit them up with a ghastly crackling sound.

Suddenly I noticed a smaller tunnel set in beside the platform at right angles to the rails.

'Up here!' I yelled to Crawford, desperate to get us out of the way of the pitched battle. We scrambled up the fusty foot tunnel, scarcely the width of two of us, which started out as brick, but was degenerating into brick and soil, patched together with old tiles. It was winding its way upwards. Behind, I heard Peter again. He had obviously seen where we had gone.

'Come back, Frankie!' he yelled. 'Come back, you stupid little bitch!'

But we scrabbled on, through near pitch dark now. We hit a dead end; a solid metal door.

'Stop there!' Peter was catching us up.

CAUTION said the sign. It was a heavy metal door with a

round turnstile on it, like a ship's door. DO NOT OPEN. Well, fuck that. And fuck Peter. Fuck the whole damn lot of them. I threw myself on it, with the last remnants of my strength, twisting and turning the heavy, sticky circular handle as hard as I could. Finally, painfully, the door loosened – and then the sky fell in.

I had the presence of mind to grab Crawford, for I don't know if he'd have made it on his own. As the high-tide Thames swept around us, I shut my eyes and held my breath. The last thing I heard was Peter's ungodly scream as the sheer weight of water caught him and carried him away, back to the depths, then it was up, up, up, through the dark water to the cold open sky and the breaking air.

Epilogue

It was kept quiet, of course. They took me back at MI6 – it was the only way they could keep my silence. It turned out that Peter had bribed some ex-railwaymen to run the trains, thinking that this would solve some of his public health problems quite neatly, albeit in a completely illegal, unethical fashion. Immigrants who showed signs of infection and weren't best placed to speak up about their experiences were taken to Waterloo, dumped on a late-night Eurostar and left to fend for themselves as best they could in Lille, or Brussels – or anywhere, really, as long as it wasn't London. Not quite throwing them into the river, but hardly more merciful. It was his unbelievable bad luck, really – and mine – that it was me who got on that train. Other people had caught it before, by mistake. Hence the escape route at the Old Vic. I found out later that there'd been rumours about it for years. And when I asked why this hadn't been dealt with by MI5 – since they're the national secret service, after all – I was told that since Peter's plan had simply been to dump the problem back out of the country, it had been classified as an MI6 operation. Passing the disease and passing the buck.

Pinkie's funeral – seen as part of the tragic accident which paralysed the Tube network that day, also killing several police-men and flooding the network as far as Holborn – was a quiet and sedate affair, his parents too devastated to speak. Crawford – heavily bandaged and just about shipshape – came with me. We spend a lot of time together. We don't talk a lot, but I feel safe with him and, I think, vice-versa. My days of Scandinavian students seem a very long time ago, sadly. But I can sleep when Crawford's there and I don't dream of tunnels. I'm less afraid of the dark.

I go to Pinkie's grave often. He's the only person I want to talk to about that one late night when I made a mistake, and spent half an hour in a coffin full of tubercular people. However sorry I feel for them, the worry uppermost in my mind is whether I caught . . . anything. This fear is with me every day. So when-ever I feel a cough coming on, I like to go to Pinkie's.

Just to talk.

KATY MUNGER

The Man

Damn, he looked good in his tuxedo. James Bond could kiss his ass. Bronzed god, indeed. That week on the yacht off Corfu had been worth having to pork the old lady every night. Christ, she was so fat he'd been tempted to roll her in flour and look for the wet spot. But she'd also been loaded. The diamond cufflinks he wore proved that in spades.

Too bad she'd had a nosy son. An overprotective, black-mailing little bastard of a son. If not for that smug piece of shit, he'd be driving a new Viper by now. No matter. She was history. It wouldn't take him long to replace the old bag with a new bank account.

Thank God for prominent cheekbones, The Man thought to himself. He turned first one way and then the other, examining his profile in the mirror. He was aware of his allure, God knows. After all, he made his living from it. But he was realistic, too. In a year or so he'd have to get an eyelift, he decided. But, for now, the old magic was working. He'd walk as a god among them tonight. He'd shine. He'd dazzle. And he'd find a way to pay the rent on his condo if he had to fuck the Queen Mother to do it.

Lovingly he stroked the sleek black waves that feathered back from his temples. The Rogaine was more than worth it, better to be safe than sorry. Bald men worked in offices selling insurance. He'd been meant for more.

Eyebrows were another matter. Was that a stray hair marring the perfection of his face? He was distracted by the graceful

contour of his now Roman nose, a feature that had cost him
weeks of frantic coupling with the plastic surgeon – a trim and
very married little man who'd moaned like a goddamn pig every
time they had sex. God, but some people were never satisfied.
The Man plucked the errant eyebrow hair with determined
precision, then dropped it in the toilet. The uno-brow look was
for Neanderthals.

Almost there. His Patek Philippe watch beeped discreetly,
reminding him that the limo would be downstairs in ten minutes.
Just enough time for a final check. Like a Concorde straining
against the bonds of gravity, he was sleek, primed and brimming
with unimaginable power. The Man was ready for a spectacular
take-off. Hair. Moisturizer. A little foundation along the chin. A
smattering of blush, certainly not enough for anyone to notice.
Neutral shadow in the creases of his eyes. The tiniest hint of
eyeliner beneath his lower lids. Shoes shined. Fly zipped. Teeth
bleached. What more could anyone want?

He patted his cummerbund thoughtfully, wondering if he
needed to increase the number of crunches he burned through
each morning. He knew a lot of guys at the gym who added
twenty more per day for every year they aged. At forty-three,
that would add up to a lot of crunches. He'd rather spend the
time researching the Social Register. Besides, let's face it: he had
perfect abdominals. Because he had the perfect body. He was, in
fact, perfect. Fate had been kind in that regard. His father – who
had been nothing but a hillbilly sharecropper – nonetheless
strode those Appalachian slopes as confidently muscled as a
goddamn viper. There wasn't an ounce of fat on the old man,
ever, not even the day he died at eighty-two. The Man had
inherited his lean and lanky looks – no wonder he looked so
goddamn good in his tux – and he knew he was lucky for it.
Better yet, from his mother's side he had inherited an astonishing
bone structure, the sort of angular beauty that poverty and
deprivation often produce in a spectacular fuck you to the fates.

In short, when it came to the great genetic lottery of life, The Man had scored the Grand Prize. It gave him satisfaction each and every moment of each and every day.

As the limousine sped along the highway headed for the heart of the city, The Man watched the skyline of New York unfold in front of him – beckoning like one big glittering candy box of opportunity. God, but the men in this town were idiots. All they did was work. Work all day, work all night, talking of nothing but work, spewing endless tales of numbers and incomprehensible strategies, blabbing about their markets and ratios and risk appetites . . . leaving restless wives, bored girlfriends and plenty of credit cards lying around. For him. Because he was The Man.

In fact, The Man realized, if not for him, their lives would splutter to a halt. The women would baulk, unsatisfied and uncooperative. The men would be unable to concentrate, nagged and distracted. The markets would collapse. Profits would fall.

He was the key to all, he realized. He kept this great centre of commerce humming. He was The Man.

Another sniff of the powder and his head took flight. How much was left of this latest batch? he wondered vaguely. God bless that bond dealer's wife from Miami. She'd been a dumpy blonde and a lousy lay. Built like a fireplug, with thick thighs that squeezed his ass like a carpenter's vice. But she'd also been a great connection. Did he have enough left for the night? For the weekend? Until his next big score?

Could he go back for more?

No. There had been tears. Lots of tears. He remembered a pouty mouth twisted, wailing like a cat being slaughtered. And there had been a boot, a pointy-toed missile that missed his forehead by inches. Worse, he recalled as the warm flush of cocaine reached his brain, there had been threats of telling her husband, who was also connected – though in a much different way.

Best to leave that one alone.

But what if he ran dry? He'd think about it tomorrow.

Tonight he had more important matters on his mind. It was time to make his move. The big move. After this weekend New York City would die for the season. Anyone who mattered would be heading out to the Hamptons, or up toward Bucks County, or taking private planes to their estates in Virginia and Delaware. What he needed was someone recently divorced, with a big fat settlement under her belt. And, please God, he thought to himself, let it be a small belt. Don't let her be a cow. He was sick of flabby thighs. It was always the thighs that gave away their real ages.

'Just send me a trim divorcee with a love of liposuction,' he asked the gods above. 'Then I'll take care of the rest.'

'Here we are, sir,' the limo driver announced in a too obsequious voice that dripped with a knowing smugness. The Man knew the jerk was hoping for a tip in the form of some powder. Fuck him. He barely had enough for the evening as it was.

'Be back at midnight,' The Man ordered, preening in the rearview mirror. 'Make sure there's plenty of cold champagne.'

'Yeah, sure,' the driver said sullenly, as if suddenly recognizing The Man for what he was: a poor tipper and an impostor on the prowl.

The Man ignored him and emerged from the limo into a spring night in the city. He breathed in huge lungfuls of fresh air, expanding his chest, psyching himself up for the quest before him. 'Enjoy it while you can,' he thought. 'Soon it will be time to move on.'

This was all too true. New York was getting a little, well, thin for his tastes. He'd run through almost every suitable candidate he knew of, unable to settle for less than what he'd scored the year before, and if he didn't find a mark soon he'd have to move on. Or make do with someone a little less well-heeled than he deserved. Neither option appealed to him. Nor did he want to leave the city. He loved its brashness, the tacky way people threw money around to prove their worth, the bright night lights that proved so kind to his complexion, the endless streams of pampered women fresh from the day spa, bored and drunk and looking for love in all the wrong places. Like him.

They stood before him now, clustered in delicious groups, their gowns glowing like a vast tray of *petits fours* stretching to the doors of the gilded grand hotel. It was a good night to be looking good. He straightened his bow tie and began the long walk.

The Man looked incredible and he knew it. So did the women gathered on the sidewalk, waiting for their escorts to finish their cigars so they could sweep inside, cooing and kissing cheeks, scrutinizing dresses, bidding on god-awful donated art for some pathetic charity whose name The Man had already forgotten. He knew he was on the auction block, too, in a sense: the stares of the women told him that. Let them look. They ought to look. He walked as a god among them.

He passed by a group of three women, who stopped talking to stare. Flashing them a brilliant smile, The Man sauntered past, his eyes sweeping over them, quickly pegging them as unworthy of his attentions. Two were married, he recognized them from previous galas, and the third . . . well, he had a vague recollection of some night spent together, maybe last year. Had it gone well? He could not remember, though he had a sudden and unpleasant vision of some sort of medieval undergarment threatening to burst, flesh squeezed tight, the woman spilling out at both ends like a split tube of raw biscuit dough. It had been hard as hell to pry her off Ole Ollie, he remembered suddenly, and his disgust had showed. She had left in a huff. Just as well. Her name was Dolores, he finally remembered, and though wealthy she was not nearly rich enough to justify thick thighs and stringy, over-bleached hair. Much less a repeat performance.

Still, he was a gentleman.

'Ladies,' he purred as he set his sights on another group of women. They, too, fell silent, watching his approach. 'No,' he thought. 'No, no, and . . . no.' But the fifth woman looked interesting. He'd never seen her before. Tall, lithe, red hair twisted upward and secured with what looked to be real diamonds, though it was so hard to tell these days, especially from a distance. His eyes swept expertly over her hands. Rings galore. But none on the finger that counted. Emerald green gown, perfectly fitted to a twenty-eight-inch waist.

She was a possibility.

He let his eyes linger on hers. She turned away. Good. He liked thcm shy. Shy ones could be ever so grateful.

As he entered the hotel and moved toward the ballroom, he felt as if he were Moses parting the Red Sea – clusters of women moved back to let him pass between them, their eyes lingering on his form, drinking in his face, staring at his ass as he walked by. It was like taking candy from a baby, he thought, like taking candy from a room full of goddamn babies.

By ten o'clock the charity ball was in full swing and he had identified three possible candidates for his night's attentions. One was the tall red-head, whose date seemed to be a horsy-faced geek in a wide tuxedo, no doubt a mergers and acquisitions expert who, given the current climate, could not really afford the woman on his elbow. Well, neither could The Man, for that matter, but that was not the point. She could afford him and that was what counted. Two other women had also caught his eye. Neither one seemed to be with escorts, and though they were well into their forties and a little tattered for his tastes, both wore that sour, suspicious look that made him think 'recent divorcees'. And that was what he needed.

It was time to make a move. He snagged a glass of champagne and approached a brunette he knew named Mimi. He'd had a fling with her once over a weekend in East Hampton, but she'd gone back to her husband soon after, despite The Man's best entreaties. He had been inspired to beg her to stay since, after

all, she was loaded as only someone descended from the Whit-
neys could be loaded. It was really too bad that she would not
even play around, but at least the husband returning had given
The Man an excuse to stay friends with her. Mimi was an
invaluable source of information on the other women – and their
bank accounts.

'Those two?' he asked, nodding at the chattering pair of over-
forty damsels. 'They seem so . . . disgruntled. What gives?'

Mimi cast them a disinterested look. 'Those are the Lauder
sisters. Pay them no heed. They're visiting from Pittsburgh, for
God's sakes, and they've run through their money. Which is why
both just got dumped by their husbands. They're nobody. Or will
be soon. I'll tell you who you ought to be flirting with . . .' She
pulled him to one side and he marvelled at her good humour.
She was not always so friendly about introducing him to other
women, reacting instead to his subtle questions with suspicion.
Yet tonight she was downright effusive. Perhaps his time really
had come.

Mimi pointed out a tall figure across the room: the stunning
red-head dressed in emerald green. His time had come indeed.

'That's Caroline Halsey. She just divorced her husband and
inherited half of the third most successful Internet start-up
company in the history of the world.'

Holy shit, The Man thought. *In the history of the world?* That
would do. With that much money, he wouldn't care if she was
flat-out pug ugly or busting out of a hot-pink catsuit. He'd fucked
a lot worse for a lot less money.

But she wasn't pug ugly. Jesus. Not even close. Up close, the
woman was incredible. He stopped and stared. It was too much
good fortune for a single night.

'Caroline,' Mimi trilled, lightly touching the red-haired woman
on the arm. 'Have you met my friend?' She murmured the name
he'd been using for the last five years. 'He's an investor. And
single. Isn't he just too divine?'

Caroline turned to him: she was all long lines and triangles, cat-shaped eyes, a generous mouth, younger than him by at least ten years. And she was dripping with more diamonds than the fucking windows at Harry Winston.

Hot damn and double damn.

'Forgive me for staring,' he purred, taking her proffered hand and raising it to his lips. Her skin was warm and smelled of freesia. You could only get that scent custom-mixed at Bergdorf's. She was expensive. 'I didn't expect to see someone quite as . . . stunning as you tonight.'

It was a good line. He used it often. 'Stunning' was so much better than beautiful. It covered a lot of bases. And a lot of flaws. Hell, he could use 'stunning' to describe a mad cow. But this one, well, she really was stunning.

Her smile was brilliant. 'A smooth operator,' she cooed in a husky voice that promised a hell of a lot more than conversation. 'I like that in a man.'

Mimi drifted away with a barely muffled snort, her hand covering an incipient smirk. The bitch. The Man reminded himself to ignore her next time they met. That would teach her a little respect.

For now, he had better things to do. The party swirled around them, the noise and colours framing Caroline's upturned face for one perfect moment. The sheen of passing ball gowns, the tinkling of drunken women, the bellows of men in their black-and-white splendour, the entreaties of overworked waiters trying to make their way through the crowd: all of it merged into a single splash of sensation behind her then faded until all he could see was her perfection before him – her perfection and billions upon billions of dollars stacked in a bank somewhere.

'An investor?' she said, taking his hand and turning it over to scrutinize his palm. 'Let's see if you're going to get lucky this week.' She ran a perfectly manicured fingernail along his lifeline, a smile curling the corners of her scarlet mouth. 'I see you are a lucky man. A very, very lucky man.'

'Really?' He tried to sound bored, but his pulse was pounding. This was really too much. Beautiful, available, filthy rich – and horny? There was a god, after all.

There were not even any laugh lines at the corners of her perfect green eyes. She was the real thing: a rich divorcee in her early thirties. Ripe for the plucking.

'Could this be the one?' he suddenly thought to himself. The one he could settle with permanently? Shit, if she kept her looks and was that loaded, he might even stay faithful to her. For a while, at least.

'Do you feel it?' The Man asked, moving so close that he basked in the heat of her body.

'Feel what?' she asked coyly, dropping his hand.

'The spark when we touch hands,' he said, bending closer to whisper in her ear: 'tell me you feel it. Don't pretend. It's as if the plates of the earth are moving beneath my feet. Is there such a thing as an emotional earthquake?'

It was an old line and she deserved better, he knew, but between the cocaine and the champagne he was too high to think of anything better. He prayed it would be enough.

It was. Her laughter sounded pleased. 'If you're promising to make the earth move beneath my feet, you're on,' she whispered back.

The lady moved fast. He stepped away. You had to reel them in slowly, he had learned, or inevitably they woke up the next morning complaining of being used. He wanted nothing to go wrong with this one. Best to slow it down now.

'Are you here with anyone?' he asked, plucking two glasses of champagne from the tray of a passing waiter and handing one to her.

She sipped, gazing at him over the rim. Her eyes were bright and it seemed as if small gold flecks glittered among the green. 'Why do you want to know?' she asked with a ladylike smile.

He smiled back, his hundred-mega-watt, mirror-perfect, never-fails-to-slay-them smile. 'I refuse to answer on the grounds that it may incriminate me.'

'Oh, really?' Her laughter was deep. 'Then don't answer. I'd much rather you incriminate me.'

'So you're alone?' he guessed, thinking of the horsy man who had been at her elbow earlier.

She touched her lips with her tongue. 'Let's just say my escort is lost in the crowd. And I plan for him to stay that way.'

It was as if she could read his mind, as if she were feeding him set-ups for his very best lines. They were two of a kind in some odd sense, he realized. Perhaps she had married her husband for the money. That would mean she understood the game. It thrilled him to think of having met his match. It made Ole Ollie hard. This would be a different kind of battle.

'Lost in the crowd?' he repeated as he caressed her hand. 'Have you ever dreamed of getting lost for weeks and weeks, with a special someone? Nothing but sun and sand and making love for days and days?'

She stared at him without speaking. He had gone too far.

'I'm sorry.' He dropped her hand. 'That was forward of me. I never come on this strong. I just . . . got carried away. You're so incredibly beautiful. I seem to have lost all my fabled charm.'

There. That should do it. Blame it on her beauty.

But she surprised him again. 'No,' she protested, taking his hand back. 'I'm not offended at all. It's just that I was thinking the very same thing at the very same time. Do you like Anguilla?'

'Oh, yes,' he said eagerly. 'A charming island. Unspoiled. With that delightful resort at the western end.' Yeah, that delightful resort with a $4,000 a night price tag. He'd been there once. And talk about meal tickets. The woman he was with did nothing but stuff her face all day at the all-you-can-eat buffet.

Which gave him plenty of time to work on his tan. A lot of people had stared at him on that trip. Well, fuck them. Sex with a seventy-four-year-old was no big deal. Not for $4,000 a night.

'That's the place,' she said. 'I'm thinking of getting away. But it gets so lonely, you know?' Her eyes met his.

'I know what loneliness is,' he admitted. He sounded sad, pensive. It was just the right touch. Perhaps he should invent a dead wife? It had worked well before.

'Ever since I got divorced, my standards have gone way up,' she was confessing. 'I'm much more careful. It's so hard to find men who make the cut.'

He tried to look taller. 'I wouldn't presume,' he began.

'You're top choice,' she interrupted. 'Prime meat.'

He was taken aback by her crudeness. Though it was his line, in fact, he realized. He liked to use it when he sensed a woman was into humiliation as a way to get off. He'd never had it used on himself before, though, and he wasn't sure he liked it. But her challenging stare was irresistible. Besides: the third largest Internet start-up company in the history of the world? He calculated quickly. That could mean a divorce settlement in the billions. He felt his hard-on growing in his custom-fitted boxers: Ole Ollie was bursting at the seams at the thought of waking up each morning next to a gorgeous woman who also had billions in the bank.

'Did I shock you?' she purred, running a long fingernail over his cummerbund, her eyes dropping demurely to his crotch.

'No,' he said, heat spreading upwards from his groin. 'It takes a lot to shock me.'

'Can I try?' she murmured, licking his ear.

'Sure,' he stammered. His eyes slid around the room. A few nosy women were watching from an adjacent alcove, although they were pretending not to. Bored old cows. But, otherwise, no one seemed to notice. Free booze guaranteed near anonymity.

'Come upstairs with me and I'll suck you off,' she whispered into his ear, her breath deliciously damp. The incongruity of her elegant appearance combined with her gutter language electrified him. He was harder than he had been in decades. 'If I like what I see,' she murmured, 'you're on for a long weekend in Anguilla. My treat.'

Jesus Christ. Women were changing. Let's hear it for the modern world. Dazed, he followed her wordlessly. 'Where are we going?' he finally thought to ask as they reached a bank of elevators.

'My room,' she said, pulling him closer. She took one of his hands and laid it across her breasts. He jumped. Ole Ollie leapt in his pants like a trout at the end of a fishing line. 'There are times when I like it quick and dirty,' she said, her breath hot in his ear. Ollie almost exploded. 'What about you?'

He nodded dumbly, glancing around to see if they were being watched. It would ruin his reputation to be seen succumbing like this: he was the hunter, not the hunted. But she had led him to the back elevators, away from the crowd. Not even a waiter would see them heading upstairs.

The room was dark and expensive, perched high above the city. The Man sat on the edge of the bed, his eyes focused on the lights that twinkled beyond the huge picture window. They spread out endlessly before him, stretching towards the heart of midtown. This must be heaven.

The woman moved to the windows and pulled the curtains shut briskly.

What was her name? he suddenly wondered to himself. Had he even asked? His head was fuzzy. She'd offered him a toot from a silver cylinder stored in the bedside table. The drug had flowed through his nostrils with a hot, liquid buzz, taking half his head off before settling down to a mellow afterburn. His cock throbbed as if it were plugged into an electric outlet on the wall.

Jesus, but she was a wild one for someone so tastefully dressed. He'd be lucky even to keep up with her.

She was back in front of him, invisible in the artificial darkness. He could feel her hands on his knees, the nails scratching the silken fabric of his pants. 'Darkness,' she whispered hoarsely. 'The heart of darkness.' Her hand stroked his cock and he gritted his teeth, willing himself not to come. Usually coke made him last for hours, but he'd be lucky to make it five minutes with this woman.

'I'll be right back,' she purred after brushing her fingertips up and down the zipper of his pants. 'Here. Have another hit.'

The room was pitch black. He could see nothing. She wrapped his fingers around the cool cylinder, then uncoiled and rose to her feet. As The Man tilted his head back for a hit, he imagined her walking into the bathroom, doing all those secret things women do before they spread themselves for him.

It drove him crazy just thinking of her lifting her dress, touching herself down there.

He sniffed deeply of the powder. A darkness spread through his mind in great lazy swirls, like a whirlpool pulling him under. He blinked and then, as if hours later, someone was taking the cylinder from his hands. Her laugh was low and pleased. As if from a distance, he felt hands tugging at his pants, the zipper pulled down with one expert tug, the trousers eased over his legs. Pillows were placed behind his back then she pushed him prone. He groaned and sank back, aware that Ole Ollie stuck straight upward, as hard as a blue steel rod.

Jesus. What was she doing with her hands? The woman was a goddamned genius, more skilled than that kid he'd met in Bangkok, the one who'd been selling blow jobs since he was eight. Where had she learned to . . .? His mind flew. Images merged and pulsed, they evaporated and morphed. He was vaguely aware of a low-grade buzzing in his brain, then something else nibbling along the edges of his consciousness. Laughter? Whispering? It was hard to say and who really cared anyway? Nothing mattered except the warm pull of her mouth, the sharp strokes of her hands, the deep massaging . . . he groaned and cried out, losing it in a heartbeat, his back arching as he climaxed in slow, lazy spurts, his mind taking flight as his body lost control. The release was astounding. What had been in that vial? He was falling, falling upward into an inky darkness. He closed his eyes and gave himself to the void. His last thought was a single, practical flame that sputtered and died with his consciousness: did she really have all that money, too?

The drumming was intense. It nagged at the edges of his dreams, a persistent pounding that snatched him from the warm honey of his fantasies back to an unwanted world. His eyes seemed glued together, the edges of them crusty and dry.

The Man struggled awake, unsure of where he was.

The pounding intensified.

He was in a hotel room, he realized, squinting into the darkness. But where?

Voices rose outside his door. Someone with a Spanish accent was shouting, '*Muerte! Muerte!*' over and over.

What the fuck was going on?

He struggled to a sitting position, dimly aware that his upper torso was trapped in some sort of stiff, starched garment: his tuxedo jacket and shirt. He'd been wearing his tuxedo. He stroked it, eyes closed, trying to think.

Where in God's name was he? And why the hell was half the world gathered outside his door, shouting? More clamouring had joined the ceaseless pounding. Let them all go away.

As he opened his eyes, The Man glanced down automatically, checking to make sure Ole Ollie was intact. Strange. His stomach and thighs were coated with something sticky and dark, a pungent liquid that seeped over the sheets. He dipped a hand in the liquid and raised it to his nose. It exuded a thick, iron-tinged odour. What the fuck was it?

The door burst open amid more noise. Lights blazed on. The

Man shielded his eyes as bodies flooded into the room. The shouting grew even louder than before.

'Jesus Christ!' a male voice said. Someone gagged. The Man was confused. *Where the fuck was he?*

'I tell you, I hear the screaming. I tell you, I hear it,' the Spanish voice insisted before lapsing into a rhythmic mumbling that sounded like prayer.

The Man opened his eyes again, his pupils adjusting to the brightness. A ring of people stood, open-mouthed, around his bed. Staring. Had they never seen a naked man before?

'Get out of my room,' The Man managed to croak. They ignored him. He followed their gaze.

A naked woman lay sprawled on her back across the foot of his bed, her head dangling off one side so that her unseeing eyes stared upside down at a wall. Her arms were flung back over her head, her fingertips resting in tiny crimson pools that seemed to almost shimmer against the white carpet. Her breasts were smeared with blood, The Man realized, as if she were covered in fingerpaint. Blood ran in rivulets down her thighs, creating tiny streams that meandered and marked her pale, bare flesh in a kind of surrealistic, almost wild beauty. Her chunky legs were spread open and the dull brown of her pubic hair glowed in the lamplight. Her bush did not match the harsh blonde of the teased helmet that stuck resolutely to her lolled-back head. Her facial features were coarse and unattractive. She looked like what she very probably was: a street whore on her way down. He had never seen her before.

Who in God's name was she?

The Man lifted his hands and stared at them. His fingers dripped with her blood.

The crowd seemed frozen, unable to move, their eyes locked on the bloody tableau displayed before them, stunned at the inconceivable reality of what they saw.

The Man's eyes lingered on the dead woman and panic rose in him – a hot, burning panic that flooded his gut and clogged his lungs, choking, blinding, crippling him.

He was, he realized numbly, covered in her blood.

'Don't touch anything,' a gruff voice commanded, breaking the silence. He was a broad-shouldered man wearing a badly cut brown suit. And holding a handgun on The Man. 'And you – don't even move. The cops will be here in a minute.'

They were there within seconds. A swarm of blue uniforms burst through the door, accompanied by high-intensity lights that stung his eyes and shouting voices that froze his heart. The Man sat dumbly on the bed, unable to take it all in.

'Everyone step back,' someone ordered. The bodies around The Man moved, leaving him alone in the centre of the room. He stared at their retreating faces.

Was no one going to help him?

Rough hands grabbed him, twisting his arms behind his back. He was lifted from the bed, thrown clear of the carnage, tossed face-down on the floor. 'My nose,' he tried to cry out, his voice muffled by the carpet. God, what if they broke his nose? It would ruin everything. His wrists were locked between metal bands.

'What's going on?' he croaked hoarsely.

'Shut the fuck up,' a deep voice said.

The Man heard a series of clicks and fought to control his bladder. They were holding guns on him, he realized. *On him. The Man.* As if he were a common criminal.

'It's bad,' a calm female voice announced. 'She's been stabbed repeatedly in the abdomen and groin. Signs of sexual assault and tearing around the vagina. And it looks like there's semen sprayed all over her face, with some still in her mouth. We're getting samples now.'

'Get these people out of here,' an authoritative voice ordered.

Someone kicked him, then dragged him to a standing position. 'Put these on,' a voice commanded.

The Man could not comprehend what was happening. Where was he? Who were these people? What had happened to the woman? Who was she?

'Lift a leg, scumbag,' a gruff voice said.

Numbly, The Man obeyed. Hands guided undershorts over his bloody thighs as a video camera recorded it all.

Crunches, The Man thought vaguely, would all those crunches he had been doing make his abdomen look good on film?

'Get him out of here,' the authoritative voice said in disgust. 'Jesus. Talk about being caught red-handed.'

The Man's head was clearing. It was starting to come back to him. There had been a red-haired woman in an emerald gown. Where was she? What was her name?

'Start moving,' a voice commanded in his ear. He was thrust forward rudely, shoved to the door.

'Don't push me,' The Man mumbled, trying to straighten his shoulders.

'Shut the fuck up,' his captor hissed back. 'You're lucky I don't take you apart with my bare hands.'

They were waiting for him in the long hallway: everyone he had ever known, it seemed, everyone he had ever wanted to be. The rich. The indolent. The lucky. The high-born. The men who possessed all the money he'd never had. The women who spent it. They lined the hallway in a silent, accusing row. The men, stunned into passive observation, stared at him as if he had come from another planet. The women gripped the arms of their escorts as if The Man were somehow a danger to them.

He stared at them as he passed. They stared back, eyes glittering, mouths wet and astonished.

The silence was overwhelming. He could hear his brain roaring inside his skull. What was happening to him?

'You're a real piece of work,' he heard suddenly.

He twisted to one side, searching for the speaker. An ageing

woman in a red gown smiled at him. She looked familiar: that
mousy brown hair, her sagging cheeks. Had she just said? . . .

'You look stunning tonight,' another voice whispered, soft
and feminine.

He craned his neck. A blonde woman dressed in black velvet
and diamonds stared steadily back at him. Her eyes were flat
and dark.

He knew her, he thought dully, he knew her from somewhere.

'This must be fate.'

'Can you feel what's happening to us?'

'God, but you're incredible.'

'Did you just feel the earth move?'

The whispers grew louder, bolder, as he was dragged down
the long corridor, the words echoes of his past, each comment
hoarded and thrown back at him now.

They had done this to him.

It hit him with the force of a club swung at his gut: they had
done this to him. Everything he had ever said. They remembered
it all.

They had done this to him. And they had done it to her – he
was overwhelmed with the memory of the dead woman's hands
trailing across the crimson-stained carpet. Her nails had been
ragged, the edges blackened with grime. Hands like his mother's.
The hands of someone left to claw and scratch out a living. The
hands of the grasping and poor. And they had done this to her,
these wealthy women, they had discarded her as easily as a bag
of garbage. Just to get to him.

They saw him as just like her, he realized. All those years, all
those charades – it had been for nothing. He was still just like
her. Poor. Beneath them. Disposable.

'Yum-yum,' a woman sneered as he stumbled by. 'Looking
good tonight.'

'Top choice,' another high voice ventured. 'USDA prime
meat.'

'Now that is something to see.'

He tried to pull away from the mocking voices, but massive arms held him firm.

'This is going to be a beautiful experience,' a willowy brunette whispered as he reached the elevator. The surrounding phalanx of cops threw him inside. He bounced off the far wall, then twisted to catch a glimpse of her. He knew her. He remembered a tearful morning in Dallas. A sunlit bedroom. It had been years ago. Hadn't it?

She looked back at him – and winked.

As they pushed him further into the elevator, the assembled crowd rushed forward, anxious for one last look at the man dressed in half a tainted tuxedo – his lanky legs dribbled with blood, his face smeared with incontrovertible evidence that he was a killer, his DNA filling the mouth of the ravaged woman left behind him, his eyes dull and glazed with the knowledge that his life was over.

'I didn't do it,' he croaked.

One of the cops laughed.

'I didn't do it,' he insisted. His voice broke.

A woman in the crowd giggled. The Man looked up. A dumpy blonde stood framed in the elevator doorway, her arms crossed triumphantly over her chest. 'Is there such a thing as an emotional earthquake?' she asked, her mouth curving upward in a grin that seemed to grow as the doors inched their way shut. 'You'll be one fine piece of meat for those boys in prison. You'll never know what loneliness is.' Other voices laughed and she blew him a kiss.

As she pursed her lips, his mind flashed back to an image of her silhouetted against a boat . . . there was something about a boat in Miami.

'I know you,' he whispered.

She wiggled her fingers goodbye. The doors struggled to close, found the way blocked by a boot, and re-opened.

There she was, behind the dumpy blonde – the red-haired woman from the hotel room. Her expression was impassive, her hair still wound in a meticulous knot, her emerald gown hugging her lithe body like the skin of a snake. Her perfect face was as still as the water in the bottom of a long-forgotten well. When her gold-flecked green eyes locked on The Man's, he saw nothing in them. Not even curiosity.

'Who is she?' he wondered. '*Who is she?*'

As if hearing his unspoken question, The Woman raised a man-icured hand smartly to her forehead and snapped off a perfect military salute. She smiled at him warmly. Mission accomplished.

The doors closed and the elevator car lurched into motion.

The Man was on his way down.

JESSICA ADAMS

I Do Like to Be Beside the Seaside

Constable Peter Warlow knocked gingerly on the velvet curtains at Madame Romodo's psychic booth on the Brighton beach front.

'First of all you don't need to knock because I think you'll find you don't get much volume from velvet,' a voice said, in a strong Liverpudlian accent, from inside the booth. 'Secondly I knew you were coming anyway. I'm psychic.'

Smiling, Constable Warlow walked in and immediately attracted a fat white Persian cat, rubbing up against the trousers of his uniform.

'His name's Robbie. He only does that,' Madame Romodo observed, 'to people I'm about to sleep with.'

'Robbie?' the constable asked, secretly enjoying this last piece of information.

'After Robbie Williams. In his porky period.'

The policeman smiled politely and sat down.

'What are we after then?' Madame Romodo asked, pulling out her tarot cards from a green silk bag. 'If it's Wall's ice cream I'm afraid I can't help you, but there's a booth five doors down on the sea front does a very nice raspberry ripple.'

'We've got a murder.'

'Well, I know that. I saw it in the paper last week.'

Madame Romodo pulled at her bra strap. She was wearing what looked like a tablecloth, Peter Warlow thought, over a low-cut black swimming costume.

'I'm always helping you lot,' she continued, bending down to pick up Robbie and getting white fur all over herself in the process.

'Job's always open for you if you want it,' Peter smiled.

Madame Romodo shook her head. 'I couldn't stand the foot-wear, dear,' she sniffed. 'Now, before you go any further, I'm seeing a lot of furniture vans, a lot of very expensive chairs and a lamp in the shape of a flamingo.'

Peter drew up his chair. 'They'd just bought a house off Millionaire's Row. Graham Shirley and Angus Hunter. Every-thing was new, they had it all delivered straight from Harrods—'

'Very camp,' Madame Romodo observed.

'And of course they were a couple,' the policeman contin-ued. 'Graham had met Angus in Sydney. Angus was from one of those big, landowning Australian families. They met at the Sydney Gay and Lesbian Mardi Gras.'

'Angus was wearing satin shorts and fishnet tights,' Madame Romodo interrupted.

'Right again,' Peter admitted.

'Angus is shy,' she continued. 'I see him as a very attractive, very appealing, quiet sort of man. Loads of money.'

'It paid for the house.'

'Neighbours didn't like them,' Madame Romodo sniffed, stroking the cat thoughtfully.

'Yes,' Peter nodded. 'Shall I fill you in on the rest?'

'Please do,' she agreed. 'And put the kettle on. I fancy some Lemon Zinger.'

'Their neighbours knew that Graham had a history in Brigh-ton,' the policeman explained. 'And when some people saw this big new house he was buying, and the Harrods van parked outside, there was resentment. It didn't take long for the gossip about Graham's past to come up. The fact was, long before he met Angus – long before he had gay relationships – he was a straight man.'

'I suppose people wanted to let Angus know,' Madame Romodo observed.

'All very subtle.'

'I suppose they said it was for his own good, that type of thing.'

'Oh yes. The fact that Graham Shirley had once been engaged to a local girl was very much on the neighbours' minds.'

'And who gave you all this information about the neighbours?' the psychic asked, wrinkling her nose. 'I'm getting a Gemini type, born in June.'

'I don't know his birth date,' the policeman replied.

'Also gay, another Brighton lad.'

'Well I can tell you that much is true. Neil Pascoe owns a pub called the Oscar Wilde up past Brighton Marina.'

'He likes the nude beach as well,' Madame Romodo said. 'I'm seeing an all-over tan.'

'Well that's how Neil Pascoe and Angus Hunter met,' said the constable. 'Angus missed the Sydney beaches, so he'd always be down at the nude beach, and he and Neil got to know each other.'

'Neil's a good listener,' Madame Romodo said. 'The sympathetic type. He was worried about Angus taking all the gossip about Graham's past seriously.'

'And then there was more nastiness,' the constable added. 'At their house-warming party.'

The white Persian cat jumped off Madame Romodo's knee, nearly knocking over her cup of Lemon Zinger as he thudded on to the carpet.

'Everyone went to the party, of course,' Constable Warlow continued. 'They threw a very big bash, no expense spared. But right in the middle of it there was a gatecrasher.'

'A strange man,' Madame Romodo said thoughtfully. 'Frightening, too.'

'All of that. His name's Lang Jeffreys and he's been around

for years. We've had him on the files since 1979, mostly for hanging around the nude beach. But there have been harassment calls to local gays as well, anonymous letters to the paper.'

'Repressed homosexuality of course,' Madame Romodo waved a hand dismissively, 'and you don't need to be a psychic to see that.'

'Lang burst into the house in the middle of the party and threatened Graham and Angus. Called Graham a pervert and spat at Angus. He had his Rottweiler with him as well. Angus, in particular, was badly shaken.'

'I suppose he told them to piss off back to Australia, that kind of thing,' Madame Romodo said, sipping her tea.

'Oh yes. He said he'd been watching them on the beach with his binoculars.'

'Well of course!'

'And their kind was ruining Brighton, bringing property prices down, introducing perverts, all that kind of thing.'

'And he spat on Angus?'

'Yes, but it was never reported,' Peter Warlow explained. 'Graham, in particular, didn't want any fuss.'

He sat back in his chair. 'After the party Lang began a period of proper harassment. Angus was the main target. If he went jogging, Lang would follow him. If he went swimming, he'd see Lang hanging around on the beach, watching. In the end it got to Angus. He was having difficulty adjusting to life in Brighton, anyway – not to mention England. The neighbours hadn't made them particularly welcome. And now there was this lunatic with a Rottweiler who had it in for him. One day Angus snapped.'

Madame Romodo leaned forward, flicking the switch on the kettle for more tea.

'He told Graham that he had to take it to the police, that he couldn't put up with it any longer. He said that it was ruining everything for both of them.'

'Angus is the type to fall passionately in love,' Madame

Romodo mused. 'A Libran. Maybe with a Pisces moon. Romantic, sensitive, emotional.'

'However you paint his character,' the policeman replied, 'he was upset.'

'But Graham sorted it out without having to go to the police?'

'He suggested to Angus they should buy Lang's bedsit in Brighton – at a good price. They could both afford it, given Angus's private fortune and Lang would be able to move out of the area.'

'Lang took the deal?' Madame Romodo asked thoughtfully, staring into the distance.

'Well, wouldn't you?' the policeman asked. 'Anyway, as far as Graham was concerned, it was sorted.'

'There was a problem with Neil Pascoe's budgies wasn't there? Food poisoning?' Madame Romodo asked.

'Correct,' the policeman responded, wondering how Madame Romodo's psychic powers could extend to detecting the digestive problems of budgies.

'He had them behind the bar at the Oscar Wilde and one night a customer threw some peanuts in.'

'Yes, and Neil Pascoe was distraught. Here were his budgies on their last legs and he couldn't drive.'

'So he asked Angus and Graham to run him up to the vet.'

'That's exactly what happened,' the policeman continued.

'It gave Graham a chance to deal with his past, anyway,' Madame Romodo observed, 'because she was married to the vet, wasn't she? The woman who was once engaged to Graham Shirley.'

The policeman smiled. He had a feeling he was going to walk out of the little booth on the seafront with a solution – Madame Romodo really was on fine form today.

'I can see the scene in the vet's surgery,' the psychic said, speaking slowly. 'There's a little television in the waiting room, and copies of *Reader's Digest* in the magazine rack. I can see

Neil holding up the birdcage, talking to the budgies. They were
bright blue. Now, what were they called? Mickey and Moya?'

'Mickey and Minnie,' Peter Warlow confirmed, marvelling at
the detail the psychic was receiving.

'Angus and Graham are sitting next to Neil, trying to calm
him down, and then the vet comes in – tall chap, red hair – and
his wife after him, quite attractive, glasses, short blonde hair.'

'Correct.'

'And it could be such an awkward scene, but it isn't,' Madame
Romodo continued. 'The wife and Graham have a few jokes
about their past together, getting in first before anyone has a
chance to feel embarrassed.'

'Defusing the tension,' the policeman nodded.

'Angus feels much better,' Madame Romodo said. 'Yes, I can
see his face. Poor Angus. He'd been put through hell with all the
neighbours' gossip. Really suffered.'

The kettle boiled and Madame Romodo made two more cups
of Lemon Zinger tea. Her fake tan stopped just below her ankles,
Peter Warlow realized, but for all that she still had the best legs
of any psychic in Brighton.

'You're looking at my legs,' Madame Romodo said, without
turning round. She put the tea down in front of the policeman.
'You really do want to sleep with me, don't you?' she pondered
aloud, stirring a teaspoon in the cup.

'Let's get back to the crime, anyway,' Peter said quickly,
before she could pick up any more about his – frankly unpro-
fessional – intentions.

'It was so sad,' Madame Romodo said, gazing thoughtfully
into space. 'The very next day after they'd been to the vet Angus
was drowned. Not at the nude beach – at a place near Hove,
where there are very powerful currents. It was terrible weather.
Wind, rain. Three teenage girls were jogging and they saw poor
Angus having an argument. It was Lang's final gesture, really.
One last piece of harassment before he sold up and moved out

of Brighton. The Rottweiler was let off the lead and the girls saw Angus run for it, into the sea, swimming further and further out.'

Peter Warlow winced, remembering the photographs of Angus's body in the police files.

'Sensitive, nice people like Angus don't like confrontation. So he just swam off. When Graham Shirley finally turned up at the beach – he'd gone to get some cigarettes for them – he saw Angus struggling in the water, almost half a mile from the shore.'

'He swam out to him,' the policeman observed.

'Well of course he did. Held him in his arms as he was drowning.' Madame Romodo shook her head. 'Taureans will do anything for money.'

'That's April and May isn't it?' Peter Warlow asked. 'Graham Shirley was born on 13 May.'

'Of course he's inherited the lot from Angus, hasn't he?'

The policeman nodded.

'Even after Lang had been given all that money for the bedsit – not to mention the bribes – there was still a lot of cash in Angus's bank account.'

'Bribes?' the policeman asked.

'Well, Graham had to bribe Lang to keep up the harassment. To divert attention away from himself. Having Lang turn his dog on Angus, forcing him into the water, was a risky idea, I suppose – but it paid off.'

'You can't just count on rough seas, though,' the policeman offered.

'Well, of course not. That's why Graham had been sleeping with the vet's wife for all those weeks.'

'The neighbours were right to gossip, then.'

'Oh yes. People really were very fond of Angus. They didn't want to tell him the whole truth, of course, but half of Brighton knew what was going on. Graham's bisexual – Mercury in Gemini trine Uranus in Libra – and he used his relationship with the vet's wife, whom he'd once been engaged to, to get the ketamine.'

'Animal tranquillizer,' the policeman nodded.

'When he swam out to rescue Angus, he had it ready, and the needle too. It's all in a little black rubber waterproof belt case. It's washed up down past Rottingdean somewhere. Get the police dogs out, or the beachcombers, you'll find it soon enough.'

Constable Peter Warlow shook his head.

'We'll need a confession from Lang. He's gone to Wigan, apparently.'

'Weymouth,' Madame Romodo corrected him.

'We're getting close with Neil Pascoe.'

'Now that's the real love story,' Madame Romodo said softly. 'Graham's been crazy about him for years.'

'Waiting for his chance.'

'Yes, and I suppose he thought that with poor Angus out of the way, he'd get it.'

'You know,' Peter Warlow said, stretching his legs, 'I was never happy with the doctor's report.'

'Not the doctor's fault. Looked like a straightforward case of death by drowning.'

The policeman winced as Robbie the Persian cat rubbed up against his trousers again.

'We won't sleep with each other right away,' Madame Romodo said, putting her tarot cards back in the pack – the last card she had drawn was The Lovers, Peter noticed.

'Tell me more,' the policeman said, trying not to notice how much white fur had ended up on his right trouser leg.

'Pay up,' Madame Romodo said, getting out her cashbox, 'and I'll think about it. But I won't charge you for the Lemon Zinger.'

LAUREN HENDERSON

Talk Show

It was always going to be a disaster. I couldn't understand why I was the only one, out of everyone who worked on the show, who had seen it coming. But they were all too caught up in the celebrities who were participating, the originality of the concept, the miracles our booker had performed in coaxing even the most reluctant guests into the spotlight by dangling the carrot of a large juicy fee in front of their noses . . .

Didn't it occur to anyone, I wanted to say, that if it were such a good idea, it would have been done before? By people who were much better qualified than us? But that would have sounded negative, and we were big on positivity at the *Jillian Jackson Show*. Besides, I didn't need to cover my back. I was too lowly for anyone to try to dump the blame for this fiasco on to me. I could watch the slow-motion train wreck unfold on the screen before my eyes and, in a twisted, perverse, altogether skin-crawling kind of way, actually enjoy it.

'Well, it wasn't just *me.* She cursed my whole family,' Phaedra was explaining. 'She made my mother fall in love with a bull. Not even Zeus as a bull, but a real one. Imagine the shame. And then she got pregnant and before you knew it we had a Minotaur half-brother with horns and a tail down in the dungeons. Disgusting. Why my father didn't just kill it I never really understood.'

She paused in case the interviewer wanted to make a comment, but Jillian was lost for words. Her hands were clamped tightly on to the armrests of her chair and her lips were drawn back in an unnatural smile which looked halfway to a rictus.

'It was supposed to be a particularly attractive bull, though,' Phaedra continued. 'That was the point. Or that's what my mother always said. But I was too young, really, to be able to judge what made a bull good-looking or not. I saw him a few times, in a field behind the house. Big and white. I expect he was handsome, if you like that kind of thing. But I wouldn't have seen it. No child likes their mother's lover, do they? I mean, he was the cause of so much trouble and upset in the family. And my father felt terrible too because he thought he had brought it on his own head.'

She looked at Jillian.

'You see', she explained, 'my father was given the bull by Poseidon to sacrifice, but he – my father – couldn't bear to kill it. He said it was too beautiful to die.' She sighed. 'And then my mother had an affair with it. I expect modern psychologists would have a field day with that, wouldn't they?'

Medea, sitting next to her, made a harsh, guttural noise of amusement and flicked her fingers, dismissing modern psychologists in one comprehensive gesture.

I actually felt sorry for Jillian. It was such a new experience for me that it took me some time to recognize the emotion. Clearly she had realized that she couldn't sit still for ever, like a woman turned to stone in one of Phaedra's family anecdotes of life in ancient Greece. With her best serious expression, she was now saying in a voice which, despite her professionalism, quavered a little, 'And *who* did you say had cursed your family?'

Phaedra stared at her briefly, as if unable to believe the depths of Jillian's ignorance, and then raised her eyebrows slightly, like a miniature shrug.

'*Aphrodite*, of course,' she said, as if speaking to a backward child. 'She cursed all of us. We were fated to fall in love with the wrong people. Or bulls, in my mother's case,' she added.

Jillian winced.

'There was my poor sister Ariadne, as well,' Phaedra said. 'Abandoned by my husband on an island in the middle of nowhere, left to starve for all he cared, after all the help she'd given him in killing the Minotaur. God, you'd think my father would have been grateful! It was such a relief to have that creature finally out of the house!'

A certain degree of light was dawning on Jillian. I knew that expression; when she tilted her head to the side and gazed off into the middle distance, it meant that she was trying to remember her briefing notes. I bit my fingernail crossly. I had done such a good job on this research; it was scarcely my fault if the material wouldn't condense down into a couple of pages. This was a little more complex than 'Help! My Husband Keeps Sleeping with the Teenage Babysitter's Brother!' or 'My Grandmother's Toy Boy Is Younger than Me!', two of the *Jillian Jackson Show*'s most successful programmes to date.

'This was the "curse" that made you fall in love with your husband's son, wasn't it?' Jillian said, more cheerful now that she was back on the familiar ground of family sex trauma. She emphasized the word 'curse' and smiled at the audience, inviting them to join her in shared amusement at what she considered a weak excuse for bad behaviour. Jillian kept trying this conspiratorial look, even though by now it must be clear that it wouldn't work. Her teasing jocularity was based on the presumption that everyone, even the most recalcitrant of guests, shared certain common beliefs, such as that sleeping with your babysitter's brother, or your husband's son, was not only wrong but entirely your own fault.

But her guests on this particular show took what they were saying completely seriously; they weren't open to be coaxed into a reluctant admission of culpability. And the audience could sense that. I snatched a glance at the other monitors. They were riveted. Not an ironic smile in the house.

'Yes, that's right,' Phaedra was saying. 'Aphrodite had a grievance with him. My stepson, that is. Hippolytus. He was a virgin, you see, he worshipped Artemis. That's the virgin goddess,' she added kindly for Jillian's benefit, having seen that Jillian's knowledge of Greek mythology was scanty. 'And Aphrodite was jealous. He was terribly, terribly handsome and a wonderful athlete, and she was furious because he wouldn't worship her instead. Admit the power of love, as it were. So,' she gestured loosely with her long elegant fingers, 'she made me fall in love with him.'

'Wouldn't it have been better to make him fall in love with you?' Jillian suggested.

Phaedra's hand halted in mid-air, an arrested expression on her face. She was still an extraordinary-looking woman; she reminded me of an ageing French film star who has made no effort to reverse the effects of time by resorting to plastic surgery, but wears her lines with a weary pride. Her eyes were heavily outlined with black, her hair a thick and cascading dark auburn which, though it could not be real, was wonderfully decadent in its defiance of the ageing process. Her long, wide mouth turned down slightly at the corners and now it pulled into a grimace as she thought over Jillian's idea.

'Certainly for me it would have been,' she agreed. 'But – oh no, you see, he was in love with someone else. That little mouse of a girl. So it wouldn't have worked.'

'I see,' Jillian said, now getting into her stride. She flicked her golden bob behind her ear and smiled archly at the audience. 'So that's how the "curse of Aphrodite" works? You can't make someone fall in love if they're in love already?'

'Well, of *course* not,' Phaedra said, looking at her now as if she were a lunatic. 'Love is love. It's more powerful than any other force in the world. Not even the gods can alter that. Don't you know that? I mean, isn't that what you talk about on your show all the time?'

I snuffled to myself with amusement at this snub. Checking the other screens, I could see the audience nodding gravely. They were as quiet and sober as if they were in the theatre, rather than at a daytime talk show. No restlessness, no hurling of insults. Ancient royalty was a different kettle of fish from the usual eagerly obsequious minor celebrities or troubled mums whom Jillian handled so effectively. Phaedra and Medea were behaving as if they were granting an audience to Jillian, rather than the other way round, and she still hadn't got the measure of this different atmosphere.

Jillian crossed her legs the other way and turned to Medea. Between them, Jillian looked like a life-sized doll in her pale-pink suit and beige high heels, her pretty but unthreatening make-up and blonde streaky bob. Phaedra and Medea were real women, with crow's feet edging dark eyes which had seen countless centuries, more than Jillian could possibly imagine. Phaedra was beautiful, in a wasted, world-weary way, the elegant, experienced older woman sitting in a Parisian cafe, chain-smoking Gauloises, drinking anisette, and looking for the next fresh young man. But Medea was beyond mere beauty. You didn't notice her features, apart from the dark, dark eyes in their web of lines. She radiated power. Tired, old, bored with everything, well beyond her glory days, she was still the most powerful person I had ever seen. I found it hard to take my eyes off her.

'And would you agree with that, Medea?' Jillian asked. 'After all, you did everything in the name of love, isn't that right?'

It was awful how Jillian's banal, daytime TV questions sometimes actually summed up the truth of an entire situation.

Medea's eyes flashed.

'Of course,' she said. Her voice was hoarse, as if rusty from disuse.

Jillian raised the clipboard on her knee and turned to the camera.

'I have a list here of your main, um, activities, just to summarize for the audience,' she said. 'You fell in love with Jason when he came to your father's kingdom, and you helped him defeat your father's plot to kill him, right? And then you escaped with him, and when your father chased after you, you killed your brother. Well, to be exact, you cut him up into pieces and scattered him in the sea so that your father's boat would stop to, um, collect the pieces, and Jason's boat could escape.'

There was a gasp from the audience, half-suppressed. I heard people shift in their seats. Medea, caring nothing for anyone else's opinion of her deeds, nodded indifferently.

'Can we just talk about that for a moment?' Jillian asked. 'How did it feel, exactly, to kill your brother and cut up his corpse?'

Medea shrugged. 'We needed to escape,' she said. 'My father would have killed us all. Besides, I never liked him.'

'Your brother, you mean?'

'That's right.'

Jillian leaned forward. Her expression turned sympathetic, her voice confiding. This, again, was one of her most familiar moves.

'Had your brother – did he do anything you didn't like?' she asked gently. 'Was he – inappropriate with you?'

Medea looked blank.

'Inappropriate?' she said. 'What do you mean?'

Jillian put a perfectly manicured hand on Medea's knee. Medea looked at it as if it were a dead cockroach, and the hand slid away.

'I mean, did he – touch you, you know, was he – did he try to—'

Under Medea's stare of contempt, Jillian's voice was withering up.

'I was a *witch*,' Medea said coldly. 'I was the only witch I, or anyone else, ever knew about. Apart from Circe, and she never left her island. Do you really think that anyone would dare do anything to me that I didn't want?'

God, the list of things we would need to cut was piling up to the ceiling. Anything that made Jillian look bad; any mention of witches; and I had the feeling that the whole bestiality thing would have to go too. We were a daytime programme, but even the late-night ones drew the line at woman/bull action.

'But despite that, you weren't able to resist falling in love with Jason,' Jillian said, persisting, though feebly. 'That was the curse of Aphrodite too, wasn't it?'

I noticed that the inverted commas were missing now.

Medea nodded. 'She made Cupid shoot an arrow at me,' she said. 'Jason needed my help; without me my father would have killed him. So Aphrodite wanted to be sure I was on his side.'

'And why did she want—'

'Oh, he was the most handsome man in the world,' Medea said simply. 'He was a hero, incredibly beautiful – no wonder she didn't want him to die. She didn't even need to bother with Cupid; I would have fallen in love with him anyway. We all did.'

Her voice softened when she spoke of her husband, I noticed, despite everything that had happened between them.

'Jason was a hero,' she repeated. 'No one nowadays can possibly imagine what that was like. He yoked my father's two bulls as they breathed fire, wrestled them one by one to their knees and forced the yoke on them and made them plough. Can you imagine what it was like for me, watching that, to know that I was the one he loved? We were invincible together.'

'You were happy for a long time, weren't you?' Jillian said, finding familiar ground with obvious relief. 'You had two sons, you were in love, and everything was wonderful.'

Ben, the producer's assistant, was coming towards me, back from the coffee machine with a brimming cup. I thought he would just pass by, but instead he paused, not wanting to miss a moment of what was happening on screen. I knew what she was going to say; it was always the same thing. Jillian was incredibly predictable. I mimicked her voice and gestures word for word as she murmured:

'And then—', pause, tilt of head to side, hands turning palms up, 'and then it all began to fall apart, didn't it?'

Behind me Ben had burst out laughing at my imitation of Jillian. I felt myself flush with pride.

'He wanted to leave you for another woman,' Jillian said.

'I killed her,' Medea said with great satisfaction. 'She died in agony. And her father too,' she added with equal relish. 'Screaming.'

It was awful, but I couldn't help it. I was sniggering at the appalled expression on Jillian's face. Ben put down his coffee to cool.

'Jill *knows* all this!' he said impatiently. 'It was all in your notes! If she'd bothered to read them. Good work, by the way,' he added. 'Really interesting stuff you pulled up.'

'Thanks,' I mumbled.

I was training myself to say 'Thank you' when paid a compliment, instead of something self-deprecating. I had got that out of a book called *What To Do If You Don't Fit In*, whose author had been a guest on the show last year. I was pleased I had managed it, even with Ben standing that close to me; his presence intimidated me because I admired him so much. He was exactly what I wanted to be: cool, funny, liked by everyone.

'So why the hell is Jill looking so flabbergasted? This is a disaster,' he said cheerfully.

'Blame the network,' I said.

'Yeah, right,' Ben said. 'No, actually, you know what?' He lowered his voice. 'I blame Dennis.'

Dennis was the executive producer of the show and, since his arrival two years ago, the ratings had gone stratospheric. The catch was that Dennis had utterly ignored the 'quality mandate' our network demanded. After a run of tabloid-worthy shows about grandmothers dating their grandsons' best friends and the one on bulimia, which showed most of the major vomit-inducing techniques, Dennis had come under a lot of pressure from the network and panicked. 'Tragic Heroines Tell All' had been his idea for adding enough quality and culture to the programme to last us for years to come.

'Jill went to Cambridge!' Dennis had said bluffly in the strategy meeting. 'She can cope with it!'

The fact that Jillian had been to Cambridge was always made much of, by Dennis and herself, when the show was accused of plummeting downmarket. I didn't know you could do degrees in domestic science or interior decoration at Cambridge; these seemed the only two subjects on which she could cope without lavish amounts of research. No, that wasn't quite fair of me. She had seemed unusually well informed when we were doing the show on bulimia, too.

Ben pulled a chair up and sat down next to me, sipping his coffee. Panicky excitement flooded me. What if I couldn't think of anything to say to him? Or – worse – what if I tried to be funny and got it wrong?

I could think of clever comments; it was just that I had a hard time getting up the confidence to come out with them. Other people seemed to do it so easily. They didn't seem to have to think over everything they said in advance, testing it out in case it sounded wrong and they got blamed for it. But I was practising. And I was definitely getting better at it. Look at what I had just said to Ben about the network. It would seem tiny to anyone else, but even that was the kind of comment – airy, cynical – which I wouldn't have dared to make two years ago, in case Ben contradicted me.

'He told me he was divorcing me in my and the children's interests,' Medea was telling Jillian on the main screen. 'He said that by marrying the king's daughter – we were in Corinth at the time and that trollop Glauce took a fancy to him – he said it would be the best thing for all of us. He would be settled financially and he could provide for all of us. Hah! As if she wouldn't have banished my sons immediately as soon as she had children of her own! And then he told me that all I was worried about was the sex. Missing him in my bed. He said I was obsessed with sex, like all women.'

'And how did you feel about that?' Jillian asked in a game attempt to be sympathetic.

Medea stared at her.

'How do you *think*?' she said. 'I killed his little virgin bride, and then I killed our children, to punish him.' Her dark eyes burned the screen. 'I told him our children died of a disease they caught from their father.'

'Jesus,' Ben whispered.

Jillian – even though she knew this fact perfectly well – was speechless. I looked at the cameras trained on the audience. They, too, were shocked into utter silence. It wasn't merely the revelation; it was Medea's attitude.

All of the sinners we had ever had on the show had been, to some degree, repentant. That was the point. Even the most recalcitrant ones knew what was expected of them and could be coaxed into some sort of shame by the time the closing credits rolled. And they were cowed by what they had done, their defiance masking their guilt. It was hard to believe they had really committed the crimes; the constant refrain from all of us who worked on the show was always a baffled 'But they seem so normal!' That was where Medea differed from all the rest. You looked at her and saw an infanticide. No shame, no guilt. Naked power emanated from her. It was like looking straight into a spotlight. She scorched your eyes.

'Oh, everyone agreed that Jason behaved very badly,' Phaedra chipped in, the only one in that whole studio capable of speech. 'Very badly. And such a banal thing to do – marry for money.

I mean, they all did terrible things then, the men, but that was particularly shabby and unheroic. My own husband Theseus kidnapped Helen when she was just a little girl. He said he meant to marry her when she was grown. That was before he married me, of course. But *still*. And my poor sister, Ariadne, whom he abandoned – and, oh, countless rapes and seductions. Well, we hardly ever said "rape" then, in those days. Zeus was always supposed to have taken all those women willingly. And Apollo – God, no wonder all the girls were always running away from him and getting transformed into something or other. He was an animal. No woman was safe. The gods were worse than the rest of them. They set the example, I suppose.'

Jillian seized adroitly on the most sensational and TV-friendly part of this.

'Now, it's interesting that you mention rape, Phaedra,' she said thoughtfully, 'because you actually accused your stepson of rape, didn't you, when he refused to sleep with you? How do you feel about that now?'

Phaedra looked horribly embarrassed. She hung her head and started toying with one of her elaborate gilded bracelets.

'It wasn't actually me,' she said finally. 'It was my maid. It was her idea.'

'Yes?' Jillian urged. 'Can you tell us more?'

Phaedra pushed back her long auburn hair and sighed deeply.

'It was just after Hippolytus – my stepson – had rejected me,' she said. 'I was ready to kill myself with shame. And then we heard that my husband was alive and had just landed in the harbour. He had been away so long we all thought he must have died, you see. Gone down to hell again to kidnap some girl and got stuck there this time. Naturally, I panicked at the news he was still alive. The thought of Hippolytus humiliating me by telling my husband how I threw myself at him – oh, I wanted to kill myself then and there. But Oenone – my maid – convinced me to let her try something else. She said she would go to my

husband and tell him that Hippolytus had raped me, so that if
Hippolytus tried to tell the truth it would look like a pathetic
attempt to cover up his own crime.'

She looked up at Jillian, her great, beautiful, black-circled
eyes full of pain.

'I stayed silent till it was too late,' she said. 'I didn't actually
lie myself, but I let her lie for me. I know it was wrong.'

Jillian was nodding empathetically. She reached out and took
Phaedra's hand. 'It was wrong,' she said gently. 'But you regret
it, don't you?'

'Yes,' Phaedra said. 'Yes. I tried to hang myself, but they cut
me down and smuggled me out of the country and told my
husband I was dead. Look.'

She pushed back the collar of her silk shirt and showed a scar
round her throat, presumably from the rope burn.

'What would you say to Hippolytus if you had him in front of
you now?' Jillian said, moving in for the kill. 'Pretend he's there.
Look there and tell him what you'd like to say.'

'Wow,' I said to Ben. 'An authentic *Jillian Jackson Show*
moment in the middle of all this. You've got to admire her.'

Ben sniggered. I felt wonderful.

Phaedra, meanwhile, was staring into the camera as if hyp-
notized by it.

'That I'm sorry,' she said, 'but I loved him so much I was
driven mad by it. I literally couldn't help myself. I couldn't eat
or sleep, I really was going mad.'

Jillian patted her hand and turned to the camera for one of
her pop-psychological summaries, but Phaedra had only just
started.

'From the first time I saw him – at my wedding – it was like
a lightning bolt through me,' she was continuing passionately.
'I went red all over. I felt myself burn with heat. He was so
beautiful, the spitting image of my husband as a young man, but
so smooth, so unspoiled, a virgin. None of my husband's sordid

history – the rapes, the betrayal of my sister – Hippolytus was totally innocent, so pure and beautiful. I tried everything I could to put him out of my mind – I built a shrine to Aphrodite and sacrificed animals all day long to try to placate her—'

'That'll have to come out,' Ben muttered in my ear. 'We'd never hear the end of it from the animal rights lot.'

'He was like a young god – a male Artemis, a virgin god—' Phaedra was saying, her cheeks flushed.

Jillian cleared her throat loudly.

'Well, that's great,' she said over-emphatically. 'Really cathartic. I'm sure he hears you and understands. And now it's time to bring on our third guest, another tragic heroine who's managed to turn round her life after a very dramatic series of events. Will you all please help me to welcome Lady Macbeth to the *Jillian Jackson Show*!'

Ben let out a little whistle through his teeth as Lady Macbeth, smiling graciously, entered stage right and crossed to her chair. Unlike Phaedra and Medea – whom Wardrobe and Make-up had practically had to arm-wrestle to get them to wear a little powder and blusher, let alone a structured jacket – Lady Macbeth was a veteran of the interview circuit and looked as perfectly groomed as an American chat-show guest. Her silvery hair would look smooth and silky on TV, but if you had seen her in real life you would realize that there was half a can of hairspray in there. A tornado couldn't have shifted a strand. She was wearing a smart red jacket with a white blouse underneath and a skirt of the Macbeth tartan – perfect colours for television. Her manicure and lipstick matched her suit.

'I saw her in Make-up,' I said to Ben. 'She was giving Karen a terrible time. She knew exactly how she wanted everything. Karen was nearly crying.'

'She's *terrifying*,' Ben said in awe.

She reminds me of my mother, actually,' I said without thinking.

'*Whoah*. Really?' He looked at me. 'You must have had a pretty scary childhood. Bet you couldn't do anything right.'

I made a grimace I had seen Sophie, the deputy floor manager, pull. Sophie was pretty and flirty and funny and she would roll her eyes comically when asked to do something she didn't want to do. I had been practising the eye-roll for a while and this was the first time I had used it.

It worked fine. Ben smiled in sympathy. I bloomed inside. It didn't matter if the gestures weren't mine yet, or if I had had to practise them. Eventually they would become second nature to me, and I would turn into the person I was pretending to be. That was what the book had promised, anyway, and so far it seemed to be working.

'Is your mum still on your case?' he asked sympathetically.

'Oh, she died a couple of years ago,' I said. 'It's OK. Really,' I added lightly, not wanting him to feel embarrassed, and shifted my gaze back to the screen.

'Lady Macbeth, welcome to the show!' Jillian was saying as the latest guest smoothed her skirt over her legs and smiled at the camera. Jillian was visibly more confident; at least Lady Macbeth looked the part of a guest who knew how to behave on a daytime talk show. No bestiality, animal sacrifices or overt displays of lust for teenage boys.

'Jillian, how nice of you to invite me on,' Lady Macbeth purred back.

'Now, we're here to talk about great tragic heroines, of course, but meanwhile you have a book just coming out, don't you?' Jillian said breezily. 'Why don't you tell us all about it?'

This was code for 'I haven't read it and I don't intend to', but Lady Macbeth was too much of a pro to be fazed.

'Well, Jillian, it's been a very exciting project for me,' she said, smiling. 'After my first book came out, my publishers were very keen for me to tell the public more about myself.'

'And that of course was your motivational book, wasn't it?' Jillian snatched a glance at the teleprompter. '*Infirm of Purpose?* Which was a *great* success.'

'Oh, thank you,' Lady Macbeth said, all faux-modesty. 'It's just come out in paperback, actually.'

'Yes, we have some copies here,' Jillian said enthusiastically, her whole posture expressing relief that finally this programme was following normal lines.

One of the cameras swivelled obediently to a display table where copies of *Infirm of Purpose?* and the latest book, in hardback, were propped. Lady Macbeth indicated the latter.

'I was asked to write an autobiography,' she explained. 'Naturally, I had used incidents from my life in writing the motivational book, which is, of course, about how to set your goals and then motivate not only yourself but the people around you into achieving them.' She smiled toothily. 'But apparently, according to my publishers, the public wanted more about me. And so I wrote *Give Me the Daggers*.'

'That's a very intriguing title, isn't it?' Jillian prompted, steepling her fingers together to show off her manicure. 'Can you tell us a little about it?'

'Well, like *Infirm of Purpose?* it's a quotation from the Shake-speare play *Macbeth*, which of course was based on my and my husband's tumultuous life. My husband died young, in battle, as I'm sure you know.'

Ooh, a death in the family. This prompted Jillian's head-tilting, sympathetic look.

'And how did you feel about that?' she said gently.

'Well, I was pretending to be mad at the time, so my husband or his enemies wouldn't kill me,' Lady Macbeth explained. 'So I really didn't have much time to grieve. I actually staged my own death and escaped to France, where I had relatives. It was a very hectic period of my life. I had to lie low for a long time. But the play is obviously very famous and I was glad of the opportunity to set the record straight, since many of the events it depicts are not at all true to life.'

'Hmmn, fascinating,' Jillian said. 'I look forward to diving into it! I'm sure it's a great read! And it's already heading up the bestseller charts, isn't it?'

'Apparently, yes!' Lady Macbeth said. 'It's very exciting.'

'Wonderful! Now, you've obviously been the subject of a play, and so have my two other tragic heroine guests!' Jillian said, gesturing to Medea and Phaedra. 'I wonder if you have come across each other at all in your exciting lives?'

This was a cue for a little light celebrity gossip.

'Well, I—' Lady Macbeth started, faltering but game.

'No,' Medea said flatly. She had clearly not taken to Lady Macbeth.

'I'm afraid not,' Phaedra said more politely.

'Oh, there isn't some place where all of you – um—'

'*Please* don't let her say "tragic heroines",' Ben muttered.

'—ex-heads of European royalty gather to, um, get away from the common round?'

Medea and Phaedra just stared at her. Lady Macbeth, having a book to publicize and wanting to be invited back, was visibly trying to think of an answer, but not succeeding.

'Cue brittle laugh,' I said to Ben, a second before Jillian erupted into that tinkling laugh she used when she had dropped a brick and wanted to pretend she had been joking.

He grinned at me. 'You're good at this.'

'Well, let's throw this open to the audience, shall we?' Jillian said brightly. 'I'm sure they've got loads of questions they're dying to ask.'

Normally, they would have been champing at the bit by now. But this was a unique show, in all senses of the word. Jillian, mike in hand, had to range up and down the aisles for a good five minutes – an eternity – to find someone willing to ask the first question. No outbursts, no angry mums, no feminists furious with Phaedra for making a false rape accusation. They were all petrified. Finally, with great relief, Jillian managed to prompt a pedantic older man into asking Lady Macbeth how she could write books for money based on a murder she and her husband had committed.

'Hmm, that is an interesting point he's raised, isn't it?' Jillian said, addressing Lady Macbeth with her serious, I'm-pretending-to-be-an-investigative-journalist expression. 'How would you answer that?'

Lady Macbeth, smiling sweetly, explained that actually the murder had been a very long time ago; that she, even in the Shakespeare play, had only been an accessory to a crime; and that her lawyers and those of the publisher had advised her that no one would prosecute her on such minimal evidence. However, she had donated a portion of the royalties from both books to various charitable causes, as a symbolic gesture of restitution.

'How generous of you,' Jillian said. 'I'm sure we all applaud that!'

She managed to get a few ragged claps from the audience. Another awful pause ensued. Then, finally, a woman raised her hand tentatively. Jillian rushed over so fast she nearly tripped on the stairs and went flying. Dragging the poor woman to her feet, she shoved the mike into her face.

'I just . . .' the woman said in a trembling voice, 'I just . . . I mean, I'm sure we're all thinking this, but I just want to know – I have three kids myself and I love them to death – I mean . . .' she tailed off, horrified by her own expression.

'Yes?' Jillian prompted between gritted teeth.

The poor woman was shaking from head to foot. Ducking her head, she muttered to her feet that she didn't know how Medea could possibly live with herself after having killed her children.

There was a subdued, intimidated murmur from many of the women. No one wanted to call attention to themselves, but everyone wanted to know the answer. Jillian, visibly bracing herself, said, 'Hmm, that certainly is a question I'm sure we all wonder about. Medea, would you like to answer that?'

Medea, who had been staring into space, finally turned her head slowly and fixed the woman with a long, dark stare. The woman sat down so fast that in the silence we could all hear the rattle of her chair.

'It was my pain to bear,' Medea said, in that hoarse, rasping, oddly compelling voice. 'Mine and his. No one else's.'

Jillian was clearly irritated. The *Jillian Jackson Show* was not accustomed to its guests refusing to answer questions on the grounds of personal privacy. The *Jillian Jackson Show* was about public confession, repentance and absolution, and guests who were unaware of that should not be on the show at all.

'But—' she began.

Medea shifted in her chair and looked at Jillian intently. The words seemed to catch in Jillian's throat. Everyone in the audience suddenly found the contents of their laps to be the most interesting thing in the entire room.

'Maybe she's going to turn Jill into a pig,' Ben whispered in my ear. 'That's what that other witch did, yeah?'

'Circe,' I said automatically.

'Right.'

Jillian coughed, as if repudiating something.

'Well, I can see that Medea feels this very deeply,' she said, avoiding Medea's gaze. 'And I'm sure this show has helped her to come to terms with things. Any more questions?'

Various guests, emboldened by Lady Macbeth's civilized answer to the first question, gradually gained the confidence to give testimonials to the effectiveness of the points outlined in *Infirm of Purpose?*, to which Lady Macbeth responded graciously. She spoke for a short while on what she called her key insight, which was a creative visualization exercise designed to help one focus one's goals and intent.

The final questioner was a schoolteacher, who was accompanying a party of teenagers and who pointed out rather angrily that the title of the programme did not perfectly reflect its contents.

'I'm actually doing tragedy with my class this term,' she said, indicating the class. Some of them shrank back into their seats, embarrassed at having been mentioned by their teacher. Others, more bold, waved or stuck out their pierced tongues at the camera. Something else to edit out.

'And I have to say that this is not exactly what we would call tragedy, based on the principles we've been studying. I mean, a tragic heroine – OK, tragedy is when you bring your fate onto your own head, by innate character flaws, and that's clear enough here. But a true tragic heroine, or hero, in my view, undergoes some sort of character change, some sort of realization, transformation, by the end. They grow as they come to understand what they have brought down on themselves. I mean, that's the definition of tragedy as we understand it. And their fate is inevitable, I mean, Lady Macbeth in the play actually pays for her crime, unlike what we're seeing here today . . .'

Her voice tailed off. Jillian looked expectantly at the guests. Lady Macbeth was about to answer, but Phaedra, surprisingly, cut in first.

'Well, she dies, in the play. What I think you really mean is that a tragic heroine dies, isn't it?'

Phaedra had been silent for a long time, presumably in a trance contemplating her remembered vision of Hippolytus's young, naked, virgin body. Now she added with a completely aristocratic hauteur, 'If you want dead heroines, I suggest you try grand opera. I'm sorry we've disappointed you by being alive.'

'Well, I—' the teacher stammered.

Jillian went for another tinkling laugh.

'There certainly are a lot of dying heroines in opera, aren't

there!' she said. 'Mimi – um, and all the others – fascinating!
Well, sadly that's all we have time for. I'd like to thank my
wonderful guests – Medea, Phaedra and Lady Macbeth – and
thank you all for participating in this really unusual programme.
So, till tomorrow—'

'I'm Jillian Jackson,' I mimicked, turning down the sound,
'and this is – laugh – my show!'

Ben grinned, acknowledging the accuracy of my imitation. He
stretched his arms above his head and let out a long whoosh of
breath.

'I wouldn't like to be the guy who has to edit that,' he said
ruefully.

Ben stood up, pushing back his chair carelessly. That was
what people did who were really confident; they just pulled
chairs where they wanted and left them; they didn't worry about
putting them back, or what other people would say.

'Sophie and I and some other people are going to the Crown
for a bevvy,' he said casually. 'Want to come along?'

'Sure.' I managed to mimic his casual tone, though my heart
was pounding.

'Great. See you in there when all this has wound down, then.'

He wandered off, leaving the empty polystyrene coffee cup on
my desk. I pictured myself one day calling, 'Oi, litterbug!' and
making him take it with him. Dizzy imaginings. I was so excited
I could barely breathe. It was the first time ever that they had
asked me to the pub and I had never been confident enough to
go without an invitation.

Back on the screens the guests were leaving the stage. I
watched Medea walk offscreen, her carriage as regal as if she
had an iron bar in place of a spine. She was like a magnet; she
drew me despite myself. I had been thinking of little else since I
knew she was definitely booked to come on the show. Now was
the moment. I got up and traced my way through the maze of
corridors to the green room. Phaedra and Lady Macbeth had

been taken there by an assistant for the customary post-show wind down with coffee and sandwiches, but there was no sign of Medea.

'Did Medea go already?' I said, panic rising. I had been planning this for months. I had to find a moment to talk to her.

Felicity, one of the gofers, shook her head. Through a mouthful of croissant, she said, 'Dennis's office. Only window that opens.'

She mimed raising a cigarette to her lips.

The door of Dennis's office was closed. They must have warned Medea about the smoke alarms. She was standing by the open window, the wind catching her dark, silver-streaked hair, her eyes closed. In her fingers a cigarette smouldered, its strong, aromatic scent unfamiliar to me. As I came in, her eyelids flickered open and she considered me for a brief moment, one long assessing gaze, before she turned her attention to the fiery point of her cigarette.

'I wanted—' I began. 'I wanted to say—'

'Oh, I can guess what you want to say,' she said wearily.

It was like an oracle speaking, the voice of centuries, worn and harshened and altogether powerful. She exhaled smoke from her nostrils in twin jets.

'I expect you've got something to confess, haven't you?' she said cynically. 'Something you've never told anyone else, but feel that I'll understand?'

I stammered an agreement. It felt as if she had made my tongue swell in my mouth; I could hardly speak.

'I should have expected this,' she said, inhaling deeply. 'I should never have done this ridiculous programme. But they offered me so much money, I would have been a fool to say no.'

She sighed.

'Let me guess. Your boyfriend? You don't look old enough to have a husband. Times have certainly changed. He left you and you killed him? Or did you kill his girlfriend? The story's always the same. I'm the goddess all the murderers worship, you know.

All the ones who have murdered for love. They make dark little sacrifices at my altar. I'm so bored with it. How I wish someone would bring me something original for a change.'

'I've never had a boyfriend,' I managed to say.

'Really? Then someone you loved, I expect, who rejected you? No?' She looked more closely at me. It was like having two cigarette points pressed into my eyes.

'But you have killed. I can see that. So.'

She gestured with her cigarette. Strangely, it was the same length it had been when I had entered the room; it didn't seem to be burning down.

'Tell me. Perhaps it will even be original. A child, maybe? A sibling you hated?'

'My mother,' I mumbled.

Medea recoiled.

'Your *mother*?' she hissed.

I was dumbfounded at her reaction. Seeing how revolted she looked, I tried to explain.

'She wouldn't let me go out, ever. I had to do my degree by post. She wouldn't let me take a job, or have any friends, or do anything she didn't like. She wanted to bury me alive – to make me her slave, really. She didn't want me to have any life that wasn't about her. And I couldn't – it had always been like that, I didn't know how to tell her I wouldn't put up with it any longer, she just had to look at me and I would cave in, no matter how much I'd practised beforehand telling her that things had to change. It was the only way. *Really* it was. I thought – you'd understand—'

'What?' she said contemptuously. 'Because I killed my children?'

She laughed bitterly.

'They belonged to me. I had made them, in more pain than you can ever imagine now. I'd rather go into battle three times than give birth to one child, the way things were then. Ripped apart by them, and my husband wanting a virgin, nice and tight and new. My children belonged to me. They were *mine*. And you, a *matricide*, confess that to me, as if I would understand – the worst crime imaginable—'

She took a long drag on her cigarette.

'*Zeus*,' she said in exhaustion. 'Enough. Young people today are so *decadent*.'

Smoke poured out of her nostrils like dragon's breath. It was a dense, aromatic cloud, strong as incense, filling the room, blinding me, swirling thickly around me and wrapping me tight. I coughed frantically, unable to lift my arms to wave it away from my face, terrified that she was choking me to death.

Then, suddenly, it sucked itself away as fast as it had come, lifting and swirling in a spiral out of the open window and into the sky. Medea had vanished with it. I doubled over, coughing up phlegm. When I finally stood up, there was no trace of anything; no smoke, nothing that had been hers. Not even ash on the carpet.

I opened the door and went slowly back to my desk. Strangely enough, I felt oddly calm. I had tried: I had done my best. As with my mother, I had practised what I would say in advance. I had given her every chance, and it had failed. Confession hadn't worked. And if Medea wouldn't absolve me, or give me the penance I had almost been expecting, no one would. I remembered my mother, tumbling down the stairs to her death, and shrugged. I would just have to learn to live with it.

And, meanwhile, they were all gathering in the pub and I was invited. I had some blusher in my bag I had just bought, meaning to copy the way Sophie wore it, bright highlights on the apples of her cheeks. I could try that out in the loos. I thought it would suit me.

JENNY SILER

Africa

It was raining over the straits, the clouds dense as wet wool. Gibraltar slid by the windows of the ferry like the sea-battered head of a drowned corpse bobbing in the swell. A pair of gulls hovered in the ferry's wake, then suddenly plunged from view. It was warm inside the boat, the air thick with the smell of too many damp humans, of cigarettes and sweat. A group of German Rastafarians lounged on the floor to Neely's right, their heads propped on grimy backpacks. On the other side of the cabin, a woman in a djellaba and a headscarf was changing a baby's diaper.

There was a time when Neely had made the crossing regularly, from Tangier to Algeciras and back at least once a week. She'd been one of Joshi's perpetual tourists, with a knapsack full of dirty clothes and uncut heroin, a thick stack of hundred-dollar bills just in case, and a mental list of every official along the way who'd been taken care of. It had been an easy run, easy to slip through with the hundreds of other dirty white kids nursing their Costa del Sol hangovers.

That had been five years ago, five years since she had met Brian in the bar at the Hotel Continental. A few months later he'd offered her a job at Transarms. Working for democracy, he'd told her, for the cause of freedom. She got the feeling he actually believed what he was saying, and it fascinated her.

She'd just seen a movie about three Americans on a joyride in some backwater Asian country. When one friend was arrested for drug possession and thrown in an even more backwater prison, it fell to the other two to own up to their share of the hashish. The rub was that to keep the one friend from being executed, the other friends had to give up their cushy American lives and do their share of the time in the Asian prison. The movie hadn't scared Neely, but it had made her think. She had seen the characters' predicament not as a misfortune but as an act of grace, a choice that, once made, would define them as no other could. It seemed to Neely that Brian's life had that kind of definition.

The job with Transarms wasn't exactly legitimate, but it was a government job of sorts, a big step up from working for Joshi, and she could put her skills to work. Anything, she'd told herself, to get off that ferry. And yet here she was again, slipping through, on her own this time, and with something different in her baggage.

Neely had forgotten how much she hated Tangier, the hustlers at the ferry docks, the rug dealers and black market money changers who clogged the putrid streets just outside the medina, the listless illegals from Senegal or the Ivory Coast waiting for a chance to make the crossing to Spain. Making her way from the boat to the Cafe Africa to meet Joshi, she was reminded of all these things.

'He'll love you,' Joshi said sarcastically, eyeing her frayed jeans and tie-dyed sweatshirt. 'You're just his type.'

'Don't worry,' she told him. 'I brought a dress.'

'Clean and classy, that's how Werner likes it.'

Neely propped her elbows on the table and lit a cigarette. 'How's business?'

The waiter brought two glasses of mint tea. Joshi fussed with his, carefully mixing in three cubes of sugar. Neely had forgotten how delicate and feminine he could be. 'Business is good. Better now. No more exports, just the girls.'

When Neely had worked for him the girls had been a perk,

a way of greasing the wheels of bureaucracy, of paying off all the various government officials who looked the other way so he could run his business.

Neely glanced around the bright cafe. A group of men in brown burnouses were playing cards at a table in the back. Two boys sat near the front door, taunting a fat Senegali whore who was parading her wares on the street outside.

'What's a nice boy from Osaka doing pimping white girls in the armpit of Africa?' she asked.

'I'm simply supplying dinner companions,' Joshi corrected her.

The waiter appeared again, with two greasy tagines and a platter of spongy bread. 'Don't these things usually have something to do with love?' Joshi said, as if this explained everything.

Neely took a last drag off her cigarette and stubbed it out in the cheap tin ashtray. *What things?* she wondered. *The girls? The drugs? The circumstances that had brought him here?* Sometimes the gap between Joshi's English and what he was trying to express was too big to cross. 'Or money,' she added, too tired to help him out.

He smiled from behind his round glasses. 'Either way, I guess it's lucky for you I am in this business.'

'Yes,' she said. 'Thank you.'

Joshi lifted his glass to his lips. The tea was cheap, made with dried mint instead of fresh. 'It feels good to help out an old friend,' he said. 'Besides, Werner is merely a customer and not a very good one. Let's just say he has bad manners. Some of my girls have been hurt. You will be doing me a favour.'

They ate their meal in silence. When they had finished, Neely paid the bill.

'A drink at the Continental before you go?' Joshi asked as they rose.

'My train leaves in half an hour.' It was a lie, but Neely didn't want to go to the Hotel Continental, not on this trip.

They stepped out of the cafe together into the bustle of the old city. It had started to rain again, making the streets and sidewalks soupy with mud and grime. A *petit taxi* pulled up and Neely swung her backpack on to the luggage rack, then folded herself into the back seat. '*La gare*,' she told the driver.

From her room on the fourth floor of the Sheraton, Neely had a view across the Avenue de la Menara to the bleak silhouette of the Atlas Mountains and the moonscape of olive groves and makeshift football fields that marked the ragged boundary of the city. It was just past sunset and the only faces on the Avenue were European. Even the camel drivers had gone home for harira and mint tea. A white woman in a satin ballgown stood outside the hotel gates, trying unsuccessfully to hail a cab. It was a bad time to be in Marrakesh, midwinter and Ramadan, too cold for sunning by the pool, and everyone was hungry and mean.

Neely turned from the window, from the now frantic woman in the street below. It had been a long trip down on the train. She'd tried to sleep, but even in first class she'd felt as if she was riding a paint mixer. She wanted to lie on the king-sized bed, put her head on the down pillows and close her eyes. Later, she promised herself, checking the mirror one last time. She smoothed a stray wisp of hair, adjusted her breasts inside the strapless bodice of her dress and put on a final coat of lipstick. She pulled her Beretta Tomcat from the bottom of her pack, shoved a fresh clip into the stock and stuffed the gun into her beaded evening bag.

Werner was waiting for her in the bar. She could see him when she got out of the elevator. He had his back to her and he was talking to the bartender, a young European woman in a short black skirt and a red vest. Neely sat down on a velvet banquette in the corner and waited for him to turn around.

She'd met him once before, on a weapons deal in Amsterdam,

but she was certain he wouldn't recognize her. Transarms had been buying Chinese hardware for Foreign Materiel Acquisitions. It was an American programme, a way of getting a sneak peek at the other guy's technology. Werner was the willing seller. She'd been a minor player in that meeting and she doubted she'd even registered on his radar screen. Men like Werner tended to have selective vision and only saw what was useful to them.

There was just a handful of customers in the bar. A table of bored and overdressed expatriates. A group of Japanese businessmen in grey suits and paper party hats. Neely signalled to the Moroccan waiter and the movement caught Werner's eye. He turned towards her and smiled, then made his way across the bar.

'You must be Joshi's friend.'

She nodded. 'Leila,' she said, extending her hand. She'd chosen an Arabic name for the meeting, the word, she had once been told, for night.

The waiter came over and Werner ordered a bottle of Taittinger. 'It is New Year's Eve, after all,' he told her, settling back in his chair, pulling a cigar from the breast pocket of his evening jacket. 'Do you mind?'

'Of course not.'

'You know, our holiday means nothing to them. As far as they're concerned it's still the fifteenth century,' Werner explained. 'They hate us for our excess.' He motioned toward the waiter. 'But if it weren't for us, he'd be home right now with his family, gorging himself on couscous and pea soup.' He snipped the end of the cigar and fingered it gingerly before lighting it.

Neely slid her foot from her shoe and found Werner's ankle under the table. She smiled as if she meant it and ran her bare instep up under his pants leg. Until now she had never thought about what it might mean to pay for another person's affections, or the price of such capitulation. The pleasure here had only to do with his power and her lack of it. And yet, she could make him want her.

Werner looked over at her. 'You're not like the girls Joshi usually sends, are you?'

'Smell the Sahara!' he exclaimed, gazing out towards the invisible mountains, sniffing at the cold air. A few of the camel drivers had returned and were waiting for tourists in the dark fields across the Avenue. 'Have you ever been across the Atlas?'

'No,' Neely said, but it was a lie. It had taken three years after their first meeting at the Continental for Brian and Neely to become lovers. Their first trip together had been to the Sahara. The spring before Brian was killed they'd flown into Marrakesh, then driven over the mountains to Ouarzazate and on to Zagora.

'That's where Africa truly begins,' Werner remarked, pretentiously. 'The real Africa.' They were standing just inside the Sheraton's gates, waiting for Werner's driver to pick them up.

Neely shivered. She could remember Brian next to her in their tiny bed in Agdz, a lunch they'd eaten one day beneath the rustle of date palms. Somewhere along the way they'd spent the night in a whitewashed room inside an old kasbah.

'I suppose it is,' she agreed.

A black Mercedes pulled off the Avenue and stopped. The driver, a tall, muscular Moroccan with a neat goatee, climbed out and opened the door for them. The bulky shape of a handgun was plainly visible through the expensive fabric of his well-tailored suit jacket. Werner took Neely's hand and helped her into the dark interior of the car.

Technically, it wasn't Werner who had killed Brian. As far as anyone could tell it was one of Werner's flunkies who put the bullet in his head, then threw him from a plane somewhere over Zaire. But no doubt it was Werner who had ordered the execution.

Brian had called her from an airport in Bulgaria the night

before to say he'd had enough. He'd rolled on a shipment he'd arranged between Transarms and Werner's company, a mixed-cargo freight that had a Nigerian end-user certificate, but was headed somewhere even Brian couldn't stomach.

'Christ, Neely,' he said on the phone, his voice thickened slightly by Bulgarian brandy. 'We're supposed to be the good guys.'

She laughed at the outrageous innocence of the statement. 'We buy and sell the machinery of war,' she reminded him.

'Not this war. I'll call you when we land. I've arranged a nice welcome for Werner.'

But Brian didn't call. He was spotted getting into the plane after it had stopped for refuelling at an airfield in southern Sudan, but was conspicuously absent when the plane touched down in Kigali. And there was no sign of Werner either. The professional in Neely told herself it was part of the job, that these things happened, that somehow, if she waited, she'd get lucky and Werner would pay in the end. That was the official line at the company. But she didn't want to wait.

Werner slid in beside her and laid his arm across her shoulders. The car rolled forward, down the Avenue de la Menara and in through the gates of the old city, past the gardens of La Mamounia, its Moorish facade lit up like a stage set for the millennium party.

They ate at a French restaurant, a homey imitation of a farmhouse in Provence, with a stone hearth and wood beams in the ceilings, and a doting proprietress who kissed Werner twice on each cheek. There was white linen on the tables and vases with small pink roses, and yet something was not quite right. It wasn't until the second course, poorly cooked slabs of foie gras, that Neely realized there were no windows, not one single opening through which the reality of their surroundings might intrude.

At eleven everyone stood up and sang the Marseillaise.

'It's midnight in France,' Werner explained, with a sarcasm she could appreciate. 'Welcome to the new millennium.'

Neely had studied Werner's Interpol file before coming. She thought she knew what to expect, but when they pulled in through the walls of his villa and the lights of the Mercedes washed across the house and perfectly kept grounds she was overwhelmed by their opulence. *This is what money can buy*, she thought. *This, someone to have dinner with and a civilized fuck, all financed by a few small wars.*

The house was Moorish in design, but obviously built for European tastes. There was a large open courtyard on the first floor, thick with poinsettias and palms. From somewhere in the dark foliage Neely could hear the splash and gurgle of a fountain.

'Why don't we go upstairs?' Werner proposed, as if it was her decision to make, as if the outcome of the evening was uncertain. 'We could draw you a bath.'

'Yes, that would be nice.' She followed Werner up to the second floor and down along the gallery. From the balcony she caught occasional glimpses of lights in the rooms that ringed the courtyard.

'Do you have staff?' she asked, gripping her bag, working through her options in her mind. She was thinking about noise in the open house, about an easy way out.

'Just Mustapha, my driver, and a woman who does my cooking and cleaning.' He looked at Neely, his eyes glittering like an animal's in the half-darkness. 'But don't worry. We'll be left alone.'

He stopped walking and ushered her through an ornate, curved portico and into a large bedroom. 'Make yourself at home,' he told her and again his consideration seemed inane, this pretence of tenderness, of some kind of affection. 'I'll get your bath,' he said, disappearing through a side door.

Neely surveyed the room's furnishings, the goatskin lamps, leather ottomans and handloomed rugs. A hand of Fatima hung over the bed's carved wooden headboard. A peg on the back of the bathroom door held a robe-like burnous. On the far side of the room two open doors revealed a large veranda and a glimpse of the Koutoubia mosque's minaret, its dour shape towering over the city like a night watchman.

Neely crossed to the balcony and stepped outside. It was a long drop to the ground below, too far to jump, even if she had no other choice. The villa's terracotta tiled eaves hung low enough to climb, but she had no way of knowing if there was a way off the roof. A door clicked open in the garden below and a broad-shouldered shape emerged from what Neely assumed was the garage. The man made his way towards the front of the house. When he stepped into the light of the driveway, Neely could see that it was Werner's driver, Mustapha.

'There you are.' Werner's voice sounded from the doorway behind her and Neely turned towards it.

'Yes. Here I am,' she smiled.

Werner had taken his jacket off for the first time that evening. The sleeves of his white shirt were rolled up over his elbows. 'Your bath is ready,' he said. 'Why don't you come inside?'

Neely nodded. The breeze picked up and she could suddenly smell the sweet odour of the gardens that surrounded the house, the faint yet pervasive stench of the leather tannery. *That's where Africa truly begins*, she heard Werner say, *the real Africa*. She thought again of that trip with Brian, of the vertiginous ride back across the Atlas, the road's edge dropping precipitously to snowfields and scree. She had been uncharacteristically afraid, conscious of all she had to lose.

Werner turned, heading across the bedroom to the bath and Neely followed, slipping the Beretta from her bag. She could hear the driver inside now, his voice and a woman's voice muffled by the walls of the villa.

'I suppose Joshi told you,' Werner said, 'my tastes are some-what unusual.' He stopped walking and looked back at Neely, as if to monitor her response.

'Yes,' she said. Raising the barrel of the gun to the level of Werner's chest, she slowly eased the safety off with her thumb.

Panic flickered across his face, then he smiled at her as if she'd just told a joke.

Who could say what the real Africa was? she thought, feeling her fist harden around the Beretta. The red walls of Marrakesh? The acrobats in the Djemaa al-Fna? The thin light of the Atlas? The hashish dealers in the Petit Socco? Two dozen Frenchmen singing the Marseillaise? Or the hum of a plane crossing Zaire, the door sliding open to reveal the black terror of night?

'Amsterdam,' Werner said, his voice full of satisfaction. 'I knew I'd seen you before.'

'Yes,' Neely agreed. Somehow his knowing bothered her more than anything, the fact that he recognized her for who she really was.

'You work for Transarms,' he said, taking a step forward. 'No wonder you're such a good whore.'

She wanted to be able to tell Werner that he was wrong, that this was personal, that it had something to do with love. But in the end she knew he was right. *We're supposed to be the good guys*, Brian had told her. She had loved him for believing this, but she had never shared his faith. Even now it was her own dark rage that drove her.

Neely squeezed the trigger and the gun leaped in her hands, once, then a second time. Two dark blooms of blood erupted on the front of Werner's white shirt. He let out a high-pitched squeal, the sound an animal might make when wounded. There was a moment of profound silence after the eruption of the gunshot, then footsteps pounded up the stairs.

Neely grabbed the hooded burnous off the bathroom door and raced out on to the veranda. Slipping out of her high-heeled shoes, she hoisted herself up over the eaves and on to the roof. She could hear yelling from Werner's room, Mustapha's throaty Arabic, and the woman again, her voice shrill with panic.

She crept along the perimeter of the roof, peering down into the garden. Along the back of the house was another veranda, and below it some kind of storage shed that backed on to the garden wall. *A moment of grace*, Neely thought, *a way out*. She leaped from the roof to the balcony, to the shed, wrapped the cloak of the burnous around her shoulders, pulled the hood down over her face, and slipped over the wall and on to the street.

KARIN SLAUGHTER

Necessary Women

I was fourteen years old when I watched my mama die. Her pale skin turned white as a pitcher of buttermilk as she clutched her throat, blood seeping through her fingers like she was squeezing a sponge instead of trying to hold on to her life. She was barely thirty years old when she passed, but my daddy had put age on her. Streaks of silver shot through her dark hair like lines on a blackboard and there was a hardness about her eyes that made you look away fast, before you could be drawn into the sadness.

I try not to think of Mama this way now. When I close my eyes, I think of Saturday nights sitting on the floor in the living room, Mama in the chair behind me, brushing my hair so it would look good for Sunday services. Mama wasn't particularly religious herself, but we lived in a small border town, smack on the line between Georgia and Alabama, and people would have talked. I'm glad we had nights like this because now that she is gone I can think back on it, sometimes even feel the bristles of the brush going through my hair and the soft touch of Mama's hand on my shoulder. It comforts me.

We lived in a three-room house made of cement block, which kept heat in like a kiln. Thankfully, pecan trees shaded the roof, so most days we didn't get the full intensity of the sun. In a county that routinely saw hundred plus temperatures, this made a difference. Come summertime we would pick the pecans, salt them and sell them to vacationers on their way to the Florida Panhandle. Sometimes Daddy brought in peanuts and Mama would boil them. I can still see her standing in front of the cauldron, stirring the peanuts with a long two-by-four, her shins bright red from the open flame beneath the pot.

Our life had a settled routine to it and while I can't say that we were happy, we made do with what we had. At night, sometimes we would hear people beeping their horns as they crossed into Alabama and Mama would get a wistful look on her face. She never said anything, but I remember the first time I saw that look I got a pain in my gut as I realized that maybe Mama wasn't happy, that maybe she didn't want to be here with me and Daddy. Like most things this passed, and soon we learned to ignore the honking vacationers. Around about the middle of summer, every supper would go something like, 'Pass the—' honk-honk. Or, 'Can I have some—' toot-toot.

Daddy was a long hauler, driving semis across the nation for this company or that, and he would be gone for weeks, sometimes months, at a time. Mostly when he was home I slept on the couch, but when he was gone I would sleep with Mama in their bed. We would stay up at night, talking about him, both missing him. I think these are the happiest memories I have of my mother. At night with the lights off there was no work to do; no floors to scrub, meals to fix, shirts to iron. Mama had two jobs then, one cleaning the restrooms at the welcome centre on the Alabama side, the other working nights at the laundry. When I would lay with her, I could smell an odd mixture of Clorox bleach and dry-cleaning solvent. I often think if that knife had not killed her the chemicals she used would have sent her to an early grave.

About a week before she died, Mama had a talk with me. We had turned in early, just as the sun was dipping into the horizon, because Mama was due at work around four the next morning. A hard rain was sweeping across the tin roof, making shushing noises to lull us to sleep. I was just about to nod off when Mama rolled over in bed, nudging me awake.

'We need to talk,' she said.

'Shh-shh-shh,' the rain warned, none too softly.

Mama spoke over the hush, her voice firm. 'We need to have that talk.'

I knew what she meant. There was a boy at school, Rod Henry, who had started to pay attention to me. With no encouragement from me, he had gotten off the bus at my stop instead of his, which was three miles down. I had no particular interest in Rod Henry other than in the fact that he was an older boy, about sixteen. He had what could on a generous day be called a moustache along his upper lip and his hair was long enough to pull back into a ponytail. When he pulled me behind the pecan shack in our front yard, I did not stop him. Out of curiosity, I let him kiss me. Out of curiosity, I let him touch me.

'That Rod Henry,' Mama said. 'He's no good.'

'He has a tattoo,' I told her because I had seen it. 'I don't like him much.'

'I didn't like your daddy much when I met him, either,' Mama said, 'but things happen.'

I knew that I was the thing that happened to her, the thing that took her out of school at the age of fifteen, the thing that put her in the welcome centre cleaning toilets instead of working at the Belk over in Mobile like she had planned to do when she got out of school. Her sister Ida worked there as a manager, and it had been lined up for years that Mama would go over and help Ida out as soon as she finished school. She would live in Ida's apartment and they would save their money and one day they would meet nice, respectable boys and settle down. The plan was perfect until Daddy came along.

To hear Mama tell it, there was no romance in the way Daddy got her. It was a night of firsts that changed her life. Her first cigarette, her first beer, her first kiss, her first time having sex.

'That's all it takes, baby,' Mama said, her fingers digging into my arm, her stubby nails like slivers of hot metal. 'Just one time is all it takes.'

I closed my eyes, crying for no reason, thinking about what it must have been like for Mama, just a little older than me, to feel my daddy on top of her for the first time. He was not a gentle man, and he was large, six-four at least with a wide chest and arms so big around he had to cut the sleeves of his T-shirts just so he could get into them. Daddy was twenty-two when he first met Mama and he had tricked her, she said, with his worldly ways.

'The pain,' Mama said, mumbling. 'He about ripped me in two.'

I nodded my understanding. She was a small woman, with delicate wrists and a thin waist. There was a look of fragility to her that had fooled more than one person. Daddy liked to say that she was skin and bones, but I thought she was more like skin and muscle. I reached out and stroked her arm, which was wiry and hard from working. A sliver of light came from the window. With the weight of the day off her, her face was relaxed and I could see the young woman she was before Daddy got to her. I could see how beautiful she must have been to him and how she was totally the opposite of me. I felt like a monster next to her.

Her head turned suddenly, the slackness gone, a furrow set into her brow. 'You listening to me?' she demanded, her tone low and sharp in the small room.

'Yes, Mama,' I mumbled, drawing my hand back as if from a snake. She kept that look on me, paralysing me momentarily with the sudden flash of anger and fear I could see brewing inside of her. Though she had never hit me, I felt violence radiating off her, like she might lunge and throttle me any minute.

'Don't be me, baby,' she said, 'Don't end up in this house with your daddy like me.'

Tears came in earnest now. I whispered, 'I won't, Mama.'

Her look said she didn't believe me, but that she knew nothing could be done about it. She turned her back to me and fell asleep.

Of course, Mama's warning had come too late. Neither of us knew at the time, but I was pregnant.

After she died, Daddy sat me down at the table. He leaned his elbows on the table, his hands clasped in front of him. I noticed that together, his hands were bigger than my head. He smelled of pipe tobacco and sweat. His beard was growing in though he was a man who liked to be clean-shaven. Mama's passing had been hard on him.

'Now that your mama's gone,' he said, 'you gotta be the woman of the house.' He paused, his broad shoulders going into a slight, almost apologetic shrug. 'The cleaning, the cooking, the laundry. They's just necessary things a woman's gotta do.'

There was true regret in his voice that sent shivers of pain through me. I ran from the table and vomited into the kitchen sink. Looking back, I don't know if it was the baby or Daddy's words that brought such a rush of bile up from my gullet.

Daddy was on a long haul about six months later when I started to have pains. It was just me in the house and had been that way for the last three weeks. I had stopped going to school and nobody had bothered to find out why. Being big anyway, carrying my weight in the front like I did, nobody remarked upon the fact that I was showing. I had no idea that I was pregnant and had taken the stop of my monthly flow as a gift from God rather than a sign of impending childbirth. I was fifteen by then, same as Mama when she had me, and with her gone, I was still naive to the ways of nature.

The two hundred dollars Daddy had left for food was gone by the third week of his absence. I was a child and did not know how to buy groceries. There were packs of Kool-Aid in the cabinets and sweet tea was in the fridge, but no nourishment to speak of lined the shelves. We were in the middle of an unseasonably hard winter, and except for the pecan shells I was burning in the fireplace, there was no heat. Between the cold and my hunger, I think I brought on the worst for the baby. I take responsibility for it.

That morning I had taken Daddy's .22 rifle and shot a squirrel, but the meat had been sparse and I don't think I cooked it long enough. The pain hit me hard around six that night. At first I thought it was cramps from the bad meat, but soon the sharp contractions took hold. I thought I might die. I thought of Mama and that seemed OK to me.

Night passed, then another day, then another night. Pain seized me so hard at one point that I broke a chair trying to get into it. We never had a phone in the house and even if we did, I would not have known who to call. I didn't know where Daddy was and I had no friends from school.

The baby came around one in the morning on the third day. She was a tiny little thing with only one arm and a knob where her left foot should have been. When I pried open her eyes, they were a deep blue, but that can be said of most babies. The cord was wrapped around her neck, which I suppose is what made her pass. I said a prayer over her head, begging God to accept her into His house, even though she was deformed and had no father.

The ground was too cold to bury her. I wrapped her in an old blanket and set her behind the cauldron in the pecan shack. At night sometimes I would wake, thinking I heard her crying, realizing it was only me. Two more weeks passed before the ground thawed and I buried my baby next to Mama in a tiny little grave out behind the house. I put a stone on top of the mound and I prayed on my knees for them both to forgive me. I took it as a sign that they did when Daddy came home the next day.

I made him chitterlings out of a pig he had kept off the back of his truck.

'These'r good chitlins, baby,' Daddy said, scooping a forkful into his mouth. 'Just like your Mama used to make.'

His eyes watered, and my heart ached for him at that moment more than it ever had. He had loved my mama. No matter what the drink made him do or where his temper brought him, he had loved her.

'I remember you made these when your Mama—'. His voice cracked. He managed a smile for me. 'Come sit on my knee, Peanut. Tell me what you been up to since I was gone.'

I did not tell him about Laura Lee, my baby girl that lay in the back field alongside Mama. I made up stories for him about classes I had not attended, friends I had not made. He laughed with me, smoking his pipe, and when I put my head on his shoulder, he comforted me.

After a while, he moved me off of him, and I sat at his knee as he spoke. 'Listen, honey,' he began, using the same phrase he always used when there was something difficult that he was about to say. I remembered he had used those same words with me that first time. I was laying on the couch, Mama asleep in the next room, and Daddy came in, shaking me awake. 'Listen, honey,' he had said then, just as he said now.

'I met this lady,' he said, and my heart dipped into my stomach. 'She's gonna be coming by some.' He gave a low laugh. 'Hell, she might even move in after a while if things work out. Take some of the chores of your shoulders. What do you think of that?'

I wiped my mouth with the back of my hand as I sat back on my heels. I remembered Mama in the kitchen that day, washing her hair at the sink. I remember how angry I had been, hearing them the night before. He had promised me that he wasn't with her any more, said the only reason he needed me was because she wouldn't let him touch her. And then I had heard them together in bed, snorting like pigs. And then I had walked into the room, and watched him working his mouth between her legs until her body went taut and her hand snatched his hair up in a tight fist.

I clenched my hands now and I could feel Mama's hair between my fingers as I jerked her head back. Daddy was due back that night, so I had acted fast, knowing even as small as she was that her hands were stronger than mine. The blade was sharp, but cutting a person's neck is a lot like cutting up a chicken. You have to whack it good in just the right place or it won't slice all the way through. I hacked six times before her neck separated.

By the time I had taken off her head, the knife was dull, but not at the tip, and when I used it to cut out between her legs, the flesh folded in on itself like a piece of liver. I used the cauldron to fix dinner that night, giving Daddy the same thing to eat as he had had the night before.

Daddy scratched his chin, giving me a tight smile. 'With Mama just taking off like that,' he said, shrugging. 'No note, no goodbye.' He sat back in the chair, smiling apologetically. 'I got needs.'

'I know, Daddy,' I answered, buttoning my blouse with shaking fingers.

'I mean, nothing's gotta change with us. You know you're still my girl.'

'I know, Daddy,' I mumbled back.

'That OK with you, baby?' Daddy asked, zipping himself into his pants as he stood.

'That's fine, Daddy,' I said, forcing some cheer into my voice. I looked up at him, giving him my best smile. 'Why don't you invite her over next Sunday? We can have her for dinner.'

JEN BANBURY

Take, for Example, Meatpie

I knew that the five girls draped like baloney slices at the bottom of the high school steps had to be popular. The right make-up. The cell phones. The cutesie backpacks and sexy baggy clothes and cheerleader tits. I put on my Jackie O sunglasses and ambled up. Four of them had their phones earringed to their heads and one pressed some buttons on a pager. That one, she looked like she might cry. Having a pager instead of a phone could kill you with that crowd. She pretended she enjoyed tapping a text message to somebody, but I could sense the desperation. She probably wore a one-piece bathing suit to the beach, too. In these thoughts, I felt hope for her future.

'Hello, ladies,' I said. The five of them looked up at me. Four continued tweeching into their cells. 'I said "hello".'

'Someone's trying to talk to us,' one of them said into her phone. She and two others hung up. One just said, 'Hang on,' and set the phone down on her books.

'I have a question I hope you can help me with,' I said. The longest of the girls lifted a small gold cross that hung from her neck and put it in her mouth. 'The school's inside,' she said, talking around her jewellery.

'That's correct,' I said. 'I don't want that, though. Listen,' I said, 'I'll cut right to the chase. Which boy in the junior class is the biggest loser? Who eats his lunch alone? Who's awful doofalicious?' They giggled nervously. And a tiny voice came out of the phone on the books, yelling something unintelligible.

'Why?' they said. 'What?' 'Who?'

'The biggest loser,' I repeated slowly. I made an 'L' out of my thumb and finger and held it up to my head. These girls would not be in honours' English.

'Kevin!' one said. 'Whathisnamekevin! Who carries his books in the bowling ball bag!'

'He's not really a loser. He's just totally gay,' said the girl with the cross in her mouth. She worked hard at her boredom.

'Gay's no good,' I said. They seemed disappointed. One said, 'It's OK to be gay, you know.' 'Yeah!' the other girls choired in. 'Yeah, inCREDibly OK.'

'Ladies,' I said, 'you're right, but that's not the point.' I put my hand in the air. 'Ladies, let's focus. Please. When the hand goes up, the mouths go silent.'

'Fuck you,' said the long girl with the cross.

'Yeah. This isn't fucking school.'

I heard the girl who was still on the other end of the phone yell something again. I was going to pick up the phone and throw it, but then I realized she was saying a name. It sounded like a name. 'Hold it!' I said. 'What's it saying?' I pointed to the phone. We all leaned towards the phone. Closer, and now a little closer . . .

It took three school days to get Meatpie into my car. He was suspicious, of course. He had been taught to refuse rides from strangers. The first day I found him waiting for the bus alone on the grass next to the school. He sat tearing up the red leaves that fell within reach. Tearing them up and throwing them over his shoulder like spilled salt. Big for a sixteen-year-old, with light brown spastic hair and a certain flabbiness. The way he sat – cross-legged and hunched over on the grass – he looked as though someone had stolen his bones from the neck down. I watched him for a while. I'm sure he knew I was there but had learned to avoid looking at people who might be looking at him.

October had begun to kick the cold around, and Meatpie

pulled the back of his sweatshirt up over his head to make a kind of hood out of it. When I finally asked him directions, he peered up at me like a chipmunk coming out of its hole.

'A gas station?' he repeated. I was wearing red boots, short skirt and a faded corduroy coat with a fake fur collar. I believe I looked both sexy and kind. He could see my knees and a little bit of thigh, but he avoided looking at these bits of skin. In fact, after that first peek, he avoided looking at me altogether. He began, instead, slowly to tear the fabric of one leaf away from its veins and spine. That could be a good sign (a careful undresser) or a bad sign (de-fleshing fantasies). He spoke quietly to the leaf. 'What kind of gas station?' he asked.

'Any kind,' I said. I squatted in front of him and hugged my knees – a position I have found to be very non-threatening, but potentially condescending. I look younger than thirty-five, especially in those boots. My face contains some attractive bits. Overall, it's forgettable. Photographs do not flatter me. I have a nice ass, though.

'There's McGill's,' he said. 'That's that way.' He waved the naked leaf in a circle with his right hand.

'I just moved here,' I said. I allowed myself to fall over sideways as though I had lost my balance. Despite this winningly goofy manoeuvre, he refused my offer of a ride home.

The second day he was sitting with a kid holding a Gameboy so I just kept driving.

The third day I got lucky. It poured rain and I found him inside the school entrance, reading a comic book and pretending the teenage furies were not running and screaming around him. I hate the sound of teenagers yelling inside on a rainy day. Shrinking and exploding rooms and hallways with their exaggerated noise. An arrogance.

'Why don't you let me give you a ride?' I said. He stood up

without a word, shouldered his backpack and followed me to my car.

My windshield wipers didn't wipe. I drove slowly and asked Meatpie if he would come to my place for tea. 'Don't you work?' he said.

'I work from eight p.m. to two a.m.,' I said. It was true. I worked the late shift at a convenience store in the next town, but I didn't say that out loud and he didn't ask. After flicking at the passenger window for a while, he said, 'I have to let the dog out.'

The dog ran in circles around my apartment. Its muddy paws left dance instructions on the floor. Meatpie sat on the couch. I gave the dog some crackers and it stuck its moustached snout in my crotch. 'Your dog has a lot of energy,' I said.

'The dog is crazy.' Meatpie ate a cookie, turning away from me so I wouldn't watch. When he was done, he said, 'My dad loves it, though. It's a breed.'

'Who named the dog "John"?'

'Me,' said Meatpie. I had put a Replacements record on. I replayed the song 'Unsatisfied' three times while he sat and picked up his coffee cup and put it back down again. And scratched the back of his head and counted the buttons on his shirt. He probably realized that I kept restarting the song, but had been taught not to question authority. I played with the dog and said, 'Good BOY, John. Good boy.' I let Meatpie sit and get used to the surroundings. The apartment was a small but comfortable place, like all my other places had been. Some of the things I owned were: one good couch, some books, old photos, my grandmother's dishes, a comfortable bed with soft sheets and a mattress partially filled with cash. All of it fitted inside a small U-Haul trailer.

I sat down next to Meatpie on the couch. Our shoulders touched and he didn't move away. I looked straight ahead with

my hands in my lap, projecting a non-aggressive confidence.
'I thought you were beautiful when I first saw you,' I said.

'Oh no,' said Meatpie.

'I thought, "There's someone I would like to spend time
with."'

It's important for sex to enter into the process right away.
Hormones . . . gratification . . . investment. Meatpie came while
I was still pulling his pants down. He sat absolutely still. He held
his right arm straight to the side, as though making a turn signal.
John, the dog, jumped up on the couch and took the half-eaten
cookie from Meatpie's fist.

Before my sweetie could start crying about any of it, I began
to suck him and he became hard again.

I always made sure Meatpie and John got home before Meatpie's
parents returned from work. It wasn't easy. Meatpie loved sex.
Meatpie loved it. And though he never became much of a talker,
he soon made it obvious that he was highly capable of following
directions.

The first week, the programme demanded constant fucking.
I believed that Meatpie was, indeed, a virgin because he was
considered such a loser and the town only had one high school.
I was on the pill and had a clean bill of health. Still, I made
Meatpie wear condoms to get him into the habit of practising
safe sex. On a typical afternoon that first week Meatpie and I
might have sex five or six times. A good way to tackle the basics.
Soon it got so that, by the fourth time in the afternoon, he could
last up to twelve or fifteen minutes. Mostly I taught him to
go slow. Porn has a terrible influence on boys – they grow up
believing they should aspire to jackhammer humping speeds.

Also, during that first week, I taught Meatpie how to make
coffee and put the cookies on the plate. I told him that we would
trade on and off who made the coffee and put the cookies on
the plate, but that, sometimes, we should try and surprise each

other. After having sex, Meatpie acted less embarrassed about me watching him eat cookies. We would eat in bed and let the dog sit in between us.

Meatpie's flabbiness didn't bother me. I figured he would grow out of it. In the course of each afternoon I made a point of telling him how much I liked his body, his belly, his ears, lips, feet, cock. Everything but his eyes. (Forget that 'windows of the soul' business, telling someone they have beautiful eyes is like telling them they have a nice personality.) Because I was an authority figure, he began, slowly, to believe me.

We took showers together and I taught him how to use a washcloth the right way.

And how to unclasp a bra without fumbling.

And to avoid picking his nose when he was nervous (an unconscious distancing or defence mechanism, I believed).

And cunnilingus.

Early on I asked, 'What's the meanest name they call you?' Meatpie bent his arms over his head as though waiting for the grenade to explode.

'Asshole?' he said.

'More specific,' I said.

'Shit Skid?' He had a habit of speaking very slowly. Each word became an entire sentence, often a question. 'Adam. O'Downey? Calls. Me. Shit. Skid?'

'Less disgusting,' I said. 'Maybe something girls call you . . .'

He gave up the name 'Meatpie', but he wouldn't tell me its origins. From then on, whenever he was on the verge of orgasm, I would gently whisper, 'Yes, Meatpie, yes.' The first time he said, 'What are you doing?' The fear came out of him hot and sad. He sounded like a tiny boy trapped in the land of endlessly stolen lunch money.

'Shh,' I said. 'Trust me Meatpie, you beautiful boy. I'm just teaching you how to read again. I'm just shaking your snow-globe.'

The second week, I introduced poetry. Between fucks I would read a poem – a different poem each day. If he remembered some of it or could talk about it, I would do something special. One day I said, 'This is a great poem.' Then I read aloud a terrible poem. 'Well?' I asked.

'It's nice,' he said.

'No,' I said, 'That poem sucks the icing off a cupcake.' I found the use of slang helpful in communicating with all the boys.

'It does?' I read it aloud again, very slowly.

'It does suck,' he said.

'No it doesn't. It's da *bomb*. I was kidding when I said it sucked.' I made him read it out loud.

'Yeah,' he said. 'That's pretty good.' I got out of bed and got dressed. We hadn't fucked yet, merely undressed (and to my relief, he *was* a careful undresser).

'That's it for today,' I said. 'Get John, we're getting in the car.'

'But. Trombone . . .' he said. Trombone was his nickname for me. I had encouraged him to come up with one and it certainly was lousy, but he had struggled and I'm a strong believer in positive reinforcement.

'You need to figure this out in your own room.' I gave Meatpie a stack of photocopied poems to read and said that I would pick him and his opinions up after school the following day. Before I dropped him off at home, I said, 'I'm not mad at you. But I will ask things of you.' I used that phrase often in the course. I think I first came across it in some Fifties sci-fi movie.

Meanwhile, at work, I was skimming an extra thirty to forty dollars a night. I would tell people the cash register wasn't working and make change from my pocket. The store sat just off the highway so most of the customers were passing through on the way to their real lives somewhere down the road. The store's owner, dumbass, looked like a bald version of the jock who always threw cheese at me when I was a fat kid. What did he expect? Dumbass.

Now, if you ever have the opportunity to sit naked on a bed next to a teenage boy with a hard-on and watch him pick out and understand and get heady on a truly good line of poetry, well, I suggest you take advantage of it. Of course Meatpie had studied poetry at school, but most people who love poetry love it in spite of school. It took me years of teaching in a traditional classroom to understand that. Meatpie had mediocre to fine taste that would improve as he grew older. So far, he was wary of himself. As skittish as John the dog. They both rolled on to their backs at the first sign of trouble.

We didn't stop at poetry. In the following few weeks I expanded the curriculum. Next to the bed I kept the picture books. Photography, then art. I don't skimp on these books. I only steal the best and it's worth it. The quality allowed Meatpie to really see the pictures. I made him flip the pages and told him he could go at any speed he wanted. At first he flipped quickly – finishing a book meant fucking, after all. But soon he slowed and even stopped at the pictures he liked. When he stopped at one of my favourites, I would point to the picture and smile big and kiss him somewhere and say, 'Good!' John's tail would flap against the bed like the arm of an old woman who had just been told a dirty joke.

I had few rules for him. They were: no telling anyone, no wearing any clothes that had logos, no skipping school to come over and have sex, no skipping school for any other reason, no talking about television, no talking about guns, no talking about my family, no talking about his family, no talking about my friends (or lack of them), no talking about his friends (or lack of them), no weekends, no wishy-washyness, no anal sex. These rules left us free to focus on what I believed to be the most important subjects.

Meatpie struggled the most with his opinions disability. I could not get him to argue with me or articulate why he liked something. Over and over again, I tricked him into agreeing with me when he knew better.

'Meatpie,' I said, 'pretend you're the dog.' I picked up one of John's balls so I could use the dog to illustrate my point. 'I throw the ball and you bring it back.' I threw the ball out of the bedroom and into the living room. John jumped from the bed, skittered across the floor, hit the couch and returned with the ball. I threw the ball three times. I said, 'Then, ahah, I only pretend to throw the ball. I don't *really* throw it.' I gave John the old fake-out and he went for it. 'And, see? You run. You run for the ball.' John sniffed around the corners of the living room and scratched beneath the couch, looking for my little lie. 'Don't run for the ball if you don't see it. Do you understand? Don't trust that I'll keep throwing the ball. Trust that you can see the ball.' Meatpie fussed and scratched the back of his head.

'I'm not a dog,' he said. It was better than nothing. I climbed on top of him and gave him the business.

I lived in the next town over and rented from a woman who had split her house into two units. She worked long hours. In the past Meatpie had spent his afternoons watching television alone at home. In other words, we didn't have to worry about getting caught. No one noticed when I picked him up at school. He had become invisible in that world. What made Meatpie such a loser in the eyes of his classmates? He was socially dysfunctional. Shy. Flat. But I've grown to understand that, in most cases, becoming a school pariah can be as arbitrary as getting hit on the head by a falling air-conditioner. Fate demands its victims. Meatpie had goodness, but not strength.

Those weeks, I felt as though we were knee deep in a hidden stream, the time rushing past like water. Now it seems like the whole thing lasted a year. Or a few hours.

In some ways Meatpie opened like a locket. I felt proud. Accomplished. He grew to love his nickname. He picked up photography books all by himself and paused for minutes at certain pages. Soon he had seen all my books and I had to spend a Saturday driving around to malls and lifting more.

On a dark afternoon we lay in bed and used a flashlight to make shadow puppets on the ceiling. I encourage any creativity, however childlike. Meatpie could make a good rabbit and an OK bird. The rabbit and the bird fought viciously.

'Oh, Meatpie,' I said. School had been worse than usual that week and he still cared. I put his chubby rabbit-ear fingers in my mouth and tried to swallow whatever sadness they possessed.

In the fourth week, way ahead of schedule, Meatpie decided he loved me. I told him, 'You love doing it.'

'No,' he said. 'I mean, yeah, of course, but if I can love, like, a Robert Frank picture, why can't I love you?' My little Meattie had gotten the photographer's name right and I began to cry. When he realized what was happening, he made soothing gestures – hugging me and patting my head and saying, 'Trombone, Trombone, my lovely Trombone.' None of the others had comforted me in such a manner. None of the others had comforted me. I cried harder. The boundaries of the relationship were in danger of becoming blurred. The course would be a short one. I'm in favour of using unorthodox methods, but there are limits.

The next day at my place Meatpie shyly withdrew a box of cookies from his backpack and gave them to me.

'I bought these for you,' he said.

'That's so frigging excellent!' I said. I sucked him off right away. Later, when we were eating the cookies, I said, 'Honey, you don't have to bring me cookies. I steal them from work.'

'Oh,' he said. I saw his mind Ferris wheeling slowly behind his eyes. I jumped off the bed and recited some poetry while turning in circles. The dog barked and Meatpie laughed in his magical closed-mouth way. I wanted him to think about the cookies later, alone in his own room.

After Meatpie began declaring his love, the formaldehyde scent of his insecurities returned with increasing pungency and, really, he bugged the shit out of me. When I asked him to play some music, he agonized over his choice and second-guessed himself.

I said, 'Meatpie, what do you believe in? What really knocks your balls up your ass?'

Meatpie said, 'S—'

'Besides sex.'

'Arrg. Dunno. Buncha stuff.'

I loaded him and John into the car. On the drive to his house he said, 'I believe I love you.'

'It's OK, Meatpie,' I said.

'Robert Frank?'

I kept driving in the direction of his house. The rain cried down the windshield. A reminder that I didn't belong anywhere and never would.

'The end of capital punishment?'

'Why?'

'Am I wrong?'

I dropped him at the end of his driveway. He wouldn't get out of the car right away. When he finally tugged at the door handle, he mumbled, 'I love you. I believe *that*, Trombone.' He shut the door harder than usual. That night at work, I got stinking drunk off beer taken from the cold case.

What is it that I do? I am a teacher. It's all I've ever wanted to be. Teaching means sacrifice and heartache. The most a teacher can hope for is to start someone down a road, a clean well-lighted road, and know that she will never see the end result.

We had one last good week. Coffee and cookies and new positions and poetry while some lost ocean wind creaked through the ugly tree outside the window. I stopped questioning him and allowed him a sort of simple happiness. I used softly moderated tones when I spoke. I gave him full body rubs with high-priced olive oil. Meatpie had joined the school photo club all on his own, and I let him take close-up artsy pictures of my ass. He played music I knew he didn't quite like yet – James Brown, Patsy Cline, Velvet Underground. And danced with a loony full-speed abandon that he could only sustain if he kept his eyes closed.

Sometimes I let him fall asleep in the bed so that I could watch him and feel sorry for myself.

After dropping him off in the evenings, I drove to nearby towns to get more licence plates.

That last day before our break was a Friday and I wore the red boots. When I picked him up, he complimented me on them. In the car he held his hand over mine on the gear shift. His skin looked better.

Instead of going to pick up John, I headed toward the convenience store where I worked nights. 'We're out of cookies,' I said. Meatpie had never discovered my place of work. I pulled into the parking lot and patted his gorgeous angel-boy hair. 'I'm going to distract the clerk,' I said. 'You steal cookies.' Meatpie began to laugh inside his mouth, then stopped. 'I mean it. It's time for you to steal the cookies.'

'I . . . I have money,' he said.

I shook my head. 'Do you want to get laid today or what?' I asked. 'C'mon, dude.' I put my hand over his crotch and squeezed him through his pants. 'Animal Crackers even,' I whispered. Before he could say anything, I walked inside and began speaking with Egan, the clerk on the day shift. I pretended to be asking directions. Poor Meatpie. He waited five minutes, then entered the store and tried to wrestle a package of mini-muffins into his backpack.

Because Egan was wise to the whole thing, he hopped right on the kid and gave him a balling out. Shook him by the shirt a little, too. I waited outside. After a while, I tapped on the glass and signalled Egan to stop. I had to repeat the gesture a few times until Meatpie saw.

He got into the car. Sad, yes, but, even better, he was angry. He hit the dashboard with the flat of his hand. 'I didn't even want to!' He spoke so quickly I could barely make out the words. 'IDIDNTEVENWANTO!' I wouldn't tell him that, no matter what his actions had been, we were finito.

When we got to the top of his driveway, I said, 'I'm not angry at you. I just want you to think about it in your own room.' I leaned over and we made out for a while. Then he pulled his hand from under my shirt and said, 'Yeah. Yeah, I think I want to go think about stuff in my room.'

After he got out of the car, he tossed the bag of mini-muffins through the open window. 'I had pay for these,' he said. 'You take them, Trombone.' Ooh, he certainly was pissed, glaring right at me as I drove away. My little grown-up boy.

I imagine that, by Monday, he had forgiven me and waited as usual for the car. (It's not that easy for a sixteen-year-old to give up that kind of good fucking.) I lived somewhere else by then. Worked one last night and made my way, more-or-less untraceably, to the next island of misfit toys.

What is the best thing we can teach someone? Something small, I believe. Like how to find a light switch in the dark.

LISA JEWELL

Labia Lobelia

Lobelia pulls open the display cabinet and slides Joan Crawford's bustier on to the middle shelf, next to Lana Turner's bedjacket. Then she puts Judy Garland's hairslides into a small drawer with Rita Hayworth's toothbrush, Jayne Mansfield's mascara and Natalie Wood's paste brooch. She breathes in deeply, inhaling the heady aroma of rosewater, mothballs and Chanel No 5 – the aroma of another time. When women were women and men were gentlemen and clothes were fully lined.

The sun pours in through her windows, highlighting the dust she's agitated arranging her possessions in her new home. Flat 4, 126 Violetta Road, London SE20. Her first flat. Her first mortgage. It's a vast conversion in a huge detached mansion opposite a small park in Anerley. Yes – Anerley. Not nearly as awful or as suburban as the name might suggest. Quite a pretty part of London, in fact – she loves the old-fashioned aura of the area, all the old Twenties houses, deco features here and there, the Edwardian road names.

And just look at what you get for your money down here, in the so-called sticks. Living room big enough to play football in. Vast bedroom with windows on *two sides*. Huge kitchen/diner and not one but *two* bathrooms. It's going to take her months to fill this place up – all her possessions fitted very easily into the boot of her friend Cathy's Peugeot estate this morning. But that's not exactly going to be a hardship. Shopping for bric-a-brac is one of Lobelia's favourite hobbies. In fact, shopping for bric-a-brac is her job.

Lobelia is a memorabilia dealer. She goes around the world picking up dead film stars' detritus – saucepans, knickers, bobby pins, golf clubs – at auctions and junk shops and sells them on at a profit. It's a lucrative line of work, or it would be if Lobelia didn't allow herself to get so attached to things. She probably sells on only half of what she buys. Which is why it's taken her this long to save up enough cash to put a deposit down on a flat.

So – the name – Lobelia. It's a flower. A very beautiful flower. Lobelia's parents wanted to name their daughter after a flower, but not a Daisy or a Violet or a Poppy. They wanted to name her after an *original* flower. And they found Lobelia in a book, checked first to make sure that it was a *beautiful* flower and it was and that was that. And Lobelia loves her name. She loves the fact that it's different. And possibly, if her parents had called her Louise or Clare or Julie or something, she'd have changed her name anyway, by deed poll, to something equally unusual. Because Lobelia is an unusual girl. She always has been. She came out of the womb unusual. Actually, she tried to come out sideways and had to be removed manually through a C-section. She was ten days late, too. And she weighed over ten pounds. Massive. Like carrying a small car around for nine months according to her mother.

She's still a big girl. Not a fat girl. She doesn't know how much she weighs because she never weighs herself and she doesn't know what size she is because she only buys vintage clothes that are cut for completely different proportions from the ones they use these days. The last time she knew what size she was was about eight years ago, when she was a bridesmaid at her cousin's wedding and had to be wedged into a duck-egg trouser suit from Joseph, and she was a size fourteen. Or was it a sixteen? She can't remember. The three other bridesmaids had thought it was just the best idea *ever* to wear trousers. How chic. How refreshing. How *modern*. But Lobelia had thought it was disgraceful. As if there wasn't little enough glamour in the world today as it was, without making bridesmaids wear trousers. Lobelia wanted to be festooned with lace, trimmed with roses and crinolined and meringued in lilac and apricot. Because Lobelia likes feminine things. She likes old-fashioned things. A lot.

She loves the smell of old clothes. She loves the yellowing satin labels – *Cecelia May Fashions* – stitched into the inside pockets. She loves the craftsmanship, the bias binding, the hand-stitching, the little brass hanging chains. She loves the starched corsets and pencil skirts and waisted jackets. And she loves the fabrics. The brushstroke roses, nubby tweeds, slubbed silks and girlish ginghams.

Her hair is another major preoccupation – she's been a bleached blonde since she was fifteen, since she first clapped eyes on Doris Day, in fact. She used to wear it in a pin-curled helmet but she wears it a bit longer now, either pinned back in a neat backcombed chignon, or kicked out with a styling brush and plenty of Elnett. Her lips are always, *always* red – her Lancôme Very Cherry would be her desert island request – and her eyes are slicked with liquid liner. Lobelia is not a classically pretty girl, but she makes the most of what she's got. She makes an *effort*. Which is more than you can say for a lot of people these days.

She preens her fringe now in the mirror, pulling it over her wide forehead. Her clear blue eyes sparkle back at her. There is a kohl spot on her cheek, just at the corner of her mouth. She adjusts her fantastic 42DD breasts inside the poppy-print camisole she's wearing with white cotton pedal pushers, picks up a small cactus in a pot she decorated herself with sequins and pink gloss and heads for the front door.

She's going to make the acquaintance of her next-door

neighbours. She always does this when she moves into a new flat, even if she thinks she's only going to be there for a few months. It just makes life so much *nicer*, especially in a city like London, where everything is so anonymous.

Her weeny kitten-heeled sandals make a clip-cloppy noise across the wooden floorboards as she crosses the landing. She presses her fingertip against the doorbell and breathes in.

'Hi.' A young man clutching a can of Red Stripe is looking at her quizzically. He seems a bit thrown. Probably not used to people ringing directly on his doorbell without coming via the intercom.

'Hi,' beams Lobelia. 'I'm your new neighbour. I thought I'd just pop across and say hello.'

The young man looks over her shoulder at her front door, which she's just gestured at. 'Oh,' he says, 'right.'

He's not bad-looking, thinks Lobelia, eyeing him up and down subtly. Thick wavy hair, a bit long perhaps, but nothing that a trip to the barber couldn't sort out, a large nose that sits well on his large-featured face and what looks like a very promising physique peeping out of his loosely buttoned shirt. Bit young, though. Probably not much older than twenty-two, twenty-three. She beams at him again and proffers her cactus. 'Here's a little cactus', she says, 'in a little pot. Just to say hello.' She giggles and he takes it from her outstretched hand.

'Wow,' he says, running his other hand casually through his thick hair, 'wow. That's really nice of you. Thank you.'

Lobelia smiles and makes dismissive facial expressions. 'My name's Lobelia, by the way,' she says offering him her hand to shake.

'Sorry?' he says, smiling uncertainly, taking her hand.

'Lobelia. It's a flower. My parents were a bit hippy-dippy,' she says, not for the first time in her life.

'Oh,' he says, his hand still inside hers, 'right. I'm Dom. Dominic. Dom.'

'Oh,' she says, 'that's lovely. And do you live alone?' She peers behind him into a large hallway filled with masculine clutter; mountain bikes, golf clubs, a carjack, a pile of travel brochures, skis.

'Er, no. There's three of us. Me, Mike and Joss.'

'Friends?'

'Uh-huh,' he pulls his hand out of hers and uses it to scratch the back of his neck. A huge male roar goes up in the background and Dom looks at Lobelia apologetically. 'Actually,' he says, 'we were just watching the er, football. So, er . . .'

'Oh. Gosh. Sorry,' she says, 'don't let me keep you. Please.'

He nods gratefully.

'Well,' she says, 'I hope we'll bump into each other from time to time. And maybe you could recommend some places in the neighbourhood. Restaurants. Bars. That sort of thing. I'm new to the depths of south-east London.'

'Yeah,' he says, backing into his hallway, his hand clasping the edge of the door, 'yeah. Sure. No problem.'

'Nice to meet you, Dom.' She puts her hand up and gives him a little wave.

'Yeah. You too . . . Lob . . . Lab . . . Lobbi . . .'

'Lobelia,' she grins.

'Yeah. Right. And thanks. For the plant. It's really cool.' And then he smiles again and brings the door to a close between them.

Lobelia smiles to herself and clip-clops back to her new flat, feeling a little fluttering of excitement and pleasure in her stomach. New flat. New neighbours. New life. She has a good feeling about this place.

She enters her flat and picks up a cardboard box that contains Bette Davis's wigs. There's a cupboard built into the wall in the hallway and as she pulls the door open Lobelia can hear whistles and shouts. Football. And then she can hear male voices. Laughing. And somehow, even though the vent in the

cupboard through which these noises are being carried from the
next door flat is very, very small, through some little aural trick,
she can hear every word they're saying. Clearly. As if she were
in the room with them:

'Oh. My. God.'

'Who was that?'

'The question, my friend, is not who – but *what*.'

'What?'

'You will *not* believe what has just moved in next door. Aw –
Jesus!'

'What? *What?*'

'I dunno how to describe it – it's kind of like a . . . a drag
queen. A drag queen with these two *huge* . . .'

'Cool.'

'No. Not cool. Horrible. Big, blubbery – actual cellulite on
them.'

'Aw . . .'

'A hound. A moose. A pig. A dog. A pigdogmoosehound. It's
a fucking *monster*.'

'And what's it called.'

'Well – that's the thing – I'm pretty fucking sure she said her
name was – *Labia*.'

'NO!!!!'

'Yeah – I even asked her to repeat it. Labia. Her name's
Labia.'

'NO FUCKING WAY!!!!'

'Yes fucking way . . .'

Lobelia turns slightly to view her reflection in the mirror. She
puts a hand to her cleavage, examines the creamy skin for signs
of blubber or cellulite, neither of which are apparent to her. And
then she looks at her face: her mouth, her cheeks, her long
eyelashes, her dazzling baby blues. She has so many redeeming
features – looking like a supermodel, or some such stupid,
modern thing is not one of them – but she has so much else.

Hasn't she? A lump forms in her throat. She tucks her hair behind her ear, takes a deep breath and walks circumspectly towards her kitchen. She suddenly and uncharacteristically needs a drink, so pours herself a Bailey's Irish Cream. She breaks the viscous, velvety surface with a dainty fingertip and sucks it off, between scarlet lips. And then her doorbell rings.

She opens it to two young men – one small and lean, one tall with a slightly middle-aged physique, both wearing jeans and loose shirts and both smelling of cigarette smoke.

'Er – hi,' says small and lean. 'We just wanted to er – we live next door. With Dom. I'm Mike.'

'And I'm Joss,' says tall and tubby. They both shuffle around a bit and crackle with a hidden agenda.

'Hi,' beams Lobelia, puffing out her bosom. She smiles at them expectantly.

They glance at each other. 'Yeah,' says Mike, eventually, 'we just wanted to say – thanks. For the plant thing. Really nice of you.'

'Yeah,' says Joss, 'thanks a lot.'

'Oh,' smiles Lobelia, 'you're very welcome. Really . . .' She smiles even more brightly.

There is a moment's silence during which it is entirely obvious that Mike and Joss have something they'd like to ask her.

'Anyway,' says Lobelia, trying to hasten them along.

'Yeah,' says Mike, gulping, 'thanks and er – what was your name again?'

'Lobelia,' says Lobelia, 'my name is Lobelia.'

'Cool,' says Mike, his face distorted in the manner of one trying to control last night's vindaloo, 'see you around.'

Lobelia closes her front door on them, leans against it and sighs. From the open cupboard in the hallway, she can already hear them next door, snorting and hooting and gasping for air as they try to control their hysterical laughter. She feels all – horrible. All sort of angry and violent and – ooh – *horrible.* And there's only one thing a gal can do when she's feeling this blue – and that's to get the girls over. They're a mixed bunch of women, Lobelia's friends. There's sweet-hearted Judy, ice-maiden Lana, cruel Joan and highly strung Bette. But they're all gorgeous, glamorous, beautiful and incredibly loyal. They're also all dead.

She heads towards her display cabinet and pulls it open. 'Is there anyone there?' she calls inside. 'Girls – anyone?' She runs a loving finger over tortoiseshell barrettes and Pucci print silk scarves and polka-dot plastic sunglasses. 'Please,' she says plain-tively, 'please. I really need to talk to someone.'

'I'm here, honey,' it was Judy.

Lobelia tells her tearfully about the boys next door and the mean things they said and Judy strokes Lobelia's hair and murmurs into her ear. 'They're just dumb, is all, Lobelia. Just big and dumb. They can't see your inner beauty shining out the way that we all can, sweetie.' Judy's rosebud mouth curls upwards into a reassuring smile and her eyes twinkle with mischief. 'What you need to do is show 'em. Show 'em how special you are.'

'But how?' Lobelia sniffs and breathes in the scent of Judy's signature perfume, which she has made specially for her. It's sweet and flowery and feminine. Just like little Judy.

'The three Gs, sweetie. Generosity, Grace and Genuine-ness . . .'

A sudden blast of cold air bursts forth from the cabinet and, in a puff of dry ice and blinding blue light, Joan appears. Joan absolutely *loves* being dead – she can make such dramatic entrances.

'Three Gs my big fat *ass*, Judy Garland,' she says, whipping her gold satin cape around her. 'What those boys need is the three Ts. Torture, Torment and a Taste of *hell*. Crawford-style.'

'Oh, Joan honey. Lobelia's not like you. You know that. She's a sweet girl, a gentle girl, a kind soul. Let her deal with this *her way . . .*'

Joan blows smoke from her lips and narrows her eyes at Judy. 'OK,' she sighs, adjusting her satin cape, 'OK. I've a million and one things to haunt and horrify this morning. But Lobelia, honey, take it from me. Those boys are bad to the core and there isn't any amount of human kindness you could show them that would change the way they see you. I'll be here – when you see the light.' She kisses Lobelia and throws Judy daggers and then she disappears in a whisper of heavy satin.

'OK,' says Judy, 'here's the plan . . .'

Lobelia doesn't watch television or listen to the radio at all during her first few days in her new flat. Instead she sits in the hallway, by the vent in the cupboard, and learns a lot about her neighbours.

Dom is the dominant member of the household – his name is very fitting. Mike and Joss clearly see Dom as the good-looking one, the funny one, the disseminator of catchphrases and nicknames that fall quickly into common usage. And the most popular phrases of the moment all seem to involve the word 'labia'.

Joss is the butt of all the jokes that don't involve Lobelia – his lardy exterior is obviously an outward manifestation of a lardy mind.

And Mike – Mike is the abrasive one. He seems to be angry with everyone and about everything. His jokes have an edge to them that Dom's do not. Lobelia imagines him to be the sort of man who would marry some really nice girl, be really nice to her for a few months and then suddenly turn round one day and hit her in the face. You know.

Their conversations strike Lobelia as being horribly cyclical. Ten or twelve topics that roll round and round and round, incessantly. No conclusions ever reached, no decisions ever arrived at, no progress ever made. Just random words, artlessly assembled, like those fridge magnets. Mainly about things they hate and things they love.

Things they *hate* include: Graham Norton, the smell of Mike's farts, phone calls from their mothers, Joss's boss Miranda, having to pay road tax, Jamie Oliver, anyone in a boy band, anyone off a reality TV show, cooking, going to work, their 'piece-of-shit' TV set, not having any money, that 'ugly' bird off the AOL adverts, Ronan Keating, Chris Evans, living in Anerley and not being able to get hold of any spliff.

The things they *like* include *Trigger Happy TV*, Cat Deeley, the Garlic Duck from the Himalaya Tandoori House around the corner, extra jalapeños on their pizza, Dom's new company car, Joss's new snowboard, Tamzin Outhwaite, Sarah Michelle Gellar, the new album by the Avalanches, anything with Robert de Niro in it, Britney Spears, Kylie and finally getting hold of some spliff.

Lobelia has a theory about people – they're all basically good. She's had this proved to her time and time again. Judy's right – if you're genuine and generally nice to people, you'll bring out the best in them. So the following day she decides to remedy their dislike of cooking, lack of cash and liking for hot food in one fell swoop by making them a bowl of super hot chilli. And not just chilli, but sour cream, tortillas and salsa too. She puts them in her best chinaware and even gives them a packet of fresh coriander to sprinkle on the top. Joss answers the door and accepts her offering very politely, with lots of wows and gods and cools. See, she thinks to herself, see. That's all it takes – just a little civil behaviour.

She totters back to her flat, opens the cupboard and listens to their reaction:

'Aw *fuck* – what is that?'

'Looks like dysentery.'

'Ohmigod – Labia shat in a bowl and brought it over.'

'So, what d'you reckon that white stuff is?'

'No. Man. Please. Don't go there. *Don't go there . . .*'

'Bin?'

'Bin. Definitely. You are the weakest shit – *goodbye.*'

Lobelia calls round to collect her bowls the next day and Mike tells her how it was the best chilli any of them have ever tasted.

Lobelia has three TV sets – a result of a long and not very interesting series of events – and, since the boys hate their TV so much, she decides to offer to lend them one. It's only small, but it's very modern and won't cause them the same level of problems as their existing TV.

Joss looks genuinely excited when she knocks on their door and mentions the spare TV set that's 'cluttering up her flat'. There are loads more wows and Gods and cools and he actually smiles at her. He comes back with her to her flat to collect it. He turns down her offer of a cup of tea, but is perfectly pleasant and even makes a little small talk about how much lighter her flat is than theirs.

Excitedly, Lobelia goes to the cupboard to hear their reaction:

'What – is that *it*?'

'Christ – I've got a bigger screen on my mobile phone.'

'What brand is it? Jees-us – I've never even heard of it.'

'What a piece of shit.'

The next half-hour is filled by the boys making what they appear to think are fantastically funny jokes about small screens and big beef curtains. Lobelia sighs and pours herself a Bailey's.

After a pep talk from Judy on Sunday morning, Lobelia's flagging spirits are perked up again and she decides that the most effective way to the boys' stubborn hearts would be to sort out their ongoing drug-flow problems. Her ex-flatmate has a man called Sweet, who drops off. Very reliable, same-day delivery, always in a hurry so never stops to chat and always gets really good stuff. Apparently.

Dom looks like he's going to faint with excitement when Lobelia mentions Sweet to him in passing on Wednesday. 'Really? Same day? Home delivery? And you don't mind putting in a word for us. Wow. God. That's so cool. *Thank you.*'

For a while all Lobelia can hear through the vent is full-blown excitement:

'Yeah – he delivers. Same day. Reliable. Doesn't hang around.'

'Just think – no more driving out to Catford. No more hanging around pissy estates, risking our lives. We can just sit here and order it in – like *fucking pizzas*!'

Lobelia smiles warmly to herself. Now she's done it. She's broken the ice. They'll see beyond their petty prejudices now and see the real Lobelia inside – her inner beauty. And then Lobelia's life will be all lovely and perfect, just like Judy said.

'Can I just say something?'

'Shoot.'

'Er – has anyone stopped to wonder why exactly Labia is being so, you know, *helpful.*'

'What d'you mean?'

'You know – the cactus, the chilli, the TV, Sweet. Like – *why*?'

'Aw, fuck. You don't think she's after us, do you? After our bodies?'

'Oh Jesus – I feel sick just thinking about it. Just imagine – Labia – naked, her breasts pendulous and flabby, her legs spread, her piss flaps all red and hairy and wet and—'

'STOP! Jesus, please stop. I'm gonna puke . . . urgh.'

Lobelia doesn't sleep well that night. She's a tolerant girl, but she's never before encountered such unpleasantness. She was convinced that she could make them see her inner beauty – absolutely convinced that all it took was a little kindness, a little consideration, a nice smile and she could spread her own sunny outlook on life around her. But these boys – they're really not interested in sunshine or smiles or Lobelia's inner gorgeousness. Lobelia's tried everything. She's tried her hardest. And now it's time for Plan B.

'Joan,' she whispers into her display cabinet, 'Joan – are you there?'

'Oh, Lobelia honey. *Please.*' Joan is gripping Lobelia's knees and pleading with her.

'No,' says Lobelia firmly, 'no physical damage. No injuries. And most certainly no *death.*'

Joan pouts and sighs. 'OK,' she says finally, 'but I can really scare them, yes?'

'Yes.'

'And I can be really *gruesome*?'

'As gruesome as you like.'

'And vulgar.'

'Yes. I don't care any more. I just don't ever want to hear the word labia again. That's all.'

Joan's face suddenly lights up. 'Can it be themed?'

'A themed haunting?'

'Uh-huh,' she says brightly.

'Yes,' sighs Lobelia sadly, 'it can be themed.'

'Oh goodie!' says Joan, clapping her hands together in excitement. 'This, Lobelia my darling, is going to be the most fabulous haunting *ever* . . .'

Joss answers the door this time. He's wearing some kind of sportswear – Lobelia doesn't know what kind, she's not particularly au fait with sportswear or sports, generally, for that matter – and he's looking rather red and sweaty.

'Er, right,' he says, when she makes her dinner invitation, 'I'll have to – er, check with the others. Tuesdays are no good for

Mike and Thursdays are bad for Dom and weekends are just generally – you know . . .' He licks his lips, nervously.

For the next few days, Lobelia can hear them through the vent. Her dinner invitation is about the only thing they talk about. 'Fuck – how are we going to get out of this – *this is a nightmare . . .*'

But eventually, after repeated invitations, and much compromising to be heard through the vent – 'Look, I'll say I'm feeling a bit under the weather, right, and you say you've got an early meeting, I reckon we'll be back in time for the *Adam and Joe Show* – yeah?' – they settle on a date.

Joan appears that afternoon with a tartan shopping carrier and a wicked grin slapped on to her alabaster face.

'What's in the bag, Joan?'

'Dinner,' she purrs, with an air of finality. She pushes the bag towards Lobelia and urges her to have a peep inside. Her long fingers are fluttering with excitement.

Lobelia pulls it open and her eyes widen. 'Is that . . .?'

'It most certainly is. And I even managed to find you a recipe. It's a darling little medieval Italian recipe I picked up from Lucrezia Borgia.'

'But where on earth did you find them?' says Lobelia, still peering into the bag with fascination.

'Oh, for heaven's sake, Lobelia,' says Joan, her painted-on eyebrows knitting together impatiently, like two fat slugs squaring up for a fight, 'I'm *dead*. I have means. I have contacts. Stop asking stupid questions.'

'Yes,' says Lobelia, concern oozing from her, 'but what about—'

'Will you stop worrying yourself with the whys and wherefores and just cook the stuff – OK?'

'OK.'

'And while you're doing that I'm going to pay a little visit next door. Get the boys in the *mood . . .*' Joan's steely eyes twinkle for a second as she sucks the last three millimetres from her cigarette, stubs it out on a dinner plate and floats from the room in a haze of aquamarine chiffon.

Joan's back a few minutes later, wiping her hands on a linen napkin, her face a picture of self-satisfaction.

'Well,' she growls, 'that should whet their appetites.'

'What have you done?'

'Go listen,' smirks Joan, indicating the hallway cupboard with her eyes.

Lobelia puts down her boning knife and heads for the hall:

'Poargh.'

'Aw. Jesus. What the *fuck* is that smell?'

'Christ – that's *disgusting.*'

'It wasn't me.'

'Jesus, Mike – even you couldn't manage to make your farts smell like a crusty old cunt.'

'God – it really does. It smells like a funky fanny.'

'Open a window for fuck's sake.'

'Oh no – not the Kouros, Dom – please, not the Kouros.'

'Oh Christ. Get the Neutrodol.'

'We haven't got any Neutrodol.'

'Yes we have, you tosser – in the toilet.'

Lobelia smirks to herself and heads back to the kitchen.

'You like,' says Joan, sliding a shot glass off a shelf and peering around her.

'Yes,' beams Lobelia, 'I like. How did you do it?

'Oh – I found these fabulous little droplets in de Sade's apothecary. They're called Aroma du Cunte. Just a couple of drops and the whole flat will reek to high heaven for at least forty-eight hours.'

'Lovely,' says Lobelia.

'Isn't it just?' beams Joan, 'Should put them all off sex for life.

Now, honey,' she simpers, waving the bottle of Bailey's around carelessly, 'I've been scouring your dear little kitchen here for a decent drink and all I can find is this odd-looking *brown* stuff. Now tell me, surely this liquid is not *alcohol*?'

The boys arrive dead on the dot of eight. They all smell of Kouros and Neutrodol and look slightly edgy.

'Brought some wine,' says Dom abruptly, handing her a bottle of wine with dust on it and 1980s style graphics, which looks as if it's been festering on the bottom shelf of the food and wine shop over the road for at least a decade.

'Thanks,' says Lobelia, 'make yourselves at home.' She heads towards the kitchen and stirs the saucepan on the hob, leaning over it to breathe in the delicious aroma. She adds a little more water and a touch more basil and leaves it to simmer.

'I hope you're all meat eaters,' she says sweetly, strolling nonchalantly back into the living room.

They all nod and say 'Sure are' and try to look enthusiastic.

She heads back to the kitchen, where she pours them all a drink.

Lucrezia's medieval recipe turns out to be a real success. The meat is finely sliced into strips, simmered with fresh herbs, chopped tomatoes, onion rings and mounds of garlic.

'You not eating the stew?' says Dom, indicating Lobelia's plate with his knife.

Lobelia shakes her head and cuts herself another slice of smoked fish terrine, 'Vegetarian,' she says.

'Pity,' says Joss, tucking into his casserole, 'because this is absolutely delicious.'

'This is the tenderest chicken I have ever eaten in my life,' gushes Mike.

'Mmmmmm,' says Dom.

Lobelia smiles.

Over dinner they talk about the area, they talk about their jobs, they talk about all sorts of civilized, grown-up things. The boys are on their best behaviour. But sure enough, no sooner has Lobelia cleared way their dinner plates, than they start excusing themselves.

'Big meeting,' mutters Dom.

'Headache,' murmurs Mike.

'Beauty sleep,' grunts Joss.

'Oh,' says Lobelia, 'what a shame.'

She sees them to the door and they're all very sweet and say thank you again and even lean in to kiss Lobelia on the cheek.

She's holding a large rubbish bag in her hand. It's full of onion skins and tomato tops and old packaging. As she sees them off she swings it on to the floor. 'I'll take it down later,' she smiles. They all let their eyes fall to the bag. The bag which Lobelia has deliberately left undone. There's something there. Something that none of them can be entirely sure about. A couple of boxes. Like frozen-food packaging. Slightly obscured. They can see a brand name – Otherside Gourmet Products. And a picture, which looks like . . . No. Can't possibly be. They all look up and smile at Lobelia, who smiles back at them.

'Night,' she says, closing the door on them.

'Night,' they say, backing away slightly uncertainly.

She can hear them the minute she closes the door:

'Did you . . .?'

'In the bag?'

'Yeah.'

'Me too.'

Brief pause.

Lobelia can hear them scuttling back across the hallway. She can hear the rustling of the bag.

'*What!!*'

' "Finest Fillets of *Labia*".'

'This is a joke – right?'

'"Prime Cuts Taken from the Purest Vestal Virgins."'

'"Tender and Delicious."'

'"Guaranteed Hair-Free." Urgh – Jesus. This *has* to be a joke.'

'Yes – but – if it was a joke, then when was she going to tell us about it?'

'And it was really . . . *unusual*, wasn't it – that meat?'

'Tender.'

'Juicy.'

'Melt in the mouth—'

'Yes, but – *where*? I mean—'

'Oh. Fuck. I'm going to be sick—'

Lobelia hears them sprinting across the hallway, frantically searching for keys, all three of them silent for once.

The moment they disappear into their flat and the door clicks closed behind them, Joan arrives.

'Well,' she says, 'We've been having *the* most marvellous time.'

'Have you?'

'We have.' She pulls open the cupboard door and gestures to Lobelia to come and listen. 'Me and the girls have been working very hard.'

'The girls?'

'Yes. Bette, Marlene, Greta and me. Next door. While you were eating.'

'Doing what?'

'Just some interior design touches. A bit of rewiring. Some special effects. I left the girls in there, actually. Listen,' she beams, 'they've started already.'

'What are they going to do?'

'Oh you know. The standard performance. Moaning. Chain clanking. Hot breath against their faces. That kind of thing . . .'

They lean into the cupboard and listen.

'Oh great – a fucking power cut. Have we got a torch or anything. Candles?'

'What is this *shit* on the walls?'

'What?'

'This – urgh – this slimy stuff. It's . . . urgh—'

'Jesus – what was that noise?'

'What noise?'

'Oh fuck.'

'Who dropped that?'

'Mike? Mike – where are you?'

'Dom – will you stop pissing around.'

'*Me?* I'm not doing anything.'

'Argh!'

'What!'

'What was that?'

'Oh. God. What is going on?'

'Fuck. Where's the fuse box?'

'Guys? Guys? I've just been sick on the stereo.'

'Somebody find a fucking light.'

'Oh. Jesus. What is that – there's something growing – growing out of the walls. It feels like – *hair*.'

'Will somebody – oh God – Mike – is that you?'

'Who's that? Dom – are you wearing a *bra*? Dom?'

'Urgh – the floor – my feet are sinking into it – it's all spongy and wet and—'

'Help me!'

Joan and Lobelia clutch each other and giggle like naughty schoolgirls.

A minute later Joan clicks her fingers and the lights go on. There is a moment's stunned silence.

'What the fuck?'

'Is this a nightmare?'

'Is this hell? Are we dead? Are we in hell, Dom?'

'No, Joss. We're in a cunt.'

'Eh?'

'Look. Touch. Smell. Our flat has turned into a huge twat.'

'I'm getting out of here.'

'Me too.'

'Where's my jacket?'

'Car keys. Quick.'

'What about our stuff?'

'Fuck our stuff. Jesus. Let's just get out of here.'

Joan and Lobelia wait until they hear Dom's Audi Quattro squealing away into the night before taking the Bailey's into the dining room. Lana, Bette, Greta, Marlene and Judy join them and the girls sit and talk about their triumph into the early hours.

Lobelia clip-clops across the landing clutching a small cactus in a pink pot decorated with sequins and knocks on the door.

'Hi.' The door is opened by a young woman wearing pyjamas with a toothbrush in her hand.

'Hi,' smiles Lobelia, 'I just thought I'd pop over and introduce myself. I live across the landing. My name's Lobelia.'

'Lobelia?' says the girl in the pyjamas. 'What a beautiful name. It's a flower, isn't it?'

Lobelia beams. 'That's right. My parents were a bit hippy-dippy. Living alone?'

'No,' she says, 'there's three of us. Me, Tamara and Beulah. I'm Angelica, by the way. My parents were a bit hippy-dippy, too.'

Lobelia feels her insides warming up with happiness.

'So – tell me,' says Angelica, moving towards Lobelia, conspiratorially, 'what happened with the guys who lived here before us?'

'What do you mean?'

'Well, the landlord told me that they did a runner. And that when he let himself in the whole flat was covered in jelly and blancmange – like they'd had the greatest food fight of all time. And there was sick everywhere. And they'd left all their stuff.

Apparently it took a team of six professional cleaners nearly two days to clean it all up.'

'Well I never,' says Lobelia, eyes all wide and incredulous. 'Goodness me.'

They make small-talk for a moment or two before Lobelia says goodbye and returns to her flat. Inside, she pulls open the cupboard in her hallway and puts her ear to the vent.

'Our neighbour's just been to introduce herself.'

'Really?'

'Uh-huh.'

'What's she like?'

'She seems lovely. Really sweet. Very glamorous. She looks like Jayne Mansfield. And she's got the most incredible blue eyes . . .'

Lobelia smiles and gently closes the cupboard door.

LIZ EVANS

Pussy Galore

'Bad things happen.'

Well I couldn't argue with that one. Bad things had been ganging up on me for the past twenty minutes. Top of the list was a curry-eating hamster.

It was nestled in the armpit of the bloke strap-hanging in front of me. Each movement brought another blast of vindaloo-scented BO from the hamster-hair.

In my experience Fate is a malicious bitch who sees to it that every good happening is balanced by a bad one. I'd just spent three days living it up in a four-star hotel in London's West End – courtesy of Mr Henry Birdman's chequebook – getting the goods on Mrs Henry's non-marital bonking and now it was pay-back time.

The plan was to take the tube to Victoria, catch the first train going south and be home in Seatoun in time to scrounge supper at my favourite greasy spoon. The reality was I'd been stuck on an Underground train that seemed to be trying to establish squatter's rights on the platform at Leicester Square for the past twenty minutes. Being British we were sitting in total silence pretending to read the overhead adverts for insurance, language courses and pension schemes. All except my neighbour.

'Yes,' she hissed in a whisper that could be heard three stops down the Piccadilly line. 'Bad things happen. Most people don't notice what's going on under their noses.'

Lucky old them, I thought silently.

'But I've been trained, you see. Special Operations.' She leaned closer. 'Ian Fleming based Pussy Galore on me.'

She was seventy plus, with leathered skin, grey hair and a body designed to stuff a duvet (tog 13) rather than a secret agent (tag 007). You had to admire Ian's powers of imagination.

'She's missing,' Pussy said in that piercing whisper.

I played along. 'Who is?'

'Susie. And there are others too. Six at least. It's the black ones they take. They don't see the pattern, but I'm trained. I can see it's the same pattern.'

'Yeah,' I murmured back. 'That Special Ops training. Does it every time.'

She smiled. 'I knew you'd understand. You've got that look. Sharp. Are you in the business?'

I put my lips to a whiskery ear. 'I'm a private investigator.'

'A gumshoe!' Pussy exclaimed, not bothering to lower her own voice. 'That's what I need. I've tried to tell people about the disappearings, but they don't listen. I was going to make contact with the old firm. But I'll hire you instead. You can find what happened to them.'

'Good thinking. Mind you, my rates are kind of high.'

'That doesn't matter. I have money.' She fumbled with the stained tapestry bag on her knees. It fell open and revealed a green plastic carrier bag, a tin of salmon, a can of furniture polish, a duster, and what looked like about five thousand pounds in bundles of notes. A dozen pairs of eyes locked on to the booty like heat-seeking missiles, whilst the tannoy told us what we'd all known for some time – this train was going nowhere.

I felt obliged to see Pussy to wherever she was going. If it hadn't been for my crack about my rates, the rest of the carriage wouldn't have known she was toting a small fortune around. As it was, we had hamster-man trying to look inconspicuous on the opposite pavement and I was pretty certain we'd got half a dozen other ex-passengers somewhere in the mass of window shoppers. Suddenly no one wanted to use public transport. We'd all turned into fitness freaks.

I kept my own duffel swinging loose from the left hand, ready to use as a flail if anyone came in for a fast snatch, and tried to keep Pussy corralled against the right-hand walls so no one could rush her from that side. She'd flatly turned down my suggestion that I carry her bag.

'The evidence is in here. Names. Times. Pictures. I have to preserve it. You don't need to worry. I've been trained in counter-espionage. I can kill with my bare hands if I have to.'

'Right. Well, let's hope it doesn't come to that.' Personally I thought a heavy bag in the kneecaps, followed by my boot in the family jewels should just about do it. I swung to walk backwards, staring out a ripped-denim hyena who was getting too close for my comfort – and his. He dropped his eyes and swerved away to browse a window display – pink sequins and a feather boa – clearly the guy wanted to get in touch with his feminine side.

Pussy stomped along beside me, oblivious to the threat to my luggage and her loot. 'What should I call you?' she asked.

'Grace. Or Smithie if you prefer.'

'Check. I had cover names when I was on active service. I was Tamara when I seduced Colonel Mikhail Zaikov in Finland. He was KGB. Loved Bournville chocolate. He used to melt bars of it in the sauna and brush it all over me. Big paintbrush it was. Not the tiddly little tickle-your-arse jobs they sell in sex shops these days. I've always thought that was where Ian got the idea for Goldfinger's body-painting from. Once I was coated, Mikhail would make me go outside. Cold enough to shrivel a polar bear's whatsits. Chocolate used to set solid in seconds. Mikhail cracked it off me with his teeth. He always started on my bum.'

Looking at her broad butt swaying under the purple anorak,
I knew that eating a Magnum ice-cream bar would never be the
same again.

I don't know London all that well, but Pussy appeared to
navigate without the need to check street names. We wove
through back alleys, down side streets and across small squares
that I wouldn't even have known existed. I'd just started praying
this was her idea of anti-surveillance measures rather than a
scouting expedition to check out possible doorways for tonight's
doss-down, when she disappeared.

I'd only taken my eyes off her for a second – having been
momentarily distracted by the flashing pink adverts in 'Sensuarama – the Ultimate Sex Shop'. Alarmed I hurried past the
enticing smells coming from the Indian restaurant next door and
found a small alleyway burrowing between it and the entrance
to a dry cleaner's. Pussy's large butt was swaying halfway down
the passage.

It was another of those hidden squares. Opposite us, across
the paving stones and scrubby garden patch, was a high building
of narrow windows and small nineteenth-century brickwork.
To the right was a dilapidated chapel and to the left were the
walkways and doors of a bland modern four-storey block of
council flats. The whole place stank of cats' pee.

Pussy pointed to the facing doorway. 'Check it out. I'll stay
here. Cover you.'

'Received,' I murmured back. 'What is it? Safe house?
Entrance to an underground complex?'

'Don't be stupid. Go on, get a move on. See the snake isn't
lurking.'

It looked like espionage had given way to hostile fauna. I
glanced around. There was no sign of the would-be bag snatch-
ers. 'OK. Back in a mo.'

Pussy seized my wrist again. 'Please, promise you'll stay.
There's bad things happening here. Promise.'

'Sure. My name's Smith. Grace Smith. Licensed to snoop.' I gave her a reassuring wink and gently eased my arm free.

The door was unlocked. There was a girl halfway up the stairs, smoking in a desultory fashion, and a dish perched up a stepladder changing the lightbulb in the hall.

I targeted the dish. 'Erm . . . Pussy Galore?'

'Connie. Right.' He jumped down. Normally I go for the tall dark type. He had my own colouring – fair hair and brown eyes – but what the hell, he was six foot plus of tanned muscles and a tight butt. I was prepared to compromise.

He wiped a hand on his jeans and extended it. 'David Wadlow.'

'Grace Smith.'

'I take it you've brought Connie home?'

'It seemed best. She's got a lot of money on her.'

'Really? Heaven knows where that's come from. Where is she?'

'Outside. She seems to think a snake's going to get her.'

'That would be Dayna Vipra. She's the administrator of St Benedict's.'

'Which is what exactly?'

'A hostel for women.'

I hadn't expected that. It provided an unexpectedly substantial basis for Pussy's 'disappearings'.

David looked beyond me. I glimpsed feet descending the treads. 'Ah, Dayna. Connie's turned up.'

Dayna looked like this news hadn't exactly made her day. If they ever bring out a mag called *Supercilious Bitches* I figured she was a cinch for the launch cover.

'Milly, you know the rules. No smoking in public areas.'

The girl dropped her half-smoked ciggie and deliberately ground it into the carpet. She was bare-legged and bare-midriffed under a tatty black denim mini-skirt and jacket, but she had those full-lipped, high-cheek-boned looks that had put the likes of Iman and Naomi Campbell into super-star status. And she used them now to stare down Ms Vipra as she swaggered insolently past her up the stairs.

Ms Vipra switched her attention to me. 'Is this another one?'

Did I look like a candidate for a hostel bed? I checked out the outfit – pink vest with fairy motif, camouflage green trousers, jacket and cap, desert boots – sort of Bambi meets the SAS. Three quid the lot, courtesy of my local Oxfam shop.

'*Grace* kindly brought Connie back to us. She's . . .?'

David cocked an eyebrow. I was being invited to share my CV with them. I didn't. 'Outside,' I said blandly. 'I'll get her.'

They both followed me out. The quadrangle was deserted apart from half a dozen cats that were circling in the restless, tail erect, fashion that cats have. One drifted towards us. Beside me I felt Ms Vipra stiffen.

'Get away!' She threw a balled-up tissue. The cat patted it and then stalked away in disgust. Two others padded closer. Dayna backed away into the hall.

'There she is.' David nodded to our left. Pussy (or Connie as I guess she'd better be now) was peeping at us from around the corner of the chapel building. He beckoned encouragingly. Clutching her bag to her chest, Connie came slowly across, her eyes downcast like a naughty kid, until she stood in front of David.

'Grace was saying you'd got money in there, Connie. Don't you think it would better in the safe? May I see?'

Connie opened the bag wide. The bundle of notes had shrunk to a thin roll worth about two hundred pounds at most. My first thought – that one of the train muggers had caught up with us – was dispelled when I caught Connie's gaze through the curtain of grey hair. A glint of mischief twinkled in one violet eye. The old devil had stashed the stuff somewhere.

She meekly handed the remaining cash over at David's suggestion. He tried to steer her inside. Connie dug her trainers in. 'She's stopping too. She's my friend. She's a detective.'

'That's impossible,' Dayna snapped. 'We can't . . .' She was interrupted by a terrified scream from inside the building.

'That's Caro.' Dayna hurried back inside as the scream reverberated from above again. I went after her, with David springing after me.

Upstairs the original walls had been supplemented by partitioning to form dozens of small rooms just wide enough to hold a couple of bunk beds and a cabinet. Milly was dragging on a pair of tights in the first room we passed and seemed unconcerned that we all got to see her knicker-free zone. Instead she turned back to a jumble of sweater, tights and underwear strewn on the bed. It was hard to tell whether she hadn't registered the screams or she just didn't give a damn.

Dayna pushed through a fire door, allowing it to swing back in my face. In the next section of corridor two women were circling each other. Behind them a collection of spectators were either jeering, grinning or just looking plain scared.

The girl facing us was young, dark and pretty – apart, that is, from several nail gashes that were stripping her left cheek like red icing on chocolate cake.

'Sharon! Stop that!' Dayna grabbed the other woman and tried to pull her back.

Sharon struggled free and took a small, short-bladed knife from her waistband.

It's good to talk. But there are times in life when a knuckle-shout works better. I brought my duffel bag back and then forward before Sharon could register what was happening. The weight hit her full in the stomach. She doubled over with a retching gasp and breathed out enough pure alcohol to constitute a serious explosion hazard.

David picked up the knife. 'Are you all right, Caro?'

Dayna examined the gashes. 'I don't think it's too deep. Come with me.'

'It will not matter? I will get apartment?' Caro sobbed. 'It is not my fault.' There was a rime of accent around her vowels. Not Caribbean. Eastern Africa maybe?

Leading her away, Dayna made reassuring noises. Sharon made obscene ones. 'Apartment . . . apartment . . . give me apartment,' she mimicked. 'Bloody foreigner. That should be me. But oh no! Not pretty enough. Giving her one, are you?' she yelled after Dayna's back.

'That's enough, Sharon,' David said. 'Come with me.'

'You ain't locking me up again. You try it and I'll 'ave the coppers on you.'

'Please yourself. Pack your things.'

Along the corridor doors were opening and other occupants were crowding back now the danger of ventilation with a knife blade had passed. The age range was between Connie and teen jailbait. The chatter was in a dozen languages.

Connie suddenly materialized at my side and tugged my sleeve. 'This way.'

She led me forward and then down a back set of stairs. We ended up in the front hall again. I checked we were alone, then asked her what she'd done with the money.

'Hid it. And my evidence. I couldn't risk it falling into their hands. Come on.' Her hand was wet and cold in mine.

I assumed we were heading for wherever she'd hidden the cash and goodies. I was still assuming it, when she fetched up before the front door of the corner ground-floor flat and produced a key.

'You live here? I thought you—?' I waved towards the hostel.

'I do. This is the Sky Jockey's place. Come on.'

It was furnished in the worst possible selection of Seventies naff; Dralon curtains, nylon carpets, kitchen units fitted on the glue-it and be-damned basis. Connie trotted over to one, removed several tins of pilchards and pushed them into her bag. Then she cut the top off a tinned steak pie, thrust it into the oven and put the tin opener in her bag as well. A tin of peas was stabbed with a technique that any vampire slayer would envy and dropped into a saucepan of water.

'What are you doing?'

'Getting his supper. It's my job.'

'What is?'

'Housekeeper,' said David's voice behind me. 'Connie looks after my flat and cleans the chapel for me.'

I processed this information. 'You're a vicar?'

'The Reverend David Wadlow.' He looked over Connie's venture into catering. 'I meant to say Connie, I'm going out for a pizza. Have you eaten yet, Grace? Or would you like to join me?'

He looked at me in way that vicars aren't supposed to look at you. At least they aren't according to my rules. But if the world was fair a dog collar wouldn't be wrapped around a cute smile and a tight bum.

I hesitated. Now I'd delivered Pussy Galore safely home, part of me wanted to be heading out myself. But what if there was a glimmer of truth in her fantasy world? What if she *had* stumbled on a serial kidnapper – or worse? I'd already spotted there was at least one odd thing going on in the hostel.

Connie settled the matter by announcing, 'She wants to use your lav before she goes.' And giving me a large wink behind David's back.

I half-expected to find coded messages scrawled in lipstick on the mirror, but the room looked as normal as turquoise tiling and orange sanitary wear allowed. What did James Bond do in the bathroom? When he wasn't sharing the hot tub with sex-bombs whose mascara never dissolved in the steam, that is. I was just considering dismantling the bath panel when I noticed the water splashes on the top of the cistern and remembered Connie's cold, damp fingers.

She'd balanced the green plastic bag on top of the ballcock. It was tightly bound with yards of clear Sellotape. Luckily I was still dragging my duffel bag around with me. Thrusting the package inside, I flushed the loo, ran the taps and trotted out ready to be plied with crispy crust and garlic bread.

Connie was attacking the carpet with a vacuum cleaner. Behind David's back she raised her eyebrows. I winked and was rewarded with a smile. I'd passed the apprentice secret agent's first test.

We stepped out of the front door. The pigeons strutting and cooing over the yard rose in a startled whirr of wings as an unearthly yowling erupted from behind the chapel. A moment later two black streaks sped through the alleyway.

'You've sure got a lot of cats. Are they wild?'

'Sadly not, or the council might round them up. The woman who owns the sex shop outside has three unneutered queens. She's given kittens to everyone in the block. And now they're breeding. See.'

He waved upwards. I tipped my head back and felt the hairs on the back of my neck tingle. There were cats on practically every balcony staring at me through the metal railings with an unwinking – and vaguely sinister – expression. It looked like a moggie Alcatraz.

We ate looking out over the ornate ironwork and garish advertising posters of the Cambridge Theatre. I was conscious of the weight of my duffel, with the evidence of Connie's 'disappearings', leaning against my legs, but I figured it might be best to get a little background before I opened it. Besides David was paying for dinner. I've never let anything come between me and a free meal.

Once we'd both got large slices of 'The Works' in front of us, David said, 'I hope you didn't mind my dragging you out to dinner. It's just I couldn't face Connie's cooking. I've always thought if I go to hell I shall find Connie running the restaurants and Dayna running the brothels.'

I guess my face revealed my prejudices. He grinned over the melted cheese and pepperoni. 'You looked shocked.'

'Sorry. You're not what I imagine a vicar should be.'

'Middle-aged? Anally retentive? Dull?'

'Something like that. Cliché-prone, that's me.'

'You're not what I imagine a police detective to be.'

'Not police. Private investigator,' I admitted through a mouth-ful of crust. 'I used to be in the police.'

'Then shouldn't you be a cynical male with a battered leather jacket and a complicated private life?'

'I'm working on the jacket.' I smiled back at him, felt the lump of stringy tomato caught between my front teeth and clamped my lips shut again.

'Why did you leave the police?'

'Corruption.'

'You uncovered it?'

'I was it – according to some.'

That silenced him for a moment then he asked, 'Are you working for Connie?'

'Not exactly. We sort of . . . collided. How did you get mixed up with her?'

'I inherited her from my predecessor. Together with that terrible flat. She's got some kind of connection with the chairman of St Benedict's Trust. Normally they can stay for a maximum of three months. Connie's been there for five years.'

'Was she really a secret agent?'

'I doubt it. She was probably a filing clerk in some hush-hush department. The agent thing is the career she wished she'd had. But then most of us end up wishing we'd taken other paths in our lives, don't we?'

'Do vicars?'

'Of course. The idealism wears off eventually.'

We ate in silence for a while. Then I asked what happened to the women after three months.

'We try to get them into flat shares or live-in jobs. Sadly I'm afraid many of them just end up drifting back into street life . . . and everything that entails . . .'

'How'd you find them?'

'Some are referred by agencies. Sharon, for instance, came from a prisoners' resettlement group.'

'Do you really lock her up?'

'She's an arsonist. It's lock-up or eviction. Believe it or not, she's grateful when she sobers up.'

'What about Milly?'

'She was living in a doorway near here.'

I changed tack and asked if the women kept in touch once they were fixed up.

'Most don't. If they make it, it's not a part of their lives that they want to remember usually. They become someone else, you could say.'

Or they stopped being anyone at all. Who'd notice if homeless, illegal immigrants started disappearing? They'd just be assumed to have fallen back into whatever gutter group they'd emerged from. But if you lived there for several years, wouldn't you start to notice a pattern?

'Excuse me.' I hauled my duffel into the ladies' and bolted myself into a cubicle.

The green plastic bag was swaddled up like a mummy that was into serious bondage. I used teeth, nails and curses on it. Eventually I ended up with teeth full of shredded tape and a white plastic bag that was even more tightly bound in tape. At this rate I'd be playing pass the parcel until midnight.

I headed back to the table. David had ordered coffee and ice cream.

'Lovely.' I flashed him my best smile, palmed a knife, and excused myself again.

'Are you all right?' he called after me.

'Yes thanks. Just something I ate, I expect.'

Ignoring the dirty looks from the waitress, I bolted into the lav and attacked the parcel once more. There were six photos inside and two sheets of notes written in mauve ink. I turned up the first picture. A pretty girl was cuddling a cat and smiling at the camera. Printed on the back was 'Susie'.

The next one was called Patty. She was older than Susie. Even with the heavy make-up, I'd have put her in her forties. Patty was a cat lover too. A sleek model was draped around her shoulders like a stole.

The third shot was one of those instant jobs. It was fuzzy and out of focus, but the features were just about recognizable. Quickly I flipped the others. Connie was right. They'd targeted the black ones.

'Are you feeling sick?' David asked when I returned to the table. 'You look a bit pale?'

'I'm fine. Can we get the bill? I'd like to get the nine-ten train home.'

'You're not staying the night then?'

'I don't think so. I'll come back and say 'bye to Connie. Then I'll blow.'

When we passed Sensuarama there was a bloke browsing those flashing pink adverts. He'd changed from hip huggers and vest to black chinos and dark plaid shirt, but he couldn't change the ear lobes. It was the hamster man.

Connie wasn't at the flat or the chapel.

'I shouldn't worry,' David said. 'She often goes walkabout. You could hang on if you like . . .?'

'No thanks. I'll be getting off. Can you say 'bye for me? Thanks for supper.'

'Any time.'

I felt eyes on the back of my neck as I crossed the quadrangle. David's brown ones; the glittering green, blue, amber and yellow of the cats, and – I rather suspected – another pair.

Just to be certain, I took off on another tour of the area. After an hour or so of walking my shadow's socks off, I wandered down to the Embankment and watched night taking the greyness from the Thames and infusing it with golden slicks of light riding over inky black water. I gave it another hour and then walked back to St Benedict's Passage.

There was enough light from the hostel and flat windows to see that the quadrangle was deserted, apart from the cats. Dozens of glittery hard-boiled orbs followed my progress from every corner. I started with the chapel, circling to the back of the building and flicking my torch beam around just enough to let anyone who wanted to know that I was on the prowl round here.

It was little more than a long, narrow corridor of weed-choked, crumbling flagstones bordered by the chapel's back wall and the high windowless side wall of the neighbouring building. The beam flickered over the remains of tomato sauce, fish scales and tiny bones, and half a dozen cats contentedly licking the last dregs of salmon and pilchard. There were dozens of the soggy sheets forming a tablecloth for the cats' supper. And all cut into the size and shape of ten-pound notes. I wondered who she'd have suckered into taking this job on if she hadn't met me?

I caught the slightest of movements behind me and swung the light fast. 'Hello, Milly.'

'Take that frigging beam out of my eyes. What you doing back here?'

'Just seeing if you'd take the bait. Let's have a chat.'

' 'bout what?'

'How about hacking it on the streets?' I switched the torch off and leaned against the chapel wall. 'I live down on the coast. We get plenty of dossers down there. Especially in the summer. And shall I tell you two things they've all got in common? One – they've got a special smell. Sort of a combination of stale BO and despair. You don't have it. And two . . . they wear all their clothes. And I do mean *all* of them, Milly. They don't leave them around in a hostel room for someone else to nick. I've got to say that whoever sent you in undercover must have been kind of pressed for choice. What are you? Investigative reporter? Drug Squad?'

I caught the flicker of white as she looked sideways at me and then she said abruptly, 'Vice.'

'Is your mate joining us? He's been on my tail all afternoon. Might as well introduce us.'

At least she didn't play ignorant. The 'I don't know what you're talking about' routine drives me crazy. When I'm being brilliant, I want the full audience and plenty of applause.

I didn't exactly get that, but she came back a few seconds later with hamster man in tow. 'My colleague. Steve.'

'Lovely to meet you and your fur . . . friend at last. Been staking the place out long?'

'A week.'

'And I bet you've been using the curry house for observation.'

'How'd you know that?'

'Just a hunch. Why have you taken to following me?'

'I'm not. I'm tailing the old girl. But she's done a runner on us again. We thought maybe you'd hook up with her.'

'Sadly she's given me the slip too. What do you want her for?'

They exchanged looks and telepathy apparently.

'She reported girls had gone missing from here. Black girls,' Steve said. 'The thing is . . . there's a trade in girls into the sex trade. Mostly Nigerian and Somali refugees or illegals. A lot of them just vanish from Britain and turn up all over – Italy,

Germany, Malta. We thought this place might be a staging post. Somewhere the girls are held until they can be shipped out. The old girl said she had evidence, but she wouldn't hand it over . . .'

'Care to see it?'

'You've got it?' they hissed.

For some reason we'd all lowered our voices in the dark and were conducting the conversation in whispers. I could feel their excitement tingling in the night air. I gave it my best performance as I went through the motions of taking Connie's package from my bag, unrolling the assorted plastic bags and then very *very* slowly fanning out the photos. I played the torch over them.

'Cats!'

'Yep.' According to Connie's evidence: Susie, Patty, Barbarella, Pushikins, Belle and Pepper had all vanished from the local moggie hang-outs in the last three weeks. 'Six of the finest black pussies known to well . . . known to the local tomcats I imagine. Enjoy!'

I slapped the prints in Steve's hand and turned my torch off. It was childish, but I've had a grudge against the police since they'd bounced me out for some very flimsy reasons (lying and bribery – but only a tad I promise). I just hadn't been able to resist the wind-up.

'I told you this operation was a flaming joke,' Milly hissed.

'Well, who's fault is it we got stuck with it? If you hadn't screwed up last time . . .' her partner breathed back.

'Don't you blame this on me, I'm the one who's been stuck living this shitty life . . .' Milly choked off the furious whisper at the sound of footsteps.

Glittery eyes and the tinkle of a collar bell marked the arrival of another furry free-meal bummer. A dark shape came around the corner of the chapel after it. The cats lifted their heads, hopeful of a top-up on the moggie mat.

Coming from the lighted yard to the pitch-black corridor, I guess we were momentarily invisible against the grimy wall in our dark clothing. The figure lifted its arms above its head. We all saw the glint of metal. And then there was a crunch and five of the cats streaked away.

I flicked the torch on. It was hard to say which of us was the most shocked: David caught in the light with blood dripping from the raised axe; me, Milly, Steve, or the cat. On balance I think the cat won. The expression on its face certainly suggested surprise. Or maybe it was just trying to figure out where the rest of it had gone. Its head was now a foot from the bloody, pumping stump of its body.

I smiled. 'Hello David. Decided to do your own catering?'

Steve stepped forward. 'Give me the axe, please.'

'Who are you?'

'Police. You can't go around . . .' He gestured at the fur-covered mess.

'It's kinder than poison. They're pests. They spread filth and cause traffic accidents. I'll tell the owners it was run over.'

Stooping, David snagged the collar off the head. It rolled over, its mouth forever frozen open to show tiny teeth. It had been a cute little thing, all black with a white patch over the nose and one white ear.'

I grabbed the prints back from Steve's fingers and shuffled them in the torchlight. *'I can see it's the same pattern,'* that's what she'd said.

'They're the same . . .' I held the pictures out. 'All the cats have the same white markings.'

Both Milly and Steve looked blank. David looked worried.

'Now why would you only kill those particular cats?' There seemed to be one possible answer. 'Can I have a look at the collar, Dave?'

'Why would you want to?'

'Humour me.'

He was backing away fast. But not fast enough to avoid Connie, who erupted from the dark behind him. She aimed a classic Bond babe karate chop at the side of his neck. I think he actually tripped over a cat that wove between his legs and smashed his head on the flagstones. But the effect was the same. Pussy power one – David nil.

I exchanged a high-five with Connie. 'Special training,' she beamed. Then her face twisted into a sob. 'He didn't have to kill them. They'd have come for a bit of fish. Why did he hurt them?'

For the same reason he traded in young girls I guess. Once the idealism had evaporated, what had flowed into the vacant space inside him had been pure evil.

In fact David was having a bad night all round. After three weeks of wholesale decapitation, he finally struck lucky that night. Kitty number seven was the right one.

My guess was he'd seen the note being hidden, but the cat had got away before he'd been able to retrieve it. It was sewn inside the folded leather of the collar. Six lines printed on a sheet of paper in a rusty brown shade. And in a language that I couldn't even recognize, let alone read.

'It's Hausa.' Milly said quietly. 'A Nigerian dialect.' She read aloud:

My name is Maila Okpere. I am fifteen years old. They told my mother i would go to school, but now the reverend david man says i must work for them. He says i will have a good place to live and pretty clothes but i want to go home. If anyone finds this, please tell my mother. I want to come home.

'I think this is written in blood,' Steve said. 'If we can find Maila, we get a DNA match and hallelujah, vicar . . . we got a conviction I reckon.'

'You'll be lucky,' I said.

And they were. Maila turned up in Rome six months later. The police got a DNA match, placed her in the vicinity of St Benedict's and charged David. Unofficially I heard he'd claimed he was doing the girls a favour – making sure they had a decent place to work from and protection – rather than drifting into street prostitution. Maybe he was sick enough to believe it.

And Maila got to go home. She went in a coffin. They'd found her with her throat slit in an alley.

Sorry. Were you expecting a happy ending? Tough luck. Like Pussy said, bad things happen.

Martha Grace

Martha Grace is what in the old days would have been termed a 'fine figure of a woman'. Martha Grace is big-boned and strong. Martha Grace could cross a city, climb a mountain range, swim an ocean – and still not break into a sweat. She has wide thighs and heavy breasts and child-bearing hips, though in her fifty-eight years there has been no call for labour-easing width. Martha Grace has a low-slung belly, gently downed, soft as clean, brushed cotton. Martha Grace lives alone and grows herbs and flowers and strange foreign vegetables in her marked-out garden. She plants by the light of the full moon. When she walks down the street people move out of her way, children giggle behind nervous hands, adults cast sidelong glances and wonder. When she leaves a room people whisper 'dyke' and 'witch', though Martha Grace is neither. Martha Grace loves alone, pleasuring her own sweetly rolling flesh, clean oiled skin soft beneath her wide mouth. Martha Grace could do with getting out more.

Tim Culver is sixteen. He is big for his age and loved. Football star, athlete, and clever too. Tim Culver could have his pick of any girl in the class. And several of their mothers. One or two of their older brothers. If he was that way inclined. Which he isn't. Certainly not. Tim Culver isn't that kind of boy. Tim Culver is just too clean. And good. And right. And ripe. Good enough for girls, too clean for boys. Tim Culver, for a bet, turns up at Martha Grace's house on a quiet Saturday afternoon, friends giggling round the corner, wide smirk on his handsome not-yet-grown face. He offers himself as an odd-job man. And then comes back to her house almost every weekend for the next three years. He says it is to help her out. She's a single woman, she's not that bad, a bit strange maybe, but no worse than his grandma in the years before she died. And she's not that old, really. Or that fat. Just big. Different from the women he's used to. She talks to him differently. And, anyway, Martha Grace pays well. In two hours at her house he can earn twice what he'd make mowing the lawn for his father, painting houses with his big brother. She doesn't know he's using her, thinks she's paying him the going rate. God knows, she never talks to anyone to compare it. It's fine, he knows what he's doing, Tim Culver is in charge, takes no jokes at his own expense. And after a few false starts, failed attempts at schoolboy mockery, the laughing stops, the other kids wish they'd thought to try the mad old bitch for some cash. Tim Culver earns more than any of them in half the time. But then, he always has been the golden boy.

For Tim, this was meant to be just a one-off. Visit the crazy fat lady, prove his courage to his friends and then leave, laughing in her face. He does leave laughing. And comes back hungry the next day, wanting more. It takes no time at all to become routine. The knock at the door, the boy standing there, insolent smile and ready cock, hands held out to offer, 'Got any jobs that need doing?'

And Martha did find him work. That first day. No matter how greedy his grin, how firm his young flesh, no matter what else she could see waiting on her doorstep that young Tim Culver couldn't even guess at. Mow the lawn. Clean out the pond. Mend the broken fence. Then maybe she thought he should come inside, clean up, rest a while, as she fixed him a drink, found her purse, offered a fresh clean note. And herself.

At first, Tim Culver wasn't sure he understood her correctly.

'So, Tim, have you had sex yet?'

Why would the fat woman be asking him that? What did she know about sex? And did she mean as in today, or as in ever? Tim Culver blustered, he didn't know how to answer her, of course he'd had sex. The first in his class, and – so the girls said – the best. Tim Culver was not just a shag-merchant like the rest of them. He might fuck a different girl from one Saturday to the next, but he prided himself on knowing a bit about what he was doing. Every girl remembered Tim Culver. Martha Grace remembered Tim Culver. She'd been watching him. That was the thing about being the mad lady, fat lady, crazy old woman. They watched her all the time, laughed at her. They didn't notice that she was also watching them.

Tim Culver says yes, he has had sex. Of course he's had sex. What does she think he is? Does she think he's a poof? Mad old dyke, what the fuck does she think he is?

Martha Grace explains that she doesn't yet know what he is. That's why he's here. That's why she asked him into her house. So she can find out. Tim Culver knows a challenge when it's thrown his way.

When Tim Culver and Martha Grace fuck, it is like no other time with any other woman. Tim Culver has fucked other women, other girls, plenty of them. He is a local hero, after all. Not for him all talk and no action. When Tim Culver says he has been there, done that, you know he really means it. But with Martha Grace it is different. For a start there is not fucker and fuckee. And she does talk to him, encourages him, welcomes him, incites him. Martha Grace makes Tim Culver more of the man he would have himself be. Laid out against her undulating flesh, Tim Culver's young toned body is hero-strong, he is capable of any feat of daring, the gentlest acts of kindness. Tim Culver and Martha Grace are making love. Tim Culver drops deep into her soft skin and wide body and is more than happy to lose himself there, give himself away.

Before he leaves, she feeds him. Fresh bread she baked that

morning, kneading the dough beneath her fat hands as she
kneaded his flesh just minutes ago. She spreads thick yellow
butter on the soft bread and layers creamy honey on top, sweet
from her hands to his mouth. Then back to her mouth as they
kiss and she wipes the crumbs from his shirt front. She is tidier
than he is, does not like to see him make a mess. Could not
normally bear the thought of breadcrumbs on her pristine floor.
But that Tim Culver is delicious, and the moisture in her mouth
at the sight of him, drives away thoughts of sweeping and
scrubbing and cleaning. At least until he has gone, at least until
she is alone again. For now, Martha Grace is all abandon. Fresh
and warm in a sluttish kitchen. After another half-hour in the
heat by the stove, Tim Culver has to go. His friends will wonder
what has happened to him. His mother will be expecting him in
for dinner. He has to shower, get dressed again, go out. He has
young people to meet and a pretty red-head to pick up at eight-
thirty. Tim Culver leaves with a crisp twenty in his pocket and
fingers the note, volunteering to come back next Saturday.
Martha Grace thinks, stares at the boy, half smiles with a slow
incline of her head, she imagines there will be some task for
him to do. Two p.m. Sharp. Don't be late. Tim Culver nods, he
doesn't usually take orders. But then, this feels more like an
offer. One his aching body won't let him refuse.

She watches him walk away, turns back to look at the mess
of her kitchen. Martha Grace spends the next three hours cleaning up. Scrubbing down the floor, the table. Changing the sheets,
wiping surfaces, picking up after herself. When she sits down to
her own supper she thinks about the boy out for the night,
spending her money on the little red-head. She sighs, he could
buy the girl a perfectly adequate meal with that money. If such
a girl would ever eat a whole meal anyway. Poor little painfully
thin babies that they are. Living shiny magazine half-lives of
self-denial and want. Martha Grace chooses neither. Before she
goes to sleep Martha notes down the visit and the payment in

her accounts book. She has not paid the boy for sex. That would have been wrong. She paid him for the work he'd done. The lawn, the fence, the pond. The sex was simply an extra.

Extra-regular. On Saturday afternoons, after winter football practice, after summer runs, late from long holiday mornings sleeping off the after-effects of teenage Friday nights, Tim Culver walks to the crazy lady's house. Pushes open the gate he oiled last weekend, walks past the rosemary and comfrey and yarrow he pruned in early spring, takes out the fresh-cut key she has given him, lets himself into the dark hallway he will paint next holiday and walks upstairs. Martha Grace is waiting for him. She has work for Tim Culver to do.

Martha Grace waits in her high, soft bed. She is naked. Her long grey hair falls around her shoulders. Usually it is pulled back tightly so that even Martha's cheekbones protrude from the flesh of her round cheeks, now the hair covers the upper half of her voluminous breasts, deep red and wide, the nipples raised beneath the scratch of her grey hair. Tim Culver nods at Martha Grace, almost smiles, walks past the end of her bed to the bathroom. The door is left open so Martha Grace can watch him from her bed. He takes off his sweaty clothes, peels them from skin still hot and damp, then lowers himself into the bath she has ready for him. Dried rose petals float on the surface of the water, rosemary, camomile and other herbs he doesn't recognize. Tim Culver sinks beneath the water and rises up again, all clean and ready for bed.

In bed. Tim Culver sinks into her body. Sighs in relief and pleasure. He has been a regular visitor to her home and her flesh for almost three years now. The place where he lies with Martha Grace's soft, fat body is as much home to him as his mother's table or the room he shares with an old friend now that he has moved away. Tim Culver has graduated from high school fucks to almost-romance with college girls. Pretty, thin, clever, bright and shiny college girls. Lots of them. Tim Culver is a

good-looking boy and clearly well worth the bodies these girls
are offering. This is the time of post-feminism. They want to
fuck him because he is good-looking and charming and will
make a great story tomorrow in the lunchtime canteen. And Tim
is perfectly happy for this to be the case. The girls may revel in
the glories of their fiercely free sexuality, Tim just wants to get
laid every night. Everyone's happy. And the girls are definitely
happy. It's not just that Tim Culver is good-looking and clever
and fit. He also, really really, knows what he's doing. Which is
more than can be said for most of the football team. Tim Culver
is a young man of depth and experience. And, of course, it is
good for Tim too to be seen to be fucking at this rate. To be
this much the all-round popular guy. But as he lies awake next
to another fine, thin, lithe, little body he recognizes a yearning
in his skin. He is tired of fucking girls who ache in every bone
of their arched-back bodies to be told they are the best. Tired of
screwing young women who constantly demand that he praise
their emaciated ribs, their skeletal cheekbones, their tight and
wiry arms. Weary of the nearly relationships with would-be-poet
girls who want to torment him with their deep insights into pain
and suffering and sex and music. Tim Culver is exhausted by the
college girls he fucks.

They are not soft, these young women at college, and they
need so much attention. Even when they don't say so out loud,
they need so much attention. Tim learned this in his first week
away from home. Half asleep and his back turned to the blonde
of the evening, her soft sobs drew him from the rest he so
needed. No there was nothing wrong, yes it had been fine, he'd
been great, she'd come, of course it was all OK. She wasn't
crying, not really, it was just . . . and this in a small voice, not
the voice she'd come with, or the voice she'd picked him up
with, or the voice she'd use to retell the best parts of the story
tomorrow, but . . . was she all right? Did he like her? Was she
pretty enough? Thin enough? Good enough? Only this one had

dared to speak aloud, but he felt it seeping out of all the others. Every single one of them, eighteen-, nineteen-year-old girls, each one oozing please-praise-me from their emaciated, emancipated pores. But not Martha Grace.

With Martha Grace Tim can rest. Maybe Martha Grace needs him, Tim cannot tell for certain. She likes him, he knows that. Certainly she wants him, hungers for him. As he now knows, he hungers for her. But if she needs him, it is only Tim that she needs. His body, his presence, his cock. She does not need his approval, his blessing, his constant, unending hymn of there-there. And maybe that is because he has none to give. She is fat. And old. And weird. What could he approve of? What is there to approve of? Nothing at all. They both know that. And so it is that, when Tim comes home to Martha, there is rest along with exertion. There is ease in the fucking. Martha Grace knows who she is, what she is. She demands nothing extra of him. What sanctions of beauty or thinness, or perfection could he give her anyway? She has none of those and so, as Tim acknowledges to himself in surprise and pleasure, she is easier to be with than the bone-stabbing stick-figure girls at school. And softer. And wider. And more comfortable. It is better in that house, that bed, against that heavy body. Martha Grace is not eighteen and a part of Tim Culver sits up shocked and amused – he realizes he loves her for it. The rest of Tim Culver falls asleep, his heavy head on her fat breast. Martha Grace smells the other women in his hair.

One day Tim Culver brings Martha Grace a new treat. He knows of her appetite for food and drink and him, he under-stands her cravings and her ever-hungry mouth. He loves her ever-hungry mouth. He brings gifts from the big city, delica-tessen offerings, imported chocolates and preserves. Wines and liquors. He has the money. He is not a poor student. Martha Grace sees to that. This time the home-from-college boy brings her a new gift. Martha Grace had tried marijuana years ago; it didn't suit her, she liked to feel in control, didn't understand the desire to take a drug that made one lose control, the opposite of her wanting. She has told Tim this, explained about her past experiences, how she came to be the woman she is today. Has shared with Tim each and every little step that took her from the wide open world to wide woman in a closed house. And he has nodded and understood. Or appeared to do so. At the very least he has listened and that is new and precious to Martha. So she is willing to trust him. Scared but willing. And this time Tim brings home cocaine. Martha is shocked and secretly delighted. But she is the older woman, he still just a student, she must maintain some degree of adult composure. She tells him to put it away, take it back to school, throw it out. Tells him off, delivers a sharp rebuke, a reprimand and then sends him to bed. Her bed. Tim walks upstairs smiling. He leaves the thin wrap on the hall table. Martha Grace watches him walk away, feels the smirk from the back of his head, threatens a slap, which she knows he wants anyway. Her hand reaches out for the wrap. Such a small thing and so much fuss. She pictures the naked boy upstairs. Man. Young man. In her bed. Hears again the fuss she knows it would cause. Hears again as he calls her, taunting from the room above. She is hungry and wanting. Her soft hand closes around the narrow strip of folded paper and she follows his trail of clothes upstairs, clucking like a disparaging mother hen at the lack of tidiness, folding, putting away. Getting into bed, putting to rights.

Tim Culver lays out a long thin line on Martha Grace's heavy stomach. It wobbles as she breathes in, breathes out, the small ridge of cocaine mountain sited on her skin, creamy white avalanche grains tumbling with her sigh. He inhales cocaine and the clean, fleshy smell of Martha. And both are inspirations for him. Now her turn. She rolls the boy over on to his stomach, lays out an uncertain line from his low waist to the soft hairs at the curve of his arse. She is slow and deliberate, new to this, does not want to get it wrong. Tim is finding it hard to stay face down, wants to burrow himself into the flesh of Martha Grace, not the unyielding mattress. She lays her considerable weight out along his legs, hers dangling off the end of the bed, breasts to buttocks and inhales coke and boy and, not for the first time in her life, the thick iron smell of bloody desire. Then she reaches up to stretch herself out against him full length, all of her pressing down into all of him. The weight of her flesh against his back and legs has Tim Culver reaching for breath. He wonders if this is what it is like for the little girls he fucks at college. He a tall, strong young man and they small, brittle beneath him. At some point in the sex he always likes to lie on top. To feel himself above the young women, all of him stretched out against the twisted paper and bones of the young-girl skin, narrow baby-woman hips jutting sharp into his abdomen, reminding him of what he has back at home, Martha waiting for the weekend return. He likes it when, breath forced from the thin lungs beneath him, they whisper the fuck in half-caught breaths. Tim has always been told it feels good, the heaviness, the warmth, the strong body laid out and crushing down, lip to lip, cock to cunt, tip to toe. He hopes it is like this for the narrow young women he lies on top of. Tim Culver likes this. He is surprised by the feeling, wonders if it is just the coke or the addition of physical pressure, Martha's wide weight gravity-heavy against his back, pushing his body down, spreading him out. Is wondering still when she slides her hand in between his legs and up to his cock. Is wondering no longer when he comes five minutes later, Martha still on his back, mouth to his neck, teeth to his tanned skin. Her strength, her weight, like no other female body he has felt. He thinks then for a brief moment about the gay boys he knows (barely, acquaintances), wonders if this is what it is like for them too. But wonders only briefly; momentary sex-sense identification with the thin young women is a far enough stretch for a nineteen-year-old small-town boy.

They did not take cocaine together again. Martha liked it, but

Martha would rather be truly in control than amphetamine-convinced by the semblance of control. Besides that, she had, as usual, prepared a post-sex snack for that afternoon. Glass of sweet dessert wine and rich cherry cake, the cherries individually pitted by her own fair, fat hands the evening before, left to soak in sloe gin all night, waiting for Tim's mouth to taste them, just as she was. But after the drugs and the sex and then some more of the bitter powder, neither had an appetite for food. They had each other and cocaine and then Tim left. Martha didn't eat until the evening, and alone, and cold. Coke headache dulling the tip of her left temple. She could cope with abandon. She could certainly enjoy a longer fuck, a seemingly more insatiable desire from the young man of her fantasies come true. She could, on certain and specified occasions, even put up with a ceding of power. But she would not again willingly submit to self-inflicted loss of appetite. That was just foolish.

It went on. Three months more, then six, another three. Seasons back to where they started. Tim Culver and Martha Grace. The mask of garden chores and DIY tasks, then the fucking and the feeding and the financial recompense. Then even, one late afternoon in winter, dark enough outside for both to kid themselves they had finally spent a night together, an admission of love. It comes first from Tim. Surprising himself. He's held it in all this time, found it hard to believe it was true, but knows the miracle fact as it falls from his gratified mouth: 'Martha, I love you.'

Martha Grace smiles and nods. 'Tim, I love you.'

Not 'back'. Or 'too'. Just love.

A month more. Tim Culver and Martha Grace loving. In love. Weekend adoration and perfect.

And then Martha thinks she will maybe pay him a visit. Tim always comes to her. She will go to his college. Surprise him. Take a picnic, all his favourite foods and her. Martha Grace's love in a basket. She packs a pie – tender beef and slow-cooked sweet onion, the chunky beef slightly bloody in the middle, just the way Tim likes it. New bread pitted with dark green olives, Tim's favourite. Fresh shortbread and strawberry tarts with imported out-of-season berries. A Thermos of mulled wine, the herbs and spices her own blend from the dark cupboard beneath her stairs. She dresses carefully and wears lipstick, culled from the back of a drawer and an intentionally forgotten time of made-up past. Walks into town, camomile-washed hair flowing about her shoulders, head held high, best coat, pretty shoes – party shoes. Travels on the curious bus, catches a cab to the college.

And all the time Martha Grace knows better. Feels at the lowest slung centre of her belly the terror of what is to come. Doesn't know how she can do this even as she does it. Wants to turn back with every step, every mile. Knows in her head it cannot be, in her stomach it will not work. But her stupid fat heart sends her stumbling forwards anyway. She climbs down from the bus and walks to the coffee shop he has mentioned. Where he sits with his friends, passing long slow afternoons of caffeine and chocolate and drawled confidences. He is not there and Martha Grace sits alone at a corner table for an hour. Another. And then Tim Culver arrives. With a gaggle of laughing others. He is brash and young. Sits backwards across the saddle of his chair. Makes loud noises, jokes, creates a rippling guffaw of youthful enjoyment all around him. He does not notice Martha Grace sat alone in the corner, a pale crumble of dried cappuccino froth at the corner of her mouth. But eventually one of his friends does. Points her out quietly to another. There are sniggers, sideways glances. Martha Grace could not be more aware of her prominence. But still she sits, knowing better and hoping for more. Then Tim sees her, his attention finally drawn from the wonder of himself to the absurdity of the fat woman in the corner. And Tim looks up, directly at Martha Grace, right into her pale grey eyes and he stands and he walks towards her and his friends are staring after him, whooping and hollering, catcalls and cheers, and then he has stopped by her table and he sits beside Martha Grace and reaches towards her and touches the line of her lips, moves in, licks away the dried milk crust. He stands again, bows a serious little bow, and walks back to his table of friends. Who stand and cheer and push forward the young girls to kiss, pretty girls, thin girls. Tim Culver has kissed Martha Grace in public and it has made him a hero. And made a fool of Martha Grace. She tries to leave the cafe, tries to walk out unnoticed, but her bulk is stuck in the corner arrangement of too-small chairs and shin-splitting low table, her feet clatter against a leaning tray, her heavy arms and shaking hands cannot hold the hamper properly, it falls to her feet and the food rolls out. Pie breaks open, chunks of bloody meat spill across the floor, strawberries that were cool and fresh are now hot and sweating, squashed beneath her painfully pretty shoes as she runs from the room, every action a humiliation, every second another pain. Eventually Martha Grace turns her great bulk at the coffee-shop door and walks away down the street, biting the absurd lipstick from her stupid, stupid lips as she goes, desperate to break into a lumbering run, forcing her idiotic self to move slowly and deliberately through the pain. And all the way down the long street, surrounded by strangers and tourists and scrabbling children underfoot, she feels Tim's eyes boring into the searing blush on the back of her neck.

Neither mentions the visit. The next weekend comes and goes. Martha is a little cool, somewhat distant. Tim hesitant, uncertain. Wondering whether to feel shame or guilt and then determining on neither when he sees Martha's fear that he might mention what has occurred. Both skirt around their usual routine, there are no jobs to be done, no passion to linger over, the sex is quick and not easy. Tim dresses in a hurry, Martha stays cat-curled in bed, face half-hidden beneath her pillow, she points to the notes on her dresser, Tim takes only half the cash. Pride hurt, vanity exposed, Martha promises herself she will get over it. Pick herself up, get on. Tim need never know how hurt she felt. How stupid she knows herself to have been. The weekend after will be better, she'll prepare a surprise for him, make a real treat, an offering to get things back to where they had been before. Then Martha Grace will be herself again.

Saturday morning and Martha Grace is preparing a special dish for Tim. She knows his taste. He likes berry fruits, loves chocolate like any young boy though, unlike most, Martha Grace has taught him the joy of real chocolate, dark and shocking. She will make him a deep tart of black berries and melted chunks of bitter chocolate, imported from France, ninety per cent cocoa solids. She starts early in the day. Purest white flour mixed in the air as she sifts it with organic cocoa. Rich butter, light sugar, cool hands, extra egg to bind the mix. She leaves it in the fridge to chill, the ratio of flour to cocoa so perfect that her pastry is almost black. Then the fruit – blackberries, boysenberries, logan-berries, blackcurrants – just simmered with fruit sugar and pure water over the lowest of heat for almost two hours until they are thick syrup and pulp. She skims the scum from the surface, at the very end throws in another handful. This fruit she does not name. These are the other berries she was taught to pick by her mother, in the fresh morning before sunlight has bruised the delicate skin. She leaves the thick fruit mix to cool. Melts the chocolate. Glistening rich black in the shallow pan. When it is viscous and runs slow from the back of her walnut spoon, she drops in warmed essences – almond, vanilla, and a third distilled flavour, stored still, a leftover from her grandmother's days, just in case, for a time of who-knows-and-maybe, hidden at the back of the dark cupboard beneath her stairs. She leaves the pan over hot water, bubbling softly in the cool of her morning kitchen. Lays the pastry out on the marble slab. Rolls it to paper fine. Folds it in on itself and starts again. Seven times more. Then she fits it to the baking dish, fluted edges, heavy base. She bakes the pastry blind and removes from the oven a crisp, dark shell.

Pours in warm, thick, liquid chocolate, sprinkles over a handful of flaked and toasted almonds, watches them sink into the quicksand black. Her mouth is watering with the heady rich aroma. She knows better than to lick her fingers. Tim Culver likes to lick her fingers. When the chocolate is almost cool, she beats three egg yolks and more sugar into the fruit mixture, pours it slowly over the chocolate, lifts the tart dish and ever so gently places it in the heated oven. She sits for ten minutes, twenty, thirty. She does not wash the dishes while she waits, or wipe flour from her hands, chocolate from her apron. She sits and waits and watches the clock. She cries, one slow fat tear every fifteen seconds. When there are one hundred and sixty tears the tart is done. She takes it from the oven and leaves it to cool. She goes to bed, folds into her own flesh and rocks herself to sleep.

When she wakes Martha checks the tart. It is cool and dark, lifts easily from the case. She sets it on a wide white plate and places it in the refrigerator beside a jug of thick cream. Then she begins to clean. The kitchen, the utensils, the shelves, the oven, the workbench, the floor. Takes herself to the bathroom, strips and places the clothes in a rubbish bag. Scrubs her body under a cold running shower, sand soap and nailbrush. Every inch, every fold of flesh and skin. Martha Grace is red-raw clean. The clothes are burnt early that afternoon along with a pile of liquid maple leaves at the bottom of her garden, black skirt, red shirt and the garden matter in seasonal orange rush. Later she rakes over the hot embers, places her hand close to the centre, draws it back just too late, a blister already forming in the centre of her palm. It will do for a reminder. Martha Grace always draws back just too late.

Tim Culver knocks on her door at precisely three forty-five. She has spent a further hour preparing her body for his arrival, oiling and brushing and stroking. She is dressed in a soft black silk that flows over her curves and bulges, hiding some, accentuating others. She has let down her coarse grey hair, reddened her full lips, and has the faintest line of shadow around her pale grey eyes. Tim Culver smiles. Martha Grace is beautiful. He walks into the hall, hands her the thirty red roses he carried behind his back all the way down the street in case she was looking. She was looking. She laughs in delight at the gift, he kisses her and apologies and explanations spill from his mouth. They stumble up the stairs, carrying each other quickly to bed, words unimportant, truth and embarrassment and shame and guilt all gone, just the skin and the fucking and the wide fat flesh. They are so in love and Tim cries out, whimpering with delight at the touch of her yielding skin on his mouth, his chest, his cock. And Martha Grace shuts out all thoughts of past and present, crying only for the now.

When they are done, she takes Tim downstairs. Martha Grace in a light red robe, Tim Culver wrapped in a blanket against the seasonal chill. The curtains are drawn, blinds pulled, lights lowered. She sits the boy at her kitchen table and pours him a glass of wine. And another. She asks him about drugs and Tim is shocked and delighted, yes he does happen to have a wrap in the back pocket of his jeans. Don't worry, stay there, drink another glass. Martha will fetch the wrap. She brings it back to him, lays out the lines, takes in just one half to his every two. He does not question this, is simply pleased she wants to join him in this excess. There is more wine and wanting, cocaine and kissing, fucking on the kitchen table, falling to the just-scrubbed floor. Even with cocaine, the wine and the sex have made him hungry. Martha has a treat. A special tart she baked herself this morning. Pastry and everything. She reaches into the cool refrigerator and brings out her offering. His eyes grow wider at the sight of the plate, pupils dilate still further with spreading saliva in his hungry mouth. She cuts Tim a generous slice, spoons thick cream over it and reaches for a fork. The boy holds out his hand, but she pushes it away. She wants to feed him. He wants to be fed.

Tim Culver takes it in. The richness, the darkness, the bitter chocolate and the tart fruit and the sweet syrup and the crisp pastry shell and the cool cream. Tim Culver takes it in and opens his mouth for more. Eyes closed the better to savour the texture, the flavours, the glory of this woman spending all morning cooking for him, after what has happened, after how he has behaved. She must love him so much. She must love him as much as he loves her. He opens his eyes to kiss Martha Grace and sees her smiling across at him, another forkful offered, tears spilling down her fat cheeks. He pushes aside the fork and kisses the cheeks, sucks up her tears, promises adoration and apology and for ever. Tim Culver is right about for ever.

She feeds him half the black tart. He drinks another glass. Leaves a slurred message on a friend's telephone to say he is out with a girl, a babe, a doll. He is having too good a time. He probably won't make it tonight. He expects to stay over tonight. He says this looking at Martha, waiting to see her happiness at the thought that he will stay in her bed, will sleep beside her tonight. Martha Grace smiles with appropriate gratitude and Tim turns his phone off. Martha Grace did not want him to use hers. She said it would not do for his friend to call back on her number. Tim is touched she is thinking of his reputation even now.

She pours more wine. Tim does not see that he is drinking the whole bottle, Martha not at all. He inhales more coke. They fuck again. This time it is less simple. He cannot come. He cuts himself another slice of the tart, eats half, puts it down, gulps a mouthful of wine, licks his finger to wipe sticky crumbs of white powder from the wooden table. Tim Culver is confused. He is tired but wide awake. He is hungry but full. He is slowing-down drunk but wired too. He is in love with Martha Grace, but despises both of them for it. He is alive, but only just.

Tim Culver dies of a heart attack. His young healthy heart cannot stand the strain of wine and drugs and fucking – and the special treat Martha had prepared. She pulls his jeans and shirt back on him, moves his body while it is still warm and pliable, lays him on a sheet of spread-out rubbish bags by her back door. She carries him out down the path by her back garden. He is big, but she is bigger, and necessity has made her strong. It is dark. There is no one to see her stumble through the gate, down the alleyway. No one to see her leave the half-dressed body in the dark street. No one to see her gloved hands place the emptied wine bottles by his feet. By the time Martha Grace kisses his lips they are already cold. He smells of chocolate and wine and sex.

She goes home and for the second time that day, scrubs her kitchen clean. Then she sleeps alone. She will wash in the morning. For now, the scent of Tim Culver in her sheets, her hair, her heavy flesh, will be enough to keep her warm through the night.

Tim Culver was found the next morning. Cocaine and so much alcohol in his blood. His heart run to a standstill by the excess of youth. There was no point looking for anyone else to blame. No one saw him stumble into the street. No one noticed Martha Grace lumber away. His friends confirmed he'd been with a girl that night. The state of his semen-stained clothes confirmed he'd been with a girl that night. At least, the police said girl to his parents, whispered whore among themselves. Just another small-town boy turned bad by the lights and the nights of the bright city. Maybe further education isn't all it's cracked up to be.

No one would ever think that Tim Culver's healthy, spent, virile young body could ever have had anything to do with an

old witch like Martha Grace. As the whole town knows, the fat
bitch is a dyke anyway.

A season or two later and Martha Grace is herself again.
Back to where she was before Tim Culver. Back to who she
was before Tim Culver. Lives alone, speaks rarely to strangers,
pleases only herself. Pleasures only herself. And lives happily
enough most of the time. Remembering to cry only when she
recalls a time that once reached beyond enough.

SPARKLE HAYTER

The Diary of Sue Peaner, *Marooned!* Contestant

Day One

First day on the island for the *Marooned!* TV show. It's like a paradise, palm trees, white-sand beaches, clear blue water. I really like the people in my tribe, especially Herve, the gay Filipino-American chef from Fresno, and Karen, the librarian-slash-survivalist from Ames, Iowa. The others are nice too. It's going to be hard to vote someone off. Today we sat around a campfire and told a bit about ourselves. I am awed by the experience of these people! Myron is a doctor from Atlanta. It's comforting, I admit, to know we have a doctor in our midst. Helen is sixty-six, a grandmother, breast cancer survivor and marathon runner from Houston. Bob is a forty-year-old insurance actuary from Brooklyn, who enjoys woodworking. He's a war vet and has a lot of backwoods survival training.

Today we had rice and fish for lunch. The producers gave us the fish, just for today. From tomorrow on, only rice will be provided. We'll have to find other food ourselves. Karen, the librarian, brought a book about the edible plant and animal life on the island. Smart lady. Coconuts look like they'll be our main staple, supplemented with the delicious fish that swim in these waters. Herve was ecstatic thinking about the fabulous meals he could create just from our indigenous flora and fauna. I'm so glad he's in our tribe.

We have to build our sleeping huts and dig a latrine. It sounds easier than it is. We have no shovels, hammers or nails.

Day Two

Bob is really getting on my nerves. It turns out the only war he's a veteran of is the Grenada thing. I asked very innocently if that was a real war and he got angry and defensive. He's been picking on me ever since. I was in charge of finding dinner and I thought I did pretty well, considering how picked over this island was. We haven't found most of the things in Karen's book. I think a lot of these species are extinct now. None of us has been able to make it all the way up a coconut palm to get coconuts, which was our first big test, incidentally. We've all got blisters up our inner thighs, but the guys got the worst of it. We have yet to catch one delicious fish, or even see one. Anyway, I brought back a rat, a big jar of edible insect larva and a parrot which, I think, died of natural causes (I found it, eyes closed and legs up, under a tree by the sleeping hut I share with Karen). It's not gourmet French cuisine, but jeez, Bob made such a stink about it. *Hey Bob*, Karen said, *this isn't a movie, this is reality. Make the best of it.* Herve has promised to make a nice rat, larva, parrot ragout.

Day Three

It was really hard to do today's test, after being awake half the night throwing up. Everyone was sick but Bob, and naturally he thinks it's because he skipped the ragout last night. I just know he's building an alliance to get me kicked off the island. Luckily everyone else thinks he's a pompous bore. Plus he totally bombed out on the test today, which involved walking over hot coals and jagged rocks, then standing in salt water for fifteen minutes.

Day Four

Today's test: being dropped blindfolded and hands tied on another part of the island and having to find our way home. What we didn't know is that they took us around and around for a few hours, and then dropped us just fifty feet from base camp. We bumbled around in our blindfolds, calling out to each other like a bunch of idiots for a couple of hours, unable to find our destination, which was just feet away. The TV crew taped it all. It probably would have taken us longer if the crew hadn't cracked up laughing and alerted us to their presence.

I can't believe Myron joined Bob in voting against me tonight. What a two-faced phony, acting all nice to my face and then dropping my name in the ceremonial tribal ballot box. Luckily everyone else voted for Bob. It's times like these you find out who your real friends are.

Day Five

You know what kind of doctor Myron is? A doctor of French literature. That'll come in real handy if we're suddenly invaded by an army of French writers. Boy, is he touchy. He called me a passive-aggressive manipulator and a lot of other things. His evil little scheme to project his failings on to me didn't work though; he got voted off tonight. What surprised me was Karen voting against me. She said I was a trouble-maker. That's a laugh. She's the trouble-maker. All we had to eat tonight was rice, leaves and a few insect larvae. I'm so tired.

Day Eight

All hell has broken loose. A big typhoon hit and washed some of us, maybe all of us, off the island. We were asleep in our huts when it happened. I woke up adrift, clinging to the remnant of my hut as the sea tossed me about. Made landfall on some other island. Herve, Karen and a guy from the other tribe, Tom, a minister from Alabama, landed here too. We don't know what happened to everyone else. Herve fears they drowned. The storm still rages. All I have left are the clothes on my back and my notebook and pen.

Day Ten

The storm has lifted and today we went out to see where we were. It's a rocky little island with little vegetation surrounded by miles and miles of sea. No food, but Herve almost caught a fish today. Karen is acting very strange. She's got wild eyes.

Day Eleven

No food today. Everyone is cranky. Tom is getting on everyone's nerves. He keeps praying and telling us this is all part of God's plan and talking about his college football days at Bob Jones University. Plus, he hums hymns to fall asleep. I wish he'd SHUT THE FUCK UP. Gotta stop writing now. It's too dark to see.

Day Twelve

No food again. I am feeling very weak. I thought I saw angels hovering over me when I woke up this morning. Tom was humming almost all night. I want to smash his face in.

Day Thirteen

We ate Tom today. Herve found him, apparent heart attack, on the beach this morning. He must have fallen on some rocks because his head was pretty bashed up. It's a terrible thing to eat Tom, I know, but we couldn't afford to waste the protein. Nobody knows where we are, nobody seems to be looking for us. We haven't even seen an airplane. Thank God Herve is here. He made a fire with driftwood and roasted some of the meatier parts of Tom, rest in peace. Then he made a saltwater solution to preserve the leftover pieces of Tom, and we dried them in the sun, like jerky. That and some seaweed that washed ashore will keep us for a week. I know Tom would have wanted us to eat him, rather than starve.

Day Twenty

No more Tom. We ate the last jerky last night with the last of the seaweed. Karen and Herve went out to look for more seaweed tonight. I wish the network would find us. Maybe they think we died in the typhoon. I would give anything to be able to turn back the clock and just be plain Sue Peaner, executive secretary and camping enthusiast from New Paltz, New York, again.

Day Twenty-one

Oh my God, now Karen's missing. Herve and she went out to get seaweed, and an undertow grabbed her and swept her out to sea. He said he did everything he could to save her, but the undertow was really strong. Now it's just him and me in this godforsaken place, and all we have to eat is cold seaweed (Herve is trying to preserve our driftwood supply). This is hell.

Day Twenty-two

Boy, are we lucky! Karen's body washed ashore today. Herve found it when he was out looking for ships and airplanes. Herve says she'll be very tender because she has a good layer of self-basting fat. We fashioned a dripping pan using flat stones and a piece of Karen's dress we greased up and dried in the sun until it was stiff. We have just enough driftwood for tonight's feast, but we'll make jerky tomorrow and eat that cold until we have more wood.

Day Thirty-one

We're almost out of jerky again and completely out of driftwood. Herve and I are going driftwood hunting today. I'm as good as he is at finding driftwood, and I'm better at starting a fire using a piece of broken Coca-Cola bottle and the sun. We're making the best of it and I feel like a real survivor. I wonder if the network will ever find us. If so, I am going to sue their asses off.

Day Thirty-two
No food. We've been lucky so far, with Tom and Karen both dying. Now what are we going to do? More later. I hear Herve coming up behind me and

Day Thirty-four
Herve tried to kill me two days ago by bashing my head in with a big stone! I'm hiding out behind some rocks, afraid to sleep, tired from hunger. For two days I've been on the run on a tiny island. Don't know how much longer I can elude Herve. God, I wish the network would come.

Day Thirty-six
Boy, am I lucky! Herve slipped and fell when trying to attack me today. I smashed his head in with a rock. Then I ate him. Not all of him, just an arm I roasted. Will make jerky from the rest tomorrow.

Day Forty-five
Talk about great timing. No sooner did I eat the last of the jerky and throw all the bones into the sea, than a seaplane circled above the island. I lit a fire on the beach with the last of the driftwood to make sure it saw me. It landed about twenty feet offshore and I walked out to my rescuers. The network sent them. Now I'm in a swanky hotel in Australia. Just called room service. Ordered up a steak, a lobster, a baked potato with butter and sour cream, two pieces of pie with ice cream and coffee with Grand Marnier. I know Herve, Karen, Tom and the rest of the gang would have wanted me to. Then I called my lawyer.

MAROONED! CONTESTANT TRULY IS A SURVIVOR

(AP) New York – For well over a month, Sue Peaner, an executive secretary and camping enthusiast from New Paltz, New York, survived on a deserted island with nothing but spring water, seaweed and the occasional fish she caught in tide pools. Peaner, twenty-eight, was one of the contestants who signed up to do the latest season of the popular television show. Tragedy struck shortly after the filming began – a sudden typhoon swept everyone into the sea. Peaner washed up on a rocky island. She was all alone there.

'I knew I had to make the best of it,' she said from a five-star hotel in Sydney, Australia. 'I had to survive until the network found me.' The network found her on Thursday afternoon and whisked her to Sydney to rest and recover from her ordeal, which included 'stinging jellyfish, sharks,' and other hazards.

The other eight contestants and the entire film crew of twenty-seven are still missing, and presumed drowned.

'They're great folks,' Peaner said. 'I hope they find them all safe and sound.'

The network has agreed to award Peaner the million-dollar prize. Peaner has reportedly retained legal representation to seek further moneys in damages, while Disney today made a seven-figure pre-emptive bid for publishing and entertainment rights to her story.

Notes on Contributors

Jessica Adams on 'I Do Like to Be Beside the Seaside'

'Brighton is packed with tarts and, as I've just moved there from Sydney, it was a natural setting for a Tart Noir story. I've always preferred female detectives, so this collection of saucy, crime-busting dames is too good to resist – both for a writer, and a reader. If you're ever in Brighton, by the way, do have your palm read on the pier!'

Jessica Adams is the author of two novels, *Single White E-Mail* and *Tom, Dick and Debbie Harry*, and the forthcoming book *I'm a Believer*. She is also the co-editor of two anthologies for the charity War Child: *Girls' Night In*, and *Girls' Night Out – Boys' Night In*. A third fund-raising collection, *Big Night Out*, will be published in 2002. Jessica is an astrologer as well as a novelist, and her books include *The New Astrology for Women* and *Handbag Horoscopes*. Her website is jessicaadams.net.

Jen Banbury on 'Take, for Example, Meatpie'

'I hate Nancy Drew. She always does the right thing. She never gets pissed off (even the bad guys are treated with fine girlie courtesy). And she can't punch. I used to read those books and wonder how Nancy could become involved in all those dirty crime situations and remain emotionally (not to mention physically) unrumpled. It drove me nuts.

'When I began writing, I found myself creating women characters who are Nancy Drew's opposite. Tough, sexually charged, unsunny, highly fallible . . . They wouldn't have much to say to her at a luncheon. In fact, they would probably never go to a luncheon. For me, Tart Noir describes these women, and my own sense of anti-Nancyness, perfectly.'

Jen Banbury graduated from Yale University and has since been a B-movie casting assistant, used bookstore clerk, star of an AT&T commercial, waitress, nude sculpture model and writer. Her first novel, *Like a Hole in the Head*, was published by Little, Brown in the USA and Victor Gollancz in the UK. She used to live in Los Angeles. Now she lives in New York.

Liza Cody on 'Queen of Mean'

'In all the really good noir movies, the Tart Noir is the one who sports the sexy footwear and optional chain around her ankle. She is the only original thinker in the story and, true to life, gives the simple-minded blokes a reason to live and beat each other up – for which they are not as grateful as they should be. But by that definition the Tart Noir is a male construction and the embodiment of the famous old whinge: "The woman made me do it." As such she's an old feminist's nightmare – a manipulator without shame or guilt. In fact no feelings at all.

'As an act of revenge I thought of a scenario where the Devil is a young post-feminist woman who tempts and seduces someone who wants to live with ambition and achievement but without guilt. After a process of transformation the result is a hybrid construction of testosterone, impressive teeth, new hair and very few moral scruples. A female construction? I wonder.'

Liza Cody grew up in London. She has worked as a painter, furniture designer, photographer, graphic designer, basketball coach and hair inserter. Her first novel *Dupe* won the John

Creasey memorial prize for crime fiction. In 1992 she won the CWA's Silver Dagger Award for *Bucket Nut*, the first in a trilogy which included *Monkey Wrench* and *Musclebound*.

Martina Cole, 'Enough Was Enough'

Martina Cole was born and brought up in Aveley, Essex and still lives in the area. She is the best-selling author of seven novels including *Dangerous Lady*, *The Ladykiller*, *The Jump* and *The Runaway*. Her worldwide book sales now exceed two million.

In her novels Martina Cole tackles issues more usually associated with male writers – violent crime, prostitution, pornography, child abuse, corruption – but always from a woman's perspective.

Following the successful TV adaptations of her books and her own emerging role as a scriptwriter, she has formed her own TV production company, Little Freddie Productions. She also runs creative writing workshops for prison inmates in many British prisons.

Jenny Colgan on 'The Wrong Train'

' "The Wrong Train" came from how spooky I find all the hidden areas of the London Underground – it's so old and has so many nooks and crannies, empty tunnels and long dead stations – many are apparently perfectly preserved, with advertisements and vending machines from the Thirties and Forties. I also love *The X-Files* and *Dr Who* – those old speedy jump plots with lots of shouting and running around in the dark, and I think that's probably reflected here.'

Jenny Colgan was born in Scotland and attended Edinburgh University. After six miserable years in the NHS (moonlighting as a stand-up comic and cartoonist), her first novel, *Amanda's Wedding*, was published in January 2000. Her third novel, *Looking for Andrew McCarthy*, was published in September 2001 and she is currently working on her fourth, a TV script, some journalism and trying to stop watching so much television during the day.

Stella Duffy on 'Martha Grace'

'Martha Grace happened when I put down the fourth novel that month with a thin and lithe heroine, finished reading the third story with a young, thin and lithe heroine, turned off the TV on yet another heroine – young, thin, lithe – and, still more infuriating, feisty. And not that I haven't loved those series, books, stories. And not that I haven't written those heroines myself. I just wanted to write someone who wasn't thin. Or lithe. Or young. I wanted to write a woman who was the opposite of all that we have been led to believe are the only attributes of desirability. I wanted a woman who was fat and old – and immensely fuckable. Furthermore, I grew up in a small town. Mine was in New Zealand, but I know them to be the same the world over. The outcast, male or female, young or old, is always where the interest lies. They are the unknown who draw unwanted attention, the juice that feeds the fevered imagination of the conforming rest. Which makes Martha Grace ideal Tart material – self-sufficient, secret-holding, and just looking for a good shag and a little bit of love. Pretty much like the rest of us.'

Stella Duffy has written four crime novels featuring PI Saz Martin: *Calendar Girl*, *Wavewalker*, *Beneath the Blonde* and *Fresh Flesh*, all published by Serpent's Tail, and three non-crime novels: *Singling Out the Couples*, *Eating Cake* and *Immaculate Conceit*, published by Sceptre. She has published over twenty short stories and also writes for radio and theatre. In addition to her writing work, Stella is an actor, comedian and improviser, most recently performing off-Broadway with Improbable Theatre's *Lifegame*. Other interests include attaining enlightenment and staying alive.

Liz Evans on 'Pussy Galore'

'I'd had the plot for the first Grace Smith novel (*Who Killed Marilyn Monroe*) in my mind for some time. Since it involved a dead donkey I needed a location where donkeys are generally found – hence the beach. I drew on memories of childhood holidays which seemed to suit the style of story – I needed a slightly seedy, rundown area that was desperately clinging to the illusion that it was a centre for "fun-filled family holidays". As a location for the summer holiday it might be the pits, but for moody atmospheric descriptions it's terrific. I've always felt it suits Grace's personality with her up-front humour and liveliness but with the darker introspective side lying just under the surface.

'Having said that, you'll no doubt be surprised to turn the page and find yourself on the London Underground system. But what the hell – Grace is a versatile girl with a habit of attracting hopeless cases and an inability to walk away from trouble when she should be running like hell from it. Besides, I sat next to a bag lady on the Tube the other week and started wondering, what if . . .'

Liz Evans was born in London, brought up in Hertfordshire and now lives between Herts and Bucks. She spent years in a succession of jobs, from Japanese banking to a plastics moulding company, via television and a film production company, ending up as a contracts manager for a major electronics company (the hi-tech equivalent of the living death) and spent time when she should have been negotiating mind-blowingly dull contract clauses writing crime and horror stories for magazines instead. When faced with redundancy she decided to do what any reasonable woman would do in those circumstances and attempt to write a bestseller.

Grace has featured in four novels: *Who Killed Marilyn Monroe*; *JFK is Missing*; *Don't Mess with Mrs In-Between* and *Barking*.

Sparkle Hayter on 'The Diary of Sue Peaner'

'I wrote this story during the first season of *Survivor*, a reality show popular in the USA and elsewhere, which plopped a bunch of contestants (and a TV crew of about a hundred) on an island and charted their attempts to pass painful physical tests and outmanoeuvre the other contestants in order to be the last remaining survivor and win a million bucks. Not much reality there, I thought as I ate a serving of Weird Deird's special popcorn – which consists of chocolate-covered caramels melted over hot buttered, salted popcorn – and watched the contestants vote another off the island. What would happen, I asked myself, if the contestants were really forced to survive in that environment, without the cameras? The following story is the result of all this deep philosophical questioning.

'While the narrator, Sue Peaner, is not particularly tarty, the tone is Tart, and the subject matter is noir. It is also an offbeat murder mystery and a quick read.'

Sparkle Hayter is a former journalist and stand-up comic who has published five Robin Hudson novels. The first, *What's a Girl Gotta Do?*, won Canada's Arthur Ellis Award in 1994. In the UK she won the Sherlock Award for Best Comic Detective. She does not expect to win anything else ever. Born and raised in northern Canada, she has lived in India, Tokyo and Pakistan, but for most of the last twenty years has made New York her home.

Lauren Henderson on 'Talk Show'

' "Talk Show" was actually an idea given me by my father, oddly enough. There was a great parody of the Jerry Springer show (an American talk show where various under-evolved dregs of humanity reveal terrible, Sophoclean family secrets and shout abuse at each other) doing the Internet rounds a few years ago. It was called "I Have a Philosophical Secret!" and billed as the least successful Jerry Springer show ever. When I sent it to my dad, thinking it would give him a laugh, he said, "Why don't you do Medea, Phaedra and Lady Macbeth on one of those shows?"

'He, and I, imagined it originally as knockabout farce. But when I went back to the plays, I realized that wouldn't work. There would have to be a more serious core to the story. I couldn't just joke about what these women had done. And I needed a narrator who – maybe – had a secret or two of her own. I had been tossing round the idea for so long that I was very nervous of actually sitting down to write the story; but it practically wrote itself.'

Lauren Henderson was born and bred in London. She has written seven books in her Sam Jones series for Hutchinson – *Dead White Female, Too Many Blondes, The Black Rubber Dress, Freeze My Margarita, The Strawberry Tattoo, Chained!* and *Pretty Boy*. Her anti-Bridget Jones novel, *My Lurid Past*, came out this year. Lauren has written short stories for various anthologies. She lived in Tuscany for eight years, but has now moved to New York, where her interests include bar-hopping, cocktail preparation and cute bar owners.

Vicki Hendricks on 'Stormy, *Mon Amour*'

'Writing about women who are tough and in trouble has always come naturally to me, especially when I can toss in a psychologically impaired mind and hints of a sordid past. These are the characteristics that lend themselves to hardcore passion and obsession, to me the driving forces for each tart, slut or independent woman on a mission.

'Although the story contains an element of fantasy, "Stormy, Mon Amour" is actually a gritty Tart-against-the-world tale all the way. Cherie's blend of raw need and the innocent belief that she can wash away the residue of an angry redneck husband and find freedom to live an extraordinary life bring out unexpected courage and abilities in the young woman – by my definition, essential attributes of the true tart.

'I didn't know where the story was headed until I was deep into the climax. Then I didn't want to go where I was being taken. Ultimately, I had no choice.'

Vicki Hendricks is the author of noir novels *Miami Purity*, *Iguana Love* and *Voluntary Madness*, as well as several short stories, one of which, entitled 'ReBecca', appears in *Best American Erotica 2000*. She lives in Hollywood, Florida and teaches writing at Broward Community College. An avid skydiver, having logged over 400 skydives, she features the sport in *Sky Blues*, her next novel of murder and obsession. Her autobiography, in progress, includes skydiving, dog sledging, scuba diving, sailing, and other adventure travel.

Lisa Jewell on 'Labia Lobelia'

'My agent reckons that the denouement of this story makes me sound like a man-hater. Nothing could be further from the truth. I don't hate men. I adore them. When I was younger I wanted to be one. And I am currently married to one of the finest males imaginable. He is perfect in nearly every way. Except one. And that was something I wanted to explore in this story. He is completely lookist about women. Any woman who doesn't look like the result of an experiment in cross-fertilization between Audrey Hepburn, Christy Turlington and Penelope Cruz is basically a pig. He, and many other men just like him, can see no beauty in a woman who doesn't fit neatly on the attractiveness scale somewhere between Conventionally Pretty and Goddess-like Beautiful. I also wanted to look at how ideals of beauty have changed so radically. I don't think many modern (straight) men would be fired by desire for the old Hollywood stars – too fat, too much make-up, too harsh – and I wanted to see what would happen when a woman encapsulating these old-fashioned, big-bosomed, bleached-blonde ideals clashed with Cat Deeley-loving, MTV-generation man. So I created Lobelia, a woman whom I would consider to be fantastically attractive but many men wouldn't, and placed her in a flat next to three lookist men. Funnily enough, it was only once I'd come up with the name "Lobelia" and realized that it sounded like "Labia" that the true theme for the story came to me!

'Writing this story was fantastically liberating and possibly not what people might expect. I have a very ghoulish side – I like documentaries about serial killers, I like watching operations on the television or peering underneath peoples' plasters at scars and stitches. I can launch into a conversation about anal sex with a complete stranger within five minutes of meeting them. *American Psycho* is one of my favourite books, particularly the scene with the hungry mouse and the tube. I am nearly impossible to shock (except for seeing people throw up or that snot that's kind of bright green and stringy, both of which inspire a gag reflex reaction). The original brief for these stories issued an incitement to "go for something very different from your usual – funnier, sexier, nastier, cleverer. Something perhaps that you've always wanted to write but know your editor would never let you get away with." Well – I didn't need asking twice. It was great to be able to write something a bit crude and a bit grim and not worry about losing my readership.

'And to any indignant, straight, Jayne Mansfield-loving men out there – kudos, respect and good on yer . . .'

Lisa Jewell is thirty-three years old and was born and raised in north London, where she still lives with her husband and their cat. She worked as a secretary before redundancy, a bet and a book deal took her away from all that. Her first novel, *Ralph's Party*, was the best-selling debut of 1999, her second novel *Thirty-nothing* has sold more than 250,000 copies worldwide and her third novel, *One Hit Wonder*, was published in September 2001.

Laura Lippman on 'What He Needed'

'The first line of this story came to me in a large electronics store called Circuit City as I watched a friend shop for a DVD player. Those who know anything of my life story may be tempted to read it as autobiography, but that would be a mistake. This is very much a road-not-taken story, inspired by spineless bosses who have built themselves neat little prisons of possessions and propriety. I've made a lot of mistakes in my life, but becoming addicted to the middle-class norm of more, more, more is not one of them.

'Strangely, given the nature of this collection, the result is one of the "politest" stories I have ever written. The unnamed narrator of this tale is much more ladylike than my series character, Tess Monaghan. She dresses impeccably, she does not use profanity or smoke dope, she doesn't carry a gun, she draws a veil across her sex life. But she is tough, far tougher than anyone would imagine, seeing her on the train with her travel mug and her red coat, the one with the black velvet collar. Which makes her a true Tart. Probably more of one than I am, but I'm trying. I'm really, truly trying.'

Laura Lippman has been a reporter at the *Baltimore Sun* since 1989. Her books about Baltimore-based private investigator Tess Monaghan have won the Edgar, Shamus, Anthony and Agatha awards. She may well be free of the newspaper world by the time you read this. *The Economist* has called her 'one of the most polished and consistently interesting writers of detective fiction in America today'.

Val McDermid on 'Metamorphosis'

'Girls are supposed to be sugar and spice and all things nice. Which is bollocks, really. We're just as capable of anger, viciousness and all-round meanness as men. But we're conditioned to believe it's not acceptable to reveal that side of ourselves in public. So we don't generally expose our dark sides in acts of physical violence. That's not to say we don't dream about them. And that's one of the refreshing things about the new wave of women's crime writing. We've broken out of the straitjacket of cosiness and started to confront those dark places that lurk in all of us.

'I've never shied away from writing directly about the desperate, murderous things people do to each other. But for me the taboo area has always been sex. Not because of embarrassment or squeamishness, but because I know how very hard it is to write well about sex. It's so easy to become toe-curlingly coy, clinically anatomical or queasily saturated with bodily fluids. And, although writing about murder does not provoke the belief in readers that you are a serial killer, writing about sex invariably makes them think they know exactly what you get up to in bed. But the invitation to contribute to this anthology felt like a challenge to me, an opportunity to push my own boundaries. So I've chosen to write a story of sexual obsession.

'And just for the record – this is a work of fiction.'

Val McDermid considers herself the sad old slapper of Tart Noir in that she's been doing it the longest. Born and raised in small-town Scotland, she escaped to sow her wild oats, and any other cereal she could get her hands on, at Oxford. She was a national newspaper journalist for fourteen years, labouring under the misapprehension that journalism had something to do with writing. Her first novel appeared in 1987, since when she has published sixteen novels, several short stories and a non-fiction book. A regular broadcaster for Radio Four and Radio Scotland, she also reviews for the *Los Angeles Times*, the *Express* and the *Herald*. She has won several awards, including the Gold Dagger, the Grand Prix des Romans d'Aventure and the *Los Angeles Times* Book Prize. Oh, and let's not forget the Ted Bottomley Memorial Prize for Use of English. She divides her time between a rock and a hard place.

Sujata Massey on 'The Convenience Boy'

'I learned about the provocative slang term "convenience boy" when I was gathering intelligence from the cheerful Japanese child-minder who comes to our home every now and then. Although the Japanese have many whimsical, slightly deprecating labels for all kinds of people – "education mamas", "salarymen", etcetera – "Convenience Boy" struck me as especially humiliating, but in my story the question of who, in a no-questions-asked sexual relationship, is being humiliated or empowered intrigued me.

'The sexual mystery that engulfs the passionate, yet constrained, Japanese woman is a play on a very old fantasy – the fantasy of female subjugation, of being able to enjoy yourself thoroughly because it's impossible to say no. In all sorts of everyday situations in Japan people really can't say no because to do so is bad manners. When I lived there, and I realized that people wanted to say no to me in all kinds of situations but simply wouldn't, I felt quite frustrated. I tried to liberate the people around me . . . with varying results.

'Now that I'm a few years older I know better. There is no way to force rapid change in communication and relationship patterns in Japan. Yes, it's possible for a woman to be a Tart there, or in other Asian countries – but it must be done with the utmost finesse. Women seeking power – or sexual gamesmanship – make their moves discreetly, often through a veil of subterfuge. Japan is full of young girls selling their underpants to the highest bidder, and middle-aged ladies who drink in "host" bars where gorgeous men pamper them for a few hours. Yes, they're wilder than we Westerners are. But to look at a Japanese woman's face made up to be purposely blank – smooth foundation, precise lipstick, but nothing to shadow or enhance the eyes – you'd never guess.'

Sujata Massey was born in Crawley in England to parents from India and Germany. She spent her early years in England, but later emigrated with her family to the United States, where she studied writing at Johns Hopkins University. After a brief career in newspaper journalism, she moved to Japan and began writing her mystery series featuring Rei Shimura, a young Japanese-American woman who solves crimes that involve Japanese artistic and social traditions. The books have won the Agatha and Macavity awards and been nominated for five other prizes. The latest one is *The Bride's Kimono*, which uses the culture of kimono to explore East–West attitudes toward infidelity and marriage.

Denise Mina on 'Alice Opens the Box'

'"Alice Opens the Box" was inspired by a recent Glasgow case. A young mother became the ultimate Tart noir; a feared woman refusing to conform to all the sexual and social mores demanded of her.

'She was young, working in a busy city bar. She killed her three young children and hid them in her flat. She kept going to her work. She was quiet but well liked. No one knew what she had done until she moved house and the new tenants found a tiny mummified body in a kitchen cupboard. Everyone in Glasgow was wondering how she could do it to her own kids, how she could get away with it. The woman had thrown off the mantle of valiantly coping single mother. Almost immediately, her sexual behaviour was being speculated about. The children had different fathers. She had named ten men as the possible father for one of them and none of the DNA matched the baby's. There were rumours of incest because she came from the Islands. None of this was in the papers, it just grew out of chat in bars, urban myth-making, someone who knew someone who'd worked on the case.

'The case made me think about how we assume that there is a social consensus in our values. But we know that there is no consensus because we all deviate from the dominant value system in some way; some people smoke hash, some people are gay, some campaign for the minimum wage. We all know that we don't conform totally and yet we expect everyone else to. Some deviations are positive. Social progress is impossible unless there is deviation by people brave enough to push the boundaries, so maybe we're specifically designed not to conform.

'In "Alice" I wanted to explore the sort of deviation that develops in the dark, unchecked by outside influence, the sort of alienation that leads to Rosemary West-ish domesticity. I wanted to imagine what sort of justifications a person would need to do what the barmaid did to her kids.'

Denise Mina has worked as a nursing auxiliary in geriatric and terminal care nursing homes, in a meat factory and in a thousand bars. Fed up with getting sacked for being cheeky, she got into university, studied law and ended up teaching it while studying for a PhD in mental illness in female offenders. Her first novel, *Garnethill*, won the John Creasey Prize for the best first novel of the year. The trilogy was completed with *Exile* and *Resolution*. She won the CWA Gold Dagger for the Best Short Story of 2000.

Karen Moline on 'No Parachutes'

'Nothing like a little lust in a moving yet confined space to get the juices flowing. An elevator ride is such a short thrill; cars have windows and knobs in uncomfortable places; trains can be swell if you've got a sleeping compartment but hell on the gluteus if not. Which brings me to planes. This story was inspired by an incident at 35,000 feet when I was returning from New Year's Eve revelry in Brazil many years ago. Never mind what I did – or didn't – do. (I'm sure my blame-it-on-Rio memory has embellished certain aspects of the flight and conveniently forgotten the most egregiously naughty). What interested me is the body's response to criminal and terrifying behaviour when there's no place to run. I soon found out that my body, at least, had a will of its own. And, in retrospect, given the events of 11 September 2001, this story takes on a dreadful innocence about horrifying events high the the sky. How I wish it weren't so.

Karen Moline is the author of the novels *Belladonna* and *Lunch*, and formerly a film critic for www.movieline.com < http://www.movieline.com > and BBC World Service Radio; columnist for < http://www.nerve.com > and interviewer for *The Big Breakfast* on Channel 4. She is also a freelance entertainment journalist who has ghosted many books and written for dozens of magazines and newspapers in the US, UK and Australia, including, most recently, *W*, *Nylon*, *More*, *Tatler*, *Nieman Marcus the Book*, and *Marie Claire UK*. She is currently writing her third novel, *Game Over, You Win*.

Katy Munger on 'The Man'

'"Noir" has traditionally been used to describe those books and movies that attempt to look at the darker side of life without flinching. Such stories are bleak and grim, and inevitably end unhappily. This, of course, makes noir the ideal milieu for exploring female power: women are no strangers to the darkest corners of life. In fact, it is in our most hopeless moments – those involving death and disappointment and illness and betrayal – that we often discover how deeply capable and resilient we truly are. So, to me, Tart Noir is more than an attitude. It's about women finding power within their lives – whether that means in the bedroom, where we have traditionally held our greatest power, or outside it, during those moments when life and death hang in balance.

'Sometimes Tart Noir will bring you women who use power for evil, and who see the world in the deepest possible shades of traditional noir. But, sometimes, Tart Noir will bring you women who use the power they have discovered within themselves for the greater good and who illuminate the darkness of noir with their own unique brand of laughter and cynicism. Believe me, the darkness is still there – but, like millions of women before us, we simply choose to laugh at the night.

'Whether Tart Noir is lighter than traditional noir – or just as bleak – the one thing all Tart Noir stories have in common is that they revolve around women who have discovered and are consciously using their power over other people and within the confines of their worlds. There is little room for self-victimization or helplessness in Tart Noir and that's a good thing – the world is unforgiving enough to women as it is. And no one knows that better than a woman.'

Katy Munger is the author of nine mystery novels, including the award-winning, hard-boiled Casey Jones series set in the

Research Triangle area of North Carolina. She is a native of Raleigh, North Carolina and a graduate of the creative writing programme at UNC-Chapel Hill. The first Casey Jones novel, *Legwork*, introduced Casey Jones – a raunchy, cynical, bottle-blonde brickhouse of a private investigator whose soft heart hides beneath 160 pounds of muscle and moxie. The fifth book in the Casey series, *Better Off Dead*, was released in the United States in June 2001.

Katy Munger is also the author of four books in the Hubbert & Lil mystery series, written under the pen name Gallagher Gray. In addition to writing mysteries, Munger writes a regular mystery review column for the *Washington Post* and is a proud founding member of Tart Noir. Visit www.katymunger.com or www.tartcity.com for more information on her work.

Chris Niles on 'Revenge Is the Best Revenge'

'My tart days were behind me, or so I thought. I was going straight. Writing serious tales about big-hearted girls who volunteered for overnight shifts in animal shelters and knitted socks for Nicaraguan women's cooperatives. I'd not counted on the ruthlessly resourceful Stella Duffy and Lauren Henderson. How they managed to track down the photographic evidence of that 1997 evening in Zagreb and why the story leaked to the *News of the World* so soon after I had submitted my contribution to Tart Noir are questions that must be directed to them.

'A few words in my defence: the South American police chief was on the verge of leaving his wife. The Bulgarian twins had assured me they were at least sixteen. The crate of premier grand cru, the flame-thrower and the patent leather lederhosen were, in contrast to scurrilous media reports, paid for entirely out of my own pocket. And I emphatically deny that a single one of the marsupials was hurt in the making of the video tape.

'But what's done is done. I leave it to the reader to judge

whether Ms Duffy and Ms Henderson's unorthodox methods of conscription were worth it.'

During the last fifteen years Chris Niles has wandered in a seemingly aimless fashion from New Zealand to Melbourne, Sydney, Budapest, London (twice) and on to New York City, where she now lives. In addition to her active life in fiction, she occasionally musters the odd fact, working freelance as a print and television journalist. She is the author of four novels, *Spike It*, *Run Time*, *Crossing Live* and *Hell's Kitchen*. She is working on a book about a woman who is hired to find her own worst enemy.

Jenny Siler on 'Africa'

'I confess, I'm a movie junkie. Though I more than appreciate Raymond Chandler and Dashiel Hammett, my heart belongs to Clint Eastwood and Cary Grant. If anything informs my idea of noir, it's the opening scene of *North by Northwest*: the unsuspecting Grant raising his arm at exactly the wrong moment, identifying himself as someone he isn't, an error upon which the rest of the movie hinges. For me, that momentary yet fatal confusion is the essence of noir: the ordinary man minding his own business, who is suddenly thrust into another, more treacherous life; or Ingrid Bergman in *Notorious*, the rich party girl who sobers up to find herself married to a German agent, playing spy for the Americans. There's a truthfulness to this kind of confusion, the scrim of middle-class life pulled back to reveal the grimy realities of crime and betrayal, the ugly underbelly that supports our comfortable existence.

'If the American in me grew up inhaling stories of everymen turned unlikely heroes, then the Montanan in me feasted on the Spaghetti Western. I still have a soft spot for the bloody morality plays of *Fistful of Dollars*, *High Noon*, and *Pale Rider*. As a Westerner, and a human being, I can't help but feel a poignant connection to the angry loner, the gunslinger with a score to settle. Even if the settling of that score often amounts to nothing more than an exhaustion of rage. Think Eastwood in the last scene of *The Outlaw Josie Wales*, his guns spent when he finally confronts the man who killed his wife and children.

'What does this mean for my own writing? Partly it means that my characters' personal journeys are often infused with these two very different traditions. Part gunslinger, part innocent, they muddle through situations they often seem to have fallen into. They are generally outsiders, plagued by their pasts. Often, they are the fallen middle class. They hurtle toward resolutions that are more revelations of self than good triumphing over evil. What this particular fusion also means is that I frequently find myself writing in a profoundly male world. The real challenge, then, is to create female characters who are more than just male characters with women's names. To my mind, this distinct femininity is what separates Tart Noir from noir. Say, Ingrid Bergman seducing the ageing Claude Rains while she scours his house for Nazi secrets. Or Neely, the heroine of 'Africa', slipping on the mask of a high-priced call girl. Call her Annie Oakley in an evening dress, or Doris Day with a grudge and a gun. Whatever, she makes no apologies.'

Jenny Siler lives in Missoula, Montana with her husband, Keith, and her cat, Frank. Besides writing, she has, among other things, tended bar in Seattle, graded salmon in Alaska, picked grapes in the Pyrenees, driven a forklift in Key West and worked as a sketch model at an art museum in Frankfurt. She is the author of several novels, including *Iced* and *Easy Money*.

Karin Slaughter on 'Necessary Women'

'I've always thought of noir as a male-dominated genre; not because women can't do noir, but because the moral of these stories generally seems to be that men are basically solid, upstanding citizens until they meet the Wrong Woman. It's a classic retelling of Adam and Eve, only with more liquor and sex. Eve, in the guise of the helpless victim who needs to be rescued from her abusive husband/loveless marriage, tricks poor Adam into doing her dirty work. Once Adam has developed a taste for the forbidden fruit, Eve is revealed to be a monster. Of course, she must be punished for this in the end, preferably stabbed, beaten and/or shot before she gasps her final, unrepentant breath.

'The women of classic noir were defined by the men in their lives: they were dames and broads, singled out as real lookers for their gams that wouldn't quit. To get away from one man they had to latch on to another. Only through guile and blatant sexuality could they achieve any power and then they were punished for it. In contrast, Tart Noir is all about rewarding women for taking power. Men are more likely to be accessories at best, nuisances at worst. Tarts are quite capable of getting in and out of trouble on their own. They may often make the wrong decisions, but they at least have the opportunity to make these decisions for themselves.

'"Necessary Women" embodies the spirit of Tart Noir. It is about a young girl whose fate is decided not by the men in her life, but by the choices she makes. The narrator reminds us why it was Eve and not Adam the snake chose to tempt first.'

Karin Slaughter, a Georgia native, lives in Atlanta. Her first novel, *Blindsighted*, was published in 2001. *Kisscut*, the second in the Grant County series, will be released in the autumn of 2002. She is currently working on *A Faint Cold Fear*.